WILL JONES

Journey of a Young Englishman to Rebel Patriot

BY

Cecil Burton "Burt" Jones

Editor: Alayne Merestein

Cover Design: Ira-Rebeca

Library of Congress : 2021917615

ISBN: 978.1.7360013.7.0.

Cover Art: Maxwell Burton Jones

Map Images: Geography and Map Division

Interior Designer: Muhammad Faizan Altaf

Acknowledgments

I'd like to thank my family for supporting me in this endeavor. It was their support and encouragement which enabled me to finally complete the task. And to all the other members of my large extended Jones Family, who by any standards are great storytellers. A special tribute to my late cousin John Paul Jones, who was our family genealogist, and keeper of the family secrets and legends.

Preface

While deployed to the Middle East in 2002, I started a story to entertain my wife. I was interested in the Revolutionary War since it was rumored that one of my distant grandfathers had fought in the war as a young man. Each night after work, I would write a page on the fictional exploits of a young colonial boy in an email and send it to my wife. She began collecting those emails and when I returned, she presented them to me in a little booklet. This became the genesis of my book.

Over the years, I found little time to write. Upon my retirement, my wife pulled out the booklet of collected emails and told me it was time to finish my work. With renewed vigor, I set about the task. While working on the book, I found time to research my distant grandfather's military record which verified his service in the North Carolina militia. With that, I applied for entry into and was duly initiated into the Sons of the American Revolution.

While the book does not follow the adventures of my grandfather, it does present a fairly accurate picture of the emotional challenges of being an Englishman during the Revolutionary War and the desire to break free of an unappreciative monarchy.

Contents

Chapter 1

Early Years

Looking back over my early years, things just seem to fade into memories of hot, humid Virginia summers, crisp colorful autumns, cold bone-chilling winters, and warm resuscitating springs. These first 15 years of my life were wonderful; at least I wanted them to have been so.

I was born on the 14th of May in the Year of our Lord 1759, the first son of William Nathaniel Jones and his wife, Molly. Four brothers and three sisters would follow me. At my birth, without fanfare or fuss, I was named after my father and became known as Will. Although my family history may be of little importance or relevance to my later life, I always thought the character of my parents played a significant role in my development.

Father … we all called him father, for we dared not call him anything else. Father is what he wanted us to call him, and we did. We dare not call him Pa or Pappy as other children called their fathers. As you can imagine, Father was stern, but at night when the work was done and our chores were finished, he would show us his softer side. There were always the special moments for a hug or a tussle of our hair. Most importantly, Father was a storyteller by nature. The stories he would tell us of distant lands, ships at sea, and skirmishes with the Indians all had a basis of truth. Just how much was Father and how much was the story, we could never tell.

What we did know of our parents we picked up as bits and pieces caught by eavesdropping on conversations they had when neighbors came a-calling.

Father, was old by the time I was born, 30 to be exact. He and Mother had only been married 10 months when I arrived. This situation was necessitated by Father's previous status as an indentured servant. We pieced together that Father, as a young lad of 15, penniless, unemployed, and with no hope of survival during the next winter in Wales had sold himself to a ship's captain for passage to America in hopes for a better future. Father's particular period of servitude, originally for only 10 years, was extended by a sentence of an additional five years for an attempted escape, which Father referred to as youthful folly and a bad escape plan. Although Father never outwardly bore any hatred or ill-will toward his master, he nonetheless bore the physical scars of the 10 lashes that accompanied the additional sentence. It was always a reminder to us children that Father had paid a heavy price for his fortune, a lesson we would always carry with us.

Mother, on the other hand, was still a young woman, by most counts only 19 or 20 perhaps when she married Father. Since Mother had been orphaned as a baby and all records surrounding her birth had been destroyed in a fire, there was no real telling just how old she was. But she was young when she married my father, so everyone said.

A good Quaker family had raised her, even though she did have family somewhere in North Carolina. The Quakers were good people who believed in hard work, religion, and education. As a result, Mother could even read, write, and cipher. As a consequence, all of us, even Father suffered under her strong-willed determination that everyone in the family would be literate. The Holy Bible was our reader, as it had been hers as a child. We learned to cipher by counting our harvest of apples and pears.

Chapter 2

February 1775

The winter night was cold already, even though the sun had set only a couple of hours prior. Inside our small one-room cabin the family was settling down for the evening. Mother, who was pregnant with child, had just finished our evening prayer service, a holdover from her Quaker upbringing. The children were all nestled in their beds on the far wall of the cabin. Since there were so many of us, there were four to a bed. Father, the world traveler as he liked to call himself, had constructed a ship's bed, two beds, one on top of the other, like he had seen on the British merchant ship that had brought him to America when was a young lad. One was low to the floor and the other on posts was a little higher. The older children were granted the place of honor above. "It wouldn't do to have a little one fall out at night from such a great height" was what Father always said when one of the little ones begged to sleep on top. In actuality, I think it was more for protection of the older ones. It was the infrequent accident of one of the little ones that would have made sleeping below them an occasional wet affair.

I, being the oldest, had a special place. Although deer hides were worth a whole half a shilling, Father had allowed me to keep two hides that I had cured. I stitched them together with rawhide. This was my bed, which I unrolled each night in front of the fireplace. In Winter I could roll myself up in the fur like a caterpillar in a cocoon.

Things seemed the same, at least on the surface, as Father announced he was going outside for a spell for a breath of fresh air and to smoke his "damnable pipe" as Mother called it.

"Will, come with me outside and sit a spell. You need to feel the crisp air on your cheeks for a while," said Father as he packed his pipe and headed to the cabin door.

"Yes, Father." I had been conditioned to respond to my Father without question. Only on those rare occasions when he asked me what my thoughts were, was I allowed to freely state my opinions, most of which were answered with a "Humph" or "So." Father never really supported my opinions nor did he ever criticize them. As I grew older and, as he would say, bolder, I did once ask what he thought of my opinion about some now forgotten subject.

Father had responded, "Son, your Mother and I raised you children by trying to set a good Christian example. We can only hope by giving you the benefit of our experience and the teachings of the Bible you will grow up to be good Christians. There is, by necessity, some latitude to be given to each of you to explore the world around you and form your own opinions. As long as those opinions fall within that latitude then you are doing well."

What that latitude was or just how close we got to it was

never quite clear. We were rarely punished and never severely for our minor transgressions. Although Father always said he held to the proverb, "Spare the rod and spoil the child." I cannot remember ever seeing a rod in our house. An occasional swap with his hand on the rear was the most corporal punishment any of us ever received. Extra hard work was the punishment of choice for our infrequent transgressions.

Tonight was different. Father seemed too preoccupied with something and had a worried look on his face. I hurriedly put on my worn buckskin jacket and went out to the porch to join him. As I closed the cabin door behind me, I saw Father perched on the porch rail just to my left. With an ember stick in his right hand, he was lighting his beloved pipe. The first draw on his pipe disappeared for a second in his lungs, then he cast out the smoke in a bilious cloud, which filled the air with the heavy sweet smell of fine Virginia tobacco.

"Come, Will, sit with me on the rail. We have things to talk about tonight that your Mother does not need to hear," said Father, as he patted the rail next to him.

As I threw my legs over the rail and perched myself next to him, he handed me his pipe. This sort of gesture had only been offered on special occasions, first when I turned 15 and then again after I had killed a particularly large black bear that had been menacing our cow. Whatever Father wanted to discuss I knew it had to be of extreme importance. I took a deep draw on the pipe as my Father had taught me and handed it back to him. I was allowed only a "taste;" Tobacco was too expensive to waste. As I tried not to erupt in coughing, my eyes watered. I managed to blow out the smoke with only a small series of coughs attached. Father made no comment; He merely accepted the pipe and took another draw, held in for a second, and stared out over the now barren fields shimmering in the light of a nearly full moon. He was contemplating how to start the conversation. He exhaled a cloud of bluish-white smoke, hesitated a second, and then began.

"I learned that tonight the Tories plan to raid several Whig farms looking for stockpiles of arms and ammunition. As far as I know, they have no intention of coming this far west, but I can't say for sure. Even if they did, we should be left alone."

His pronouncement ended as quickly as it had started, but it was an encompassing commentary on the "troubles" as father called it that had been festering in our county for the past several years. Tories, the loyalists supporting the King, had always been an outspoken lot in our county. Fiercely loyal to the King regardless of the news of excessiveness of British troops in New England, the Tories were active in trying to stamp out any hint of rebel activity in the more populated eastern part of the county. Rarely would a Tory enforcement raid ever venture forth far from Charles.

The fact that Father used the word Whigs to describe the rabble that was opposing the King was truly remarkable. Ever since the beginning of the troubles in Boston, Father had distanced himself from those who called for a resort to violence. Father was an Englishman, but indifferent toward the King. Zealousness of the Tories did not appeal to Father either. As families in Charles were labeled Whigs and then summarily dispossessed of their property by the Crown, they headed west past our homestead to start a new life beyond the mountains. Seeing this exodus of the poor and dispossessed caused Father great concern and it weighed heavily on his soul. "It's not right" was all he said.

The cold, crisp evening air seemed to amplify the sounds in the valley below us. Almost three miles away, Mr. Jenson's dog barked, probably at his own shadow. Then, Old Man Henley's cow bellowed two farms away in the direction of Charles. Momentarily, all was quiet and the light wind blowing through the bare limbs of the oak trees could be heard.

Father and I must have sat there a good 20 minutes while he smoked his pipe. Nothing was said; we only stared into the distance.

As Father began to tap his pipe on the porch rail to clean it out, the sound of a faint crack echoed in the distance. Then there was another crack followed by a crescendo. Father stopped cleaning his pipe and listened intently.

"Damn it all. Musket fire. It sounds like it's coming from Benjamin Brown's farm near the crossroads. I was afraid they would raid his farm." Father was visibly upset.

Mr. Brown's farm was five miles down the road toward Charles, lying on the crossroad between the east-west oriented Charles Road and the north-south oriented Post Road. The musket fire continued for a good 20 minutes. The raiding party must have been sizable because the firing was steady and consistent. There was no way to tell how Mr. Brown was fairing. Occasionally I would hear his old blunderbuss explode, but after about 10 minutes, I didn't hear it anymore. We sat and listened. Father did not move.

The firing died down and finally stopped. Now we watched as the night sky in the direction of Mr. Brown's farm began to glow.

The raiding party was burning him out.

"Damned old fool," is all Father said as he eased off the porch rail and turned to go inside the cabin. I waited a moment, stared in the distance at the orange glow that was once Mr. Brown's farm, and eventually followed him into the house.

As I entered, I saw Father sitting close to Mother on the wood bench, his arm around her shoulder. He was offering her comfort and solace. Mrs. Brown had been the midwife for the whole community and was a tireless woman of good works and spirit.

"I spoke to Benjamin just this morning and tried to warn him to be watchful. He would hear none of it. He said, 'Let those Tory roosters come near my farm and I will greet them with my old blunderbuss full of shot.' I could not persuade him to leave the community for a couple of days. He would hear none of it. He even refused the offer of help from other farmers in the community. 'Nothing to fear,' he said. 'They won't dare to show their faces in these parts after dark.' I tried at least to get him to send his wife and children away. He was stubborn."

At some point in time, Father had taken a small but now perceivable step away from the excess of the Crown and toward a neutral stance. He was not willing to support the Whigs, but he was not willing to turn his back on his neighbors. How he knew the Whigs would be out that night was never explained.

"William," it was Mother's turn to speak her mind. "If we stay here, I fear that we may be drawn into this disagreeable situation whether we want to be or not." The whole county is choosing sides. It will be most uncomfortable. I have no use for violence and will not tolerate my family being drawn into this fracas. As far as everyone is concerned, we are good Christian people and will not take up arms against our neighbors. I know we have worked hard to build our farm, but if we must move, then I think it would be best."

"Molly, I will not be drawn into this fight. I had enough during the Indian campaign. Nothing can be resolved by violence," said Father with commitment in his voice.

It was then that we heard the approach of a wagon traveling at a fast rate of speed. As it turned into our yard, we heard the desperate cry of Mrs. Brown. "Help me, please!"

All three of us bolted to the cabin door. I was the first through, unmindful of any trouble that might lie on the other side. Father was right behind me as Mother followed closely with a lantern.

There in our yard was the Brown family in their two-horse wagon. Mrs. Brown jumped down from the seat into my Father's arms.

"Oh, William, the Tories came and raided our farm. Benjamin is shot. I fear he is dying."

Without a moment's hesitation, Father went around to the back of the wagon. In the pale light of the lantern, we could see Mr. Brown laying in a blood-soaked bed of straw as his six children watched helplessly.

"William, is that you?" uttered Mr. Brown.

"Yes, Benjamin. I'm here." Father's voice cracked a bit.

"I was a fool, William. I should have taken your advice and left. I did at least have Molly and the children hide in the woods with the wagon just in case. William, there were too many of them.

There must have been 20 to 30 Tories bent and determined to rid the county of one more voice of reason." Mr. Brown coughed and frothy blood erupted from his mouth.

"Quiet Benjamin! Save your strength. We'll get you inside where we can attend to you properly," said Father.

With that, I moved to one side, as instructed by Father and with the assistance of the two Brown boys we gently slid Mr. Brown out of the wagon and carried him into our house. Mother preceded us and cleaned off our eating table to serve as his resting place. The light from the overhead lantern was increased. The sight of Mr. Brown's bloody clothes was not a pretty sight. Just a quick glance and I saw at least eight bullet holes spread out over his upper torso. The wicked one was in his chest in the area of his right lung.

We sprang into action. First, Mother situated the Brown children around the room out of the way, told my siblings, who were now fully awake, to go back to sleep. She then took her fine bed linens off her bed and directed Mrs. Brown to start ripping them up into long strips. As Mrs. Brown undertook that task, I stoked the fire in the fireplace and got it roaring. Mother added water to the black kettle and swung it over the fire. Father began the difficult task of removing Mr. Brown's clothes. As he cut away the clothes and exposed the upper torso each grisly wound could be clearly seen.

Father somehow knew what to do. Quick work with his hunting knife and Father cut a leather patch and placed it over the chest wound. We worked a strip of cloth under Mr. Brown and then tied the patch in place. Father then went about the work of checking each wound. Several wounds were superficial and didn't require more than to be cauterized. Thankfully, Mr. Brown was unconscious and the ember red iron rod caused him no visible pain.

Three wounds were serious and required immediate attention. Mother, knowing the precise routine, handed Father one of her prized French knitting needles. Father used it as a probe to locate each piece of shot. Before he started to dig out the shot, Mother and Mrs. Brown quickly washed off the blood covering Mr. Brown with rags soaked in hot water. As they gathered a rag filled with blood, they would dip it back in the water, wash it out, and continue the process until Mr. Brown was fairly clean.

Father gave his first orders for the upcoming surgery.

"Will, as soon as I get the shot out, there is going to be a lot of bleeding. I need you right by my side with the rod to cauterize the wound. When I tell you, bring the rod from the fire as quickly as you can. Listen to me Son; Mr. Brown's life depends upon how fast we get the bleeding stopped. We'll do the wound to the left shoulder first. I need to practice. It's been a long time since I had to dig out a bullet."

As I prepared four rods in the fire, Father moved to the family chest. From there he extracted two strange-looking thin-bladed knives with lips instead of points. Fitted together they formed a perfect loop on the bottom.

"Son, get the first rod ready. I will have to fit the first knife in, rotate it, and then fit the other in until both are underneath the shot. Once I have them positioned, I should be able to lift the shot out quickly. As soon as I have the shot out, I will need the rod. Will, you ready?"

"Yes, sir" was my only response.

Father began to work. He carefully inserted the first knife in the wound, found the shot, and positioned the lip underneath the ball. Leaving the knife standing in the wound, he inserted the companion knife and deftly worked it into the right position. Father looked in my direction and nodded. I knew he was getting ready to pull the shot out. I carefully watched his quick, but gentle progress. Just as the shot was lifted out, I was at my Father's left shoulder with the rod. He quickly inserted the rod in the wound and slowly drew it out, ensuring the surfaces of the wound were closed properly. With a second rod, he burned the wound closed. The stench of burning flesh was strong, but we all knew it meant that a life was being saved.

Father repeated the surgery two more times with little fanfare. The fourth wound presented a problem.

"Sarah," Father was speaking to Mrs. Brown, "This last wound is too difficult to remove the shot. The shot is deep within the wound and I cannot get to it with my knives. It looks as if it almost went all the way through the upper chest. It has broken his collarbone and may be lodged against his shoulder blade in the back. If I try to dig it out, I could possibly cause him more harm than good. The only thing I can do is cauterize the wound. Benjamin will just have to live with it."

Mrs. Brown just nodded her head. Father then nodded to me and I brought over the first rod and then the second. The wound was thoroughly closed. That only left the wound to the lungs to be dealt with. Father had done all he could.

"Sarah, we'll have to get Benjamin to a doctor in another community. It's too dangerous to go to Charles after last night.

We'll need to wait until it is light and then go. Right now, cover him up and keep him warm. You can wipe his lips, but don't give him anything to drink. If he were to vomit it up it could cause him to start a coughing spell and he could drown in his own blood. Keep him quiet and still."

Father motioned to me and I followed him outside as Mother cleaned up the mess and Mrs. Brown covered her husband up to protect him against the chill in the air. The Brown children were all huddled together in shock. I felt a pain in my heart for them as they were too small to fully understand what was going on and surely didn't deserve seeing their father near death on our eating table."

I reached the porch as Father lit his pipe. He was staring out into the blackness of the woods beyond our fields. For a moment he didn't say anything, only smoked his pipe as if he was in deep thought.

"Will, we need to prepare to take Benjamin into Fredrick tomorrow at sunrise. Unhitch the Brown's horses and take them into the barn, give them plenty of water, and feed them some good hay. They will need strength; it's a long trip we have to make. Before you take care of the horses, sit down with me on the steps. We need to talk again. Things have gotten a mite out of hand too quickly."

As we sat down together, he handed the pipe to me. Twice in one day, this was indeed serious.

"What I am about to say, you will not repeat to anyone. Do you understand, son?"

"Yes, Father," was my reply.

"There are bad things afoot in this county, which are only

partially related to the troubles in New England. Greed and avarice are the forces we will have to tend with if we are to survive. Benjamin Brown is a good man, a little too vocal perhaps, but a good Englishman nonetheless. As I have not, neither has he taken sides, nor as far as I can tell would he have not done so unless he talked with me first. Ours is a solid friendship that goes back to the Indian War. It is a brother's bond that can't be broken. This whole affair is not over a question of loyalty; it is over greed for more land. That Tory bastard, Squire Morris, has wanted Benjamin's bottomland to add to his plantation for years. He found an excuse and used it to take what he wanted and has nearly killed to get it. No one in this county with bottomland is safe for very long. It is only a matter of time before the Tories divide all of the good farmland between them. They will call it spoils of war. Son, we are faced with the choice of standing up to this swill of humanity or pulling up and moving over the mountains to a safer place. Judge your Mother and me not too harshly, but she is right. We have too much to lose if we fight. Once we get Benjamin to a safe place in Fredrick we will return and pack up everything to move to Cumberland. There is good bottomland just beyond there for the taking. Hard work and a little luck, we'll have a better place than this in two years."

For some reason, tears welled in my eyes. Anger built in my chest and I exploded.

Chapter 3

The Indian War

"Father, the Bible says 'An eye for an eye and a tooth for a tooth.' As good Christians we have to stand our ground. We can't let them run us off our land." Although I wanted to pour out my emotions, I collapsed into stunned silence.

"Son," said Father as he put his arm around my shoulders, "This is not the time nor the place to fight. We are only a few and there are many. Listen to what I say and learn well. I was a lad not much older than you when my Master sent me to the militia to fight the Indians in order to save his eldest son in the service.

"At first it was a lark and as close to freedom as I had enjoyed in years. I trained in marching, shooting, and marching some more. And food … there was always a feast. We definitely had good hunters in our militia company. Things changed when we were dispatched to the frontier. Life was harder, food scarcer, supplies undeliverable, and the elements made our lives miserable. It was on the frontier that I met a young Benjamin Brown, a freeman, called on to protect Virginia. We soon became best friends and shared the good and the bad. It took six months before we hardened to the elements. The frontiersmen who soldiered with us taught us soft lowlanders Indian crafts and survival skills in order to help us survive under adverse conditions. These are the same skills I have taught you; remember them well.

"Even with the help of the frontiersmen we were not prepared for the warriors we were to face. Many will say the Cherokee and the Shawnee are savages who deserve to be run off the face of the earth. Those who would say that they are ignorant cowards have never had to face a fiercely proud Indian brave defending his homeland.

"Our first skirmish with the Cherokee came in the Spring of 1755 as we broke bivouac near Cumberland and headed into Indian country to destroy a village deep within. We had made it no more than two days, before we ran into an Indian scouting party. They were only 10 to 15 braves to our 200. They attacked the middle of our column just in front of me. With the suddenness of a tornado, they swooped down upon the column and wreaked havoc. The whole skirmish lasted only seconds. We suffered five dead, 24 wounded. The Indians lost one brave. They were gone as soon as they had appeared. They were ghosts who appeared out of nowhere and faded back into the fog just as quickly. My squad at least managed to form a line. Alas, the Indians had gone before we could fire.

"Our noses were bloodied and our nerves were shaken. Our frontiersmen now reorganized us. Squads were put to either side to prevent another ambush and we were now ordered to fire at will rather than wait to form the line. They were only small adjustments. Talking was forbidden and we walked with a renewed effort to silence every footfall. To make ourselves more invisible, we even took to dyeing our white shirts red clay brown to make us less of a target.

"For three weeks we kept up the march, always shadowed by Cherokee scouting parties. On the 25th day of the March, we reached the convergence of two small creeks, the reputed location of the village, which was the target of our maneuver. Overlooking the creeks from a small hill we could see the village at a distance. It was a well laid out village of bark longhouses and huts full of life. Through the Captain's spyglass we could see women and children scurrying around as they sensed danger. There was perhaps a mile between our position and the village; a dense forest to our front and the two streams impeded our forward progress. The frontiersmen advised our Captain to turn back and wait for another day. They explained the village was larger than expected and by all rights there were at least 400 braves or more. Unperturbed and forgetful that the Cherokee had long shadowed our advance to the village, the Captain ordered us to advance on line toward the village.

"We formed our lines at the base of the knoll and began to march on line to the village. No sooner had we reached the edge of the forest than the ambush was sprung. The Indians armed with French muskets laid down a writhing fire. In the open we suffered terribly. We fired one volley at the hidden enemy, to no avail. They waited until we had emptied our rifles and then descended upon us with tomahawks and trade axes. The ensuing melee was horrific. Fighting as best we could, we repulsed the Indians and retreated with only half the company back up the knoll and made a hasty defense. There over the next four hours we struggled to survive repeated attacks by the Indians. As night fell our chances of survival dimmed. Before us lay over half of the company dead. The wounded below us had been dispatched without any consideration of the rules of war. Of the 90 or so left on the knoll most everyone had some sort of injury. Our frontiersmen had long since disappeared, last seen beating a hasty retreat.

"The light faded and the Indians slipped from the battlefield back into the forest. It appeared most had merely returned to their village to get a good night's sleep before continuing the assault in the morning. Indian sentries were posted in the tree line, who fired occasional shots in our directions just to remind us they were still there. An attempt to send a party to the rear was met with utter disaster. That party had made it no more than 30 yards before they were set on by a volley of fire. We were surrounded and cut off.

"Around two o'clock in the morning we were rousted by a returning frontiersman. He told us to prepare to move out quickly. The plan he said was for our frontiersmen to attack the village and torch it and in the confusion, we were to slip back down the trail we came in on and set up an ambush for the pursuing Indians. Only those who could walk would be taken. There was no mention of the fate of those wounded, who could not walk. It was a hard decision, but it was a decision of life and death; life for a few or death for all. Quickly, we moved the badly wounded to hiding places in the nearby forest, gave each food and water, and covered them with leaves to at least offer them some protection from discovery. Nary a man complained; most asked only that someone take care of their families back home in case they did not make it out.

"Now down to 60 men, we quietly gathered our remaining equipment and made a hasty retreat up the path. At that time the frontiersmen, some 15 to 20 strong, attacked the village. They sounded like a whole army with all the noise they made. There was mass confusion in the village as it was set afire. In that confusion, we made good our escape.

"Tired as we were, we were still able to put about 10 miles between us and the Indian village as the dawn began to break. Now it was time for us to set up a deep ambush. The trail at this point favored us; here it wandered between two overhangs for about 100 meters before it opened into large glades surrounded by dense wood. Careful not to give away our ambush, the whole troop passed beneath the overhangs on through the glade. Thirty men then concealed themselves in the dense foliage at the edge of the glade, giving them an open view. The other 30 men, carrying fowling pieces loaded with buckshot, circled back deep in the forest to the overhang and set their ambush. The hope was that the Indians, in their haste to catch up with us, would run into our ambush before they realized what had happened. Only when the Indians presented themselves in the glade would we open fire. The men by the overhang would wait until the Indians bunched below them and would then open fire. It was risky at best.

"An hour after sunrise, the Indians discovered we had escaped, and began their search for our retreat. We rested the best we could, waiting for the inevitable.

"I was on the edge of the glade, armed with a musket, a pistol, a hunting knife, and an ax; and a strong will to survive.

Benjamin Brown lay not too far away. Even on the knoll fear had not affected me because there was no time. Now as we waited, knowing the enemy was approaching, fear began to smother me. Benjamin must have been feeling the same. He crawled closer; an arm's length away. There we lay next to each other, two scared boys. As fear manifested itself, we both began to sweat and we got the shakes. Sensing our fear, an old grizzled frontiersman crawled to us. 'Steady. Everything will be alright lads. Keep your heads down; fire as fast and often as you can. When you hear the signal for retreat, run as fast as you can for 100 yards down the road and regroup there. Be good lads now,' he said as he clopped Ben and me on the backs and left to reassure the others.

"The end to our waiting came about mid-morning. With the suddenness of a deer emerging from the woods, two Indian scouts in dark buckskins appeared at the far end of the glade as the trail emerged from the overhand. Soon another appeared. Never did I hear any of them. Had they not appeared in a small opening, I would not have seen them. They were truly the invisible ghosts of the forest.

"No one moved on our side. We too, had to remain invisible in order to survive.

"Soon another Indian appeared, who appeared to be in charge. Unmindful of the cautiousness of his scouts, he berated them and urged them forward. Blindly obedient, the scouts quickly caught our trail and began to run across the glade toward our positions. The main war party soon began to emerge from the confines of the overhang. The scouts sticking to the trail passed our ring without discovering us and proceeded down the trail into the woods. More of the war party was now in the open. Perhaps 20 to 30 braves were casually walking the trail unaware of the ambush. It was only a moment before the frontiersmen waiting in ambush set on the scouts. The unmistakable war hoop of one of the scouts sent the Indian scurrying for cover. We opened up as if on cue. The blasts from our muskets and those of the Indians filled the glade with a dense cloud of smoke. Now standing next to a tree and reloading, an Indian brave appeared out of nowhere and attacked me with his tomahawk. Ben fired his pistol and saved my life.

"There were shouts of anger and cries of pain all around us. A volley of fire erupted to our front as the other ambush was sprung. I could not see well in front of me; the smoke covered the glade. Time and again I reloaded and fired blindly into the glade. Whether I hit someone or not, I will never know. After firing no more than five or six times, the hunting horn blared and Ben, still next to me, and I turned tail and ran for our lives. Visions to the right and left of us were also running. It was then I noticed a brave carrying a tomahawk in his right hand and his musket in his left hand, running parallel to me not more than 10 yards away. It seems we noticed each other at the very same moment. He immediately swerved toward me as I pulled out my pistol. Not stopping, I quickly fired on him and luckily hit him in the shoulder, knocking him down. I did not hesitate to finish him off, but kept on running as fast as I could, hoping to find the rally point.

"Ben and I managed to make the trail and continued to run for some distance. It was soon apparent we had overrun the rally point and were now way beyond the rest of the company. We could hear the sounds of battle far in front of us. Exhausted, we stopped and immediately set about reloading our weapons and trying to catch our breaths. We agreed to wait no more than 10 minutes for others to appear before we continued our escape. Less than a minute later, a volley of fire came from our front. Soon we heard the shouts of approaching men. To our sides the men from the overhang appeared, not too worse for the wear. They saw and began to fall in around us, quickly reloaded, and took up positions ready to continue the fight. Orders were shouted, men repositioned themselves, wounds attended to.

"It was not long before men came running down the trail. The bulk of 15 men, some being carried, appeared first. Then came the remainder, some on the trail, some through the woods, all intently looking behind them for any approaching enemy.

"As they approached our hasty defense, the Captain barked out simple orders. "We hit them hard. They'll be more cautious for a while. Ten miles ahead on this trail is a creek crossing. We'll rally again there. The main body with the wounded will go now. The rest of you hold here for 15 minutes and then come running. You should catch us in about a couple of miles. When you reach us again, break off and continue to act as a rear guard. If something happens and you get separated, we'll join up again at Pearce's Ford on the Cumberland. That's about 25 miles due east of here. Try to stay together if you can.'

"To my luck, Will, the Captain, looked at our grizzled scout and gave him an order. 'Take the two young lads there and move on ahead as quickly as you can. Try to reach Pearce's Ford by sundown. If the militia is there, send them back to us. If no one is there, move on to Cumberland and try to raise the militia there.'

"We took off on a slow run, following our scout. We raced through Pearce's Ford by late afternoon. No one was there and there was no sign anyone had been there in recent months. Two hours later, exhausted, we stopped by a small creek. Clear cold mountain water refreshed us only a little. Only halfway to Cumberland and civilization and unable to move any faster, we moved out again at a fast walk. Throughout the night we marched, ever mindful of the fate of our neighbors lay in our hands. We made only an occasional stop. Finally at daybreak we came to our first farm along the trail. It was only a matter of time before we were in Cumberland. There our scout made his report to the British magistrate, who quickly called out the militia. A 60-man relief column was formed and by late afternoon was dispatched to aid our company.

"Four days later, the remnants of our militia company arrived in Cumberland. Of the 200 we started with, 60 returned, 20 were seriously wounded, 100 or so were known to have died, and the remaining 40 were missing and presumed dead. We lost over half of our militia company in a punitive raid on the Cherokee. The Cherokee lost perhaps as many; we were never sure. But as a result, the Cherokee moved their villages deeper into their territory and raids on farms dropped off. It was a high cost to pay for peace in the mountains, but one we made none-the-less.

"Will, when we went after the Indians we had a purpose, we were bound together by that purpose and were willing to endure great hardships to see it through. At a great loss of life, we succeeded. If there's anything you learn from this story it is that now is not the time to fight. There is no consensus of opinion as to what any of the Whigs are fighting for that we can't go to a fair and equitable court of law and obtain relief. We live in a civilized society and even though the Tories are grabbing land on the flimsiest of excuses, the law is bound to finally catch up with them. We must bide our time. End of sermon. Now go and attend to the horses. We have a lot to do in the morning."

Chapter 4

Confrontation

Morning came early for us. Shortly before sunrise, a horseman came riding into our yard, dismounted, and rapped heavily on our door. I rose to answer the door, as Father reached for his rifle. Gingerly I opened the door to find a weary Donald Sullivan, a farmer from down in the valley at the door.

"For God's sake Will Jones, open the door. I've no time to spare and neither do you or your family." Mr. Sullivan literally burst into the cabin and surveyed the surroundings. He spoke to my father directly, ignoring the rest of us. "William, trouble is headed this way. I see that poor Benjamin has taken shelter here. The Tories are scouring the countryside for him. They know he has escaped, but they don't know which way he went. It seems he put a load of shot into the Squire. Caught him full in the chest. Kilt him dead. Good riddance, I say. Now they are threatening to jail anyone caught harboring Benjamin. They are only two farms away and there is no stopping them. You better get him moved and quick."

"Donald, if we move him, he will die. He needs medical attention. I had planned to take him to Fredrick this morning after he had a chance to calm down a bit."

From his deathbed, Benjamin Brown spoke with a labored voice. "Let the damn Tories take me. I've stopped the Squire and I've done my service. I don't have much more time left. They can't hurt me anymore. William, when they come, turn me over and save your family." He stopped momentarily and turned his head to his wife, "Darling, I can't bear to leave you alone, but at least you won't have to pay for my folly. You and the children must move to my brother's over in Story. He will take good care of you. Just remember I will always love you." Exhausted, Mr. Brown passed out again.

"We can't move him; he's too weak. We'll have to hide him. Any place we try they will surely find him." Father was thinking out loud. "There is a chance we might be able to save Old Ben if we can keep him quiet. It will be hard, but it's the only chance we have. Donald, get back on your horse and ride back to Charles, slowly, full of emotion and pain. Intentionally run into the Tories and tell them Ben is here, but they are too late because he's already dead. They'll not believe the story, so they'll bring a party to see for themselves. If we can make Ben look dead and if Mrs. Brown can weep convincingly, we just might pull it off. Donald, take off, do your job. We need about 30 minutes to make things look real. Now go and everyone get busy."

Donald Sullivan wished everyone well and was out the door without another word. Father grabbed Benjamin Brown's blood-soaked clothes and with the help of Mother and Mrs. Brown started to redress him. It was truly a gruesome sight to see Mr. Brown in the crimson red clothes. To add pallor to his skin, Mother went to the fireplace and carefully extracted gray ashes. She and Mrs. Brown then carefully rubbed the gray ashes on his exposed skin. The effect was dramatic; Mr. Brown now indeed looked dead. Darker ash was used to give his eyes a sunken look. Father then took some of the precious writing ink, diluted it with water, and gently damped Mr. Brown's lips. Although not blue like a dead person's, it did make the lips less red. In the darkened cabin, it might just do the trick. Our only cause for concern was that if Ben woke up during the "Troy wake" or moaned.

Father pulled himself up alongside Mr. Brown and spoke softly. "Benjamin, we have a difficult situation ahead. No less dangerous than we faced during the Indian War. Do you understand me, Ben? Please tell me if you can hear me?"

"You haven't offered me a pint of ale yet so; they'll be no talking till then." Ben spurted a small cough.

"You old fool, this is serious. The Tories will soon be here. You got to be quiet as a real dead man. No moving and no coughing. Try not to breathe too deeply."

"Easy for you to say. I've only got one good lung. To make it real, don't forget our burial traditions. Be sure to place a hay penny in each eye, that is if you have such wealth to spare. And don't think of taking them from me, they'll be mine after this."

The final touches were readied, even down to the hay penny in each eye as required by tradition.

Our wait for the inevitable confrontation was not long. Less than half an hour after Donald Sullivan left our cabin, we heard the approach of a band of riders on horseback. Soon a band of 10 weary, angry men rode into our yard. Father, carrying his rifle in both hands and with a pistol in his belt, greeted them before they even got off their horses.

"There'll be no need for any of you to dismount. Benjamin Brown is dead and I will not allow any of you to disturb his grieving family. Now be off with you. You have done your deed."

As would have it, one horseman ignored Father's warning and acted as if he would dismount. Father, without further warning, fired his rifle, nicking the man in his left upper arm. Father handed the empty rifle to me as I handed him a freshly loaded one. We were no match for the Tory band, but Father's marksmanship was legendary in these parts. Everyone knew had he wanted, he would have put the bullet square into the man's head. No Tory reached for a weapon, and all sat a little uneasy in their saddles.

It was a county constable who spoke first. "William, I know you to be a fair man, a good loyal subject of the Crown. We must see Whig Brown's body to make sure he is in fact dead. He shot and killed the Squire last night and if he's not dead then he would surely hang. At least allow me to confirm his death. That's not too much to ask. I will be very respectful of the Widow Brown."

The Squire's disheveled son, tauntingly called the Peacock for his peculiar mannerisms, spoke up in an acrid tone. "The traitor Brown ambushed us as we rode up to talk to him about some missing livestock. Without warning, he shot my father dead. The old bastard deserves to be placed on a pike in the town square for all to see."

As the Peacock moved in his saddle, Father leveled the rifle on him. The constable quickly interceded and pushed the Peacock upright again.

"There'll be no need for further violence. I wasn't there last night and can't vouch for what transpired. All I know is that if Ben Brown is alive then he returns with me to Charles to face trial. If he's dead then justice has been served. I'll have no more of this bitterness today," said the constable turning his head toward the Peacock.

From the back of the band, a man with a powerful, resonant voice spoke up. "William, we have known each other for years. As a doctor and the county coroner, it is my duty to pass judgment on the dead. I think it would be more appropriate if I took the examination." Dr. Miller moved his horse closer to the front so Father could see him more closely.

The constable spoke first, "William, we need to confirm the death. I'll accept the doctor's word."

The Peacock spoke next, "I want to see for myself, I don't trust any of you. You were all against my father."

"The doctor may view the body, but no one else. I won't have the grieving widow disturbed by anyone else," said Father.

What disturbed me was that the doctor would surely see the ruse and poor Ben would be hauled off to face the hangman. I dare not move or say anything. Father knew what he was doing, I hoped.

"Will, prop the other rifle next to me and show the doctor inside. Stay with him. I'll keep these fine gentlemen entertained outside."

The doctor dismounted and carried a small black bag with him as he mounted our front steps. As he made the front porch, we shook hands and exchanged greetings as they were. He and Father never looked at one another, Father was preoccupied with staring down the Tories. The doctor followed me inside without further comment. I held my breath.

It took only a second to see the horror in the eyes of Mother and Mrs. Brown when the doctor appeared inside the cabin. All was lost. I see the hope drain from the women's eyes. Mrs. Brown started crying uncontrollably.

Instead of going to the "corpse," the doctor went to the assistance of Mrs. Brown.

"Sarah, there is no need to have fear. As far as I'm concerned Ben is dead. The only question is how do we get that stubborn old bastard out of here safe and sound. By the way, the make-up job would have fooled most in this light."

Mrs. Brown looked into the eyes of the doctor with amazement. Without a word, she embraced him and then began to sob again in earnest.

"Enough now. Let me do a quick look, see what this is about, make my death report and then we'll see what we can do. So, Benjamin, you cut the poor Squire down as he was making a social call with 20 of his friends."

A labored whisper was all Ben could manage. "Like hell I did. The bastard rode up and started firing without even a 'How do you do.' I was lucky to have hit him at all."

"You hit him perfectly in the chest. He was dead before he hit the ground," retorted the doctor. "I examined him earlier this morning at your old place, which I'm afraid is completely burned down. I only wish you had taken us up on our offer of assistance.

We might have ended this reign of terror last night for good. At least you chopped off the head of the main rattlesnake."

It was then I knew that Dr. Miller was a Whig. There were rumors that a secret Whig organization existed in the county, but no one knew for sure who was in it. Sure, some more vocal small farmers were thought to be members, but no one ever suspected any of the professionals in the county were. I guess my Father knew a lot more than I gave him credit for.

Dr. Miller did a thorough exam of his new patient.

"Sarah, I will depend on you to give me a reason to stay. You must lie down and appear comatose, just in case the rabble outside wants to check on you. If all goes well your old curmudgeon will be fit as a fiddle in three to four months. I have a lot to do. Now get to bed, while I go and report Ben's untimely death to the crowd outside." Without waiting for a response, the doctor turned and went to the door.

I followed close behind him. As we walked onto the porch, the scene outside had changed a little. Father had relaxed his aim and held the rifle to port, across his chest. The horsemen were more spread out. This caused Father to be a bit more anxious.

The doctor began to give his report. "Gentlemen, Old Ben Brown is dead. There were eight gunshot wounds to his upper torso, one of which penetrated his right lung. I will write in the death records that he died from loss of blood due to injuries sustained in a confrontation with Crown authorities. Does anyone have any further questions for me regarding this matter? If not, I must return inside to attend Widow Brown. She is suffering from either shock or else she has had a minor episode. In either case, she will need my attention." As the doctor prepared to move back in, Peacock spoke up.

"Not so fast Dr. Miller. You need to remain here for a moment to witness the next proceeding. Constable, I am preferring charges against Farmer William Jones for interfering with a duly constituted Crown search party, assault with intent to cause harm, and harboring a treasonous criminal in his home. These charges are duly presented in front of witnesses, the Crown party, our duly appointed constable, and also a respected professional member of the community. Constable, do your duty and arrest him."

Although the Constable heard the charges and the demand to arrest Father, he sat very still in the saddle and did nothing to enforce the Peacock's demand. "Young Squire, due to the situation we have right now, it would not be beneficial to either the Crown or the good order of the Community to forcibly take Farmer Jones into custody," said the Constable.

Before Father could say anything, the sound of two flints being cocked off to my extreme right suddenly changed the whole complexion of the standoff. There at the edge of the porch stood two Tory marksmen, one with his weapon trained on Father and the other trained on me.

It was an eternity before an even more confident Peacock spoke up. "Constable, as you can see the situation has changed dramatically." He then addressed Father directly. "Jones, if you do not surrender your rifles immediately, a Crown marksman will cut you down as you stand. Please notice one rifle is aimed at your eldest son, who will also pay for your sins. I advise you very strongly to consider the consequences."

At this moment, all of the horsemen shouldered their weapons and aimed at Father and me. There was but one choice under the circumstances. Father slowly released the hammer on his rifle and leaned the weapon against the porch post. The confrontation had ended to our disadvantage.

The constable spoke quickly. "Now lads, he has duly surrendered, so put your weapons away. I will have none of this so-called quick justice as long as I'm on duty. William Jones will accompany me to Charles where I will present him to the Magistrate. Young Squire, if you wish to prefer charges, you may accompany William and me to Charles. The rest of you disband and go home. Your services are no longer needed."

One by one each Tory horseman released the hammer on his rifle and placed it across his saddle. The marksmen at the edge of the porch did not budge; they kept their rifles trained on Father and me.

Dr. Miller spoke to my Father loud enough for everyone to hear. "William, take my long jacket and use my horse. I will have Will bring me in with Old Ben's body later today if Widow Brown is doing better." With that, Dr. Miller slipped off his long coat and gave it to Father.

Mother, who had been watching from inside the house, cautiously eased out the front door and up to my Father. Father tried to console her as they embraced and told her he would be back home by nightfall. Mother only told him to hurry home, but the anguish showed in her face, tears streaked her beautifully pale cheeks. As Father walked to Dr. Miller's horse, I followed behind.

He mounted the bay gelding and then looked down at me.

"Son, take care of your Mother and the children. You are the man of the house while I'm gone. I am depending on you and I expect you to do the right thing. Don't worry about me, the laws protect us common folk from the power of tyranny." He reached down and tousled my hair as he reigned the horse out the front gate of our yard.

Slowly, the Tory horsemen disappeared. I saw the two Tory marksmen ride by as they too headed back in the direction of Charles.

"Don't be concerned about your father, Will. There is a brace of fully primed pistols in the jacket and my bay is the fastest hunter in the county. If your father feels the need to escape, he can do so at will. I don't think the Tories will risk another embarrassing incident this soon after last night's fiasco. Come, Will, we have a lot to do to get Old Ben ready for his trip to Fredrick."

As if things were not bad enough, the situation worsened. As we entered the cabin, the first thing both Dr. Miller and I noticed was Mother sprawled out on the floor near the fireplace. Mrs. Brown was tenderly attending to her. It took us a moment, but we finally noticed the pool of blood oozing out from under Mother.

"A miscarriage," said Dr. Miller compassionately. "Will help me with your mother. We will have to work hard to save her. I'm afraid the baby may not survive."

Quickly, Dr. Miller and I moved Mother to a more comfortable position on the floor as Mrs. Brown readied a new pot of boiling water. There were still plenty of clean rags from the surgery. Like the well-practiced doctor that he was, Dr. Miller prepared to deliver a premature baby as he had done hundreds of times before. I took a position just to his left and waited for my instructions. Mother came to and immediately knew what was happening.

"I'm afraid I couldn't help Dr. Miller. I guess this child was not meant to be. I'm so sorry to have imposed upon you, what with all the problems we have right now." Mother's voice was soft and weak. She couldn't continue; a sudden labor pain racked her body.

"Sarah, never you mind. I'm afraid though you are right. There's not much chance for this poor child to survive. I'll do the best I can. Now you have to help and push so the child will come out. Your labor is starting, so work through it and remember to push and breath, push and breath. Will, get some clean rags and a small blanket ready. Helen, hurry with that water. We will need it soon."

Dr. Miller's calculation of "soon" lasted for five hours. During this time the kids, both my siblings, and the Brown children stayed out of the way and remained quiet. Occasionally one or another would whimper a little and Mrs. Brown, dear soul that she was, would go and comfort them. In between, she attended her gravely wounded husband still perched on our kitchen table, no better, yet no worse. Benjamin, as tough as his reputation was and to his credit, remained relatively quiet and even managed to sleep just a little. He was truly a tough farmer.

As the sky lighted and the morning rays of early dawn came through our cabin window, Mother delivered a very tiny, stillborn baby girl. The poor thing was not even the size of a grown man's hand. Dr. Miller quickly handed my baby sister to me. In turn, I gently cleaned her off and wrapped her in a small piece of discarded cloth.

"Will, give her to me. I want to hold her just a second," wept Mother softly. "Go prepare her a place near the big oak. When you have it ready you can come back for her."

I didn't respond. Tears welled in my eyes. Whether the tears were all for my little sister or the whole combination of Mr. Brown, Father being arrested, the baby's premature birth, and death, I didn't know. I could not ever remember being so emotional. My whole world, in a matter of hours, had crashed around me. My life, I felt, would never be the same. I retrieved an iron spade from the barn and walked slowly down to the big oak. I scarcely remember digging the tiny grave beneath the spreading branches of the oak, nor do I remember making a small cross to go with it. I returned to the world as I took the long walk back to the house. Still not fully myself, I gently retrieved my little sister from Mother. As I did, we spoke no words. She merely gave me a gentle stroke on my arm and then closed her eyes to rest.

I carried the precious bundle down to the oak and laid her gently to rest. Quickly I covered her with earth, gathered a few heavy stones to place over her grave to keep it from being disturbed, and then said a short prayer for the poor little waif.

I returned to the cabin to find Dr. Miller cleaning up the afterbirth and Mrs. Brown cleaning up Mother as she rested on the floor. The children were stirring, but being very quiet and mindful of the delicate situation that existed. Mr. Brown, now semi-conscious, was staring at the ceiling of our cabin, tears running down his cheek.

"Will," he said to me as I entered the cabin, "I'm a pig-headed old fool. Had I listened to your father, none of this would have happened. I am so sorry Will." He reached for my hand, which I gave him. His firm grip showed the sincerity of his personal grief.

"Mr. Brown, it's not your fault that all this has happened. It was only a matter of time before the Tories would have struck. If anyone is at fault, it is the Squire, and he has paid dearly for his mistake. As Father would say, now is not the time to wallow in anguish, but time to raise our heads and see our future whatever it may be."

"Words well-spoken, Young Will," said Dr. Miller. "Given the circumstances, we must plan our escape. No doubt the Tories will soon learn that Benjamin did not die and will seek to gain revenge for Squire's death. Will, you and your family are now as much in danger as Benjamin and his family. I, being the giver of false proclamations likewise, am in danger. Fortunately, my wife and children are visiting her family further up in The Piedmont. They are at least safe for the time being. When we deliver Benjamin and his family to Fredrick. I will then join my wife and family. I suggest you also flee. Your father will be safe for the time being, but I fear he may be detained for some time. In either case, we will send word to him once we reach Fredrick. Will, do you have a place to go?"

Leave my home of 16 years, the place that Father and Mother had struggled to clear and plant. The only home I had ever known? I could not think or make a decision.

"Dr. Miller." It was my mother's voice. "We will go with the Browns as far as Fredrick and see what happens. I don't want to go too far away from our farm. We will take only those things we need for the trip and pray that our good neighbors watch over our homestead in our absence. When this is over, we will return, if God is willing."

Mother had made her decision. It was time for me to carry it out. By mid-morning, we were ready to go. The Browns and the Joneses would leave together and go toward an uncertain future.

Dr. Miller and I loaded Benjamin carefully into the back of the Brown wagon, as the Brown children nestled around their injured father. Mrs. Brown climbed to the seat to take control of the horses. Mother, now mostly recovered, was given a soft bed in the back of our one-horse wagon among the few essential possessions we owned and the six littlest children. The two older children, Andrew and Sarah, would sit with me on the bench. The cow was tied to the back of the wagon. The three best laying hens came with us; I released the rest of our chickens to forage for themselves. As I looked at our meager possessions loaded on our wagon, I realized the most prized possession was the family itself. It was Mother's decision to save this prized possession that meant she could turn her back on 13 years of bone-numbing labor without much of a second thought. She became the staff of our family, the strong-willed spirit that would keep us together.

Chapter 5

Escape to Fredrick

As we left the cabin and headed west toward Fredrick, I took one last look at our 40-acre homestead. I felt a strong pang in my heart, unsure whether I would ever see my home again.

The trip to Fredrick was long and trying for both Mother and Mr. Brown. Both wagons creaked along over the rough, hard-packed road, which was more a trail in places than an actual road. Several times the children had to dismount our wagon in order for us to make it up a steep incline. The Browns, with two horses in their team, fared much better. We had to stop every three hours or so, give the horses water, let them eat a little grass on the side of the road, and let both horses and humans rest for a while. Mr. Brown, despite the rough trip, was showing signs of recovery. His color was now returning to normal and amazingly there were no signs of infection. Mother too was looking better. Despite her haggard, worried look, Mother's color was also returning.

Just as the Fredrick Presbyterian church bell tolled eight

o'clock, we arrived on the outskirts of town. It is there that we first noticed a radical difference between Charles and Fredrick. The guard post stationed nearly a mile from town was manned by 10 Whig militia in, of all things, what would pass as uniforms; dark black cockade hats, blue homespun waistcoats, and dark blue homespun greatcoats to shield against the evening cold. That is where the uniform look ended. Pants were of the individual's choosing, as was footwear. Even the choice of weapons was personal. There was an eclectic collection of hunting rifles, trade muskets, captured British muskets, and even a fowling piece or two. The officer or perhaps the militiaman in charge was distinguished by the two rather expensive French dueling pistols stuck in his waist belt. His countenance also underscored his authority.

As we approached the torch lite checkpoint, I noticed several militiamen fade into the shadows and take up firing positions behind two rather imposing oaks that dominated the site. The commander in charge of the post stood firmly in the middle of the road behind a singletree wagon used as a barrier. The other militiamen milled around a bonfire trying to keep warm disregarding our approach. It was not until we were approximately 25 yards away did they leave the warmth of the fire and meander to the wagon barrier. We were finally challenged as we pulled to a stop at the barrier.

"Halt!" cried the watch commander. "Who might you be and state your business?"

Having taken the lead since our wagon was slower, which necessitated us setting the pace, I was at a momentary loss for words. Behind me, Dr. Miller spoke in a clear and resonant voice that carried beautifully in the crisp night air.

"I am Dr. Miller of Charles. We have two critically ill people with us. One is Mrs. Jones, who suffered a miscarriage and the other is Farmer Benjamin Brown, who was wounded near Charles when attacked by Tory raiders last night. We need to get both medical assistance and shelter."

"We understand that Mr. Brown was killed in the attack?" questioned the commander.

"I will not debate the success of our ruse. I can only say that Mr. Brown's heroic effort to save his farm from the Tories ended in the death of our most despised adversary Squire Morris. Now I am struggling to save both these brave people and need your assistance, sir."

"My father, William Jones, was taken prisoner by the Tory Constable for providing shelter to Mr. Brown and threatening the raiding party," I added.

"So, it must be true," laughed the commander. "There is only one man that could stop a Tory raiding party in their tracks. It is a great loss to know that William is now in Tory hands. We welcome you to our small hamlet and hope that you find your needs taken care of. Go to the town square and inquire at the pub Cock and Rose for Mr. Cramer; he will see to your requirements. You are free to pass friends. God be with you." With that, the commander ordered the wagon barrier moved to let us pass.

Our wagons rolled slowly through the checkpoint. Militiamen lined the road and wished us "Good Luck," "God's speed," and tipped their hats at Mrs. Brown and Dr. Miller. One militiaman casually walked next to our wagon and spoke directly to my mother.

"Mrs. Jones, I am saddened by the news that William was arrested. I'm sure he will be fine. If there is a man alive that can come through unscathed it is William. Don't worry." He quickened his pace a bit and came forward to me. "Young Will, you must be. From what I see, a young man cut from his father's cloth. I'll be around to see you and your family within the next couple of days. We have a lot to talk about, young Master Will." With that, he was gone like an apparition into the darkness which now surrounded our wagon. I didn't have a chance to even respond.

Within the hour we arrived at the quiet Fredrick town square. Most of the lights in the houses and shops surrounding the square were dark. The Cock and Rose, the local tavern, was the only establishment with lights shining in its windows, but even the noises coming from the tavern were low and muffled, unlike the taverns in Charles with which I was familiar.

Dr. Miller and I quickly jumped down from our wagons and proceeded to the tavern, leaving the families momentarily on the empty street. With mild trepidation, we entered the tavern to find it surprisingly full. There appeared to be some sort of meeting going on, a closed meeting at that. Nonetheless, Dr. Miller boldly strode in and announced us in a very confident tone.

"Good evening gentlemen," bellowed Dr. Miller trying to be heard over the disturbance our entry had made. "I am Dr. Miller of Charles and this is my companion Master Will Jones of our county," he continued. "The commander of the guard instructed us to ask for Mr. Cramer. Farmer Benjamin Brown, the noble defender of his farm, who was severely wounded by a Tory raiding party, is in need of additional medical assistance which I was unable to give him, due to our flight from the county. We also seek shelter for the Brown family, the wife, and six children; and the Jones family, Will, his mother, and six children."

"I'm Cramer," came a voice from behind the bar. "Where is William? Why is he not with you?"

I spoke up to establish myself as the head of my clan. "We gave shelter to Mr. Brown and for that act of kindness, the Tories arrested my Father and took him to Charles and charged him with assisting the rebellion. My mother is in ill health and needs a clean warm place to stay; the children and I can stay in a barn if necessary.

"We'll have none of that lad," said Cramer. "Boys, you heard what the doctor and young Will has said. Now go take care of these good people. Dr. Miller, I have some of the boys bring old Ben around back to the cottage. It is warm and dry there. He and his Mrs. can stay there. We'll have to farm the Brown children out to the neighbors. Ben needs a quiet place I'm sure, and there'll be enough room for you too. I'm afraid as far as more medical assistance, there is none. We have had no doctor hereabouts for the past three months, ever since Dr. Henry left to join the Continentals. I stored all of his equipment and medical supplies in my cottage, so they are there for your use."

Without another word of encouragement, one after another townsmen volunteered to take a child or two and donate blankets, clothes, or any necessity we had not brought with us. Their charity was from the heart and certainly well appreciated by all of us.

The Brown children were split up between two neighbors who had children the same ages, as were my siblings. I stayed with

Mother in this, her hour of need. We were given the front room in the house of Mrs. Jamison, a kindly old widow. Mr. and Mrs. Brown and Dr. Miller were safely placed in the cottage behind the tavern. Resigned that the children were being cared for by others, Mother, still weak, collapsed on the small sofa bed and was fast asleep. I took my customary place before the fireplace and wrapped myself in the deerskin bag.

Chapter 6

Settling In

I must have fallen asleep as my head hit the floor. I remembered nothing more than wrapping up in my deerskin bag as I awoke early the next morning with the crowing of the roosters and the sound of impatient milk cows ready to be milked. Mrs. Jamison was quick to hit the floor. I heard her stirring around upstairs doing her morning business. After she emptied the chamber pot out the back window she closed it ever so gently, I decided it was time for me to get up. Mother was still sound asleep. She needed her rest. Since I was still in my clothes from yesterday I only had to put on my boots and I was ready to go. I left Mother sleeping and quietly closed the door to the front room. Mrs. Jamison met me in the hallway as she descended the narrow staircase.

"Well, good morning to you, Master Jones," said a cheerful Mrs. Jamison. "I hope you slept well after your ordeal."

"Good morning to you, Mrs. Jamison. Despite our hardship, I slept exceedingly well, thank you. Mother is still asleep and I think it would be best if she got as much rest as possible."

"Such a nice young man to care for your Mother so well. Of course, she can sleep all she wants. Why don't you come with me back to the kitchen and I will make you some breakfast. What would you like? How about eggs, a little Virginia ham, and some biscuits?"

"That is breakfast fit for the King," I said absent-mindedly.

"My son, be extremely careful with whom you use such phrases. There are many a man here that take offense to the King and would just as quickly label you a Tory sympathizer."

"Perhaps I should have said 'That breakfast is fit for a militiaman.'"

"My you do learn fast. I like that in a young man. So come and let me make a real militiaman breakfast. Do you drink tea or coffee?"

"I'm afraid, Mrs. Jamison, that I have only had tea on a few occasions and have never been introduced to coffee. Both were a luxury in our home and I have not acquired a taste."

"Then you must have coffee; it is a very patriotic drink. The tax on tea still goes to the Crown and we cannot be supporting the Red Coats in their war against us, can we? Coffee is so-to-say an untaxed commodity that the King derives no revenue. Now go busy yourself in the barn and milk the cows. Your good cow was brought to me last night and if she did not go dry from the walk all the way here we will have plenty of milk and some left over to trade."

Dutifully, I picked up the milk pail and headed to the barn at the back of Mrs. Jamison's small yard. The morning air was crisp and clear. Fredrick was slowly waking up from its long winter night's slumber. The smell of wood smoke from the kitchen stoves perfumed the air. Barn doors creaked open as each household sent someone out back to milk the cow. These were the morning farm noises I was used to except they were repeated 100 times over.

Both cows were in a most disagreeable mood; full to capacity and demanding attention. As quick as I could I prepared each cow for milking making sure each tit was clean and free of any dirt or trash. "Cleanliness is next to godliness, which includes the cow too!" was what Father always told us. We never had any problem with milk going bad too soon, nor did any of us children get sick from drinking milk as other children did from time to time in our small community. After half an hour of milking, I was rewarded with two buckets of fresh, wholesome milk. Carefully, I fitted the buckets on the old milk yoke and walked ever so carefully back to the main house with my treasure.

Several of the neighbors had also finished their milking and were headed back at the same time. "Good morning!" shouted one stout fellow to my right. "Top of the morning!" said another rather tall, thin man, an obviously new transplant from an English jail. I waved to both the best I could as I steadied the yoke and gave a "Good morning to you sir!" in reply. We went our separate ways without further comment.

I arrived at the kitchen door and was suddenly struck with the dilemma of how to negotiate the door when, as if by magic, Mrs. Jamison opened it for me and stepped aside.

"Oh, wonderful! Two buckets of milk! Aren't we fortunate this morning? After breakfast, you'll need to run some milk around to the Griffins for your brothers and sisters. Not that the Griffins need the milk; they have two cows of their own, but it's a good gesture and I'm sure they will appreciate it. We must assure everyone that you and your family will pull their own weight and not depend only on the goodwill and charity of the community."

Somewhat taken aback by the statement, I bristled a bit too much. "We are not charity cases Mrs. Jamison! While we might not have much money (*which in fact we had none*), my brothers and I can hold our own against any man in the field and my mother is an excellent cook and seamstress."

"Young Will, I'm sorry I offended you. I meant no harm, nor was I making a judgment about your good family. I'm certain that you and your family will not be a burden, but a real asset to our community. Forgive me for the misunderstanding, but we are a delicate balance in our small community at the moment. Every day, good people, displaced by the Tories, stream into our hamlet seeking refuge. Most, like your family, are prepared to contribute to their support. Some unfortunates come with nothing. Those are the ones that create a burden for us all. We turn away no one, but our own stores are running thin."

Mrs. Jamison came forward and pressed both of her generous hands to the sides of my face. She gently relieved one and then the other pale from the yoke, placed them on the hutch, and covered each with a small towel. "We'll take care of these later; now we eat breakfast."

It was a most wonderful Fredrick breakfast. The little bit of ham turned out to be four huge slices of excellent shank Virginia ham fried to a crispy brown, eggs enough to feed the militia, and a large pan of biscuits.

"Eat your fill young Will. There will be enough for your

mother. Your brothers and sisters will be doing fine. I will fill the extra biscuits with ham and you can take them with you this morning as you explore the town. Besides, you might find work and won't be able to come back here for your noon meal."

It was transparent that after my chores around the house, I was to go to the center of town to find day labor to earn my "community keep." Mrs. Jamison and the community were right, even in their hour of need, the displaced families needed to earn their keep. The charity of the community had to be stretched for more new arrivals. Anything we could do left more for those that came behind us.

By seven o'clock I had finished a few chores around the house for Mrs. Jamison. Mother, still exhausted from the miscarriage and the trip, was sound asleep.

"Now Will, take this bucket of milk around to the Griffins; third house past the square on the Cumberland Road. It's a pretty little white cottage with green trim. They'll be expecting you. You can visit with them for a half-hour or so then be off with you."

"Yes ma'am," was my only reply. What was not said and need not be said is, "Don't dawdle around, find some work to do, and be useful!" I lifted the milk pail carefully so as not to split any of my precious cargo and went off to the Griffins. As I passed the front door I reached for my rifle, pouch, and powder horn.

"No need for that today. You just leave the rifle here. There are enough militiamen about."

Yes, ma'am." So much for slipping away to go hunting and exploring in the countryside, I thought to myself.

Now Fredrick was a town of moderate size, perhaps 600

residents and maybe 100 homes. The town square was the commercial center of the town and 10 to 15 businesses clustered around the perfect acre square. Roads went off generally in the four cardinal directions from the square. Each road was named for its destination; Roanoke Road, Cumberland Road, Camden Road, and Wilderness Road. Four city roads and the unknown.

Finding the Griffin house was easy – or it should have been. Fredrick was composed of only cute, white cottages with green trim. It was obvious community pride that required each house to be similar in appearance to the other. Later, as I grew to know Fredrick better, I did learn that each house had its own personality, but my initial impression was that each house was exactly the same, which led to my confusion. I just cleared the square on Cumberland Road when I was faced with a long, uniform row of cute, white cottages trimmed in green. There I stood in the middle of Cumberland Road with a confused look on my face. A kindly old gentleman in a long black coat, noting my obvious confusion, came to my rescue.

"So young man, you must be one of the new arrivals. Chance you be William Jones?"

"They call me Will, sir. And, yes I'm newly arrived. I'm looking for the Griffin home. My brothers and sisters are staying there and I need to take them some milk."

"Good lad. Very responsible of you! The Griffin house is the third cottage on the right. Just go in the gate and knock on the front door. I'm sure they are expecting you. Take care of yourself, young man. By the way, we expect to see you at the tavern tonight at 7 o'clock to give us a complete account of what happened at your homestead. Good day young man," he said, tipped his hat to me, and left.

I tipped my hat to him and watched him walk away into the square with his hands clutched behind his back as if lost in thought. As with all things, I should not have been too concerned about locating the Griffin house. On their white gate, painted in black was the name "GRIFFIN." I was just a little embarrassed, but not too.

Even before I could open the gate, I heard squeals and shouting. Suddenly out poured my brothers and sisters, all seven of them. Cherokee warriors could not have made more noise. It was all I could do to save the pail of milk.

From seven different directions came a whirlwind of questions. "Where is Mother?" "Is she well?" "How does she feel?" "How's Father?" "Any word from Father?" "Are we staying?" "Are we leaving?" "Can we come stay with you?"

"Wait!" I exclaimed. "I'll answer each question in due time. First, we must take this milk to Mrs. Griffin and thank her for her hospitality. Remember we are guests and we must always show good manners."

Dutifully chastised by big brother my siblings quietly parted the way and fell in behind me as I walked up the front garden path to the front door. Mrs. Griffin, a large woman of at least six feet tall and girth to match greeted me warmly.

"So you must be Will. We have heard so much about you. Your brothers and sisters have been singing your praises. Come inside for a second and have some fresh coffee with me. My husband just left for the store. You may have seen him on the way; a dear gentleman in a black coat."

"I believe he may have been the one who gave me directions to your house."

Mrs. Griffin chuckled a little. "Didn't introduce himself, did he now? That's my Samuel, a bit distant at times, but a wonderful husband and father, nonetheless."

When we got to the kitchen I gave Mrs. Griffin the pail of milk. It was as if I had given her 10 crowns. She quickly got out a second butter churn; the Griffin children were already busy taking turns at another churn. My crew gathered around "their" churn and began to bicker over who would be first. I settled the order of work knowing full well the novelty of churning butter would soon wear thin until only the older ones continued the labor to the end. Now both sets of children safely engaged in a contest of who could churn butter the fastest, Mrs. Griffin poured two cups of hot coffee and placed them on the kitchen table. She motioned for me to sit on the bench across from her.

"Master Jones, we must discuss your family's present situation," Mrs. Griffin informed me. "I realize that you and your family have escaped the Tories under difficult situations. We, here in the township of Fredrick, understand and accept our responsibilities as good Virginians to help those in need."

Somehow I got the feeling Mrs. Griffin was the appointed marshal of the village, responsible for the initial "orientation" of all incoming refugees such as us.

"It will be necessary that you and your siblings make some sort of contribution," she continued. "You understand, earn your keep. We certainly don't expect your dear mother to do anything for a while, but perhaps later after she has recovered fully she will be able to contribute a little. I don't suppose you have any hard currency, now do you?"

Her inquisition was too personal for my tastes and I had the feeling we were being indentured to the town for support. "Mrs. Griffin, I will dutifully support my family as is expected. The question of money is a family matter that I am not at liberty to discuss. As you know my father was arrested for assisting Mr. Brown. It will be no doubt necessary to send money for his support while he is in custody and try to hire a lawyer to get him freed. Both of those undertakings will, by necessity, cost money. Surely you would not have us desert my Father when my family and I are fully capable of working for our keep, would you?"

"You misunderstand me, Master Will. I am sure you and your family will more than adequately support yourselves. The money is only an issue if you are unable to do so," she said while smiling a less than honest smile.

Having done what little paring as was necessary, Mrs. Griffin proceeded to set out the rules for self-sufficiency in the Fredrick Township. As our custodian and guardian, she had already set my work schedule. I basically became her indentured servant, farmed out to other households in need of assistance or a day laborer. In return, she would provide for the care and feeding of my family. There was no mention of monetary compensation for my work. The youngsters would only be required to perform chores around her household in the same manner as her own children. It was not an ideal arrangement, but one that I had to accept, given our dire circumstances. As an afterthought, she said I would be given Sundays off for the express purpose of attending church with my family.

That formality taken care of, Mrs. Griffin relaxed a little and began to banter about life in Fredrick and the advantages of living in a township versus living on an isolated farm. I soon longed for the safety and tranquility of our "isolated" farm.

Before long, a steady stream of visitors started arriving at Mrs. Griffin's home. Each visitor seemed to need some sort of special assistance. My days were being planned and negotiated before my very eyes. Although no mention of money was ever surfaced, I soon determined that the "usual consideration" for my services would certainly enrich Mrs. Griffin at my expense. It was a bitter pill to swallow, but for the sake of my mother and family, it was necessary.

Shortly after nine o'clock, Mrs. Griffin released me with instructions to learn the township from one end to the other. "It wouldn't do if you cannot be prompt by going from one labor to the other," she said with her suspicious smile. I was sure she would have me working from sunup to sundown, non-stop.

Despite the unsettling encounter with Mrs. Griffin, I found the township to be alive with the hustle and bustle of a thriving farming community and commercial center. People were everywhere; going about their business with smiles on their faces and purpose in their gait. Men tipped their hats to the ladies, who in return nodded their heads. This was truly a refinement that I had not noticed before in trips to Charles. Perhaps I had been too young to be aware. It was somewhat disconcerting to me personally that while all these people seemed to be cheerful and industrious, they were totally oblivious to the plight of the Browns or my family. Or at least it seemed to be. I did my best to be polite and friendly, but my feeble attempts failed to hide my desolation and despair.

As I transited the town square the third time, after first checking on Mother's condition, I was confronted by none other than the man in the black overcoat, Mr. Griffin. I had not noticed him until I heard a gruff voice call my name. "Master Will Jones." Turning to the direction of the voice, I noticed Mr. Griffin standing at the door of a general store, bearing his family name.

"Sir," I replied, "You must be Mr. Griffin." I approached him and offered my hand.

Not quick to accept my hand, he sized me up first and then reproachfully extended his hand. It was certainly a quick "dead fish" handshake.

"Come inside. We have business to discuss." He was curt and there was certainly no friendliness in his voice.

As we entered the store I was enthralled by the great quantity and variety of goods offered for sale. This was truly a hugely successful commercial enterprise. I followed him back to a small office in the back of the store as an assistant busied himself with customers. He pointed to a seat next to a small settee holding a silver teapot surrounded by fine porcelain china. I dutifully sat without saying a word as he eased into an old sea captain's chair opposite me.

"You'll need to learn to drink coffee in these parts if you are to be successful in your endeavors," he said while pouring me a cup of this strange but delicious brew. "Use milk or sugar if you like. Strong, black coffee is best; none of the pure flavor is lost."

"Thank you, sir," I replied as I picked my black cup of

coffee, longing for just a sweet taste of sugar, but not wanting to ignore his advice. I continued after taking a short sip of the burning hot beverage. "I visited with your wife early this morning and she has arranged for me to do odd jobs in the community in order to provide support for my family."

He raised his hand to stop me, "We'll discuss that later, but first let us enjoy our coffee. Business will come later." The expression on his face softened and a slight grin emerged on his lips as he delicately sipped his steaming cup. "My morning does not officially start until I have had my first cup of coffee. I'm a little late today. We have been out of coffee for a week now. Finally, a fresh shipment from Jamaica arrived in Norfolk two days ago. It was all I could do just to get two small chests of beans. Those politicians in Williamsburg are hoarding the whole shipment for themselves." He stopped talking and took another sip. An angelic smile graced his wrinkled face.

"Will," he continued, "I know my dear wife has literally mapped out your life while you are here in Frederick. I will talk to her when I get home this evening. You may attend to those chores she arranges for you each morning, however, the Committee requires your services each afternoon and evening. There may be times when you will have to go into the field for several days at a time. Your knowledge of the area and people in and around Charles is of particular importance to the Committee. We will assume responsibility for your family and ensure their welfare. We also hope your assistance may even lead to your father's rescue."

The mention of a possible rescue of my father excited me. Without even a moment's hesitation I quickly responded, "Mr.

Griffin, I will do anything you say if I can just get my father out of jail." I did not know what else to say and I fell silent, hoping that my short statement of resolve would be sufficient.

"Good," he replied, assuring me that my resolve was duly noted. "We have a committee meeting this evening at 8 o'clock. I need you to do a few errands for me, but first, go check on your mother and tell her you'll be out and about for the remainder of the day on errands for me."

He reached over to his desk for a small cloth bag. "Take these coffee beans to Mrs. Jamison with my regards and give her this note. Now finish your coffee and then go attend to your mother. Be back here at 10 o'clock."

"I'm sorry Mr. Griffin, I don't have a watch."

"Humph," he grunted. "I'll attend to that later. For now, just listen for the town clock. When it strikes 10 return here. That will do for now."

"Yes sir," I replied as I gulped down the last of my still-warm coffee. I stood and, with my hat in my hand, I gave a slight bow to Mr. Griffin and quickly departed the office as he continued to slowly savor his precious coffee.

With my small half pound of coffee beans in my coat pocket and the note in my hand I quickly departed the store and ran back to Mrs. Jamison's house. The sun seemed a little brighter, the day just a little warmer. I was totally preoccupied with the thought of rescuing Father. As I reached Mrs. Jamison's front door, the town clock peeled out nine distinctive rings. A whole hour until I had to return to the general store.

I found Mrs. Jamison and Mother in the front room

chatting over coffee, a drink to which Mother had just been introduced. I gave Mrs. Jamison a short bow, although I'm not sure when I learned to bow or exactly why I adopted this strange custom. It just seemed proper for some reason. I then gave Mrs. Jamison the small bag of coffee beans and the note from Mr. Griffin. To Mother, I gave a big but gentle hug, as was the custom in our family.

Mrs. Griffin thanked me for the delivery of the coffee and politely excused herself, taking with her the unread note from Mr. Griffin. This left Mother and I alone in the small room. Over the next 45 minutes, I related all that had happened to me that short morning in the greatest detail, not leaving out a single "humph" or "sigh." Mother rested quietly and occasionally touched my cheek as if to assure herself we were safe. She listened intently as was her manner, taking in all I was saying. I got most excited when I told her there might be a possibility Father could be rescued.

When I began to repeat things I had already recounted, she held up her hand. "Will," she said gently, "there is no need to repeat yourself. I believe your recollection was extremely thorough the first time. I only caution you to keep a clear mind and a sense of purpose. Your father is in the Crown's custody. You must remember we are law-abiding citizens. Do not take lightly someone's call to break the law. It could have serious, irreversible consequences. I'm sure your father will be released in good order. Be careful of the urge to do something that is against the good order." With that, she took my face in both her hands and pulled me gently to her to kiss me on my forehead. She emphasized to me that I was still her young son, not quite the grown man I yearned to be.

I took that as a cue I could go forth and do good, mindful

there were certain limitations to my actions. I kissed Mother lightly on her left cheek as I grabbed my hat and set off on my quest, which I hoped would include my father's rescue.

Chapter 7

Prelude to a Raid

I walked back to the general store and arrived just as the town clock began to toll 10 o'clock. Mr. Griffin, anticipating my arrival, was standing on the front porch.

"Good timing, Will. I'll need you to go around back and muck out the stables quickly. Don't take too long; you need to deliver this message to Dr. Wilson, who owns an apothecary on the main square in Charles this afternoon." He handed me the note. Deliver the message to Dr. Wilson, no one else. He is a man in his early forties, about my height, a rotund belly, and a receding hairline. His hair is black with a little gray in the temples. When you meet him, tell him you have an order for some medicines from me. He will then inform you that we went to school at William and Mary. That will confirm his identity. If he fails to say that, ask only for medicine to cure the grip. Don't deliver the message. Do you understand?" he asked.

"Yes," I replied and repeated the description of Dr. Wilson and the instructions.

"Good lad! You show promise. Now here is a letter of authorization to use the bay gelding. Don't confuse the two. Can't be too careful though. There are still thieves and brigands about. Stop only if lawfully challenged. Otherwise, ride like the wind. You are most likely to run into a checkpoint as you arrive at Charles. Avoid all other contacts along the way if they look the least bit suspicious. Now, go about your business and be back here by 7:30. I'll want to talk to you before we go to the meeting. Oh, here are a few things to eat along the way. Remember don't tarry. Just a moment Lad, I almost forgot to give you something." Mr. Griffin went inside his store and came out momentarily holding a pistol lovingly in both hands. "Here, Will, take this old Queen Anne with you. It served me well during the Indian Wars. Be careful, it's loaded. And take this small powder tin and bag of shot and patches as well."

I carefully examined the pistol and found that it was an old Queen Anne pistol. The date 1717 and the name "Wayne Delaney" were stamped on the right side of the barrel. "Sir, are you sure this pistol still shoots straight? After all, it is old."

"Good Anne always shot straight as long as your target was not more than 20 feet away. Just keep her dry and out of sight until you need to use her.

I quickly tucked the pistol, which weighed a little over two pounds and was almost a foot long, into the breast pocket of my old wool coat. I was thankful there was a moth hole in the pocket; the iron barrel protruded nicely out of it. It made for a good concealed and comfortable holster.

I thanked Mr. Griffin for his consideration, nodded

goodbye, and went to muck the horse stalls. It was almost inconceivable that I would have to muck the horse stalls before I rode to Charles, but it was soon apparent that Mr. Griffin knew his business. This exercise gave me the opportunity to think. To think about the possibilities I might encounter and how I would act out each situation. Although it only took me half an hour to muck the stalls and then saddle the bay gelding, I had raced through the trip to Charles four times and played over different scenarios each time. By 11, I was ready to ride.

As I mounted the bay and rode out of the stall I caught a glimpse of Mr. Griffin in the window of his office. No wave, not even a smile, only a slight nod of the head. I tipped my hat briefly and I was off. It was with only monumental effort that I controlled the bay at a brisk walk through Fredrick. The urge to race out of town was almost overpowering. At the edge of town, still not clear of the checkpoint a mile distant, I allowed the bay to trot. A faster pace, but still too slow for my tastes. The bay, a large hunter 15 hands high, seemed to know something was afoot. He constantly strained at his bit, urging me to release him.

Soon we reached the checkpoint. As we approached, the captain of the guard meandered to the road to intercept me. The wagon, which was in the middle of the road the previous evening, was now pulled to one side.

"Ah, Master Will Jones, word has already been passed to us that you'd be out for a ride this morning. The road to Charles is clear. You'll no doubt meet a few wagons on your way. A supply wagon left at daybreak headed to Charles and then on to Williamsburg. As fast as the bay runs no doubt you'll catch up to the waggoneer before you reach Charles. If you want to save about an hour, when you reach Sandy Creek take the trail to the right just after the ford and head southeast across the Williams Plantation. It's a narrow path that takes you directly to the main house. Not really a public road to that point, but a lone horseman such as yourself won't be bothered. Tip your hat if you're noticed. The plantation road, which begins in front of the house, will take you back to Charles Road. Don't be tempted to stop at the Williams Plantation. Their loyalties are subject to much debate. Now be off with your lad and have a pleasant ride."

"Yes sir, Captain," is all I replied as I tipped my hat in respect. I gave the bay the slightest kick and slackened the reins. He responded immediately and took off like a tempest. I found it necessary to grab my hat as I tried to regain control. It took several hundred yards before he expended his excess energy and agreed to proceed at a gallop rather than a flat-out run.

The ride on the open road was a new experience for me. Never had I been allowed such an opportunity before. I had taken short rides on our horse for errands to local farms, but never over such a distance on a spirited animal.

About 45 minutes into our journey, the bay had begun to heat up. Sweat was beginning to show around the saddle and his bridle. I slowed the pace to a trot. To have the bay overheat in winter weather would spell certain disaster. This was the first moment that I really felt the cold of the day against my cheeks. No doubt it had been cold, I was just too excited to have noticed beforehand. We continued for about another 30 minutes and eventually reached the ford at Sandy Creek. The creek itself was extremely shallow and there had been no need to build a bridge. We stopped to take a drink of water, which allowed me to stretch my legs. The bay was nervous to move on and so was I. I quickly remounted, found the trail to the Williams Plantation, and easily urged the bay into a slow gallop.

We soon broke out of the scrub trees and were greeted by a broad, open vista. The naked stalks of last season's cotton crop still graced the fields. In the distance, I could see smoke rising from two huge chimneys. The Williams Plantation no doubt. Although clearly visible, it took another half an hour to reach even the livestock pasture. I had seen no one until I reached the pasture. In a distant corner, a slave tended a small dairy herd. He paid no attention to me. As we closed on the manor itself, I arrived at the slave quarters, a long row of one-room log cabins on either side of the row. Here slave children of all ages were playing assorted games of chase or tag. For the most part, the children were dressed in layers of old, worn-out clothes to protect them against the cold. Some covered their feet in scraps of cloth, but still many were barefooted. They seemed to delight at my arrival and rushed to me. I slowed the bay to a walk. The bay was wholly unperturbed by the children and didn't flinch at their approach. The children, curious as to who was "calling on" at the plantation, asked me rapid-fire questions. To the best of my ability, I was polite but avoided answering.

When I approached the area of the kitchen garden I was met by a distinguished slave in a fine black coat. It was apparent he was not going to let me pass before I explained my business.

"Well, young master, are you here to visit the family, or are you taking a shortcut to the Charles road?" he inquired.

"I'm afraid I'm guilty of taking a shortcut," I responded. I felt the need to apologize. "I hope that I'm not intruding too much upon the goodwill of the Williams?"

"No, not at all. If I had a penny for every horseman who took that shortcut, I'd be a rich old man. If you like there is water for your horse just by the barn over there. It will give you a chance to stretch your legs."

"Thank you for your kindness, but I must be on to Charles. So if you will excuse me I'll be on my way."

"Before you go young Master Will, you'll need to stick to the main road on your return trip. Tonight, the family is hosting a party for the governor. A small contingent of British cavalry is expected to accompany him."

I was shocked that he knew my name. Although we lived only 15 to 20 miles away as the crow flew, we had never been in this part of the county before. "You have me at a disadvantage. You know my name, but I do not know yours," I said somewhat surprised.

"My name is Moses. I'm the head houseman for the family. Don't worry about your presence here; only a few knew you were headed this way. None of the family was aware. It is better not to ask how we knew, only that your journey should be safe as long as you don't come back in this direction. One last word of advice, if you should happen to meet the Governor and his British escort, leave the road immediately, rein in your horse and remove your hat as they pass by. It shows respect for the Crown and will save you a lot of questions. Now be off with yourself lad and have a pleasant ride. Charles is about 45-minutes to an hour away."

"Thank you for the advice, Moses." I tipped my hat and gave the bay a nudge. We were not disturbed again as we eased past the lane to the manor house and on to the plantation road.

I reached the main road and turned right toward Charles. The bay, sensing the open road, strained to run. I let him have his head and allowed him the pleasure of running with the wind. Twenty minutes into our ride and about another twenty minutes from Charles we were racing to the top of a knoll. As luck would have it, two British dragoons topped the small hill. My errant reactions must have seemed ridiculous to the redcoats. I jerked back the reins and the bay literally skidded to a stop directly in front of the troopers, who, it appeared, were not amused. Somewhat startled, they quickly regained their composure. I immediately began to babble.

"Sorry sirs. It was my fault. I was riding much too fast, I know. Please excuse me. I hope no harm was done." My voice, several octaves higher than it was normally, accentuated my nervousness.

The troopers found something humorous in my babbling. "Move to the side pup. The governor is coming and we don't want you to run over him. Make sure you control your horse."

"Yes sirs," was my only reply, as I moved out of their way and let them proceed. We continued to the top of the small hill at a nice slow walk.

I can't remember my exact emotions as I saw 60 British dragoons accompanying a four-horse coach. The troop seemed to be in perfect symmetry. The horses trotted effortlessly in unison. The large black fur hats of the dragoons shone in the midday sun.

Most remarkable was the sea of red coats that floated toward me. It was a grand spectacle. I do remember I had an instant compulsion to flee into the woods and ride for my life, but I thought for a second and calmed down. I was not an enemy of the Crown, although my family and I had a current grievance regarding the illegal arrest of my father, we were still loyal subjects. I took a deep breath and reigned the bay to the right side of the road. I was resolved to take in the grand spectacle and enjoy the moment. Dismounted, I stood on the right side of the bay in order to watch the procession unhindered.

The column finally reached me. "Good Morning, sirs," I said in a loud clear voice so I could be heard over the noise of the troop.

"Lad, a good Dragoon always stands on the left side of his mount," bellowed the Dragoon Captain.

"Sorry, sir." For some unknown reason, I saluted and quickly repositioned myself to the left side of the bay.

"Good Lad," he said approvingly. "Now don't forget to take off your hat and bow to the Governor as he passes."

I shouted "Yes, sir. Thank you, sir!" as loud as I could, so he could hear me since he was already a good two-horse length past me.

There was a roar of laughter from the troop. Several *good lads* were also directed at me. But then came a disturbing comment. "Bloody colonial pup. Bet he'd shoot us in the back if'n he had the chance!" Someone in the troop, probably the Troop Sergeant Major, chastised the miscreant, "That's enough. This isn't a bloody London mob. We're the King's dragoons and you will keep your thoughts to yourself. The next bloody one of you that makes a rude comment will be running dismounted drills from sunrise to sunset." The troop fell silent.

As the coach came by, as instructed by the Captain, I removed my hat and executed a perfected bow.

From the coach I heard, "See Major, I told you the people love me. The lad comes from the same stock that fought with me against the Shawnee just last year. Good people, loyal to the Crown. Nothing to fear from the good people of Virginia."

"Yes, Governor." But it was not an enthusiastic affirmation, but a resignation of someone, who perhaps had a different opinion; someone a little mistrustful.

A woman's voice said, "How sweet."

The coach passed me in a flash and I did not have the opportunity to see who was inside. I had to assume it was Governor Lord Dunmore and his personal bodyguard. The remainder of the troop passed by quickly. I remounted and now, assured that no one should be between Charles and me, I again allowed the bay to run with the wind.

Chapter 8

Charles and
Return to Fredrick

As I raced toward Charles, at one point I thought I noticed horsemen lurking off to either side of the road. Thinking the worst, I urged the bay onward. It was only after Charles came into view that I had the thought that the phantom horsemen were perhaps shadowing the Governor's procession.

I reached the checkpoint at Charles, as such it was, at about two o'clock. The checkpoint consisted of two fellows in dark winter coats, sitting around a campfire on one side of the road. Their rifles were propped against a tree some distance away. Neither got up to challenge me as I trotted past them; they only waved and greeted me with a cursory "good day." I returned the greeting, tipped my hat, and continued on into Charles uninterrupted.

Charles itself was a much busier place than Fredrick. There had to be at least 3,000 inhabitants and more than two dozen stores. My first inclination upon arriving in Charles was to locate Father. I knew he was being held here somewhere, but exactly where I had no idea. I toyed with the idea of taking a few minutes to inquire as to the location of the jail, but I thought better of it and decided to contact Mr. Wilson first in hopes that he would be able to assist. The apothecary was not hard to find; it was located directly on the south side of the town square. I rode directly to the apothecary, dismounted, and tied up the bay to the hitching post that had a water trough directly under it. No one seemed to notice my existence. I was an invisible lad on an errand.

As I entered the apothecary, the door hit a small bell to announce my entry.

"Be there in a moment. Please be kind enough to close the door behind you," came a deep melodious voice from behind a heavy curtain over a rear doorway.

Rather than resort to my typical "Yes, sir" I merely closed the door, which caused the bell to annoyingly ring again.

"Ah, there we are," said the huge hulk of a man as he came forward through a back curtain. "My, what a fine-looking young lad we have here today. What can I do for you son?"

I hesitated a moment, a little intimidated by the man who must have been at least six feet five inches and weighed at least 18 stones. I caught myself staring in amazement. "Sorry sir for staring, it's just that I've never seen someone so large."

"Quite the same impression I made on everyone the first time, lad. Don't be apologizing. So what can I do for you this fine afternoon?"

"Sir, I need to speak with Dr. Wilson, who runs this apothecary," I said a little sheepishly.

"Runs this apothecary?" he questioned. "Son, I own this

fine establishment; lock, stock, and apothecary jar. I am the Dr. Wilson you seek. So who might you be?"

Rather than reveal my name to him, I first thought it prudent to confirm his identity. "I'm here on an errand for Mr. Griffin in Fredrick. He needs some stomach medication."

"Oh, I see," he replied with raised eyebrows. He leaned down closer to me. "So I guess I better give you the secret reply, or you'll scamper out that front door like a frightened cottontail rabbit."

I did not find his reply amusing. I took a step away from him and reached under my coat for Old Anne.

"Now wait, lad. I'm sorry if I was making fun of you. I sincerely apologize. No need to take offense. You see, Mr. Griffin and I went to William and Mary together. Is that better?"

I eased my hand off the pistol and then retrieved the letter I was to deliver. "Here is a letter Mr. Griffin asked me to give to you. I am to wait for a reply." I handed the letter to an outstretched hand, which seemed to be the size of smoked Virginia ham.

His demeanor became serious as he took possession of the letter. "Sit over there in the chair lad and I'll be right with you." He turned and walked back through the curtain into what must have been the back storage area of the apothecary.

While I was waiting, no one came in. Business was exceedingly slow, it appeared. I waited for what seemed to be an hour, but in reality, it was probably only 15 or 20 minutes before he returned.

"So, young William Jones. I am very pleased to meet your acquaintance," said Dr. Wilson as he came through the curtain. He extended his hand toward me as I rose from the chair. Tried as I might to give him a good firm handshake, my puny hand was lost in his huge grip. As he forcefully shook my hand, my body vibrated like a rug being shaken.

"So you are William's son. We are so sorry to hear about his misfortune. I tried to visit him before they transferred him to Williamsburg, but they weren't letting anyone near him. That bandy young Squire had the whole Tory population in an uproar. It was all I could do to place several of our most trustworthy lads on the escort detail. They left early this morning. Poor William wasn't here barely 24 hours before they moved him out. Too many Whig supporters to take any chances they said. No matter, Williamsburg has a better jail and we do have friends there. He'll be fine. And don't you and your family worry about a lawyer for your father. We've got a good one in Williamsburg that is going to help for free."

"Thank you, Dr. Wilson. I appreciate your help and concern. Is there any chance that Father will be released soon? He didn't do anything that any other man would not have done."

"That's hard to say, son. I can't answer that question. We'll just have to wait for word from Williamsburg. But now to the matters at hand. Young William, my private correspondence between Mr. Griffin and myself must be held in the strictest confidence. You have shown yourself to be very trustworthy and will in the future continue to act as a courier between us. This is an easy courier route. Now that you are with us, we will be able to switch one of our more experienced couriers to a more difficult assignment. Private communication between our various correspondents is essential to our cause. You are now one of those vital links. As you grow more experienced, so will your responsibilities. For now, concentrate on your route. Learn it well. Once you have thoroughly learned the main route, find an alternate route and then find another alternate route. Mr. Griffin will speak more about the assignment when you return to Fredrick. Here is a return letter for Mr. Griffin and his stomach medication." He extended the letter and a small parcel to me.

As I took both of them, I accepted his employment, "Dr. Wilson, although I'm not familiar with the cause you speak of, if my service will help free Father from jail, then I will ride to the ends of the earth for that cause whatever it might be."

"Lad, you have a good heart and a trusting soul. As time goes by Mr. Griffin and myself will take the time to further your education and teach you about the cause of liberty, for it is a noble cause that unfortunately not all hereabouts subscribe to. A word of caution; you perhaps have youth on your side, so remember the old saying about children, 'they are better seen and not heard.' In your case, hold your tongue and listen. And most of all report what you see and hear to us. Now is that understood? Do you have any questions? What about troop movements?"

I affirmed my complete understanding of my new instructions and then proceeded to tell him with much detail of my trip to Charles, the encounter with Moses, the dragoons, the Governor, the phantom riders in the woods, and the lax sentries at Charles.

"Lad, I'm impressed with your recall and accuracy. You'll do fine and with a little more training no doubt you will become one of our better couriers. Now when you get back, make sure you give your report to Mr. Griffin. Now, be on your way. You have a long hard ride ahead of you. And follow Moses' advice; take the long road home and avoid the Williams Plantation. Don't be surprised by Dragoon sentries on the main road near the Williams Plantation. Slow to trot as you pass them; don't want to draw unnecessary attention. God's speed."

We shook hands. Thank goodness his handshake was not as exuberant as the first one. I turned quickly on my heels and literally bolted out the front door, not taking time to close it behind me. Dr. Wilson's huge frame filled the door frame. He smiled, then waved goodbye, but said nothing further.

I was off at a fast trot through Charles. As soon as I reached the outskirts of town, I loosened the reins of the bay and nudged him into a fast gallop. I paid no attention to the sentries who seemed to be frozen in the same places as I had seen them on my arrival. I did give the courtesy of a nod and a tip of the hat as I passed by unchallenged. They in return weakly tipped their hats and returned to being bored by their duty.

The bay, sensing we were on the return trip, strained at the reins to "head for the barn." I obliged and let the bay run. The bay's exuberance was noticeable; his ears were alert and forward and his tail streamed straight with the wind. We became one as we raced across the open countryside. It was not long before we crested the hill where I nearly collided with the dragoons. It was now time to consider reining in the bay before we blundered into the sentries at the Williams Plantation crossroads. It actually took a few minutes to slow the bay; he was bent and determined to go home and nothing was going to stop him. Some horses, they say, have "hard mouths," meaning they are difficult to control. The bay had a mouth made out of iron. My arms ached as I finally got him under control and slowed him down to a trot. It was only then that I became aware of a rider coming up behind me.

A British dragoon reined in his horse on my left side. "You have a swift horse I see there, lad," he said as he slowed his horse to a trot.

My heart sank into my stomach. It was then I noticed the dragoon was the captain I had seen earlier in the morning leading the column. I managed a "Good afternoon, sir."

"I saw you a couple of miles back and thought I might have some sport and try to catch you. Your bay was too much for my simple old warhorse. Had you not stopped I would have never caught you. You seemed to be having royal fun, lad."

"Yes, sir. The bay loves to run and I was just along for the ride," I replied trying to remember not to start blabbering.

"So, are you headed to the Williams Plantation?"

"Oh, no sir. I have to be getting on to Frederick. Night is coming shortly and I'm afraid I tarried too long in Charles and now must make up a little time."

"There's a shortcut through the Williams Plantation you can take. That should cut off perhaps 30 minutes or so."

"I was told to stick to the main road because of thieves and brigands about. With night falling I'm not too comfortable going a route I have never gone."

"Thieves and brigands about? Sure you weren't warned about dragoons and goblins about," he chuckled.

I forced a laugh. "Oh, no sir. I much rather have dragoons

and goblins about; at least you can see them." We both laughed.

We continued to ride together and engaged in small talk and banter. I let him do most of the talking. He seemed comfortable talking about his family in England, his brother my age who would be starting university next September, his sister who was married to the Duke of something-or-the-other, his radiant mother who was always worried about his welfare in the colonies, and his successful banker father who was considering standing for parliament in a couple of years. I was disinclined to talk about my family and only gave the barest amount of information, certainly nothing about our recent troubles with the Crown. Surprisingly, the Captain never asked my name.

Soon we reached the Williams Plantation Crossroads and were greeted by four Dragoon sentries.

"Tis good to see you have returned, Captain. We were beginning to worry about you. Had we known you were being escorted by your young Dragoon, we'd not have been so concerned." The voice, which I recognized from the morning, was attached to the stout Dragoon Sergeant Major in all of his finery.

"Had the young lad not reined in his horse, I'm afraid you would have only seen a phantom as he passed you by. His bay is the fastest mount I've seen in the colonies. I was lucky he slowed down a bit so I could catch up with him," intoned the Captain. The Captain turned to me and spoke. "Lad, the light is failing and I'm afraid it will be nearly dark by the time you make it to Sandy Creek. Take care and don't stop for anyone. Remember there might be brigands and goblins about." All of us chuckled at his humor. "On the serious side, are you armed?" he asked of me.

Suddenly Old Anne felt as if she were the size of a musket. I blinked my eyes several times and furrowed my brow as if I was thinking and then replied. "Sir, I have my small hunting knife. Does that count as being armed?"

"No lad. Only if someone pounces on you does it count. Do you know how to use a pistol?"

"Yes sir. I've fired one several times for practice. Is that good enough?"

"Here," he said as he withdrew an Officer's Dragoon pistol from his saddle holster and handed it to me butt first. "Take this with you. I'm sure I'll see you in the next couple of days and you can return it to me then. By the way lad, what is your name?"

"Thank you, sir. My name?" I hesitated momentarily as I tucked the pistol in my belt. "Ah, Bill Smyth sir, but most people say Smith in these parts."

"Very good Bill. Now do take care not to run upon the sentries at Fredrick. They just might shoot you," He said with a smile on his face.

I wasn't sure whether he knew the sentries were more alert at Fredrick or whether he was seeking information. I chanced an answer, "Not to worry sir. If I get there after dark, I'll probably have to wake both of them up just so they can challenge me."

All the dragoons including the Captain roared with laughter.

"Now be on your way lad and let the bay have his head. The sooner you reach Fredrick the better. Have a good ride and God's speed."

"Thank you, sir," I replied and saluted the Captain and

tipped my hat to the other dragoons. "Hope to see you gentlemen soon." I lightly kicked the bay, who responded as if the devil himself was upon us. In a flash, we were gone.

The bay ran at breakneck speed for a good five miles before he began to falter. He was certainly a strong and determined mount. This time I had less trouble reining him in and slowed him to a trot with ease. In the failing winter light, I could see the bay was beginning to sweat too much. Darkness or not I had to let him cool off slowly. I would take my chances with brigands, goblins, and dragoons. We reached the fork in the road; the north fork ran to the mountains and was sometimes called the Military road, the west fork was the Fredrick Road. There was no hesitation, both the bay and I agreed in unison to take the road home to Fredrick.

We continued to trot and enjoy the cold evening air. The night sounds were beginning to awake. An owl hooted in the distance and waited for a response; a fox yipped for her mate.

Animals, they say, have a sixth sense for danger and the bay was certain proof to that saying. The bay suddenly became skittish. Without a second thought, I drew the army pistol and cocked the hammer. The loud noise made when I cocked the pistol echoed through the forest.

"Hold to, lad, take it easy, we mean you no harm," came a voice from the shadows to my front. Just then, two dark riders on equally dark horses appeared as apparitions coming out of a fog. They blocked my way forward. I wheeled the bay to the rear but found that way now closed off by two more dark riders.

"Master Will, it's okay," came a voice to my back. It was Moses.

I turned the nervous bay back around and looked for Moses. He advanced slowly. He had been one of the two riders in front.

Moses was completely invisible in the dark. I could barely make out his form, but his voice was extremely comforting. "Master Will, I don't have much time. I need to get back to the manor to serve the Governor and the other guests. Don't worry about the other men here. They'll stay here and shadow the dragoons as they ride to Fredrick in the morning. You have to alert the Committee and tell them dragoons are coming and are looking for stockpiles of weapons and gunpowder. They will be leaving the plantation before sunrise and will be in Fredrick shortly after 7 o'clock. Now go as quickly as you can."

Moses reined his horse around without another word and disappeared into the brush. There was not a trace of the other three horsemen; the night had swallowed them up. The bay and I were left alone on the road. It was an eerie feeling that neither the bay nor I liked.

Chapter 9

Report to the
Committee

The bay was nervously shifting his weight from one hoof to the other; he was anxious to leave and so was I. Darkness had descended and I could only let the bay trot least he stumble in a hole or a wagon rut. When the half-moon rose into the cloudless night, our way became more visible and I let the bay ease into a slow gallop, which for him was still too slow. I had to use all my energy to restrain him. We crossed Sandy Creek and soon came up to the Fredrick checkpoint in good time. I hesitated only long enough to give the captain of the guard a brief report on the impending arrival of the dragoons and then sped onto Fredrick to make a full report.

I arrived at Fredrick just as the town bell tolled 30 minutes past the hour, which I hoped was only 7:30. I went directly to the barn, jumped off the bay, and found a blanket to cover him up so he wouldn't get chilled. The sweat was streaming off him and I needed to protect him, I didn't have time to rub him down. The blanket is securely in place. I fetched a bucket of water and tossed some hay into his stall.

"Successful trip, I hope," came the voice to my rear. I was startled and reached instinctively for the British pistol. "Now Will, don't be so nervous. If this is how you receive your benefactor after every trip, I'll have to find you a less stressful job." Mr. Griffin laughed at his own joke.

"Sorry, sir. The trip was a great success of sorts." I then began to recount the entire trip, as Mr. Griffin would describe later to the Committee, in minute detail.

"An excellent job," commended Mr. Griffin as I handed him the dispatch from Dr. Wilson. "Don't forget to return the pistol to the good captain tomorrow when he pays us a visit. You can leave it in my office. I'm sure he will pay a visit to my store to take an inventory of weapons and powder. Come along lad, the bay will be fine. It's time I introduce you to the Committee. I guess I must introduce you to everyone else as Bill Smyth or Smith as they say in these parts." We both laughed. "We'll just put a hyphen in there and place Jones on the end. A hyphenated colonialist; our first in these parts I believe. Smyth-Jones, does have sort of a good ring."

I quickly put both Old Anne and the Captain's pistol in Mr. Griffin's office and then joined him outside for the short walk to the tavern. The pub was filled with an assortment of men, young and old, obviously well-to-do and simple farmers. The air was filled with blue, sweet acrid smoke from fine Virginia burley. Most everyone was either smoking a pipe, filling a pipe, or just finishing off a bowl of tobacco. The younger lads my age were content to share a pipe with their father or uncle. This made me remember

Father and how he had shared his pipe with me. For a moment I was lost and back on our front porch sitting next to him and drawing from his pipe. Tears must have come to my eyes.

"You alright Will. The air is absolutely suffocating in here. Open up a window and let the rest of the town enjoy some of this smoke. If you don't watch it lads we'll all end up as smoked as cured Virginia ham!" bellowed Mr. Griffin. The pub roared. A couple of windows were opened and fresh, cold night air bathed the room. It was a welcome relief from all the smoke.

Mr. Griffin continued. "Now quiet down. We have some news from Charles all of you will find interesting. First let me introduce Will Jones. Most of you know his father William, was took prisoner by the Tories after he helped poor Brown with his wounds. I must remind all of you, the Tories think Brother Brown is deceased. I can assure you the old curmudgeon is alive and well out back in the cottage. He will need some time, but it looks as if he will make it fine. The good Dr. Miller worked his magic again." A cheer for Dr. Miller went up in the pub. "Now back to the issues at hand. Because of young Will's adventures into Toryland, he will be known in these parts as Bill Smyth or Smith to you." The room laughed. "If you should make a mistake, just say his full name is Smyth-Jones. That's for those of you who have had too much ale already."

"Is Smith-Jones good enough for us locals?" The room erupted again. This was certainly a lively crew.

"Good enough! Now to the issues at hand. Rather than let Will tell of his adventures over the past two days in excruciating detail, I will summarize them and hit the high points for emphasis."

Mr. Griffin, a storyteller in his own right, kept the audience spellbound for at least half an hour relating the raid on Mr. Brown's farm, the confrontation and arrest of Father, our escape to Frederick, and my courier trip to Charles and back. He left out nothing.

"So gentlemen, it seems we will be paid an early morning visit by the dragoons around seven o'clock. I expect the loyal militia to be formed at the town square promptly at 6:45 for drill and the raising of the Union Jack as soon as the dragoons arrive. Drummers will be in attendance and gentlemen, no weapons of any sort. Mustn't let the dragoons think we are armed. After the ceremonial raising of the flag everyone will be routinely dismissed to go about their business. Now to the important issues; weapons and powder. Our town armory is next to town hall, in case any of you might have forgotten." There was a roar of laughter. "Squad leaders will ensure all excess weapons and powder are removed and secured in several different safe places outside of town. Only 30 muskets and two barrels of powder will remain in the armory. Gentlemen, we must remove those weapons and powder tonight. Tomorrow morning will be too late. I do not wish to curtail our festivities tonight, but if we are to ensure our liberty then we must have the proper instruments to protect it. The guard mount on the outskirts of town will be reduced to two men, who have the Committee's permission to be less than attentive when the dragoons appear. And whoever is on guard duty, do try to be surprised by their appearance. We wouldn't want them to think that we knew they were coming, now would we?" There was a resounding "No" in response. "Squad leaders take charge of your men and go about the business at hand.

And before anyone asks, just one more ale is in order."

The mood of the pub was jovial as squad leaders assembled their men in different corners of the pub. What was noticeable was the squad leaders were men of middle substance and the members of each squad appeared to be simple farmers and tradesmen. A group of men exhibiting more substance, as evidenced by their dress, was seated at a long table near the bar. Mr. Griffin took me to the gentlemen of the Committee. As I approached the table the lone exception to "rule of substance" was a raw-boned man in his late 30s dressed in buckskins seated at the end. He was a backwoodsman, there was no doubt about that, but his mannerisms and speech were refined; a true anomaly.

"Gentlemen, I would like to personally introduce Will to you. His success today bodes well for his continued service as a courier." Mr. Griffin then went around the table and introduced each individual. I was overwhelmed and could not remember one name by the time he introduced all 15 of them. The backwoodsman, I do remember as Mr. Paris, a correspondent on the frontier, here on a visit. I can only surmise I remembered his name because of his unique name and the manner of his dress.

"Now Will, you've had a hard day. I think you probably need to check on your Mother before it gets too late. Be at the town square promptly at 6:45. You wouldn't want to miss the festivities. The Committee and I have a little more business to conduct. I'll see you in the morning."

I offered the usual, "Yes, sir," nodded to the members of the Committee, said only, "Gentlemen," and turned and left the pub. The cold night air was refreshing. On my way to Mrs. Jamison's I stopped by the barn to check on the bay. He was still awake, so I fetched him another bucket of water and threw more hay in for him to eat. He deserved the extra attention.

Once home, I found Mrs. Jamison attending to Mother, who was already asleep. As I entered the room, Mrs. Jamison, put her index finger to her lips signaling me to be quiet. She got up and led me to the kitchen. The kitchen aroma then reminded me I had not eaten all day. I had completely forgotten about the sack Mr. Griffin had given me. All of a sudden I was weak with hunger.

Seeing my pale expression, Mrs. Jamison reproached me. "Now young Will, you must take better care of yourself. I see from your expression that you have not eaten today. Sit down and I will get you a bowl of soup and cut you some freshly-baked bread."

Over several bowls of soup and four slices of bread, Mrs. Jamison and I discussed the day's events. I gave her an extremely abbreviated version of my adventures, leaving out Moses and the phantom riders and exactly what I did in Charles. I did mention that Father had moved to Williamsburg, which she thought was a good thing. She, in turn, caught me up on Mother's condition, what the children were doing, and what was the current gossip around town. It was a rather pleasant way to spend the evening, but soon I grew too tired. As the town bell struck nine o'clock, I thanked her for her hospitality and excused myself. Mother was resting as well as could be expected. I quietly pulled out my deerskin bag and curled up in front of the warm hearth. It was only moments before I fell asleep.

The first rooster crowed long before daylight, appearing on the far horizon. I heard Mrs. Jamison rise and make her way to the kitchen. I had no desire to remove myself from the warm confines of my deerskin sleeping sack, but duty called. Slowly, I sat up and went about the business of restarting the fires from last night's embers. I was not willing to fully give up my sack so I labored with the tender and the embers half-in and half-out of my deerskin. Success was slow in coming, but I finally managed to get the tender burning. Quickly, I added kindling to the small flame and waited patiently for the kindling to catch up before I put on several small logs. The whole process took 15 minutes, after which I was rewarded with a sensationally warm fire that warmed me to my bones. I could have stayed the whole day in front of the fireplace and absorbed the heat and watched the flames leap and play on the logs, but my responsibilities called to me, repeatedly.

After I got dressed I eased back to the kitchen to visit with Mrs. Jamison. We spoke briefly as she was going about her task of starting the fire in her cast iron oven. The milk pails were by the back door waiting for my attention, as were the cows, who were mooing their displeasure with full udders. Town life was not too much different than country life.

I finished both cows in due course and returned to the kitchen to find my breakfast waiting for me. Mrs. Jamison outdid herself again and I enjoyed a delicious breakfast of eggs and biscuits with ham gravy. The cup of coffee warmed my insides as it went down. Hurriedly, I finished eating breakfast and apologized to Mrs. Jamison. I still had to deliver the milk to the Griffins for my siblings before I met the local militia at the parade field.

As I approached the Griffin's house I saw my benefactor standing on his front porch smoking a pipe. "Ah, there you are young Will. Good to see you here bright and early. It's only 6 o'clock so we have time for a little breakfast. Come inside. The children, I'm afraid, like all children, don't want to get out of bed until the sun comes up. You, the misses, and I will enjoy a quiet breakfast together."

I was not about to refuse another breakfast. Mrs. Griffin, anticipating my arrival, had already cooked a whole tray of scrambled eggs, what seemed like a side of bacon and two pans of biscuits. There was even a small saucer of bacon drippings for the biscuits. A whole pot of coffee was brewing on the counter. This was truly a delightful experience. Thirty minutes later the three of us had completely devoured the meal.

"Good show lad. That's what I like to see, a young man that can appreciate a good meal." Mr. Griffin turned to his wife, "Sweets, the dragoons are due soon. Keep the children close to the house, just to be on the safe side."

Mrs. Griffin nodded and then turned to me. "Now Will, you be careful. Mind Mr. Griffin and don't do anything foolish." She was serious.

"Mrs. Griffin, thank you so much for this wonderful breakfast. I ate more than I should have. As far as the dragoons, I will be under Mr. Griffin's complete control."

Chapter 10

Dragoon's First
Visit to Fredrick

M r. Griffin and I quickly put on our coats and went directly to the parade ground. As we approached I could see 20 or 30 militiamen mulling around in the semi-darkness of dawn not sure of what to do.

"Will, you might as well go get the Captain's pistol and stick it in your belt. Wait; on second thought let's just leave that pistol where it is. Old Anne can use the company for a while longer. We wouldn't want the dragoons to get nervous about you carrying a pistol in your belt. Caution, at least in this case, is the better part of valor. I'm not sure that is the correct saying, but you understand what I saying, don't you Will?"

"I understand absolutely, sir. One question, sir. Should I be friendly with the Captain when he arrives?"

"Good point Will. Let's first gauge the mood of the dragoons. If they are relaxed then I think it would be beneficial for you to greet our dear Captain. Watch the dynamics of the troop.

See who is in charge and what the order of business is. If they are cordial then I would recommend it; if they are surly and arrogant as they are prone to be then I would keep my distance. Certainly at some point you do need to approach the Captain and ask when he would like you to return the pistol. Watch, wait, listen, and judge. Go over to the stone wall, where the other youngsters are waiting. I expect you to keep them under control. No harassing from the side. They'll be a couple of elders there to take control, you just help them out." He turned from me and addressed the militiamen, "Now gentlemen please form up the company, if you can remember how to. Drummer sound assembly."

The drummer, unsure of the exact beat to drum, began just to tap a steady rhythm. No one seemed to mind. There were shouts by each squad leader to form a straight line and form behind the man in front. Off to one side stood a group of men who appeared to be militia officers. There were nearly half as many officers as there were militiamen. Once the company was formed, the acting company sergeant turned around and shouted, "The Company is formed, sir."

Mr. Griffin responded, "Thank you sergeant. Officers, please take your position at the rear of the company formation."

The gaggle of officers slowly sauntered to their appointed position. There was momentary confusion as to how many rows there should be and who was to be at the position of importance on the left end.

Mr. Griffin, showing the patience of a father, stood in front of the company waiting for the officers to democratically decide who stood where. Finally they situated themselves into some sort of order.

"Thank you gentlemen. I am so glad that you finally agreed on something. Now this morning gentlemen, we will march around the parade field in some sort of semblance of a well-drilled militia. When our guests arrive, I will give the order and we will form up on the south edge of the parade field, which is to my rear. There, I will greet the commander of the troop and then we will raise the Union Jack, as is our duty. Are there any questions?" Mr. Griffin did not wait for an answer; he continued. "I hope not. Now lads, let's try to look at least like a trained militia. I don't expect us to march as good as the regulars, but do put some effort in it. Officers, for the benefit of the company, you may fall out. When we do assemble again for the dragoons, be so kind as to join us. Officers, fall out. Sergeant take command of the company and drill the troops."

Mr. Griffin moved to one side as the Sergeant of the militia began his duty. The formation came to attention on command, executed a fairly successful right turn, and then marched off in good unison. The left turn at the edge of the parade seemed a bit rough as the inside squad kept their pace and lurched out in front of the whole company. As a teaching point, the sergeant halted the company in their tracks as best he could. He then explained to the company the fine points of making a wheel turn and how if executed properly the company could stay together. Most of the militia nodded, but it seemed the sergeant's words fell on deaf ears. The company reassembled to start over.

Now approaching seven o'clock, all ears strained to catch the first sounds of approaching dragoons.

As I watched the folly of the militia trying to execute the finer points of a drill, I was struck by the absurdity of the routine. I had listened to my father, and from what little he said, I was convinced the best way to fight an enemy was the Indian way. Hide in the woods, wait patiently and then attack with surprise and force. The idea of marching in a straight line in order to confront an equally amassed enemy was tantamount to self-destruction, at least in my opinion. For me, that was not a concept in which I was willing to participate.

Shortly after the town clock had rung quarter past the hour the lookout, who had stationed himself in the church tower, came running to Mr. Griffin. The lookout was vividly gesturing toward the outskirts of town. Calmly Mr. Griffin digested the information, patted the spotter on the shoulder, and sent him on his way. His duty for the day was complete. Not wanting to miss the excitement, he strolled over to the wall where most of the young men, under militia age, had assembled.

He sat down next to me on the low wall. "Well sir, they are almost here. There must be 50 or 60 of them. They don't appear to be in much of a hurry, but they don't look too friendly either."

One of the grandfatherly types, who had been placed over us, walked to the center of our group and addressed us in a loud voice. "Now listen up you young lads. Today is not to be your baptism under fire. I will not tolerate any rowdiness on anyone's part. I'll want all of you to behave yourselves. The first one of you that says anything or acts up will feel my hickory cane. Should the redcoats be in a decidedly foul mood, you will leave this field on my command and remove yourselves to McCracken's barn over on

Muddy Creek. I know that is two miles away, but it is far away enough to keep you lads out of trouble. Your families will be fine, no worries there."

The sound of an advancing troop of cavalry could be heard approaching the town square. The muffled echoes of horses' hooves on a hard-packed dirt street resounded off all the buildings. It sounded as if they were coming from all directions. Mr. Griffin signaled the Sergeant of the militia to form the company on the designated spot. Mr. Griffin himself walked slowly to his position, which would place him at the head of the company as it formed. The drummer started beating a marching beat as the company tried in vain to execute a turn in order to march into formation. The squad on the outside of the turn had to literally run to catch up with the rest of the company. Fortunately the dragoons did not see this fiasco. Just as the Sergeant of the militia ordered a halt and made quick adjustments to the formation, the commander of the dragoons and his troops entered the town square from all four directions. There would be no escape.

The Major, seeing the formation, rode directly to Mr. Griffin and halted. His personal dragoons formed expertly behind him. There was a distinct difference between our militia and the dragoons. The remainder of the dragoons formed on the other three sides of the square. Each was wearing a somber look; there were no smiles. For a moment Mr. Griffin and the Major stared at each other, each sizing up the other. The major, all decked out in his dragoon finery, was about 35, while Mr. Griffin, dressed in short pants and wearing a long dark coat with a tri-corner, appeared to be almost 60.

Mr. Griffin broke the silence first, "Major, allow me to introduce myself. I am Captain Griffin, commander of the county militia, at your service." With that, Mr. Griffin took off his hat, made a sweeping motion with it, and bowed briefly to the major.

"Captain Griffin, I am not here on a social call. Please explain to me the meaning of the formation of this rabble."

"I beg your pardon sir. We are performing our monthly drill duty and are preparing to raise the flag, as is our custom at the end of the drill."

At that moment, as if on cue two militiamen, one of them carrying a folded Union Jack, marched smartly to the flag pole next to Mr. Griffin and proceeded to raise the flag as the drummer began to beat the drum.

"Enough!" shouted the Major. "Do not attempt to deceive me with your petty performance. Sergeant Major, secure that flag immediately." Without further order, the dragoon Sergeant Major quickly dismounted, ran to the flagpole, and seized the flag from the militiamen.

"Major, I must protest. That is totally uncalled for. We are loyal subjects of the Crown. The governor shall hear of this."

"Go whine to the governor all you want to Mr. Griffin. I know you for what you really are. All of you, you are scum of the earth. Loyal subjects of the Crown, my arse. If you weren't such cowards you would ambush us every chance we gave you."

Mr. Griffin was turning red in the face as were the rest of the militiamen. It was quite fortuitous that the militia was not armed this morning. My benefactor had made a wise decision. There would have been a bloodbath.

"Major, I discern a little aggression in your voice this morning." Mr. Griffin was regaining control of his emotions. Several of the militiamen snickered. "I suppose there must be a reason you so mistrust us. Would you care to share it with us? I'm sure the company would like to hear it."

To drive his point home, Mr. Griffin half-turned to the company to get their reaction. One or two bold farmers shouted, "Please tell sir." Yes, please explain." "We'd love to hear from you, sweetie." The company roared. For the most part the dragoons remained stone-faced, however, a few smiled at the remark.

"Who said that," roared the insulted Major. "I'll have the brigand hanged."

"Not so fast major. While I admit that is a personal insult, it is not a criminal offense. Your only choice is to call out the individual and challenge him to a duel. But I'm sure you have better things to do than trade shots with one of my marksmen. Besides, I think the challenge has the choice of weapons and most undoubtedly it would be a Virginia rifle. Have you ever had the opportunity to fire one Major?"

"Enough of this banter. I will not let you or any of your men goad me. I have a mission to accomplish. And you Mr. Griffin will do as you are ordered or you will be held criminally liable. Is that understood?"

"Certainly Major. I stand at your service," said Mr. Griffin with a slight grin on his face.

"Very well," said the Major with real anger in his voice. "We have reason to believe you have a store of muskets and powder in this hamlet. You will surrender the same immediately or suffer the consequences."

"May I ask why we must turn in our armory?"

"No, you may not! Just do as I say or I will use force to carry out my instructions. Is that understood, Mr. Griffin?"

"You mustn't be hostile Major. The muskets and powder for the militia are stored in the small armory just to my rear. Sergeant, may I have the key please?"

"Yes sir, Captain. Here it is." The sergeant of the militia handed Mr. Griffin a large iron key.

"Thank you Sergeant. Major, here it is." As Mr. Griffin attempted to hand it to the Major, a dragoon stepped in front to block his progress. Without a word the dragoon snatched the key from Mr. Griffin, turned, and handed it to the Major.

"Sergeant Major, follow me. Mr. Griffin, if you would be so kind as to accompany us," said the Major with a mock smile on his face.

The Major rode straight for the armory, which meant he had to ride across the parade field and through the company formation. It was an insult of great magnitude, but the company merely parted as the Major approached. The dragoon Sergeant Major followed behind on foot, accompanied by five other dismounted dragoons. Mr. Griffin walked beside the Sergeant Major. As they approached the armory door, the Major dismounted and then stepped to one side as a dragoon rushed forward to take control of the Major's mount.

"Sergeant Major, open the door!" The Major held out the key for the Sergeant Major to take.

"I believe this is my armory," said Mr. Griffin as he stepped past the Sergeant Major and snatched the key back from the major. The major moved his right hand to his sword as if to draw it. "I wouldn't if I were you, Major. While you might be able to slice me in two, your return to Charles would be extremely perilous. Be satisfied with your bounty and be done with it." Mr. Griffin turned and inserted the key into the lock on the armory door. He then removed the lock, opened the door, and stood aside to allow the inspection. The Major removed his hand from his sword.

As the Major and the Sergeant Major were entering, Mr. Griffin spoke in a firm and authoritative voice. "As you will notice by the inventory sheet on the wall, there are 30 muskets and two barrels of powder, assorted uniform coats for ceremonial usage, our company banner, and a flag. You already have our flag. That, Major, is all of the property this militia company was issued. There never have been enough muskets to go around."

The Major spun on his heels. He was red-faced, "Sergeant Major, seize everything and load it onto the wagon." The Major stepped to Mr. Griffin and got face to face with him. "You'll pay for my embarrassment, Griffin. I'll make sure of it."

Mr. Griffin smiled and replied, "Anytime that suits you, Major; it would be my honor."

"Captain Clark," shouted the Major. "Remain here until 10 o'clock and then proceed back to Charles. I expect you to have the troop back in Charles with the contraband by sunset. I will take 10 out of the troop with me and return at once."

"Yes, sir," came the reply from behind me. I had been too absorbed in the scene unfolding in front of me to notice my captain friend had taken a position directly behind me. It actually startled me somewhat. I turned and saw the faintest of smiles on his face.

Not to be further humiliated, the Major quickly remounted and galloped back through the parade field and the company. Several in the company could not restrain themselves and called after the Major. "Sorry you couldn't stay, sir." "Come back soon." "Tootles sweetie." Needless to say, with the last remark the company roared in unison. The Major, now in front of his dragoons, reined his horse in and turned to face the company. Then as if on cue, the entire company took off their hats and waved goodbye to the Major. The insult was almost too much to bear. The crimson-faced Major wheeled his horse around and with 10 of his dragoons galloped out of the square toward Charles.

Mr. Griffin left the Sergeant Major to his task and walked over to the wall where I was sitting. He looked past me and addressed the dragoon captain. "Captain Clark, Samuel Griffin at your service. If there is anything I can do please let me know. We want to make your stay here as pleasant as possible."

The Captain relaxed and responded with familiarity. "Thank you very much, Samuel. Please call me Daniel. I will endeavor to make our stay in your village as unobtrusive as possible."

"Why thank you Daniel. You must have left early this morning in order to get here and perhaps you did not have time to eat. Would you and your men care for some breakfast?"

"I have no doubt you know exactly what time we left the plantation," he laughed. "As for breakfast, my men and I would certainly appreciate your hospitality."

Mr. Griffin looked down at me, "Will, go to the bell tower

and give the rope a good pull for two minutes. We've arranged a little breakfast for our guests." He then shouted to the sergeant, "Bailey, have the men set up the tables. Breakfast will be served in just a few minutes for our guests."

I ran as fast as I could to the bell tower and began pulling the rope. It took several good pulls before the bell began to ring. Once I got it started, the bell did most of the work. The old bell chimed loud and clear over the town. Within moments the ladies of the town started to arrive with trays of biscuits and bowls of scrambled eggs steaming in the cold February morning, there were even trays of thick-cut Virginia ham, just out of the skillet. The mood of the dragoons improved tremendously. A festive air engulfed the town square. The dragoons dismounted on order, tied up their horses, and began to assist in the preparations. Dragoons intercepted the ladies and relieved them of their heavy loads; others pitched in with the militiamen and set up makeshift tables. Short barrels were found somewhere and became chairs. The dragoon Sergeant Major quickly completed his mission, tied a tarpaulin on the wagon, and relocked the armory. The key was given to Captain Clark, who, with as much respect as could be afforded, handed the key to Mr. Griffin. I returned to hear what Mr. Griffin and the Captain were talking about.

"Why thank you, Daniel. I hope we have assured you we are loyal subjects like yourself," said Mr. Griffin smiling.

"Samuel, I never question a man's loyalty until I'm given reason to doubt it," replied Captain Clark. The Captain turned in my direction and spoke to me. "Bill, it's nice to see you this fine morning. You are looking chipper. I hope you won't let the Major's display adversely affect your opinion of us."

"No sir, I won't. It does seem the Major is an extremely temperamental man," I replied.

He leaned a little closer to me, grinned with a devilish smile. "Privately I will agree with you, but mind you don't share my thoughts with anyone else. He is still a major and very much in charge of this troop. Now come let us partake of this wonderful display of hospitality."

Although the tables had been set up with the hot food, the dragoons had reformed into a formation and awaited the arrival of the captain. The company, understanding military protocol, stood to one side in their loose formation and waited for Mr. Griffin to release them. The Sergeant Major and Bailey stood in front of their respective troops. As the two commanders approached, the Sergeant Major shouted, "Dragoons, attention!" The dragoon, in unison, came to attention and clicked their heels. Bailey then shouted, "Company, attention!" The militia company emulated the dragoons as best they could, but it was apparent that most thought the display was a little too humorous; several militiamen were grinning, barely containing their laughter.

The Captain and Mr. Griffin took positions in front of their sergeants.

Captain Clark turned slightly toward Mr. Griffin and said, "Home turf, Samuel. You should have the honor of falling out your men first."

"Why thank you, Daniel." Mr. Griffin addressed Sergeant Bailey. "Sergeant, fall the men out for breakfast."

Sergeant Bailey did a smart about turn and shouted,

"Company fall out!" The company retired in the direction of the tables.

"Sergeant Major, have the troop show their appreciation for our hosts and then fall them out for breakfast," said the Captain.

"Yes sir. My pleasure." The Sergeant Major executed an about-face and addressed his troop. "Dragoons, three cheers for the hospitality of the good citizens of Fredrick." The Sergeant Major then led the troop in cheer, "Hurrah, hurrah, hurrah."

The townspeople clapped, showing their appreciation.

"Dragoons, fall out!" commanded the Sergeant Major.

The dragoons quickly descended on the tables and intermingled with the townspeople. The Captain and Mr. Griffin seated themselves at the end of the table, which had been reserved for the militia officer cadre and the dragoon junior officers. I sat on the wall in earshot of the group. Hot pots of coffee arrived, not the typical tea. It was perhaps a small faux pas, but it was lost on the dragoons. Mr. Griffin felt compelled to offer a left-handed apology to the Captain.

"Daniel, you must try our coffee. It is fresh in from English merchants in Jamaica. Tea is so hard to find these days. I hope you will excuse us."

"Actually Samuel, I have acquired a taste for coffee. There are several good coffee houses in Williamsburg. Although a British officer such as myself finds it is more convenient to go early in the evening to drink coffee. Late evening at the coffee houses is reserved for people of less character."

I listened to what the Captain said and I wondered what he meant. I could not expect that an owner of a coffee house would allow riff-raff in his establishment late at night.

"I've heard they have actually set aside special rooms for British officers and gentry so they can enjoy their coffee in peace and not be disturbed by the common man. I hope that is an acceptable solution?" replied Mr. Griffin.

The two were skillful with words and each knew precisely what the other was thinking but not saying.

Mr. Griffin continued. "When I come to Williamsburg, perhaps we can enjoy a cup of coffee together and discuss the events of the day."

"I would enjoy that very much, Samuel. And bring young Bill there with you! I would enjoy showing him around our barracks and teaching him a little about the life of a dragoon."

The prospect of going into the dragoon camp excited me. I had no hesitations at all. My father might be a temporary prisoner of the Crown in Williamsburg and I might be able to sneak a visit with him. I was sure once the mistake was realized we would continue to be loyal subjects. And too, I wanted to experience this adventure.

Mr. Griffin saw my face light up. "Daniel, I will be glad to have Bill accompany me. And I'm sure he would enjoy a short tour of your barracks."

The remainder of the meal was taken up with small talk. Any discussions about politics were tenderly avoided. By the end of the meal, several small children had climbed into the laps of some of the dragoons to get a better view of the redcoat visitors. It was apparent that these men had families of their own that they sorely missed. The interaction between these men and the children was warm and heartfelt. However, all coins have two sides and it was noticeable to me that some militiamen and some dragoons were not being overly friendly and in fact showed animosity toward each other. Cautious hands prevailed and any confrontation was avoided without any fanfare.

As breakfast grew to a conclusion, the town clock chimed 8 o'clock. Captain Clark withdrew his pocket watch from his waistcoat and checked the time. "Very accurate clock you have there Samuel." He put his watch away. "Unfortunately my orders are to remain here until 10 o'clock and then return. I certainly don't want to impose upon your good hospitality, but I have my orders. Any ideas as to how we should spend that time?"

"I would like to say you could entertain us, but perhaps the best word is 'teach' us how to conduct a close-order drill. My lads can't get the hang of marching and it would be an excellent opportunity."

"Well then, by your leave, I'll have the Sergeant Major confer with your Sergeant Bailey." Captain Clark turned toward his left and shouted, "Sergeant Major would you please come here? And Sergeant Bailey, if you would not mind so much, could I also speak with you?"

Both sergeants got up from their barrel seats and walked briskly to Captain Clark. They reported together in one voice and saluted together. "Reporting as ordered sir."

The Captain returned the salute. "Good show gentlemen. Now then, Sergeant Major, we have two hours before we return to Charles and Captain Griffin has asked if we might be able to assist our friends in mastering close order drill. I think it would be appropriate if you two sergeants put your heads together and come up with some sort of practice drill."

"Yes, sir. I will do my best, sir. By your leave sir, Sergeant Bailey and I will confer for a moment and get right to it sir," said the Sergeant Major. Both sergeants saluted, did an about-turn, and returned to the other tables.

Captain Clark addressed his officers. "Gentlemen, there is no need for you to participate in the drill, so if you like you might consider taking a ride in the countryside. Nice to be familiar with territory you have never been in; and gentlemen, do be back here punctually at 10 o'clock; otherwise, we'll leave without you."

The junior dragoon officers responded, "Yes, sir," in unison.

Mr. Griffin addressed his militia officers. "I'm not sure which of you has some free time, but I suggest several of you accompany our guests and give them a good tour of the county; of course mindful of the time constraints."

One militia officer spoke up. "Come gentlemen, I'll take you to my plantation and show you the best thoroughbreds in the colonies."

The interest of the cavalrymen perked until someone added. "You call those nags you have thoroughbreds? They are just skinny plow horses. Now my thoroughbreds are 100 times better." The officers roared at the good-natured ribbing. It was settled it would be a two-hour tour of the local horse farms.

"Daniel, while your men are actively engaged, why don't you join me at my store? By now my clerk has a nice fire going and it will be comfortable."

"My pleasure Samuel. The thought of a nice warm fire already has a delicious warming effect."

We got up and proceeded across the street toward the general store. The sergeants had formed their units and the Sergeant Major began trying to explain the finer points of a close-order drill. The ladies of the village were cleaning up the aftermath of the breakfast feast. As I surveyed the rest of the square, I noticed three dark brown horses tied to a post at the far end of Charles Road. They had not been there before. It took me a while to find the riders. They were nearly invisible, dispersed, standing far apart from one another, watching different activities. They were dressed similarly in somber browns and blacks. There was nothing remarkable about any of them; they appeared to be just ordinary townspeople or successful farmers.

"Bill," shouted Mr. Griffin, "come along, lad. You have business with the good Captain. Mustn't forget about that."

"Sorry, sir." I jumped off the wall and ran toward the general store. I had forgotten completely about returning the pistol.

As a result of my mad dash to the store I was a little out of control and had to grab the front porch post to keep from sailing into the closed door. I took a moment, caught my breath, and then calmly walked inside.

"Close call there Billy boy. I thought sure you were coming right through the door. Mr. Griffin and the redcoat are in the back room. By the way, my name is Philip. I'm Mr. Griffin's ward.

"Nice to meet you, Philip," I said and extended my hand to him. Philip, about 16, was a little taller than me, was broad-shouldered, and had coal-black hair to go along with his olive complexion. I'm sure the young ladies in the village thought his green eyes were an attractive combination. "What's a ward?" I asked.

"They are expecting you in the back. We'll have plenty of time to talk later," he said.

Sometimes town life was awful confusing, although there was never a dull moment. I hurried to the back room and entered without knocking since the door was wide open. It didn't seem to matter to either of the men. They were seated in comfortable chairs near the fireplace packing tobacco into their pipes.

"Ah, there you are Bill. Now show off your manners for the good Captain," said Mr. Griffin.

"Oh, yes sir." I quickly went over to Mr. Griffin's desk and retrieved the Dragoon pistol the Captain had loaned me the day before. As I handed it to him I said, "Thank you so much sir for your consideration of my safety. I appreciate the loan of your personal pistol. It gave me a great sense of security and made my return trip to Fredrick that much more comfortable."

"Well done lad," said the Captain as he took possession of the pistol. He examined the pistol. "I see you did not have an occasion to fire it. That's always a good sign. Now if you will take this to my aide and have him return it to my saddle holster."

"Yes, sir." I got ready to run my errand.

"Don't tarry too long Bill. Come on back and you can listen in on my conversation with Captain Clark. Good for your further education."

I nodded my head and walked to the front of the general store. Philip was straightening stock and paid no attention to me. I wonder why I was given preferential treatment over Philip, who to me seemed much more mature and competent.

As I walked outside, I came upon a sight to behold. The Sergeant Major had intermingled his dragoons with the militia and was taking them through the steps of a close-order drill. They had been divided into three sizable companies and were doing a fairly efficient job. Separated on either side of the parade field there were two groups of men not participating. The one on the left side were militiamen sitting on the wall just watching and on the opposite side of the field were a small group of dragoons also sitting on the wall. Both groups stared at each other with animosity, which was so thick that it could be cut with a knife. There appeared to be true hatred in some of those piercing eyes. Just seeing the two groups gave me pause. Now it was my job to deliver the Captain's pistol to his aide, who was standing directly behind the banished dragoons. I did not want to walk over there and incur their wrath. I chose a half-measure and decided to walk the long way around the perimeter of the parade field rather than directly across it and have to go through the dragoons. I was also cautious to carry the pistol by its barrel with the handle pointed forward.

One or two of the dragoons noticed me and followed my progression toward them, although my ultimate goal was the Captain's aide. Something they could not have known.

When I was approximately 20 yards away from the aide, I looked directly at him and hailed him, "Excuse me sir, are you Captain Clark's aide?" Now I had the full attention of the dragoons, much to my displeasure.

"Yes lad, that I am. And what can I do for you on this fine

day?"

I continued to walk towards him. "The Captain asked that I return his pistol to you and he asked that you put it in his holster."

"Certainly lad. Just bring it over here, said the aide."

A gruff voice from the dragoons was clearly heard. "Giving pistols to these little bastards. Next they'll be making us line up so's they can shoot us. You ask me the Captain is going a little daft."

The aide, a corporal by the number of chevrons on his jacket, spoke quickly and with the full force of authority, "There'll be no more of that talk tolerated. If I find out who said that you'll feel the sting of old Maude on your back. Now lad give me the pistol."

I closed the gap between us and handed the pistol butt first to the corporal. He too examined it, opened the frizzen to look at the powder in the pan, and reclosed the frizzen.

"Is it still loaded lad?" he inquired.

"Yes, corporal. I didn't need to shoot any brigands on the way home last night, although I'm sure there are some about that need a good butt full of lead." I looked at the disgruntled dragoons."

The corporal laughed, "My, don't we have a spark. Can't say as I blame you." He leaned to me a little and said quietly, "Some of 'em are a might uneasy with the things happening up north in Boston."

"Oh!" is all I dared say. I didn't know what was happening in Boston, but I didn't want to ask and confirm that I was just a dumb country bumpkin. With nothing else to say, I nodded to the corporal and said, "Have a good trip back to Charles." As I turned to return to the store I took a moment to glare at the dragoons, who returned my glare with steely stares; these were hard, no- nonsense soldiers. Their displeasure with me sent a chill down my spine. A touch of fear briefly came over me. This was not a good feeling and I felt ashamed that it had surfaced. To compensate for it I stood a little more erect and walked resolutely back to the store.

Philip opened the door with a broom in his hand to sweep the front porch. As he came out he left the door open for me. "Careful of those dragoons; they look like they want to slit your throat. What did you say to them?"

"Nothing, not a thing," I lied. "I think they are just constipated."

Philip laughed out loud and then began to sweep the porch in earnest. I went inside and remembered to close the door behind me. The inside of the store was now almost toasty warm, although I hadn't recognized it as being cold outside. I walked directly to the back room where I found Mr. Griffin and the Captain relaxing in their chairs smoking their pipes. Each had a steaming cup of coffee within reach.

"We started without you Bill. Pull a stool over next to me and pour yourself a cup of coffee. There's a pipe for you on my desk," said Mr. Griffin.

I wasn't sure if the pipe was a gift or a loan. I chose not to ask, but to accept the pipe as a temporary loan. The pipe itself was a simple pipe with a small walnut bowl and a hardwood stem. It was nearly new, but had been seasoned. I quickly grabbed it, found the coffee pot, poured myself a cup and then pulled my stool next to Mr. Griffin. We shared a small tea stand for our coffee. As I seated myself, Mr. Griffin handed me a leather tobacco pouch. I took only a pinch of his precious Virginia burley from the pouch and handed it back to him.

"You can take a little more lad. This is a special occasion. It is not often that we have a fine gentleman from England visit us here in Fredrick, even if he is a dragoon." Mr. Griffin chuckled as his own joke.

The Captain smiled a little and continued to smoke his pipe without comment. He was absorbed in extracting as much pleasure from the pipe as was possible.

I took another pinch of tobacco and then again returned the pouch to Mr. Griffin, who accepted it without comment this time. I packed the tobacco down in the bowl with my index finger like Father had shown me. "Pack it firm, but not too tight," he had said, "Got to let a little air circulate." I tested the pipe to make sure the draw was right. Mr. Griffin watching my progress, knew when it was time to hand me an ember stick from the fire. I lit my pipe effortlessly and handed the ember stick back to Mr. Griffin who carefully placed it back at the edge of the fire for easy retrieval. Everything was in order. Blue smoke curled out of my pipe and the first taste of tobacco had a calming effect on me.

"Daniel, tell us how things are in England these days. We get so little news from there."

"All the news I'm afraid is being made in the colonies or is about the colonies Samuel. Parliament, it seems, is not satisfied with the Massachusetts compliance on the Coercive Acts and is considering new measures granting Governor-General Gage additional powers to bring the colony back into the fold. It also hasn't helped that the colonies held the so-called Continental Congress, which the King, as well as the Parliament, regard as direct defiance of the Crown. The Whigs must stop these provocations."

I listened in amazement. I had never heard of the Coercive Acts or the Continental Congress. These were new terms to me and totally unfamiliar. I felt really like a country bumpkin.

"Daniel, I understand how someone not familiar with the colonial system as it exists here might misinterpret certain actions of the Whigs. I'm not going to try to change your mind, but for just a moment look at it from our point of view, as Englishmen living abroad. We, as Englishmen, enjoy certain benefits that other peoples in the civilized world do not. Our brothers in Great Britain have full rights, which include above all the right to elect members to Parliament, which ensures their voices are heard. We, being abroad, have no such representation. Before you extol the virtues of the Colonial Office, I need only to remind you that we did not elect those officials and have the well-founded opinion that those officials are more concerned with the profits of the East India Trade Company than the rights of us Englishmen in the American colonies. True, elements in Massachusetts have brought some of their pain upon themselves, but to pass the Intolerable Acts, as we call them, only incited the mobs. Since these problems began 10 years ago, the Crown, instead of trying to solve the problems, has engaged in a system of reprisals meeting each perceived act of defiance with more restrictive, intrusive, and intolerable legislation."

Mr. Griffin was getting worked up and it was beginning to show in his face. There was a distinct red glow to his cheeks and his temples were slightly bulging. On the other hand, Captain Clark was relaxed in his chair, legs comfortably crossed. Occasionally he would take a draught on his pipe, but for the most part he did not interrupt Mr. Griffin.

"Mind you I do not subscribe to the actions of the mob in Boston, but I do feel the Crown could have at least addressed some of the numerous petitions the colonies have sent to Parliament. Why, there has been no action at all on most of the petitions."

Mr. Griffin was calming down. He must have realized he sounded like a zealot. His demeanor returned and the color in his face returned to normal, his temples stopped pulsating.

"I must apologize for my outburst, Daniel," he said. "I do get worked up when I think the Crown is making a terrible mistake and is playing into the hands of those louts in Boston."

"There is no need to apologize Samuel. I am sure Parliament will wake up someday and rectify their mistakes. Until then we must have forbearance and resolve not to let the mob in Boston destroy what all of you worked so hard to accomplish here in the colonies. You know Samuel, as I travel about the settled areas in the colonies, I am struck by a community that was carved out of the wilderness by the sheer force of will in a little over 100 years. Your progress is simply phenomenal."

"Daniel, I only hope all of the sweat, blood, and the hard work that has gone into building our colonies is not being taken for granted by the Crown. We have succeeded where others have failed and we have developed a most stubborn sense of survival. Many times our frontiersmen have gone it alone without the authority from London. We are strong-willed and I'm afraid bullheaded. Rule us with reason, not by force. Now I've said enough. You have enough to write home about, I'm sure. Let's enjoy these few minutes we have left before you have to return to Charles."

"Agreed," said Captain Clark.

I sat mesmerized as the two talked about their experiences in life. I heard about the social elite in England, about the hardships of frontier life in The Piedmont, of Indians wars and hot Jamaican nights. Captain Clark had certainly traveled a lot, but Mr. Griffin had faced adversity on the frontier. To me, one was the trained professional and the other was a seasoned veteran. I had a foreboding feeling that these two men would soon be enemies. It was a hard feeling to accept because I found I liked both of them.

When the town clock struck 9:45, Captain Clark took out his watch and checked the time. "Well Samuel, I'm afraid I must be going. I have certainly enjoyed your hospitality, although I'll not breathe a word of it to the Major. Mustn't ruin his image of the radical colonist mob. If you should ever happen to be in Williamsburg do drop by and bring Bill with you."

"Thank you for the invitation Daniel. I normally get to Williamsburg several times a year. The next time I come I will look you up and dinner will be my treat." As they got up, Mr. Griffin walked over to me and put his arm around my shoulder. "I will make sure to bring young Bill with me. He could use a little spit and polish."

They shook hands and proceeded to the front porch of the store. I followed along behind. As the Captain was getting ready to walk down the front porch steps he stopped momentarily and leaned over to me and tousled my hair. "Now Bill take care of yourself and watch out for those brigands and goblins!" he laughed. He didn't wait for a reply; he turned and skipped down the four stairs to the street.

In a clear crisp voice he shouted so all could hear. "Sergeant Major, form the company and let's ride to Charles."

The dragoons who had been lounging around the parade field talking to their militia counterparts sprinted to their horses. Without another word the company formed in front of the general store. The whole troop, standing at attention to the left side of their horses, waited for the command to mount. To the rear came a commotion. The dragoon officers came racing into the square with several fine horses in tow. The militia officers arrived close on their heels. The disruption was not unnoticed.

"Well gentlemen, so nice of you to join us. We were just getting ready to leave. Would you gentlemen care to join us?" said Captain Clark to the rowdy British officers.

One particularly senior lieutenant spoke up. "Sorry sir for our tardiness, but we are somewhat tardy due to the protracted negotiations over the purchase of three of Virginia's finest thoroughbreds. If you will forgive us, sir."

"Very well, lieutenant. You and your new additions take positions in front of the formation." Captain Clark had a smile on his face. "Sergeant Major, mount the troop."

"Yes sir! Troop, prepare to mount!" shouted the Sergeant Major. Immediately he gave the next anticipated command, "Mount!" The dragoons were precision in motion. The whole troop was mounted and ready to go in the blink of an eye.

The Captain mounted last. As he pulled away from the store

he tipped his hat to Mr. Griffin and the mounted militia officers. The dragoons followed the Captain at a fast trot out Fredrick headed toward Charles. As I watched them leave town I noticed the phantom riders meander to their horses. They chose to exit town in a different direction, no doubt a path that would allow them to shadow the troop all the way back to Charles. The militiamen patiently waited for the dragoons to disappear.

Mr. Griffin spoke to the mass milling around. "All right gentlemen, we have expended enough of our precious workday playing host to those redcoats. Now go about your chores and business. Officers, and Sergeant Bailey, I need to speak with you for a moment and then you'll be free to go." Mr. Griffin turned to me. "Will, what you have seen today is probably one of the last times British troops and our militia will ever be so civil. It saddens me to think that a fine gentleman like Captain Clark is being used to enforce unfair laws on the colonies. Enough of that for now. Go attend to your mother and your siblings. Be back here at 1 o'clock. Your education is about to begin. Gentlemen, if you will follow me into my office."

Chapter 11

A Short Respite

I was left on the porch of the general store as the militia officers followed Mr. Griffin. Philip, who had been standing to one side, came up to me.

"You missed the real show. You should have seen those redcoats drill. They were splendid. Our boys did learn a thing or two. That redcoat Sergeant Major really put them through the paces. Mr. Bailey, he learned a thing or two also. I bet he'll be a real hard drillmaster in the future. It only goes to show that with a little practice we can keep up with the redcoats." Philip had enthusiasm in his voice and fire in his eyes. It appeared he wanted to be in the militia.

"Philip, why aren't you in the militia, you're old enough aren't you?" I asked.

Philip blinked and his expression changed. "I can't," he said. "I'm indentured to Mr. Griffin for another five years and then I can't because of my Ma's family."

I wanted to ask more, but he just turned, walked slumped-shouldered into the store, and closed the door behind him without another word. I was left standing on the porch alone. Although it would have been fun to escape and go exploring my new home, I had duties and responsibilities; first to Mother and then to the children. I took off on a flat run to visit mother.

Mother was doing much better as I arrived at Mrs. Parsons' house. She was sitting in the parlor, which doubled as our bedroom, helping Mrs. Parsons work on a quilt. The quilt stand was strategically placed near the fireplace so both ladies could enjoy the warmth and still have enough room to work. I briefly interrupted, gave Mother a kiss on the cheek, and I was bold enough to even give Mrs. Parsons a little peck. I then found a comfortable seat to the side so that I was strategically placed between the two as they continued to quilt and discuss important news events going on in the hamlet. It was perhaps gossip by any other terms, but that had seriously bad connotations, which in some places was punishable by a short term in the stocks. As much as it was a favorite pastime of the local dames I could not imagine it was punishable in these parts anymore.

There was finally a break in the conversation and Mrs. Parsons, being the grand dame of the house, offered me the opportunity to tell my story about the day's events. With great zeal I told the ladies everything I could remember. They especially enjoyed the sendoff the dragoon Major had received. Both were troubled by the fatalistic view of Mr. Griffin. The thought of a looming war did not hold any attraction to Mother or Mrs. Parsons. Mother thought of Father and became melancholy; rightly so. It had only been a little over two days and yet it seemed Father had been gone a whole year. I was resolved to invigorate my efforts to get him out of the jail in Williamsburg.

Shortly before noon the quilting was at a stopping point and the ladies decided to postpone any further activity until evening. Mrs. Parsons had chores to do and Mother was anxious to see her children.

As we left Mrs. Parsons and Mother embraced and gave each other a peck on the cheek. There was true affection between Mother and her new guardian. That was a good sign to me; less for me to worry about.

We slowly began our journey with a short visit with Mr. Brown, who was safely ensconced in the cottage behind the pub. The Brown children crowded around us as we stepped inside the small front yard. It was as if we had not seen the children in a fortnight. Mother seemed to enjoy the attention given her by the children. Due to all the commotion, Mrs. Brown came outside to see what was happening. The ladies beamed. I had not seen Mother smile that much as she and Mrs. Brown genuinely hugged each other.

"Please, you must come inside and see Benjamin. He is doing so much better. Dr. Miller says it is a miracle that he is alive, much less recovering. We are very prayerful that an infection does not set in. His wounds are bad, but they are healing. The good doctor changes them at least four times a day and cleanses the wounds with some sort of solution." The hope shone in Mrs. Brown's eyes.

She led us into the sun-filled parlor where Mr. Brown lay peacefully propped up on two large pillows. His entire midsection was wrapped in a bandage that extended over both shoulders. Eyes closed, old Benjamin listened to Dr. Miller read to him from a translation of an ancient Greek novel. He seemed content for the moment. As we entered the room, Mrs. Brown spoke softly. "Benjamin, you have visitors." Dr. Miller looked up, closed his book, and stood to greet Mother and me.

"Ah, don't expect me to get up just yet. You'll have to be satisfied with a little handshake. And I mean a gentle, little handshake. It feels like I've been kicked in the ribs by 20 mules. The slightest movement brings tears to my eyes. If it weren't for the sip of brandy I get each hour, the pain would be unbearable," he said smiling.

Dr. Miller laughed slightly, "Count your blessings that you have a little pain. At least that reminds you that you're alive. Had it not been for the skills of William, Molly, and your treasured wife you'd be a sad memory."

"Don't be so hard on me Doc. I'm a very ill man. In fact, I feel a great need for a bit of brandy. The pain is insufferable."

"Benjamin Brown, you are such an awful actor," chastised Mrs. Brown.

Relenting, Dr. Miller poured a thimble full of brandy in a small whiskey glass and handed it to Mr. Brown.

"A might light on the medicine aren't you Doc? I certainly deserve at least half a glass. Don't I?"

"No, you had the half a glass less than 20 minutes ago," replied Dr. Miller.

Although disappointed by the meager ration, Mr. Brown slowly savored the medicinal brandy. As he emptied the glass there was a distinct smile on his face.

We stayed only a little while. Staying long enough just to pay our respects and learn that Dr. Miller would remain at Benjamin's bedside for another five days and then return to Charles. Trusted colleagues would explain his absence away. I only hoped they all had the same story.

As we got ready to leave, Dr. Miller pulled me aside and gave me two letters. "I understand that you will be riding to Charles every so often. Take these letters and deliver them to Dr. Wilson at the apothecary. He will see my wife gets her letter. Thank you Will. And here is a half-penny for you, the standard fee for letters."

"You're welcome, sir," I replied. "Thank you very much for the half-penny." I had no idea that I was becoming the unofficial post rider.

A little after midday we arrived at the Griffin house, our other family benefactor. I cannot emphasize enough the importance of having benefactors. Our destitute family depended on the goodwill of others and to have two dedicated benefactors was an absolute God-sent gift.

We entered the front yard and walked up the brick pathway to the front steps. No sooner had we acquired the front porch, Mrs. Griffin opened the front door. She was the perfect picture of a lady in charge of her household. Her house smock was by any descriptions frilly and ornate. Although traditional white it had ruffled sleeves and an immense amount of colorful embroidery over the shoulders onto the bodice. It was a work of art.

She exclaimed first, "My goodness, you must be Molly Jones. I am so glad to finally get to meet you. But you shouldn't be up and about so soon." Mrs. Griffin reached out to hug Mother. It seemed that was the custom in these parts. Mother responded by giving Mrs. Griffin a slight hug in return. "Now Molly my name is Rebecca, but most people just call me Becka for short. Now come in. We have just sat down for lunch. You must join us. Oh, to put your mind at ease you have the most wonderful children. Your Will is such a young gentleman, even though he did escape my clutches to go work for my husband." She reached out and gave me a gentle pinch on the left cheek. I turned beet red. It was my good fortune to have escaped her servitude, but I was a little embarrassed by it; after all, I had given her my word.

We followed Mrs. Griffin to the kitchen. As we got to the kitchen door Mrs. Griffin made a grand announcement. "Jones children, I have a great surprise for you." She stepped aside and waved her arm toward Mother standing in the doorway. "Your mother is here."

My siblings broke out in shouts. It was momentary chaos as they rudely jumped up from the table and besieged Mother. All wanted their time with Mother, so they pushed and shoved each other to be the closest. The little ones broke out in tears and were comforted by Mother. My siblings finally noticed me and came to stand by me for comfort. Right then the family needed a lot of emotional support from Mother. Any support and comfort was worth having, even if it came from the oldest brother. Mr. Griffin got up and came to introduce himself to Mother.

Remembering my manners, I spoke up. "Mother, this is Mr. Griffin." Turning to Mr. Griffin, I said, "Sir, this is my mother." Mother touched my arm and it showed she was proud that I had remembered some of my basic manners.

Correctly Mother extended her hand to Mr. Griffin and introduced herself. "Please call me Molly."

"Then you must call me Sam, which is short for Samuel. And believe me I much prefer the shorter version." They shook hands briefly as was dictated by polite customs. "Now Molly, would you join us? If you will, I'll put you right in the middle of your little Indians, who no doubt will be overjoyed." Our little ones naturally squealed with joy.

Everyone busily made room for Mother and me. Eventually we sat down to a rather large midday meal. There was no wonder why both Mr. and Mrs. Griffin were large people. It seemed their greatest pleasure, besides children, was eating enormous amounts of mouth-watering food. Mrs. Griffin was an excellent cook and Mr. Griffin was an excellent merchant, who supplied all of the good ingredients. It was a marriage made in heaven as far as I was concerned.

The meal was finished and Mr. Griffin shooed the young children from both families out of the kitchen. He asked me to stay.

"Molly, Benjamin Brown seems to be doing fine, but we can't let him stay here much longer. If the Tories get wind he is alive and in Fredrick, they will mount an arrest party and return. No doubt they will enlist the assistance of the dragoons that were our unwelcome guests today. We cannot risk a pitched battle. The Browns will move further into The Piedmont as soon as Benjamin is well enough or by the end of another fortnight regardless. That will leave the cottage free. We would like to offer it to you and your family as compensation for Will's service as our unofficial post rider between here and Charles. Of course he will have other odd jobs around the community."

"Sir," I interrupted, "Dr. Miller asked me to deliver two letters to Charles and then gave me a half-penny." I held out the half-penny to give to Mr. Griffin.

"What a fine lad you are, Will. You'll earn that and a bit more. Standard fee for a letter is a half-penny. It's just like a doctor to seek a bargain. No lad, keep the first half-penny for yourself. From now on I'll be the acting postmaster for our village and I'll make the charges. Dr. Wilson in Charles will act as postmaster there. He will charge a half-penny for letters to be delivered to Frederick, just like we charge. I'll be supplying the horse and livery. You'll earn a ha'penny a day, each day you ride. Official mail you'll carry free of charge. That's where the use of the horse comes in, to compensate you for carrying the official mail free. Is that a bargain?" Mr. Griffin asked extending his hand to me.

"Yes, sir. I'd be honored to be a post rider," I replied with enthusiasm and shook his hand to seal the bargain.

"Of course, Molly, this is all subject to your approval," said Mr. Griffin, turning his attention back to Mother.

"Sam, I have no objections and I would like to thank you and your wife for being so kind. I don't know what we would have done without you." Tears came to Mother's eyes as she gripped my hand and squeezed.

Chapter 12

Redcoat Raid

God smiled on Benjamin Brown. Two weeks later to the day he and his family loaded up their two-horse wagon and moved on into The Piedmont to seek refuge further from the town of Charles, the Tories, and the ever-menacing dragoons, which is another footnote in my recollection.

Regressing just a bit, no sooner had the memory of the ill-fated raid on Fredrick begun to fade, the dragoons showed up again and again. It was the collected opinion of the town fathers that the British were trying to intimidate the populace and quell any aberrant behavior on the part of the populace. Certainly the British did not want another Boston on their hands and they were bound and determined not to lose their grip on Virginia. That is precisely the result of their heavy-handed tactics. It came to a head at the end of February on a Saturday, several days before the Brown family left town. It precipitated their hurried departure.

Although the incident is perhaps insignificant and lost in the annals of our history, it was a catalyst for solidifying support for the Whig cause. As was the normal practice of the militia on the last Saturday of the month to drill, the men of the town duly assembled at the town square early that morning. Some looking for an opportunity to wager a few coins brought their rifles in anticipation of an impromptu shooting match. Perhaps no more than 10 rifles were stacked on the edge of the parade field. Mr. Griffin and his trusted Sergeant Bailey presided over the assembly. After roll call where most of the militia were accounted for Sergeant Bailey took over the company to practice drill as the officers retired to Mr. Griffin's store to talk about current events. No sooner had the officer ascended the steps of the general store, than an entire company of dragoons galloped into town. The sudden and unexpected appearance stunned not only Mr. Griffin but also the entire militia. The normally reliable information had failed to note the dragoons were even in the area, much less in striking distance to Fredrick. The despised Major was at the head of his troop. Captain Clark and several of his more amiable officers were noticeably missing. The dragoons surrounded the parade ground and drew their cavalry muskets; shortened versions of the venerable Brown Bess. The Major, assured his dragoons were strategically positioned, reined his horse over to the front of the store.

"Well gentlemen, so nice to see you again," sneered the Major with his teeth clenched in a forced smile. "Good to see all of you are here. Saves me the trouble of rounding up all of your ruffians and miscreants that you call a militia."

"What's the meaning of this Major? You have no right to just ride in here and draw weapons. We are loyal subjects of the Crown," implored Mr. Griffin.

"Shut up Griffin. I have had enough of your insolence. Loyal subjects of the Crown, not likely. You are no better than the rabble in Boston and it is about time all of you start showing more respect to the Crown. Now Griffin, you and your so-called officers go assemble with that motley gathering on the parade field."

Mr. Griffin and the officers removed themselves to the parade field and stood in front of the company. Philip and I watched from the safe confines of the store.

"Finally you understand obedience to the Crown. I am amazed," chuckled the Major. He raised his voice so everyone could hear, "It is the order of the Royal Governor his Excellency Sir Dunmore that there are no longer any threats upon the town of Fredrick and its surrounding area. As a result, the militia of said town will be disbanded and all equipment, weapons, and supplies previously issued to said militia will be seized and returned to the Royal Armory in Williamsburg." He went on. "The charter of Fredrick's militia is hereby revoked and all previous commissions, appointments, and ranks are vacated." The Major then added with a smile on his face, "God save the King."

The militia, no longer an organized militia; I was in shock. A part of their lives for as long as they could remember was torn out of their soul. Their duty, honor, and dedication to each other were ripped to shreds.

The Major was not finished. "Sergeant Major, seize the stacked weapons on the parade field and then conduct a house-to-house search for any other weapons. Oh, sergeant, do remember to search the general store for contraband."

The militiamen were ready to bolt for their homes and

weapons. Mr. Griffin held them in place.

"Steady men," he shouted. "There will be other days. They have us at a distinct disadvantage and I don't want to lose anyone over this minor insult." The militiamen still seething with anger steadied themselves and held tight. Their sons, who had been on the edge of the parade field and were pushed away to the outside, knew what they had to do and instantly disappeared. There would be fewer rifles than the British hoped for.

Philip and I were also of the same mind. We made a mad dash to the rifle case and grabbed as many as could and sprinted out the back of the store for the barn. Quickly we shoved the rifles under hay, behind feed troughs and even threw some down the well. We quickly returned to the store and grabbed two more rifles apiece and strapped on as many powder horns as we could manage. We left three old muskets and an old English fowler for the British. As I ran through Mr. Griffin's office I grabbed Old Anne and stuck her in my belt.

We were out the back again, but this time we headed for McCracken's barn over on Muddy Creek where we would all assemble. We skirted around the parade field far enough away that the redcoats could not see us. As we reached the edge of town there must have been 20 to 30 boys headed in the same direction each carrying at least two rifles and loads of powder horns. We were a young militia on the run.

By the time we reached McCracken's barn our numbers had swelled to more than 50 armed youngsters. Soon all of us noticed we were alone, there were no adults among us. One or two boys were 15, but most were younger, the youngest was 11. Only Philip and I were 16, but no one paid him any attention. A debate started as to what we should do. Philip stood on the outside of the discussion and nervously looked back toward Fredrick in anticipation of the redcoats. We were getting nowhere.

Finally, Philip spoke up. "We can't stay here. Someone is bound to have noticed all of us headed in this direction. We have to move up into the forest where the dragoons can't follow."

It made sense to me, but the other boys ignored Philip. I spoke up, "Philip is right. If we stay here the redcoats will find us and take all of our rifles away. We have to get moving."

I then learned part of Philip's secret. A tall lanky redheaded boy spoke up, "I ain't listening to no half-breed. You can't trust the Indian in him. He'll just lead us into a trap and the redcoats will kill all of us; worse yet he'll lead us into Indian Territory and we'll all be scalped."

I thought the last statement to be absurd because Indian Territory was at least 100 miles away in the mountains and I didn't think the Cherokees placed any value on the scalps of colonial youngsters, I hoped. I spoke up, "Most of you know me because I'm new in town and most of you know what happened over at our farm. You also know that Captain Griffin trusts me enough to make me the new post rider. Well, Captain Griffin also trusts Philip enough to let him work in the store where the rifles are kept. So the Captain trusts the both of us and now I'm telling you what Philip said was right. Half-breed or not, he is one of us and he knows we have to get out of here and into the deep woods before the redcoats come."

As luck would have it, a late arrival came running up the

path carrying a single rifle and a powder horn. Even though he was out of breath, as soon he reached the group, he struggled to get his message out, "Redcoats. They know we ran. They're looking for us. I looked back and just as I turned the corner there were about five dragoons headed our way, about half a mile behind me."

That report was inspiration enough. Philip shouted orders, "Seth, you take everyone up the old Indian Trail. You should hit pretty thick woods fairly quick. Go to the outcroppings on the trail and then go up the mountain to the caverns. You'll be safe there." In the best militia fashion, he then said, "I need five of you to pull rear guard with me and Will." All of our little company threw up their hands. Philip picked by pointing, "Harry, Scott, Andy, George, and Robert. Seth, take the rest and get gone, now! Don't stop no matter what!"

While the main party raced for the trail, Philip and I loaded our rifles as the others in our rear guard checked to make sure their rifles were still loaded and ready for action. Between us we had 10 rifles and Old Anne. It really never occurred to us what we were doing; it was something that seemed instinctive. Nor did we consider the consequences of confronting the British dragoons. Finally ready, we scampered behind the retreating groups of boys to our front. We could see they were quickly disappearing into the edges of the forest. It was a satisfying sight. We had only a few yards left before we too began disappearing when we heard a commotion behind us.

"They aren't in the barn. Spread out and search the area. They can't have gone far." It was the bellowing voice of the Sergeant Major. As we reached the edge of the forest we took shelter behind some trees to take a peek at what was actually going on. A little elevated now, we had a clear view of the barn and the surrounding fields. The five dragoons were splitting up and going in different directions. To our misfortune the Sergeant Major had dismounted and was peering at the ground.

"We got problems," said Philip. "The Sergeant Major is looking for tracks. It is only going to take him a few seconds to see which direction we went."

Then a curious thing happened. The Sergeant Major put his fingers to his mouth and gave a loud whistle. Almost immediately the other four dragoons assembled on him. We heard his instructions loud and clear. "The little rascals appear to have gone in that direction." He pointed to a scope of woods in the distance in the opposite direction we had gone. "I'll look around here for stragglers. Be careful; they are just young boys. I don't want any of them hurt. Do you understand?" "Yes, Sergeant Major" came the reply for all four dragoons. The dragoons took off at breakneck speed toward the distant and empty scope of woods. The Sergeant Major remounted and slowly headed in our direction as if he saw us hiding in the woods.

"Quick," Philip said, "we have to get up the trail a little more where there is better cover for an ambush."

"Ambush?" I questioned. "Are we going to kill the Sergeant Major?"

"Listen all of you. The Sergeant Major sent his troopers away. He doesn't want us to get hurt, but he does want us to turn in our rifles. We have to convince him that he won't succeed. When we stop him, remember don't fire. That's an order. I'm telling you he's not going to shoot, so just have your rifles ready at half-cock, but be ready just in case."

We raced another 100 yards up the trail and positioned ourselves behind trees, fallen logs, and anything else that concealed us from discovery. Philip gave us our last orders. It was only a few minutes before we saw the sergeant major nearing our ambush. As he approached the point Philip selected, the sergeant major stopped his horse.

"Now young sirs," he said in a deep baritone voice, "I sincerely hope you weren't going to shoot me out of my saddle before I had a chance to talk to you."

Philip motioned us and we eased out of our hiding places rifles at the ready position. We surrounded the Sergeant Major.

"Well done, lads! I'm sure your fathers will be extremely proud of you for this excellent display of frontiersman ship, but the game is over. You need to surrender your weapons like good boys and come on back to Fredericks with me. We mustn't keep that petulant major waiting."

No one spoke, not even Philip. I felt compelled to say something, even if it was wrong. "Sergeant major, you must appreciate the position you are in. And we truly appreciate your consideration of our health and welfare by confronting us alone. But I have to inform you that we have no intention of surrendering our rifles or returning with you. We do not wish you any harm, or any embarrassment. I am sure you are well aware that while we may be young in age, all of us cut our baby teeth on a long rifle and are therefore excellent marksmen. I suggest we call this confrontation a draw and allow each party to leave the field a winner."

"So young master Smyth, what do you propose?"

"We'll allow you the pleasure of capturing say five of our rifles and we will fade from this encounter with our honor intact."

"So you intend to negotiate your way out of this predicament. Jolly good show. I will accept no less than say 10 rifles and three of you return with me."

"Eight weapons and no one goes, last offer!" I said.

The Sergeant Major laughed, "It is a deal, gentlemen. I must say a deal that I will never repeat. Is that understood?"

"Yes, Sergeant Major," I replied. I turned to the other and barked an order, Empty your pans and take off. I'll follow."

"No," came the reply in unison. Philip spoke up, "The Sergeant Major can have his compromise, but we stay together."

Philip and I chose to give up our four rifles and quickly emptied the flash pans. Four of our comrades surrendered a weapon a piece each of which looked like an antique of dubious valve. We collected the weapons and handed them to the Sergeant Major, who strapped them to his saddle the best he could.

"Before you lads disappear, I want to give you a word of advice. Take it for what it is worth. You were very brave today, but foolish. There is no profit in trying to oppose the Crown. Soon Boston will be subdued and normalcy will return to the colonies. Don't you lads catch this radical fever. It will only get you killed. All of you have your whole lives ahead of you, go find your other friends and go home."

Philip spoke with brevity and conviction, "We'll go home when we've sent all of you home."

The Sergeant Major chuckled and said, "The impertinence

of youth."

We backed slowly away from the Sergeant Major and soon faded into the dim shadows of the forest. We left him there shaking his head.

We really didn't know whether we had won, lost, or succeeded by compromise. All we knew is that we had faced a dragoon and held our ground, at least until it was more appropriate to wait for another day. The child's play we had engaged in brought us within a hair's breadth of our own destruction, yet we didn't even know it. The world was ours and we enjoyed the sweet taste of victory however shallow it was. The bitterness of defeat and victory awaited us on another day, on another field.

Chapter 13

Into the Backwoods

Philip led the way up the path, as I controlled our rear. I'm not sure what we could have done had the dragoons fell upon us in earnest, but we acted out our parts. These were the roles we learned from listening to our fathers and uncles as they recounted endless stories about their exploits during the French and Indian Wars, the victories, the cold hard lessons of defeat, and death. These were also the skills we were taught in the woods and fields of Virginia as our fathers and uncles prepared us to defend our families against whatever foe might appear.

The journey took us until four o'clock that afternoon. It had been a torturous march. The trail had been mostly uphill or rather up one mountain and then up another mountain. As we reached the caverns, the smell of smoke and roasting venison filled the air. All of us except Philip felt overjoyed. Warmth fended off the growing cold and food filled our hungry bellies. Philip called us to a halt.

"Look, something is wrong. I know the boys could have

started a fire, but I don't remember anyone carrying any venison or hearing a shot," he said cautiously. "We should scout the site first before we go in headlong."

One of the older boys spoke up. "Who appointed you our leader anyway? You're only a half-breed. Come on, let's go. I'm hungry." The rest of the group rallied around the new leader and brushed Philip aside. I stayed with Philip. He had saved us at McCracken's Barn and I wasn't about to dismiss his cautiousness.

"So Philip, what do we do?" I asked.

"The caverns are about another half-mile up this trail, which snakes around this ridgeline before it empties right into the cavern system. The only way to really see what's going on there is to sneak around the side of this mountain and try to get above the caverns and look down into them. Over there." He pointed toward a slightly higher elevation. "We can actually see into the foreground of the caverns. That's most likely where the fires were made. Then we can judge for ourselves."

"I'm with you. Our friends will make so much noise no one will notice as we bypass the caverns."

"Let's hope not," said Philip.

Armed with Old Anne and a musket Philip had gotten from one of the boys, we dropped off the trail and began the treacherous task of bypassing the caverns. Not long after we had started, we found a small, little-used path which went along the side of a steep incline which made up one wall of the caverns above. This path was no more than a foot wide, but it was at least solid and had enough handholds to provide a quick way around. No sooner had we acquired the footpath, we heard a commotion directly above us.

There were a few shouts, but nothing more. It certainly wasn't the sounds of jubilation. Philip and I stared at each other, fear surfacing in both our faces. With nothing left to do we continued on.

As we neared the end of the path and almost to better ground Philip grabbed a bush for balance and nearly fell into the steep ravine as the bush suddenly gave way. Somehow he managed to maintain his balance. Once I got to him, we discovered he had inadvertently uncovered a small opening going directly into the side of the mountain. We looked at each other and without a moment's hesitation, Philip plunged headfirst into the hole.

He whispered back to me, "It looks like it might be part of the system, but it's dark as night in here. Grab a couple of sticks so we can make torches. See if you can find an old pine knot. I'll wait here and let my eyes adjust. Hand me some tinder and some twigs and I'll get a fire started. We'll need some way to light the torches."

I quickly gathered some tinder and small twigs from the end of the trail and hurried them back to Philip. I left to find something we could use as a torch as Philip started working on making a fire.

Lady luck smiled on us and I found a couple of old pine saplings which had been killed when lightning brought down a bigger tree on top of them and broke off the main trunks about three feet above the ground. It had been years ago and the pine saplings were now gray with age. I quickly rocked them back and forth and finally broke the roots off. I was rewarded with bulbs full of rich pine pitch. I quickly brushed as much dirt off as I could and ran back to the cave opening. Philip already had a small fire going. I could see faint wisps of smoke coming out of the rock face.

"Philip," I said as I pushed the two torches into the opening,

"I found some old pine saplings. They should do."

"Come on in Will." As I climbed in he continued to talk. "These will do fine. I'll light one and we save the other one. Grab the extra tinder and twigs and put it in your pouch. We may need it later if the torch goes out."

Philip began to light the pine torch as I gathered up the excess tinder and twigs. It only took a moment for the pine root to catch fire. It really flamed. Our torch lit up the whole passageway, not that it was much of a passageway, but at least we had a torch to push back the darkness. The passageway itself was about three feet high and three feet wide. It was not natural; it was man-made. Some ancient clan had thought it wise to make a secret entrance to the caverns.

We crawled along the shaft for a good 50 meters before we intersected a larger shaft. This shaft had a more natural look. It only took us a second to choose to go right; that's the direction of the smoke. The passageway itself varied in height from four feet to eight feet and varied in width from as wide as four feet in some places and to as narrow as a man's waist in other places. We made quick progress and soon found ourselves near an area that was getting lighter. We were either getting close to the entrance or to a hall that had a fire. Philip quickly put out our torch lest we be discovered. We crept forward until we were overlooking the foreground of the cavern system. Somehow we had managed to take a side tunnel and came out above everything.

"Cherokee," whispered Philip. "A hunting party must have been camped here. They all stumbled into them."

"Damn rotten luck!" I exclaimed in a whisper. Our friends

were all gathered in one corner being warmed by two roaring fires. At least they weren't hungry. Our newly arrived compatriots were gnawing on pieces of freshly roasted venison. Although they did not look happy, at least they weren't hungry anymore. Our arsenal of rifles was neatly stacked next to a group of Cherokee warriors lounging around their fire.

"Philip!" shouted an imposing-looking Cherokee warrior looking in our direction. "You can come out now and bring Master Will with you. We have warm fires and plenty of venison to share."

Philip surprised me by responding in Cherokee, "Thank you for the invitation Uncle, but I'm not too sure that I want to walk into the spider's web just yet."

"Philip, it pleases me that you still remember our language. I was afraid you might have forgotten. Your grandfather will be pleased to hear this news. Now please come down and join your friends. We mean them no harm and in the morning you can return to Fredrick as heroes. Tonight you will be our guests and enjoy the company of your uncle and a few of your cousins."

Another Cherokee spoke to Philip. "Hey squirt, are you going to come down, or am I going to have to pull you out of that cave like I pulled you out of that tree when you were only three?"

"Thomas, is that you? You couldn't do it then and you certainly can't do it now. I'm bigger and stronger," replied Philip, taunting his cousin. Philip spoke to his uncle, "If we are to return home heroes then we take back our rifles with us. Is that a deal, Uncle?"

"No Philip, it isn't. I heard our treaty brothers, the English, want them. We will turn them over to the Commissioner and let him deliver them to the English. The colonists' arguments with the English are of no concern to us. And I will not discuss this any further with a young pup who I cannot even see. Now get down here!" demanded his uncle.

"Yes, Uncle," said Philip, folding to his uncle's sharp rebuke. "Sorry, Will; he is my uncle and I have to obey him. I can't tell you what to do, but would you please come also. He won't harm any of us. We just have to figure a way to get the rifles away from him." Philip got up and started to walk down a small incline to the floor. "You coming or not Will?"

"What choice do I have? Old Anne and me against the whole Cherokee Nation."

"You're wrong. It's 'Old Anne and I'. At least get your grammar right. Besides, it's not the whole Cherokee Nation. There are only 15 of them. If it hadn't been my uncle and cousins, I bet we could have taken them," joked Philip.

His uncle walked over to greet him. "I'm sure the Nation will remember the day that Philip Long Walker spared us of his wrath." He embraced Philip who could do nothing but accept the bear hug from his much larger uncle.

"You joke Uncle, but these are my friends now and I would do anything to save them," retorted a humorless Philip.

"No sense of humor Philip. That is not very becoming. What are the colonists teaching you?" His uncle turned to me and extended his hand, "Young Master Will Jones, I am John Talking Bear. Someday we must talk and I will tell you about your father and the first time I met him, which was under much less pleasant circumstances. It was a long time ago, but the memory is still printed in my mind."

I shook his hand, "It is nice to meet you Mr. Talking Bear. I would very much like to hear about Father and you. He's never said much about the Indian Wars."

"I'm sure it was not any more pleasant for him than it was for me. We'll talk later, but now sit down with your friends and enjoy some supper. We have enough blankets for everyone so no one will freeze tonight. And in the morning after a little 'petit dejeuner' all of you can return home."

"With the rifles!" added Philip.

"Nephew, do not try my patience. Now go join your friends and eat."

Philip walked behind me, his head hung low. He felt to blame for the loss of the rifles and now he had to face all of the youngsters from town. I didn't feel much better. I had supported Philip and felt just as much to blame. Any hope that this sad episode in our otherwise brilliant escape from the dragoons was soon shattered. As we approached our comrades we were met with cold hard stares. There was no friendliness in their attitude.

"Congratulations half-breed," taunted the redheaded youth. "You might have saved us from the redcoats, but you gave us to your Injun friends, and now we'll traipse all the way back to Fredrick with our tails between our legs. When we git home then have to tell our kinfolks how some Injuns captured us, stole all the rifles, and then sent us packing. We didn't even put up a fight.``

"Wait! " I said, trying to defend Philip and myself. "If Philip hadn't come up with a plan, we'd lost those rifles a long time ago."

Philip put his hand on my shoulder and came forward.

"That's all right Will. They are right. My plan failed because I didn't think any further than getting away from the dragoons." Philip motioned all of us to draw a little closer. "We still have a chance to get those rifles, but it's going to take everyone working together. There can't be any room for dissenters. My honor is at stake. I can't go back to Fredrick unless I go back with all of you and those rifles. I know I'm asking a lot. I'm asking for your full trust. There is a lot at stake. We can do it if we are together. Are you with me?"

"Let's hear your plan first," said the redhead, "then we'll decide."

Philip picked up a piece of venison, sat down in the middle of the group, and pretended to eat as he began to explain his plan. All listened in silence as the plan was developed. After about half an hour we voted. One finger on the ground for "yes," two fingers on the ground for "no." The first vote was unanimous. Everyone put one finger on the ground. It was now about nine o'clock.

"Uncle, since we are your guests, at least you can provide us a little entertainment. Why don't you show my friends how to wrestle Indian style? They have heard so much about it, but they have never seen a real demonstration."

"Philip, forgive me for my rudeness. We will certainly be glad to put on a demonstration for you," said John Talking Bear. He then addressed the 10 Cherokee braves lounging around the campfire. "Your cousin would like us to show these white pups how to leg wrestle, so get off your lazy derrieres and be good teachers. Make it a good effort. We don't want these boys to think we'd do anything half-hearted."

The lounging braves slowly got up and began to stretch to loosen up their muscles. Several braves started making rude comments to each other, all in jest. Philip translated for us. It seemed they were positioning themselves for a real match. The group divided five to a side and formed a circle around an open area. We scooted closer to watch. Some stood next to the ring and some sat just outside the ring. Eight of our friends decided they didn't want to participate and curled up in their blankets to snooze the night away. A pair of braves, one from each side, entered the ring and laid opposite of each other, right shoulder to the opponent's right hip.

John Talking Bear explained the game. "As I count to three both braves will raise their right leg on each count. On the count of three they will interlock their right legs and try to flip each other. It's a game that takes a lot of skill and strategy. It's not as simple as it seems."

John Talking Bear then began the match. On the count of three the braves locked legs and one brave went flying backward over his head. The braves howled and laughed at the unfortunate loser.

John continued, "Each brave will get an opportunity to challenge each brave from the other team. A point will be awarded for each successful flip. At the end, when everyone has competed against each of the members of the opposing team, we will tally up the score and see who won."

Philip turned to me. "Cherokees are very competitive. Just watch in a couple of more bouts the betting will start. Then it gets really interesting."

After only one more bout, one team said something to the other team and two tomahawks were placed in the ring as new competitors entered. There seemed to be some negotiations going on.

"Will," said Philip, "they want to start over and extend it for two complete rounds." Philip smiled and rocked back on his heels in silent laughter. John, who was the referee, agreed to the change in format.

There was a succession of articles placed in the ring: knives, pistols, blankets, powder horns, and anything else of value that could be bet. Most of all there was always a lengthy negotiation as to the value of each article. One tomahawk might be worth three blankets, while a pistol might be worth one tomahawk and two powder horns. But the values also changed with each round. The Cherokee were legendary for their love of sport and betting and Philip knew it.

I had actually hoped to learn how to leg wrestle, but these braves were experienced and they were not about to stop to teach a group of settler children about the fine points of their sport, at least not this night. The competition and the betting continued. Eventually the red team as we called them because several of the braves were wearing red cotton shirts gained the advantage over the brown team, who were of course wearing brown cotton shirts. The game lasted a good two hours and was finally over, sort of. The winners celebrated their hard-earned victory, while the losing team groused about how the other team had cheated. After that allegation, there was what appeared to be a serious attempt by the brown to forcibly retrieve their lost goods. We scattered as both teams began a melee. John Talking Bear grabbed a nearby rifle and fired into the air to stop the fight. Captains from both sides ran to John and demanded justice as they tried to push each other away in order to gain John's undivided attention. We had scattered to the far edge of the campsite, our backs to the stone walls. It was hard for us to contain our laughter.

"Enough," shouted John. "A fine example you make for these boys. Sometimes I think you are really heathen savages. If Pastor Ames could see you now all of you would be required to do penance for two weeks. Now stop behaving like children and act like real braves." Philip whispered a translation for us. "Since no one is satisfied with the outcome of the last match, we will move on to the next event, stand-up wrestling. Here two opponents will stand opposite each other, right foot touching. They will grasp right hands and on the count of three, each will try to dislodge the other. The first one to make his opponent move his right foot wins that round. Come children, it is safe to return to the ring."

We cautiously returned to the ring. A few decided they much rather sleep. I was too excited to give up. This was really a lot of fun to watch.

Again the match started, the bets were placed and goods were lost and won with each bout. This match lasted almost as long as the other with the red team again amassing most of the bets. It was predictable that the brown team was none too pleased. With only two more rounds to go, it got ugly. Two braves faced off. As John counted to three the brown shirt brave punched the red shirt brave in the face, knocking him down to the ground. The brown shirts cheered the triumph. That was all it took to restart the melee.

This time it was a serious fight. Punches were flying. It appeared little was forbidden, except for serious biting. At least no one got an ear bitten off. We naturally scooted to the far edges of the campsite and stayed out of the fight for the most part. Occasionally a brave would be flipped by his opponent and come flying in our direction and we would try to ease his fall from grace, dust him off and push him back into the melee. Try as he could, John was helpless to stop the fight. Eventually he wandered around the fight and ended up standing by Philip and me.

"Philip, why did I let you talk me into this exhibition? I should have known better. For once, because you boys are here, I thought they would be a little better behaved," lamented John Talking Bear.

It took a good 45 minutes before the fight finally started to dissipate. Exhausted braves, unable to fight anymore, collapsed from sheer exhaustion. The last two braves collapsed on each other.

Looking at his braves, John spoke to Philip without looking at him. "Do you intend to leave now or wait until the morning?"

"We will leave now Uncle," said Philip confidently.

As if on cue the sleeping boys got up from their blankets and gingerly walked around the collapsed braves to regain possession of the rifles.

"It will be cold on the trail tonight, Philip. Each boy should have a blanket to keep him warm. May I talk to your friends before you leave?" asked John Talking Bear.

"Yes of course, Uncle," replied Philip. "Everyone, gather your belongings and grab a blanket to pull over your shoulders. It might get cold tonight. Assemble over here by Will and me, my uncle wants to talk to us."

It took only a moment or two for all of them to get things in order and assemble by us. Each boy had a self-satisfied grin on his face."

John Talking Bear began. "I look at you, with your young bright faces and see the future of your land in your eyes. Today you have earned three victories and suffered one minor defeat. First you saved your rifles from the redcoats at Fredrick, and then again at McCracken's barn, your capture by the savage Cherokee (The group laughed at that remark) was only a minor setback. Through wit, cunning, and unity you overcame adversity and triumphed without a shot being fired in anger. I am proud to have been outwitted by such a fine group of young men. I have fought against many of your fathers and have the greatest respect for their bravery and now I have the greatest respect for their sons. I fear the future holds many dark days for you and my people alike. But there will be a better day to come. Among all things never lose your honor; sometimes it is all a warrior has. Tonight you start your journey to becoming warriors. Although it will be a small hardship it will be the starting point for your future. Absorb your pain, forge ahead in silence and never stray the path. When the sun rises you will have become better men." Talking Bear finished his speech. He turned to Philip and me. "Boys, the only safe way off this mountain is to go over the crest westward to Lone Pine Mountain. At the base of the mountain there is a little settlement. You'll be safe there. I'll send Thomas to Fredrick with a message to Captain Griffin on where he can find you. Send your friends on ahead. I want you and Will to spend just a moment with us," said John plaintively.

"It's fine with me. Let Seth take charge. He got everyone here and he's probably the best woodsman among us with the exception of you and me," I said, emphasizing the correct usage of "me" in a prepositional phrase.

Seth, who had been following the conversation, didn't wait for any orders. He got torches for everyone, lit them, and got the group started over the crest towards Lone Pine Mountain. He came over to Philip and me. "Don't be too long, it's a far piece to Lone Pine. We'll be lucky to make it before sunup and then it's still a good two hours down the mountain to the settlement."

"Don't worry Seth," said Philip. "We won't be 10 minutes with my uncle."

Seth took off at a quick pace with the band of 25 boys right behind him. It took less than a minute before the lights from the torches faded into the cold night air.

John Talking Bear spoke first. "Honor is beyond value. Both of you have shown exceptional courage tonight in trying to uphold that honor. The day will come again when it is put to the test. Remember tonight and think of it as a practice and do not be too upset with me for this show," he said. He then addressed his prostate braves who still had not stirred, "They are gone now. You can get up. I have never seen a worse group of actors in my entire life."

The braves got up slowly, stretching aching bones and muscles. Still not completely exhausted, several jostled each other playfully. Thomas came over to us favoring his right leg.

"That was a great plan, boys. It only took a little while before we all realized what you were up to. Nice plan based on known tendencies of your adversary. I only wish the play-acting hadn't been so intense. My leg is killing me. I don't know who it was, but one of our cousins kicked the tar out of me. I may never be able to walk properly again," whined Thomas with a huge grin on his face.

"Uncle, I am humiliated. I thought it was a good plan and everything went as planned," said Philip dejectedly.

"Neither you nor Will have anything to feel humiliated about. It was a good plan and you have learned a valuable lesson. Just remember no plan is perfect and when a plan is working to perfection something is wrong," said John. "Now it is time for both of you to go. Enjoy your hard-earned victory and remember the lessons you have learned today." John Talking Bear gave us both a big hug, placed lit torches in our hands, and sent us on our way. The whole Cherokee band waved goodbye as we crested the ridge and disappeared into the night.

It took us almost 45 minutes to catch up with the group. We found them resting alongside the trail almost five miles from the caverns. Seth had put as much distance between the group and the Cherokees as he could manage and the group was exhausted. When we arrived everyone cheered as we moved toward the front of the line. From hero to goat back to hero all in a short expanse of time. Neither Philip nor I breathed a word about the private conversation with his uncle.

Seth addressed Philip. "Look, we're sorry about all the name-calling and everything. If it hadn't been for you we'd have lost the rifles for sure or been shot by them dragoons. Who knows what them Cherokees woulda done if you hadn't shown up? I mean your Uncle, he was nice enough to us, but still, we'd lost them rifles if'n it hadn't been for you. Thanks, Philip. We all appreciate it."

"Don't lose any sleep over it. We've had a big adventure, but we still have to get going. It's still a long way to Lone Pine. Seth, you take the lead since you know the way. Will and I will pull rear. The rest of you get up and git. We'll rest when we get there. And remember, look on this as a test of our manhood. We showed courage. Now it's time we prove our toughness."

Everyone quickly rewrapped themselves in their blankets, draped the powder horns across the blankets, and picked up their rifles. Philip and I relieved a couple of rifles from the little ones and slung them crossways across our shoulders letting slings criss cross in front. Then we carried one rifle. This at least eased the burden of two of the younger boys and set an example. Soon the younger boys were only carrying one rifle apiece, while the older boys took on more of the burden. Seth took the lead and set a good pace, always mindful that we had a long way to go and that only a few of us had gotten any sleep in the past 24 hours.

The torches gave out about 2 o'clock. Seth and Philip decided not to stop and search for more torches. It would have taken too much time. The full moon was enough to light the way. Seth took off again after a five-minute break, but at a slower pace in case the footing became treacherous. No one was complaining, not even the little ones. Everyone was watching out for each other.

Several times during the night we did stop to rest and grab some water from springs, which dotted the trail, realizing we were lucky the streams had not frozen. While the February night was cold, it must have been down to 35°F. We were blessed there were only patches of old snow every so often.

Just before sunrise, as the eastern horizon was turning pink, Lone Pine Mountain came into sight. As the crow flies it was probably only two to three miles away, but we had to follow the ridgeline, which made it another good five miles away. The only way to get to the settlement of Lone Pine was to go over the mountain and down the other side. We continued to march at the same time nearing what we thought was total exhaustion. It took us about an hour and a half to come within sight of the crest.

The smoke from the campfire at the top mountain could be seen for miles around. The smell of bacon cooking over an open fire wafted through the forest. I thought I was hallucinating, but everyone saw and smelled the same thing. We held a quick powwow. Philip and I agreed to scout forward as Seth remained in control of the boys. As we got ready to leave, a dark figure approached us along the ridgeline path.

"Hold your fire boys," said the stranger. The voice was familiar, but I couldn't place it. "I wondered when you'd be here," he continued. There's bacon and eggs waiting for you and some good hot coffee to warm your bones." It was Sergeant Bailey.

He was mobbed by 27 cold, tired, and hungry boys, all of whom wanted to tell him about our adventures. He did the best he could to hug or touch all of us that he could reach.

Finally, he had to call a halt to the festivities. "Whoa now. All of you just calm down. Sounds like to me you've got a lot to tell. Now's not the time. It's more important to get some warm food in you and let you get a little rest before we go on down to Lone Pine. Who's in charge here?" he asked.

"Philip, Will, and Seth!" everyone replied in unison.

"Well, looks like I got me three good sergeants here. Good enough, then. You boys get them organized and follow me on in." He turned, laid his rifle across his left arm, and walked off toward the crest. Seth took the lead. Philip and I took the rear to make sure no one was left behind.

As the troop lined up in a single file I heard one of the smaller boys softly crying. I went over to him and tried to comfort him. "Hey, everything's all right. We're almost there. When we get there, we'll have a big plate of bacon and eggs and sleep until noon."

The boy who was no more than four and-a-half feet tall looked up at me with his big brown eyes. "I guess I was a little scared and now I'm crying 'cause I'm so happy we're safe. I'll be alright." He stood up, grabbed his rifle, which was a good six inches taller than he was, and shouldered it. As he began to march after the others, he turned back to me. "Thanks, Will, but promise me you won't tell anyone I was crying?"

"I promise!" I said. There are certain things better left untold and this was just one of the things from our adventures which would never see the light of day in our tales.

Chapter 14

Return to Fredrick

It seemed like an eternity, but finally, Philip and I got to the crest of the mountain. There we found a roaring cook fire and several smaller fires spread around the clearing. There were other men there besides Sergeant Bailey. A few of the fathers had been fortunate enough to choose this point to come to in an effort to catch up with us. I could see the gleam in the fathers' eyes as they patiently sat with their sons and listened to our adventure. Philip and I got a heaping plate of eggs and almost a side of bacon between us. We sat away from the main group of boys by ourselves. Sergeant Bailey spied us and came over with two cups of steaming coffee.

"Here, take these cups before they burn my fingers anymore." He handed them to us and we quickly put the hot cups on the ground beside us. "Now when we get back, I want both of you and Seth to report to Captain Griffin and give him the full story; the correct story. So far I've heard at least 10 different versions of what happened. I'm sure, between the three of you, there is one version we can come up with that gets near the real facts of what happened. I want to tell you boys now, what you done was real brave. Captain Griffin will talk to all of you as a group when we get back. He has a few words for you. Just mind you he was not too happy that all of you chanced a skirmish with the dragoons over these rifles. Now as to the rest of us, the fathers, your neighbors, and your friends, well, we're real proud of you and were worried sick that you were going to be in big trouble, but when that Dragoon Sergeant Major came back and said that all of you ran off into the woods and left behind all the rifles, all six of them, we knew'd you done good. Now finish your breakfast and get some sleep. We'll take off out of here in about three hours. By the way, where did you get all these here blankets? They look like Indian trade blankets."

"John Talking Bear gave them to us," I said proudly. "He was at the –" Philip jabbed me hard my ribs with his elbow. I stopped in mid-sentence.

"You boys ran into Chief Talking Bear?" Sergeant Bailey had a perplexed look on his face. "What in tarnation were y'all doing with him? Never mind, I don't want to hear it right now. That's almost too much to believe. Now get some rest," he said, shaking his head as he walked away.

"You didn't have to elbow me in the ribs so hard that it hurt. And you didn't tell me your Uncle was a chief."

"Yeah well, it kind of slipped my mind. Just don't talk so much without thinking about what you're saying. I was sure you were going to blabber out everything. Remember, there is the matter of our honor at stake here. The less we say the better off we are. And an important point to remember when we start telling all this, use the word 'we' because all of us had something to do with this, not just you and I. The old saying goes, 'Pride goes before something or other.' I can't remember exactly what, but it's supposed to mean that someone who is prideful is doomed by his own selfishness. We did this together and we succeeded together. Do you agree?"

"Yeah, I guess so. But you've still got a lot of explaining to do about who you really are," I said as I gave Philip a little shove on his shoulder.

"Someday maybe, after you get big enough to whip me," he replied as he gave back what I had given him. We both laughed.

All of us boys slept for a good three hours before Sergeant Bailey came around and woke us up. For a company sergeant I considered him gentle. He kicked a couple boots, but softly. His gruff voice was softened somewhat for us boys.

"Now you'll be getting up. The sun is high in the sky and we have a long way to go before we get back to Fredrick. Now come on lads," he urged us. "Look lively and pack your things up. Each of you roll your blanket up and sling it across your shoulder and tie the ends at the bottom. No need to carry more than one rifle apiece. The others we'll wrap in blankets and tie them on the packhorse. Now move smartly."

It took me several minutes to wipe the cobwebs from my brain and to get all my limbs functioning. Once semi-conscious I did as I was instructed and rolled my blanket up and fashioned it across one shoulder. As we began loading rifles, the men selected the larger long rifles for the packhorse and gave the smaller lads the shorter and lighter squirrel rifles. Since I was nearly one of the biggest in the troop, I was given a full-size rifle to carry.

"Lads," Sergeant Bailey addressed all of us, "we'll be going down the mountain single file. Carry your rifles either cradled in your arm or slung over your shoulder, whichever is more comfortable. Don't be pointing any of the loaded weapons at anybody and for God's sake don't go cocking your rifle just for the fun of it. I promised your families I'd bring you back in one piece and I don't want any of you to show up in Fredrick with an ear or a toe missing because someone was careless. Now we have a long way to go, so let's get going." Sergeant Bailey took the lead and we all fell in behind him in no particular order. The men, along with the packhorse, fell in behind and brought up the rear.

It was a cold, crisp February day, but none of us was cold. We talked and joked and had a generally good time. This was a hike in the woods for most of us, something all of us had done with our fathers many times before. I found my little friend from the previous evening and saw that he was tiring, so I took his squirrel rifle for him.

"Thanks, Will," he said. "I'm called Richard, but my friends call me Rich for short."

"Nice to meet you Rich," I said.

He continued. "I'm not used to all this running around in the woods. My father has taken me on a couple of short hunts, but he prefers to go alone. He promised me he'd start taking me next year when I got older."

"What about your older brothers; do they go with him? I don't have any older brothers. I got three older sisters and four younger brothers. I guess you can say I'm the oldest, except I'm only

10, but I'll be 11 in April."

"You got three older sisters? Should I feel sorry for you or what?" I joked.

"Aw, they aren't so bad. They only torment me when they start making a dress and want me to try it on so they can hem it. I know when that's coming and I make myself scarce." We both laughed.

Then in a serious tone, Rich continued, "I just hope my father is not too upset with me. I ran off with his prized Pennsylvania rifle and if he don't get it back in good shape, I'm afraid I'm in for a licking."

"No need to worry about that Rich." It was Philip. "I saw your father's rifle loaded on the packhorse. It's in great shape. Don't worry, no one's going to give you a licking anymore. You've grown up."

Rich smiled up at both of us and even perked up a bit. We continued to walk three abreast and talked like magpies the rest of the way into Long Pine settlement. As we approached, several of the men fell out from upfront and positioned themselves at various points in the column.

As we passed one father, he spoke to us, "Now lads, look here, Lone Pine people are not exactly what you call likable sorts. They're either drunkards, thieves, or low people who live on the edge of the civilized world. They ain't people you'd invite home for Sunday dinner, that's for sure. They'll taunt ya just to git a rise out of ya. Just hold your tempers and don't let them git to you. Now you boys know how to behave yourselves, so do it. We don't want no foolishness out of any of you." He continued on past us and joined ranks several boys back. The men with the packhorse carrying the rifles moved up from the rear more to the center of the column. I noticed some of the men quietly cocked their rifles and checked the prime. This did not go unnoticed by us. I quietly handed Rich back his little squirrel rifle. Philip and I checked our prime and then returned our rifles to half-cock. Our small friend did the same.

*****

Lone Pine wasn't much of a settlement. The single street, really, was just a wide enough path for a wagon to roll down. The six or seven wooden buildings were in various states of decay. This was far from being a pristine town like Fredrick. Several pigs lounged in a large mud puddle off to the side of the road, despite the temperature. They only grunted as we passed by. The main building was a large general store with a wide porch. It was inhabited by a group of 10 to 12 unshaven, rough-looking men dressed in a mixture of dirty buckskins and soiled hunting shirts. They were passing a brown jug around I assumed to be either hard cider or rotgut whiskey. As soon as they saw us they started to hoot and holler.

"Lookie there fellers, if it ain't the Fredrick militia out for a walk through the woods. Looks like some of them kinda shrunk up."

"My, they are scraping the bottom of the barrel for recruits these days. I betcha some of them boys are still wear'n diapers. Look at that little feller carrying that toy gun."

Rich bristled. I tried to calm him down. "Rich, they're

drunk and they are only taunting us. Just leave them alone." He at least took his finger off the trigger of his gun.

Just then a large surly man walked out the general store and surveyed the column. He quickly spied the packhorse with its load of rifles and then turned to the ruffians and said something in a whisper. They quit taunting us and eased toward their rifles, which were leaning on the store's wall. "Who's in charge of these boys," he shouted. "All of you just stop right where you are." He pulled a pistol out of his belt and fired a shot in the air. The column came to a stop immediately. No one moved for a second.

Sergeant Bailey came quickly to the middle of the column and faced the man. "State your business," he called out to the man.

"Well, you people seem to be taking advantage of our good hospitality and ain't paying for it. That street you be using is a toll road," he said with a grin on his face. His compatriots, who now had secured their weapons, laughed out loud. "Now let me see, you got about 30 people in your little group, not counting the little squirts, so I guess that's going to cost you about 10 rifles."

"We'll not be paying any tolls to the likes of you or anyone else," replied the Sergeant Major. He turned to leave and a shot came from the store porch and caught him in the left shoulder. He went down. Several of our men leaped forward to his aid.

Then over the din of confusion Philip spoke up loud and clear, "Left turn, face the fire, column of twos. First column kneel. Columns prepare to fire." With the exception of me, all of the boys had watched their fathers and uncles drill on the village square. They knew the orders and followed them to the letter. Twenty-five rifles were cocked and readied; all were leveled at the 13 men on the front porch of the store. It gave them cause for concern.

Sergeant Bailey was helped to his feet. His wound was not too bad, although there was a fair amount of blood on the sleeve of his coat. He looked at us, smiled, a wicked little grin, and then turned to re-face the ruffians.

"Well gentlemen, we seem to have you at an extreme disadvantage. I dare say if one of you moves, you will not live to see another second of sunshine. I'm sure all of you are well aware of the marksmanship reputation of our esteemed Fredrick militia. Well gentlemen, these are their sons. I can quite assure you that these lads are just as proficient as their fathers, but I'm willing to dispel any doubts in your mind with a little demonstration. Richard, would you come here son?" said Sergeant Bailey.

Our little Rich stood up from his kneeling position and trotted to the Sergeant, who put his good right hand on Rich's shoulder.

"I believe you made some despairing remarks about our lad here. That, gentlemen, is a terrible mistake. You see, Richard is an expert marksman and can shoot the eye out a fly at a 100 paces. Richard if you would be so kind as to take aim at the livery sign hanging on the stable down the street. How far would you say that was Richard?"

"It's about 40 paces sir. What would you like me to do sir?"

"Blow it off its hinges Richard. You can use my pistol for the second hinge."

"Standing or kneeling sir?" asked Rich.

"Why don't we give our host the option? So sir, what will you have standing or kneeling?"

The huge hulk on the porch muttered "Standing," and then said something he perhaps should not have said. "If the little squirt can hold the rifle up."

Without any further provocation, Rich wheeled toward the hulk and fired. As the smoke cleared the hulk was rolling on the porch holding the left side of his head where his ear had been. Rich was not taking time to examine his handiwork; he was reloading as quickly as he could.

The Sergeant shouted in his loudest voice, "Hold your fire lads."

The men on the porch were trying to find anything they could to hide behind. There was nothing except a few skinning posts holding up the roof over the porch. They had a rather forlorn look on their faces; they certainly weren't smiling anymore.

"Gentlemen," said the Sergeant addressing the men on the front porch, "I wish I could sincerely say I regret this display, but I do not. Your compatriot was rude and insensitive. He should count his blessings that he is still alive. Now lay down your rifles and move off the porch to your left. Pick up your friend while you are at it."

Without further encouragement, the 12 remaining men laid down their weapons and moved off the front porch of the store with the wounded hulk in tow.

Bailey turned to us and spoke. "Someone secure the rifles. Seems like we just acquired a few additions to our militia arsenal. As soon as my arm is tended to we will continue onto Fredrick with the prisoners." He spoke to Rich in a clear voice which everyone could hear. "Young Master Richard, you must learn self-control. Don't let someone rouse your anger. Nice shot nonetheless. I do assume you were actually trying to only nick the fella?" asked Bailey.

"No sir, actually I was going to shoot his nose off, but I couldn't get a proper shot so I just took his ear off," smiled Rich.

Rich returned to the column and took up his position next to Philip and me. We gave him a good pat on the back. He seemed to grow two inches.

As expected at the mention we were taking the louts back to Fredrick as prisoners, they began to whine, made sad excuses for their behavior, and begged Sergeant Bailey for mercy for the sake of their families who would be alone in the hills unprotected. Sergeant Bailey and the men of the column drew together to discuss the matter. Eight of the men were known to have families in the surrounding area and were released on parole. Their rifles were given back to them. Two of the men, including the one that shot Sergeant Bailey, were of dubious reputation without families and retained. The other three, including the wounded hulk, were unknown drifters; they were also retained. As we were leaving it came to light that the drifters had arrived in Lone Pine on horses. These were quickly recovered from the livery stable and saddled. Sergeant Bailey, nursing his wound, mounted a black thoroughbred mare. Rich was called forward and mounted a beautiful roan gelding. One of the older men of our column was selected to ride the other horse, also a horse of some note. The horses looked a little too rich for the likes of the three drifters.

We were all anxious to get home, but Sergeant Bailey knew our limits and decided to stop at a farmhouse halfway between Lone Pine and Fredrick. The farm was a large affair with several livestock barns and two good-sized tobacco barns. We were given one of the empty livestock barns to use. Caught unexpectedly by our surprise visit, the farmer could only offer us stew and bread for supper. His servants brought a large black cauldron to the barn and set a fire under it. Soon the water was boiling. The servants then began adding corn, okra, beans and pieces of chicken to the broth along with a variety of spices. It did not take long for the stew to release a mouth-watering aroma.

A short half-hour later the Brunswick stew was ready, a meal fit for at least a youthful militia. Since there weren't enough bowls to go around, we took turns using those bowls the farmer loaned us. The stew and the bread were more than enough to satisfy our hunger. The five prisoners were fed last, but were still given enough to eat. After they finished their meal, they were bound for the night. It was not long before most of us were fast asleep in the hay. Sergeant Bailey had taken advantage of the stop and was attended to by the mistress of the house. He returned to us with a freshly bandaged arm resting in a sling. He had traded his bloody coat for one loaned to him by our host. With a watch set to guard the prisoner, Sergeant Bailey also collapsed in the hay and fell sound asleep.

I don't remember much more about that evening. I was too exhausted. All I do know is that morning came too soon. The roosters began crowing long before the sun came up, yet there was no real need to rouse us from our sleep. The excitement of returning to Fredrick still dwelled in us. The eastern sky was just showing the first shades of light as we assembled outside the barn. The three horses were saddled and the same riders mounted. Goodbyes were said to the farmer, his family, and the servants who had been so kind to us. As we marched off, our prisoners hung their heads just a little lower.

163

Chapter 15

Back in Fredrick –
End of Better Times

After a six-hour march, we reached a small hill overlooking Fredrick in the distance. There was never such a beautiful sight in my memory. Although Fredrick had only been my home for a few weeks, it was fast becoming imprinted in my mind as home. No sooner had we topped the hill than the church bell began to peel. Our approach had not gone unnoticed.

When we were about half a mile from Fredrick, Captain Griffin and four militia officers rode out to greet us. There were smiles all over their faces. First stop was with Sergeant Bailey. They congratulated him profusely, gently patted him on the back and made the required inquiries about his injury. Once done, the officers looked for their sons and Captain Griffin came looking for Philip and me. What order there might have been dissolved into a congenial festival. The four fathers devoured their sons and lavished them with hugs and more hugs. It was apparent there had been some serious apprehension about our status in the wilderness. Soon the fathers were sharing their joy with the other boys and no one was left without a good hug and a well-done clap on the back. Young Richard was the center of attention. It was obvious his status in our boyhood community had risen a notch or two. Since his father was not among those who had ridden out to meet us, those fathers present did their best to show Richard the proper attention he was rightfully due.

"Well lads," said Captain Griffin, now dismounted, speaking to Philip and me, "I'm sure you have a lot to account for. Just from the little I've heard about the adventure there will be enough grist for the mill for at least the entire summer. Tonight both of you and Seth will report to the Committee and give a full and accurate accounting. I suggest you get together this afternoon and compare your different perceptions of the events and come up with one version. Mustn't have conflicting stories. We want the real, factual story, not some tall tale. Is that understood?

"Yes sir," we both chimed together.

"I'll say one more thing for now and then we'll get on with things. I'm not very good at words when it comes to expressing emotion, but I will say that I was terribly worried about both of you." Tears welled up in Captain Griffin's eyes. "Both of you are like sons to me." He grabbed us both and hugged us. "Now enough of this foolishness." He turned to Sergeant Bailey and roared in his best command voice, "Sergeant it's time to get this ragtag group of young militia back to Fredrick. Please form them up and march them home."

"Aye, Captain, it will be my pleasure. Masters Seth, Philip, and Will front and center. Lads, due to the outstanding contribution to this exercise, these three men will head the column into Fredrick. Take your places on the road boys. Now form three columns on these lads, and be quick about it. Master Richard and myself will ride up front and lead the troops. You other gentlemen, who are not so engaged, if you would be so kind as to form in the rear and watch after our prisoners. We wouldn't want anyone taking the glory from our young lads, now would we?"

Captain Griffin and the officer good-naturedly reined their horses to the rear of the procession to oversee the prisoners.

The troop formed, Sergeant Bailey gave the order to march and off we marched with a little spring in our step. An officer rode forward from the rear and leaned down to his son in the column to hand him a fife. Within a moment we were marching to the tunes of a fife. Yankee Doodle seemed most appropriate.

We were met at the edge of town by a mass of well-wishers, but Sergeant Bailey insisted we march all the way to the parade field in the town square. After all we had passed our initial march and now it was time to show off a might. As we approached the square, Sergeant Bailey kept the commands simple so that we could look professional. At half-turn left, was then followed by a half-turn right. That put us directly on the front-side of the green. As we approached the edge he commanded halt. Another left turn and we were facing the flagpole and our admiring crowd, which for me included my mother and all of my siblings who were naturally waving and shouting. It was then I noticed Captain Clark in civilian clothes standing on the front porch of the general store leaning against a rail. At least he had a smile on his face. Captain Griffin came riding in and also noticed Captain Clark. There was a moment of anguish on Captain Griffin's face until Captain Clark nodded and smiled as if nothing was wrong.

Sergeant Bailey, still mounted, was now positioned in front of the troop and facing the general store, Richard was mounted and on his left. Captain Griffin rode up, and exchanged salutes with Sergeant Bailey, who retired to his left, nudging Richard in the same direction. Both of them finally ended up behind us, where the rest of the mounted officers had assembled.

"At ease, lads. I want to say a few things to you before you are dismissed. Your actions over the past three days have shown you to be young men of great courage, bravery, and determination. We are all proud of you!" As if on cue the crowd cheered and continued until Captain Griffin turned slightly in his saddle and raised his hand politely. Once the noise subsided he continued, "You met adversity with resourcefulness. Your quick thinking was the difference between success and failure. But most of all, you recognized one important thing; unity in purpose and the spirit to prevail above all will carry the day. If in the future, if you are called on to defend your rights, remember the challenges you faced here together and draw upon those experiences to steel your resolve that you may carry through until the job is done." He tipped his hat to us and then said, "Dismissed!"

The crowd in mass broke upon us. The only people not celebrating were the five prisoners, who were being escorted to the old armory, which would serve as their jail until their fate could be determined.

Philip and I stood on the parade field and spoke with my mother and siblings. I was trying to ignore Captain Clark on the porch. I'm not sure whether it would have been less embarrassing to approach Captain Clark than to endure my mother's unrelenting kisses and hugs. Thank goodness, Captain Griffin rescued us.

"Now lads, if you can round up the rifles that you scurried off with. Philip, since our esteemed dragoon Captain has decided to pay us an unexpected call, take the rifles to my house for safekeeping. Will, you and I have to pay our respects to the Captain, as much as it might be distasteful. Mind your manners and don't be argumentative, that's my department."

In the confusion, I helped Philip gather up the rifles with which we had escaped town. One of the other boys pitched in and helped Philip slip away from the square unnoticed. Before long there was not a rifle in the square to be seen. They all quietly and mysteriously disappeared from sight. At last, my work complete, I rejoined Captain Griffin, who was talking to some of his friends and neighbors on the square, while trying to ignore Captain Clark.

"Sir," I said, "we found all of them and Philip is taking them to your house. I still have Old Anne in my coat."

"Good job, well done, Will. Now I suppose we have no choice, but to greet our uninvited guest. This is a particularly touchy situation Will, and the less said the better. I'm not sure why he is here, but I don't like the fact that he suddenly appeared out of nowhere. So with that in mind, let's go twitch the nose of the devil himself." He laughed and put on a sincere smile.

The distance from the square to the general store was only a matter of a few yards, but it felt like an agonizing mile to me. Each step was tortuous. The hour it seemed like it took to get there was in actuality less than a minute. Captain Clark broke the ice first.

"Well done Samuel and congratulations to you Will. I'm sure your father will be extremely proud of you. The Major is fit to be tied. The Governor is having a tizzy fit and is at the moment completely incapacitated. I know both of you are wondering why I'm here. Certainly not to spy on you, I assure you." Captain Griffin and I looked disbelieving at each other. "Will, once I unraveled your little name ruse, I did my duty and checked on your father. He is doing well, but missing his family terribly as can be imagined. His first court appearance is scheduled for next week. Some local firebrand attorney has taken his defense, though it does seem your father's lawyer and the crown prosecutor are old school chums. Don't know how that will play out in the proceedings, but you can never tell about these things ahead of time. I thought I would bring you the news and just see how you fared. Actually I was extremely curious after the Sergeant Major retold of his encounter with ten very determined lads. You actually had him going there. I assured him you weren't playing, as I know you weren't. Brave thing that you did Will, but if I may be so bold as to say, you almost exceeded your abilities. If the Sergeant Major had not been wise beyond his rank there would have been a disaster. Enough said for now. Enjoy your victory and let me offer you my compliment for a jolly good job." He held out his hand to me.

I was a little slow to act, so Captain Griffin nudged me to take his outstretched hand. It was a firm handshake and I returned with one of equal firmness, I hoped. While what he said was friendly and the handshake felt sincere, something inside me just didn't feel right.

"Daniel, I know you must be leaving soon so you can be

back to Charles before nightfall, but do you have time for a cup of coffee?" asked Captain Griffin politely as if trying to hurry the dragoon along.

"As a matter of fact, I'm staying at the Williams Plantation tonight and will head back to Williamsburg early tomorrow. I came here to invite both of you to come with me to Williamsburg for a visit. I'm sure both of you would enjoy the change of scenery. Samuel it would give you a chance to file a formal protest with Governor Dunmore and Will, it would give you a discreet opportunity to see your father."

"I'm not sure I can manage to be free tomorrow, sir," I replied. "Mr. Griffin needs me to do some work around the store, in the stables, and at his home," I lied.

"Actually, Daniel, I won't be able to go to Williamsburg tomorrow, but that is an excellent idea for Will to go and visit his father. I must insist that he meet you there. I do need him around here for most of the morning." Captain Griffin turned to me and put his hand on my shoulder, "Will, would you like to see your father tomorrow?"

"Oh, yes sir, most definitely. Would it be all right for mother and the children to come along?" I asked, looking first at Captain Griffin and then at Captain Clark.

Captain Clark spoke up first. "Whoa, young man, I said a discreet visit. This will be something I will personally arrange so no one in the official establishment in Williamsburg will know about it. If your whole family suddenly arrives that will draw too much attention. I must insist you only come to visit. Samuel, do you think Will could travel all the way to Williamsburg in one afternoon?

Wouldn't it be better for him to stay overnight in Charles and then meet me in Williamsburg the next day?"

"Perhaps you're right Daniel. I'll give Will a letter of introduction to an acquaintance in Charles who will provide Will with overnight accommodations. That sound good to you Will?" Captain Griffin asked.

"Yes, sir," I said without hesitation, although I didn't quite understand the fencing that went on between the two. Both of them seemed to have ulterior motives; I only trusted Captain Griffin to be fully protective of my person.

"Now if that invitation for coffee is still open, I would enjoy hearing about Will's latest adventure. Of course, I think Will can skip over the incident with the Sergeant Major. As for a report, the Sergeant Major swore he did not recognize any of the young scamps and could not recognize any of them even if he were to see them again; a most honorable man, in my opinion. So shall we?"

"Will, lead the way," ordered Captain Griffin.

I bounded up the steps to the general store, opened the door, and stepped aside as Mr. Griffin ushered Captain Clark inside first. I followed closely behind.

As we headed back to Mr. Griffin's office, Philip came into the store behind us carrying a basket covered with a kitchen cloth. I glanced around and he smiled holding up his right thumb to signify that he had safely hidden all the rifles from the store. That was a relief. Now all I had to do was weave a story around the truth without telling the truth. My brain was running as fast as a thoroughbred. I only hoped I could get through the upcoming ordeal in decent shape.

Captain Griffin had already made preparations for coffee and the steaming water was ready to be poured into the coffee pot. In an instant the smell of roasted coffee filled the office. Philip came to the door and politely knocked.

"Sir, Mrs. Griffin noticed the Captain was here and sent a basket over for lunch for you gentlemen."

Mr. Griffin beamed as he walked to the doorway and proudly took possession of the basket. "I must say my wife is always the thoughtful one." He looked quickly inside. "Excellent!" he exclaimed. "There is enough here for a small militia. Philip go ahead and close the doors for lunch and then find a small table for us to set out this small feast. Will, find a couple of extra chairs for you and Philip. We'll have a nice quiet lunch here in my office just the four of us. Will, you can provide us with entertainment by giving us a rundown on the adventure. You can leave out any reference to dragoons!" he added with a short laugh.

It took only a moment for Philip and me to accomplish our task. Mr. Griffin unloaded the basket, arranged the variety of foods over the table, and handed out plates and forks. There were even enough knives to go around, a luxury our family didn't possess. I found it a little strange having my own knife and not having to share it with the rest of the group. Town life was different.

I was allowed to finish a plate of food before I was asked to begin my command performance. With much trepidation I began cautiously.

"I shan't go into details about how our adventure began, but for the sake of the story I must inform you that we found it necessary to split our group into two separate parties, having encountered some initial difficulties."

Both captains politely laughed at my joke. Philip sat there puzzled.

Captain Clark clarified the terms of the story, "Philip, it was agreed for the sake of the good Sergeant Major that we not refer to any incident in which he was involved. Now does that make a little more sense?"

"Oh, absolutely sir. I think the less said about that the better," answered Philip now with a grin on his face. Philip relaxed and rediscovered his food.

For the next 30 minutes, I kept my audience spellbound with my tale, which grew in character and substance. I never mentioned any names of my comrades and when decisions had to be explained I used the term "we decided" after all. I justified it as having been a completely joint adventure. Our contact with the Cherokee took on a sinister element; painted warriors half-naked ready to scalp us at any moment. Our plan of deception became a brilliant plan born of necessity and carried out with the utmost bravery. Of course the Cherokee never knew we had escaped until they woke the next day. The march from the caverns to Lone Pine Mountain was froth with danger at every corner and the night air was so cold our breath fell to the ground as ice crystals. I was beginning to enjoy spinning the tale. It was all Philip could do to keep from falling out of his chair from suppressed laughter. Only when I got to the incident in the village of Lone Pine did I not feel the need to invent any other facts. I told the story complete with our pint-size hero Richard, who, by the way, was the only participant heralded by name. I concluded with the capture of the brigands and the discovery of the three horses. I felt the overnight in the barn to be too anticlimactic. I ended with the short resolute phrase, "That's the truth of it sirs!"

The gentlemen applauded my delivery and the tale, although I suspect they thought I might have embellished the story just a bit.

Daniel spoke inquiringly, "I did notice the three fine horses that your lads brought in. I wonder if they are perhaps stolen. It would be a feather in the town's hat if the Governor had to publicly acknowledge a good deed done by the citizenry."

"I'm sure those three drifters did not buy those mounts. I will have one of my more experienced lads question them in the morning. If you would Daniel, when you pass through Charles tomorrow, inform the Sheriff of our situation here and ask him if any horses have been reported missing. I just hope they weren't taken from Georgia. It could take months before the word reaches this far if it does at all. I'm not sure we have enough information to keep those ruffians for more than a couple of weeks at the most. The exception, of course, is the sod that shot Mr. Bailey. He will be a guest of the crown for several years I suppose."

"Samuel, under normal circumstances you would be right, however, a good defense attorney might try to raise a defense of 'Protection of the Crown.' After all, the Fredrick militia was officially disbanded and while it was not 'the militia,' some militiamen were in the procession. Just food for thought. You might want to handle it locally with your justice of the peace and be satisfied with a year's labor for the miscreant. The horse thieves are a totally different issue. If it can be proven the horses are stolen, then regardless of the circumstances, the thieves will find they have a date with the hangman. So, I have thoroughly enjoyed the entertainment Will, if you and Philip will get me the full descriptions of the horses, I will be on my way. And both of you be sure to look closely at the saddles for any initials or even papers tucked in any pouches."

Mr. Griffin shooed us. "Run along lads and get the Captain his information so he can have a leisurely ride to the Williams Plantation. Be quick about it."

Philip and I took off with pen, ink, and a small scrap of paper in hand. The horses were safely tucked away in Mr. Griffin's stable for safe-keeping. They were truly beautiful horses. Philip took pains to write down the color of each animal as I measured the height of each in "hands." The weight we had to guess. We checked all three saddles, but they yielded no information. We rushed our information back to the front of the general store, where the two gentlemen were saying goodbye to each other.

Captain Clark mounted his horse and I reached up, handing him the paper. "Thanks Will. Now remember, I'll see you the day after tomorrow in Williamsburg. Meet me at the Raleigh Inn on the Duke of Gloucester Street at about one o'clock. If I am delayed, I will leave a message for you with the proprietor. Good day gentlemen," he said, tipped his hat and rode off at a leisurely pace toward the Williams Plantation.

I must admit, I admired him for his coolness under pressure. I thought it a tremendous risk for him to come into Fredrick alone. My dream world was shattered when I noticed several unfamiliar men slowly make their way to their horses and follow the good

Captain out of town. Then there was the trade wagon with the covered bed being manned by two stout-hearted lads, which seemed to join in the departure. In all, I saw five, maybe six escorts.

Captain Griffin noticed my concern. "We saw maybe five or six of his dragoons; there were probably a few more we didn't see. Bet you boys a pint of ale the wagon was loaded with muskets! Come on, we will start early today. You boys deserve a good treat and besides, let that be a lesson to you. Never walk into a hornet's nest without something to swat with. He's a very crafty man Will and he'll get the better of you if you don't watch out. Be on your toes when you're with him."

Chapter 16

The Williams Plantation

Moses was a virtual prisoner in his master's house. The unexpected company had caught everyone off guard early that morning. Even though they were dressed in civilian clothes he knew they were dragoons by the way they rode their horses. Mr. Bally, the Governor's personal secretary, arrived in a nondescript two-horse carriage. In Williamsburg, it was rumored that Bally was the power behind the throne, so-to-say. He was rarely seen even in the capital of Williamsburg, and even less so outside of the capital. Master Williams had thought it a momentous occasion that he had taken such an interest in the county and traveled all this way to personally direct a hush-hush mission.

Mounted dragoon sentries in gentlemanly hunting clothes patrolled everywhere. There was no escape and certainly no chance to warn the town of Fredrick. All Moses could do was to wait and see what information he could glean from the intrusion. Master Williams, overcome by the event, demanded that Moses be by his side so as to attend to Mr. Bally's every need and whim. Bally was a coarse, rude man, rotund, short, and balding. He wore badly-tailored clothes and had an ill-fitting dingy wig, which had not been properly washed in ages. To top it off, he had an unforgivable body odor, not dissimilar to the smell emanating from the plantation's pigpen. His one redeeming quality if it could be called that was his deep, fathomless, piercing eyes. They were not evil eyes exactly; more along the lines of a cunning and calculating gnome. What he lacked in personal appearance he made up in intelligence, but it was not to be a redeeming value since it appeared all of his knowledge and intelligence was bent toward promotion of the Crown, the Governor, and himself – although not necessarily in that order. All men were servants of some character and there to serve his every whim in the name of the Crown or the governor, whichever was more convenient to invoke.

His traveling companion was known only as the Major; a somewhat brutish, effeminate, dragoon Major. Despite his rough and forceful demeanor, the way he carried himself nullified his strong points. But for his rank and social standing, he would have been an insignificant English dandy. Here in the Colony of Virginia, he was a rising star, despite his propensity to throw tantrums. Despite their differences they were a perfectly matched pair.

It was not until four o'clock in the afternoon that a band of 20 disguised dragoons returned to the Williams Plantation. Captain Clark was in the lead; a trade wagon rode comfortably in the middle of the loose column of soldiers. There was no way of knowing where they had been or what they had been up to. The dragoons showed no emotion.

"Moses, Moses, where are you!" shouted the Master.

Moses continued to stare momentarily out the window at the arriving dragoons and wondered to himself what had happened. It would take time, but he would have his answer in due course.

"Moses!" The shrill voice again grated on Moses' nerves, just like fingernails on a slate board.

"I'm in the pantry Master. Just checking on what we can have for dinner tonight in addition to the beef brisket. I was thinking of having potatoes and casserole of sliced apples. That's about as fresh as we can get," he replied. All in all Master Williams was not a bad man as masters went. His major flaw was his indifference about the overall welfare of his 60 slaves. Moses had long ago forged an alliance with Mr. Stuart, the white overseer. Between them they had managed to improve the general condition of the plantation and reduce the suffering of family separations brought on by periodic sales of surplus slaves. Had not Mr. Stuart been a God-fearing Scottish Presbyterian, things would have been much more difficult. They had successfully placed over 30 slaves bound for auction with like-minded Presbyterians in the northern colonies, who were eventually freed of their servitude. It was good that Master Williams was unconcerned with his accounting books or he might have noticed that only 10 slaves were actually sold. It was a risky adventure, but one borne of necessity. The British were certainly not going to interfere with the lucrative slave trade. Moses knew it would take time, but at least here in the colonies there was growing unrest against Britain and that could lead to a wholesale change in the society. Change was the only way to freedom, no matter how risky it might be.

"Oh Moses, what am I to do with you? Must you always be in control of everything? You must let the kitchen servants attend to their job. Your job right now is making sure this unbearable Mr. Bally and his shadow are taken care of. I have never met more disagreeable men. Thank goodness you had the good sense to suggest the Mistress and the children go visit relatives in Charles. If I have to be nice to them much longer, I swear I will break apart and throw them out on their ears. If I hear one more 'the Crown needs this or the Crown needs that' I will surely explode. No wonder those sods in Boston are rebelling. They are surely testing my loyalty. I shall have to write the Governor about him."

Moses became familiar with his master. "Mr. John, that's exactly what they are doing. They are testing your loyalty. If you show the slightest hesitation then you become suspect. That would be a disaster for you and your family. You could lose everything with the slip of the tongue. Remember what happened to Farmer Brown just two weeks ago. People tried to warn him. They tried to get him to tone down his opinions. The Tories are not very understanding at the moment," cautioned Moses.

Moses needed the Master to stay close to the Tory cause. It provided just the right amount of disguise that he needed. As the head slave on the plantation, Moses was given a large degree of freedom and he could basically come and go as he pleased, as long as the master remained a Tory. Any crack in his Tory leanings and they would all have to flee. His network of informants from Williamsburg to Charles Town in South Carolina kept track of the goings and comings of all the prominent Tories in a two-colony area. Slaves might not be educated, but they did listen and always loved to pass on tidbits of information.

"We come from a loyal family, Moses! I will not let those poor excuses for Englishmen dissuade me. It's just that they are so insufferable. Can't we hurry them along some way?" pleaded the master.

"Mr. Stuart said that they already took over a barn and looks like they are planning to spend the night. After supper get your good port out and at least they will be a little more tolerable with port."

"Now I have to waste my good port on the louts. What is this world coming to?" lamented the Master.

"I'll go get the port now Master, while you entertain them a little more. We'll have an early dinner at six o'clock. Maybe a little sip of whiskey before dinner will put them all in a more agreeable mood."

"Go about your business, but for God's sake don't let Stuart give those troopers my good whiskey; I know he'd do it even without asking me. Tell him to use the trade liquor or something. This whole affair is going to cost me tremendously." The master walked off in disgust.

Moses gave a few instructions to the kitchen staff and walked out the backdoor to find Stuart. He found his ally in the food locker just behind the main house, pilfering several bottles of home-brewed whiskey from the ample store.

"Mr. Stuart!" announced Moses in a loud commanding voice.

"Jesus, Moses, I could have dropped a bottle. You scared the living bejesus out of me."

"The Master already knows you were going to pilfer some

whiskey for the dragoons. He only asks that you use the trade liquor and not his good stuff. I have to take a couple of bottles of the good stuff to the house for the officers and Mr. Bally. Perhaps a keg of rum would be more appropriate for the dragoons. I'm sure they won't appreciate good whiskey."

"Aye, a keg of rum! That's a better idea. Now large one or small one … large one! I want those tongues to wag a little. By morning, we should have a full report of what went on. I love doing this to these Englanders. Too bad, they're a couple of boys from Inverness in the group," said Stuart, rolling his "r's" just a bit more than usual.

"I'll do the best I can. I'll have a hard time keeping the Master with them. They aren't exactly up to his standards, although Captain Clark appears to be a fairly refined gentleman."

"Do the best you can. We'll get together in the mid-morning after they leave and figure out what's going on. I can't go into Charles tomorrow, so you'll have to go and make the report. If'n it ever comes to it, we'll at least be well-prepared with information, I hope," added Stuart.

"I read somewhere that an army fights with soldiers but prepares with information. I just hope we can get the information we need when we need it."

"Moses, we'll do all we can and when the time comes, we'll do a little more," said Stuart as he put his hand on Moses' shoulder as a show of respect and solidarity.

Stuart and Moses wrestled the large barrel of rum onto a dolly. They parted company, Stuart to the barn and his bone-weary dragoons and Moses with his Scotch whiskey to the manor house and the officer guests.

Moses entered the drawing room with the whiskey on a tray with eight glasses. "Gentlemen, Master Williams thought you might like refreshments before dinner."

Captain Clark, still in his riding clothes, addressed Moses. "Thank you very much. My officers and I are a little chilled. I'm sure the whiskey will warm us nicely." Captain Clark turned his attention to Bally and the Major. "So do you want my report now, or shall we wait until later?"

"You may leave the whiskey. Take your leave and don't bother us until dinnertime. Tell your master he is free to do what he wants until dinner. We have business to discuss and don't want to be disturbed. Is that clear, Moses?" said Bally gruffly.

"Yes sir. It's very clear. No one will disturb you until dinner," replied Moses as he prepared to leave the room. Only two other officers were present. They were lounging close to the roaring fire in the hearth. All totaled there were four dragoon officers and Bally. Moses thought to himself, not quite a company-size unit, not enough officers.

Moses slipped back to the kitchen and wondered where the Master was. He surveyed the preparation for dinner, made a few "suggestions," and hurried to the butler's pantry, which shared a wall with the drawing room. From there, if everything was just right, he could hear everything clearly, just as if he was in the room with the guests. As he opened the door he discovered Master Williams was sitting on the edge of a chair close to the adjoining wall. Seeing Moses, he put his fingers to his lips to keep Moses quiet. He pointed to the chair just across from him. Moses sat down somewhat confused by the actions of his master.

The Master mouthed the words, "Be extremely quiet. I must know exactly what they are considering. Our whole way of life is dependent upon these men. I certainly have a right to know what they are thinking.

Moses, now shielded by his master, could only savor his good fortune; Stuart was not going to believe it.

Bally spoke first after Moses closed the door and he had gotten his drink. "Please gentlemen, do have a drink. We mustn't disappoint our less than capable host. After all, it does appear the whiskey is the best this backwater farm can offer, so we might as well enjoy it." No one replied. All the officers, including the Major, poured generous glasses of whiskey.

"So Captain Clark, give me your report," demanded Bally.

"Sir, just as the Major suspected, some of the young boys of the town ran off with a number of hunting rifles and a few muskets. It does appear the Sergeant Major was able to get a number of them. Nonetheless, some boys were able to escape with their rifles. I counted approximately 20 rifles when I saw them return." Captain Clark stopped.

"Well go on, Clark," said the Major. "There must have been more than that."

"It appears the boys did run into a Cherokee trading party at a place called the Caverns. The Cherokees took possession of the rifles, but the boys tricked the Indians, got them back, and in the night escaped to Lone Pine Mountain, where members of the Fredrick militia intercepted them in the early morning." Again Captain Clark halted and took a long sip of his whiskey.

Hidden, Master Williams silently asked Moses, "The children ran into Cherokees?"

Moses shrugged his shoulders and in reply mouthed, "They were lucky."

"Yes, Clark. Now, must I prod you at every turn? Continue please and tell us what transpired on their way back to Fredrick."

"The group marched back by the way of Lone Pine village. That's the outpost just before the frontier. A lawless place full of ruffians, thugs, and thieves. A brief encounter resulted in a ruffian getting his ear shot off by one of the boys, four others were arrested for various purported crimes, and three apparently stolen horses were recovered."

"My, my, disloyal colonists enforcing the laws of the Crown," chirped Bally. "How extraordinarily ironic! I say, Major, it doesn't look like these people are too far gone for redemption, now does it?"

"Mr. Bally sir, as I have said all along, these people have a strong sense of right and wrong. They have grievances with the Crown. If these grievances are not resolved soon to everyone's satisfaction, the colonists will be pushed further from the Crown. I have endeavored to enforce the orders given me in the manner I have been directed. I do not enjoy being heavy- handed with these people. That requirement is at the direct order of the Governor and General Clinton in Boston. I will do my duty. I don't have to like it."

"While we are on the subject of colonists, there will be no further activities which might be construed by the Governor as cavorting with the enemy. Is that clear Major?" asked Bally.

"If you are speaking of Captain Clark's drill instruction given to the Fredrick militia before it was disbanded, there is a simple strategic answer to that. If I may explain?" asked the Major.

Bally nodded his head and raised his glass for the Major to continue.

"As the commanding officer of the King's dragoons, by necessity, I have to carry out the Crown's military objectives to the best of my ability. Should the troubles in Boston erupt into a rebellion then I have to be prepared to meet my enemy. The question is, do I meet the enemy on his terms or do I invite him to meet me on mine. We will not be facing a group of farmers with pitchforks and clubs. We will be facing an experienced group of militia most of whom have had service in the French and Indian Wars and have years of experience on the frontier. At the moment Mr. Bally, the colonialists have a slight advantage in knowing the terrain and how to use it. They will no doubt employ hit-and-run tactics that will reduce the effectiveness of our forces over the long run. In order to defeat them, we have to fight on our terms, in the manner in which we are skilled. We must make them face us on the battlefield where there is no place for them to run, a venue where we can use our professional skills to outmaneuver them. Take any and all advantages away from them and they can be defeated quickly. Captain Clark, playing the sympathetic English officer, under my orders, successfully initiated my plan. If we had been given leeway, we could have had all of the militias falsely believing they could have matched us on the battlefield. Unfortunately the Governor failed to grasp the brilliance of my plan. I can only hope that the colonials still look toward us as the example to emulate. If they revert to fighting the way they learned on the frontier, we could be in for a prolonged conflict."

"That is all well and good Major and I can certainly appreciate the conviction of your beliefs, but we are playing to a much larger audience. I am sure once we separate our loyal subjects from those less dedicated, then we will no doubt have separated the most talented from the chaff. Loyal colonial militias will no doubt be an essential part of the victory over any rebel band. And it is my opinion that those colonists who fought so well with us against the French and the Indians will again come to the aid of the Crown; then all that is left is a leaderless mob of ruffians. I am sure the Governor is only months away from forming loyal colonial units. Then we shall all see that we are both right. I will have my loyal colonial units, which will take the larger core of experienced militiamen away from any opposing force and you will no doubt see your prophecy come true as the remaining riff-raff try to organize themselves after the British Army, which will lead to their self-destruction. Deprived of any experienced men, a collection of disgruntled farmers and overweight merchants will by necessity have to fight the battle according to our rules and when they do, it will be a certain rout. So, Captain Clark, you have been playing the sympathetic English officer; what say you about our opinions?"

"Sir, I, a captain in the British Army, do not have sufficient enough status that would allow me to express an opinion. The Major is my commanding officer and I shall have to defer to him."

"Clark," responded the Major in a superior tone. "You have my permission to speak freely in this assembly, provided we all understand that we are speaking privately and none of this is attributable. It is important that field commanders listen to their officers and solicit their opinions from time to time as needed. So please do express your opinion without any fear of retribution," said the Major with a little laugh as he looked around the room.

Clark and the rest of the subalterns politely laughed at the Major's comment, but all knew full well that retribution was the punishment for undermining a commander's firmly held opinions.

Clark carefully weighed his remarks before he spoke. "Thank you Mr. Bally for allowing me to speak and to you Major for giving me the opportunity to freely express my opinions. I first think it is most appropriate to underscore the Major's analysis. If we are faced with a hostile colonial force, it will be essential that we quickly dispatch them on the field of battle with all haste. As the dominant force, we need to choose the time, place, and manner of the battle and invite them to meet us on our terms. We must control the battle and we can do that easily as long as we make them fight according to our rules of engagement. We must be able to find and fix the enemy force and deal him a sound defeat, bringing the affair to an early conclusion. A protracted campaign will no doubt see our advantage slip away as the colonialist become more accustomed to fighting our battles." Clark wanted to really express his heartfelt convictions that the colonialists would fight tooth and nail in any manner or configuration necessary in order to preserve their liberties. It was folly to think that the colonialists would fold, even if faced with a series of military defeats. As a last resort Clark felt a rebel force facing defeat would move *en masse* over the Cumberland and dare the British to follow, but he had said enough. "That sirs is a brief summation of my opinions. I hope they have not been too far-fetched as to put me in disfavor."

Master Williams had heard enough for one evening and signaled Moses to follow him out of the pantry. This was a disaster for Moses, who had planned to stay as long as possible to hear everything he possibly could.

As they cleared the pantry, the Master quietly closed the door so as not to make a sound. He then turned to Moses. "I am frankly appalled to think my guests would even consider allowing the rabble to assemble an opposing force. I am not too pleased with their tone. Remind me tomorrow to write to my third cousin in Sussex. He is an MP and will certainly have enough influence in the government to get a quick and final solution to these impertinent rascals in Boston. I can't believe the ineptitude of these men. They actually think it is all a game. I dare say they are actually hoping the rabble put together an army just so they can play victor. Instead of all this talk of war, they should be rooting out the leaders and hanging them on the spot. Instant justice; that would solve the problem within a week. Moses, have the kitchen staff prepare supper immediately. I want to get to the after-dinner drinks where I can have a go at these laggards. You mustn't give the rabble too much incentive. If one waves a red flag in front of a bull, then of course the bull will charge. Moses, when you and I accompanied Dunmore on the punitive expedition against the Shawnee in '62 we did our duty to the Crown without reservation. And we both know a pitched contest will only destroy valuable assets and retard our economic growth for God knows how long. So hurry up and get the table set. I'm going to interrupt this cozy conference." The master didn't wait for a reply as he stormed out of the butler's pantry with a huff.

A golden opportunity ruined by the Master. Things could have been worse; at least he understood a little more about strategic thinking, but there was definitely no information about the Army's next course of action. He did have to agree with the master, the British Army seemed to be daring the colonialist to meet them on the battlefield. This was a bad miscalculation by the British. The resolve of the militias had been noted by General Howe in his commentaries on the French and Indian War and their resolve now would be no less. Bull-headed was a term that came to Moses' mind when he tried to characterize the British attitude toward the colonies, or perhaps like an absent parent, who returns after a long journey and tries to re-establish control over a headstrong and independent child. Maybe in this case, it would be better if the British did "spare the rod and spoil the child," at least for the interim. The only hope was compromise and Moses had not heard anyone use that term recently. Moses shook his head and went about his duties.

Chapter 17

The Raleigh Inn, Williamsburg, Virginia

The inn was already filling up, as was normal for this time of day. The Burgesses, the constituent assembly of the colonialists, had long since adjourned for the day after another round of ineffective bickering among the members. The colonial legislators had retired to their homes or accommodations and were just now returning to the public arena. To see and be seen was the watchword. Here at least over a pint of ale or perhaps a good glass of Madeira wine, something could be salvaged. Then there were the lawyers, both the Crown lawyers and the ever-present defense lawyers. As in all civilized societies the lawyers in Williamsburg were both revered and at the same time despised. A truly simple matter would turn into a Crown case at the drop of a perfumed handkerchief. Add to this mixture the occasional student from William and Mary and it was indeed a lively crew.

The more the merrier, thought Harold Parker, the innkeeper. Politicians, lawyers, and students were the best drinkers.

The more they drank, the more Parker made. On the other hand, the doctors that visited the establishment were often overlooked by the crowd. Not by Parker. A good doctor was hard to find and once you found one, you hung on to him. One's life depended on it. For that reason, Parker always watched out for the doctors, the special customers, who never wanted for food or drink at a bargain price, which he was not above reminding them on every occasion he could. Politicians and lawyers, they were a penny for a dozen. Better to get your money while you could from them; same as with the students, if they had any money, which most of the times they didn't. And there were a few that had rather large chits that would probably never be settled, but then again, the youngsters were good for livening up a solemn crew.

Parker was always on duty at the front door to greet every customer, no matter how famous or insignificant. The customer was king and at least in the Raleigh Inn, everyone was someone of importance.

"Good evening Squire Randolph. Tis good the Crown's Attorney is out and about this fine night. I've reserved you a table in the Apollo room away from all of those pesky defense lawyers," said Parker.

"Thank you ever so much, Parker. I should have you be my bailiff, perhaps you could keep them at bay during the day. There is one of those pesky barristers that I do wish to converse with. Should that scoundrel Henry come in, allow him to come over. But no others. I truly want to enjoy my meal and a Madeira in peace this evening. And no students, and certainly not that Adams boy. I have never seen someone so augmentative with the exception of my brother, who by the way, you may direct to my table. At least I have learned to tolerate his opinionated pontifications."

For Peyton Randolph, the Crown's Attorney, it was increasingly difficult to find a safe haven away from the tumultuous problems facing the Governor and the Crown. Not that the Crown or the Governor ever listened to his advice. His only directions were to uphold the orders of the Crown and damned be justice. There was an ever-increasing bitterness in his mouth, not shared by his older brother John, who was as much an ardent Tory as the King himself. Tonight, if he could talk reason into Henry, then perhaps they could snatch some small victory for justice from the decaying judicial system before it completely collapsed.

Squire Randolph seated himself in his favorite captain's chair, the very chair he had so prominently carved his name into when he was a student at William and Mary. It was no doubt an antique or at least old enough to have been discarded by the previous tavern owner, rescued by Randolph, repaired, and then restored to the Raleigh Inn after he was appointed the Crown's Attorney; a small victory for the chair and a great comfort for Randolph.

Tess, probably not her real name, was the buxom waitress. She was at least 40 years old, but looked younger. The sparkle in her eyes and the effervescent smile were the most enchanting thing about her – well nearly. She was as much a fixture at the Raleigh as Parker, who was her husband. It was like yesterday, Peyton remembered old Parker buying the indenture of the buxom 18-year-old country girl fresh from the English Midlands. No sooner had Tess shown up than bets were laid as to how long before old

Parker married her. Parker had resisted a year of numerous lucrative offers for her indenture. It was the offer of 1,000 acres of prime tobacco land that convinced him he had to make the indenture more permanent and secure, if he was to maintain his best investment. Although a man of low means, Parker was loved by all and there wasn't a person in Williamsburg who had not been the benefactor of his kindness. The wedding was done in style. Governor Botetourt had insisted it be performed in the Governor's mansion. Invitations written by the Governor's secretary were distributed to every family in Williamsburg; no one was excluded. The Archbishop personally presided over the ceremony despite the nearly unfounded rumors of prenuptial activity on the part of the bride and groom. Peyton smiled at the thoughts of a wonderful, joyous time which seemed like a lifetime ago.

"Now Mr. Peyton, if you don't mind me saying, you should share those thoughts with everyone. Lord knows there's not much to smile about these days," said Tess in a friendly and familiar manner.

"I was thinking about your wedding and how it was such a different time. Everyone seemed so happy and carefree," replied Peyton.

Tears welled in Tess's eyes. "Right, you are Mr. Peyton. T'was a grand and glorious day when this poor, impoverished, and mind you, indentured servant girl from a mill town in England, became a free woman, got married, and became half-owner of such a fine establishment. It was a true success story that keeps on giving. Oh, did you know that Martha, my oldest daughter, is being courted by a planter's son. It's very formal and everything. I'll not have her traipsing around the countryside like her mother did. No, sir, she'll be a fine lady if it kills me," laughed Tess. She continued. "And little Millie is doing so well in school. My little girl, mind you. She swears she's going to William and Mary on the sly and wants to become a physician of all things. What is this world coming to?" This brought on a hearty laugh from Tess.

Peyton laughed politely and thought to himself, "the very idea of women in college, even if she was attending secretly. Indeed, what was this world coming to."

"Tess, for the moment just bring me a mug of ale and a loaf of fresh bread and some of that wonderful butter you make. That's all for now, I don't want to spoil my appetite. I'll have dinner later when Squire John arrives, but if he's not here in half-an-hour be sure to bring me another ale."

Tess reached over and patted Peyton's rather corpulent stomach, "I'll make certain that you stay just the same. Wouldn't want you starving to death. Wouldn't look good for the house."

They both roared at the private joke. When he had first met Tess, he was well on his way toward being a young man of large proportions, but as a student, he had suffered as all did, due to the lack of liquidity at certain times. At these low points in his fiscal dilemma, Tess always made sure there was enough bread and butter to keep him going. As a result of those frequent deprivations, he became virtually addicted to her bread and butter. And no matter where he was, he never started a meal without first eating a piece of buttered bread. Such habits were firmly imprinted in his personality and made him a better man for it; some would whisper a man of noble birth, but a man of common sensibilities, as it was always a compliment for a true blue-blooded Virginian.

Peyton was savoring the fine texture of the bread, noting the slightly nutty flavor, no doubt a result of finely-ground walnuts. Heaven was only exceeded by the creamy sweet taste of the fresh butter he had so generously spread on the slice.

The noise of approaching boots signaled only one thing to him. Before the man reached the table Peyton literally bellowed out with his mouth still full, "My dear Patrick, don't you even consider slapping me on the back. I have a mouth full of delicious bread and I do not want to be disturbed at this moment." Peyton closed his eyes and returned to extracting every ounce of pleasure from the succulent morsel.

"Ah, I see we're having the student special tonight," grinned Patrick as he sat down across from his best friend.

They belonged to a mutual admiration society, just the two of them. College classmates, chums, and then best friends.

His short, intense enjoyment complete, Peyton opened his eyes to see Patrick Henry seated across from him decked out for an evening of fun and confrontation. A man of normal stature, topped with brownish hair pulled into a tight ponytail, unremarkable except for those intense, devilish blue eyes. Patrick was a man of conviction ready to argue at the drop of a hat. His oratory and persuasive skills were well renowned, at least in the civilized areas of Virginia. He was a young man driven by his sense of duty and service to the community. If only his brother John had been so convicted and wasn't such a snob and a Tory on top of that.

"As a matter of fact, this is just an appetizer. I intend to dine with John later in the evening," mocked Peyton putting on an aloof demeanor.

"That sounds wonderful. I'll gladly join you for dinner. It would give me an opportunity to try out my new treatise on John. I really need the Tory perspective," smiled Patrick.

"That is not an invitation my dear Patrick. It would not please me to see my brother have a bout of apoplexy while trying to enjoy dinner. Although the thought of that would be pretty exhilarating, wouldn't it?" They both chuckled like two young college students.

"So I'm not invited for dinner. Do I at least get to have a pint of ale with the Crown's Attorney before I am banished from this establishment?" asked Patrick, uncharacteristically sheepish.

"Patrick, in all seriousness, please do not confront John tonight. When he arrives please do me a favor, say 'Hello' and then 'Goodbye.' He is not due to arrive until eight o'clock so we have plenty of time to get you mellow enough to utter those two and only two words," pleaded Peyton.

"Only if you are buying!"

"Deal," sighed Peyton. "Tess," shouted Peyton over the growing din of noise in the establishment, as was his right as the Crown's Attorney, "a pint of ale for my friend, Mr. What's-his-name."

"Keep it up my friend. I can forget I'm limited to two words," said Patrick mockingly.

As they had always done since students, they shared what remained of the bread and butter. The ale flowed smoothly and in seemingly large quantities, but to look at the two no one would have suspected they had consumed more than a pint apiece. They talked about old, more relaxed times at college, as young lawyers and their rise to the prominent steps each had reached in the legal community. Each knew the other and to Patrick, it came as no surprise that Peyton needed his assistance on a sticky legal matter.

"Now to the matter at hand. Patrick, I do appreciate you showing up on such short notice. I hope that I haven't interfered with your evening," said Peyton.

"Not at all, dear friend. I could have just as easily come to your office."

"In this situation, that would have been inconvenient. My staff is loyal to me, I think, but not above gossiping in the wrong places if you understand me. The Governor is already uneasy about my association with known 'radicals,' you notwithstanding."

"Since when is it acceptable to brand a man who has dedicated his life to preserving liberty and justice a 'radical'?" tersely asked Patrick.

"Slow down. Now is not the time to get sidetracked over labels that mean nothing to learned men. I fully agree with you. The Governor is being obstinate and anyone that does not agree with him is being placed in the opposition's camp, whoever the opposition might be that day. It varies from day to day. My job is hard enough without incurring the wrath of the Governor. If I am to do justice then I must tip the scales to support his view. Which brings me to the case at hand, the Crown versus one William Jones. Are you familiar with the case? You have been penned in as his counsel of record."

"I am so glad that you occasionally read the court dockets. That restores my faith in the legal system. To answer you directly and politely, yes, I have been retained as his consul. As a matter of fact, I was only retained today. Cash in hand as a matter of fact," replied Patrick.

"Oh, really, cash in hand? Your usual fee? How could a poor destitute farmer afford your usual fee? This is getting quite interesting."

"Someday Peyton, you prosecutors will not be able to ask those questions. There must be some sort of confidentiality between an accused and his attorney. When that day comes our legal system will protect the poor and the downtrodden from the overzealousness of prosecutors like yourself." Patrick was just warming up.

"I beg your pardon. I am not 'overzealous.' I have a duty to perform and I do it in a professional manner. I do not think that I have ever prosecuted a man that was not guilty. I am astounded that you would make such a charge!" The King's prosecutor was turning crimson.

"My, aren't we sensitive tonight? You must have some rather reserved feelings about this case. I apologize for being so argumentative."

"Apology accepted. But damn it, Patrick, you do have the most irritating manner of being able to get people inflamed so quickly. Would you please resist the temptation and not practice on me?"

"But you are so easy! I just love it when you get so indignant. That's what I like about you, you're a prosecutor with morals. One of the few I might add. So, we were talking about the Jones case, weren't we?"

"Oh yes, the Jones case. Oh, by the way, who hired you?" asked Peyton quietly as if the question would be more palatable.

"Peyton, shall we just get on with discussing the merits of the case?"

"Very well, but you do know I'm entitled to know everything."

"My friend, I would be very surprised if you didn't already know everything down to the inscription on the coin, which I was paid for by my retainer."

"Well not quite the inscription, but a round sum was mentioned, which is the reason I'm buying tonight. You must learn to charge more than a farthing for your services Patrick. Community service is one thing, a very noble thing, but you do have to feed your family."

"You old coot! How dare you mettle in my practice. What I charge my clients is my own business and none of yours!"

They both laughed. Each was well aware of the other's position and just how much each knew about the case. Theirs was a pretrial ritual played out in each case. The road to justice was much smoother when it was paved with relevant information, no matter how or at whose expense it was obtained.

Each knew that under the current situation, the Jones case had all the makings of becoming a *cause célèbre* for both the Whigs and the Tories, the fate of the accused be damned. It was up to them, the Crown's Attorney and the firebrand Defender, to find a more neutral path which did justice and silenced both sides of the issue without further unpleasantries. They conferred until shortly before John Randolph's arrival. When he arrived on schedule, true to his word, Patrick rose, greeted John, and then quietly left the Raleigh. Patrick Henry was assured that for once, if the procedure went properly, justice would be served.

"I say, brother, is something wrong with Henry tonight? He seemed a bit subdued," snorted John condescendingly.

"Might just be an off day. You know, 'radicals' do have off days, don't you John?" asked Peyton sarcastically of his brother.

John laughed quietly as the humor went over his head.

Chapter 18

Post Rider

The morning had not quite arrived when I heard a light rapping on the front door of the cottage. Since I had taken over the front living room as my private domain, I was quickly aware of the noise. Even though there was some urgency in the rapping, I was not yet willing to leave the warm confines of my deerskin sleep sack. Gingerly I slipped my legs outside of the sack and struggled to rise with the sack still wrapped around me. My eyes were at best only half-open as I peeked out the door to see who my tormenter was.

"Hey, sleepyhead, it's time to go. It's almost four o'clock. The horses are already saddled and we can be in Charles before the dragoons even wake up at the Williams Plantation." Philip was all smiles.

"A pox on you and your fleas. It's too damn early to be thinking about going to Charles," I half-pleaded.

"Such words from a young gentleman. Oh, I forgot you're a sod from the wilderness," he laughed.

"Give me a moment to get my pants on. Come on inside while I get dressed. How cold is it outside anyway? I'm still numb from being rudely awakened."

"Sailors have a saying about a 'brass monkey.' I forgot what it is, but it's cold. Better wear your heavy coat, shawl, and mittens," Philip replied.

It must have been cold; Philip was dressed as he had suggested I dress. He even had on a pair of leather leggings for additional warmth. I struggled to get my clothes together and remember where I had hidden my Cherokee leggings. I was not one to brave the cold.

"The saying has something to do with the brass ring on a battleship used to keep the cannonballs in a nice pyramid. When it was too cold the brass contracts and the balls go skittering all over the deck. My Father told me that one. The ship he came over on had a couple of cannons and the brass monkeys were always contracting and spilling cannon balls everywhere," I said, proud to share my Father's knowledge with my best friend.

When I mentioned my father, a few tears came to my eyes. But if all went well, I would be able to have a few moments with him today or tomorrow perhaps. It all depended on the goodwill of my dragoon captain. Who really knew on which side of the controversy his loyalties laid? Finally, I located my legging in a small cupboard by the fireplace. I struggled to get them on quickly.

"We still headed the long way by going to Thamesboro or are we going to tweak the noise of the lion this morning?" I inquired.

"The Captain had a change of heart and we are going to

tweak the nose of the lion this morning real hard. We're to race through the Williams Plantation, but avoid the manor house. We'll have to go across the field just beyond sight of the house. They are expecting us to be in Charles by six o'clock at the latest. When we pick up the mail, I'm to head down to Richmond while you head to Williamsburg. It is going to be an interesting day."

"I call that punching the lion on the nose myself. Anything else we can do, perhaps fire a few shots as we pass the manor house?" I added. "I just hope the fields are dry enough for us to cross them."

"Me too!" exclaimed Philip quietly. "If the fields are wet, then we'll certainly have to pass right by the manor house. That will be punching the lion on the nose for sure."

Neither one of us laughed. Although it had not rained in the past few days, and thank goodness it had not rained on us during our adventure in the wilderness, the ground was still fairly soaked from the wet winter we had. The field and roads had been thawing during the day and freezing at night. There was no telling what we would find at the plantation.

Finally ready, I headed to the front door with Philip in tow.

"Wait a second. I have to check on the family first," I whispered to Philip.

Although the family knew I would be leaving early for Charles they did not know I would be leaving before daylight. I needed to check on them just to reassure myself they were all right. I peeked in the small bedroom at the back of the house and heard the soft snoring of the bigger kids, all four of them tucked into one bed covered by a big feather comforter. I slipped upstairs as quietly as the rickety stairs would allow. Mother had the two little ones sleeping with her. There was only soft breathing coming out of the room. I tiptoed up to the bed and gave Mother a little peck on the cheek. A hand eased out from the cover and touched my face.

"Now Will Jones, you be careful and don't take any chances. If you do see your father, make sure he understands we are fine. I don't want to worry him."

"Yes, Mother," I replied.

She gently pulled my head down a little so she could kiss me on the forehead.

"Are you dressed warmly enough? I don't want you to catch a cold."

It must be a universal question that all mothers ask their children, no matter how old they are. "Yes, Mother. I even have on my leggings just in case."

We squeezed each other's hand and I backed out of the room as quietly as I had entered.

Philip waited for me by the door, not wanting to leave the relative warmth of the cottage any sooner than he had to.

We opened the door and were greeted by a cold blast of early March wind on our faces. Winter was still at hand and didn't seem to let loose of its grip just yet. The only consolation is that the wind had not penetrated our multiple layers of clothes, at least not yet.

We were mounted and on the road in less than five minutes. The shod hooves of the horses resounded off the houses as we trotted out of town. The horses needed to warm up before we let them have their heads. The sentries outside of town roused from the warmth of their fire only long enough to wave us on through the checkpoint. We were expected and they were not going to stand around on the road and chit-chat with us this cold morning. They quickly retreated to the warmth of their fire without further ado.

In due course we crossed Sandy creek, and made the right-hand turn toward the Williams Plantation. As we cleared the woods and the plantation fields came into view our worst fears were realized. There before us were fields full of ice and half-frozen mud. Traversing them would have been virtually impossible. Our only choice was to go directly through the manor, a risk we had to take. Philip and I just looked at each other, nodded, and urged the horses on toward the manor. We were thankful that the road, which was higher than the surrounding fields, was relatively dry. Under the conditions, we were able to let the horses gallop along at a safe speed. It was still too slippery for us to chance racing through the area.

We arrived on the outskirts of the slave quarters at about five a.m. just as the roosters began to crow, and the eastern sky was showing the first signs of light. At first it seemed as if there was no one about. Then we noticed a small fire off to one side of the road nearer the manor house. There, two dragoons in uniform, dressed in long coats, stood solemnly in front of their fire trying to stay warm. Philip and I looked at each other and slowed our horses to a walk and proceeded forward.

As we approached, we noticed that both of the sentries were actually sound asleep standing up using their cavalry muskets as props. No doubt the flash pans were empty, lest an accidental discharge ruin a perfectly good snooze. Our approach was somewhat muffled by the sandy texture of the road surface and did not disturb the sentries. As we pulled up next to the sentries, I noticed motion out of the corner of my eye. Two gentlemen were leaving the manor house and headed directly to the sentry post. I tapped Philip, motioned him to look in that direction.

"We've got to do something," I whispered. "Better wake the sentries up and give them a warning. They owe us their lives for the favor."

Philip nodded with a devilish grin on his face. "Dismount and make it look like they told us to get down."

'We slid out of our saddles and faced the sleeping sentries.

Philip spoke in a voice a little louder than a whisper, "Top of the morning to you gentlemen. Don't want to spoil your sleep, but you got company coming from the manor house. Wake up sleepy heads."

One of the sentries fluttered his eyes and then opened them to see us staring at him while holding on to our horses. His senses were a little slow. He blinked several times.

"Private, the Captain is coming and he's going to cut your balls off if he catches you sleeping. You better wake up your friend," I added in a little louder voice.

That startled him enough to get his attention. I would have thought he would have brought his musket up to the ready position, but he merely stiffened his back, raised to his full stature, and nudged his compatriot.

"Hey, Miller, stand tall. We's got company coming."

Without as much as a start, Private Miller stiffened his back and came to attention, then he slowly opened his eyes and blinked them as he tried to get us in focus.

The private spoke to us in a low voice, "Thanks lads, we'd been skewered for sure if'n the Major had caught us sleeping on duty. Quickly, what are you lads doin' out at this God-forsaken time of day anyway," he asked.

"Post riders on the way to Charles and beyond," answered Philip in a normal voice.

Private Miller was now beginning to wobble a little at attention. He was not quite awake. I reached over and steadied him a bit as he continued to try to shake the cobwebs of sleep from his brain.

"Thanks, lad," he said.

The dragoon private introduced himself. "Hawkins, the name. Again, thanks for the assistance. Miller and I owe you a pint. Anytime you're in Williamsburg just go to the barracks and ask for us. We'll make sure you're treated well. Now if'n you don't mind, wait for the Major to arrive. I'll explain your business and you'll be off."

Philip was in an impish mood. "Now Hawkins, what would you do if'n (mimicking Hawkins) we just jumped back on our mounts and fled?"

"Me and Miller would shoot you rascals in the arse and save ourselves a couple of pints of ale," he chuckled.

All four of us laughed out loud at the humor. This seemed to wake Miller up a bit and took the edge off our meeting. The dragoons were now assured we weren't going to flee and we were sure of a free pass. We had earned it.

"Well young Will and Philip, what brings both of you out this early in the morning?" came the all too recognizable voice of

Captain Clark. It was our time to be skewered.

"Post riders, Captain sir. They are on their way to Charles and beyond," proudly informed Private Hawkins.

We remained frozen in our tracks, still facing the dragoon sentries not daring to turn and face the Captain. The cat had caught the canaries another time. This was beginning to be too coincidental.

"Oh, how marvelous," exclaimed Squire Williams. "Why I have three letters to be posted in Charles. Captain, hold these lads here just a moment and I will quickly get my letters for them to take with them. This is so fortuitous!"

Philip and I cut looks at each other. Philip mouthed the words, *"Yeah, real fortuitous!"*

Squire William toddled off back to the manor house to fetch his letters.

"You lads are out extremely early this fine morning. Will, I distinctly remember Mr. Griffin saying you had chores to perform this morning," inquired Captain Clark.

There was nothing more embarrassing in getting caught in a lie. Even though it was truly winter morning, Will could feel himself turning red-faced. Philip came to the rescue.

"That's true sir, but Mrs. Kelley, came down with the grippe last night and Mr. Griffin is sending us to Charles to get some medicine from the apothecary. You know it takes two of us to travel at this time of day. Midday one is okay, but not this early. It's just not safe with brigands around."

"Since we had to go to Charles anyway, Mr. Griffin gave us the post to carry through. This way we get to make a little and do a good deed at the same time," added Will. "Philip will take medicine back this afternoon and I'll continue on to Williamsburg. I'll be there a day early, but I'll be fine."

Will instantly knew he had stepped into a difficult situation. But he could not figure out how to get out of it. According to what Captain Clark was told, Will was to overnight in Charles and then travel on to Williamsburg the next day and meet him at the Raleigh Inn.

Clark smiled realizing there was something afoot. Two boys out early in the morning was slightly suspicious. Although they had a believable story Clark was sure there was more to the story.

"This is rather a stroke of luck actually," replied Clark. "I was just preparing to leave for Charles myself. I planned on lunch there and then a leisurely ride on to Williamsburg. I shan't be long behind you lads. So, I insist you meet me at the town square for lunch. Of course, I will be honored to treat both of you to a fine country meal."

Philip was quick. "Sorry sir, I can't make it. I've got to get the medicine back to town for Mrs. Kelley, but I'm sure Will would like to take you up on the offer!" Philip had a wide grin on his face.

Will was sure there was an appropriate word or words for what Philip had done to him, but he couldn't think of any word but trapped.

"I shouldn't impose upon your generosity Captain Clark. You're already going out of your way by just arranging a meeting with my father," lamented Will as he tried to weasel out of the invitation.

"Will, I insist, but Philip, I will hogtie you next time and make you lunch with us." Captain Clark turned slightly and spoke to the dragoons. "It's okay, Sergeant, these two lads can be on their way." Turning back, he said, "Will, I'll see you on the square at 11; Philip take care of yourself and don't take any untried shortcuts on your way back."

We both replied, "Yes sir!" in unison.

We mounted as Squire Williams came toddling back, waving his three letters over his head. "Don't forget these letters, boys."

The Dragoon Sergeant tipped his hat to the boys as they trotted off. The private smiled and gestured as if he was having a drink. The boys nodded in return.

"Fine lads, they are sir. Good stock," intoned the Dragoon Sergeant, looking after the boys as they began to canter their horses.

"Yes they are Sergeant, truly fine patriots they are," replied Clark as he strolled away toward the barn with Squire Williams.

Chapter 19

The Apothecary and
Lunch with Captain Clark

Philip and I cantered past the manor house and up the plantation road toward Charles. Despite our close call, we were still in good spirits, after all, we were only boys and everything was a lark and high adventure. As we came to the intersection of the plantation road and Charles Road, Mr. Stuart, the overseer, was waiting by the roadside mounted on his horse.

"Well lads I see that ye're out mighty early this morning," he said with a smile on his face. "Now exactly what be ye're business?"

"Mrs. Kelley has the grippe and we –"

Philip never got to finish his sentence before Mr. Stuart interrupted. "Look lads, ye' don't have to tell tales to me. I know why ye're out and about; tis for the good of all. Now listen carefully," he said and leaned over to us in his saddle. "The redcoats are mighty curious about the goings and comings in Fredrick. Tell the Committee in Charles that there be nearly two platoons of dragoons at the Williams Plantation. Now be off with you and ride those mounts easy. Don't want to get them overheated on a cold morning like this." Without another word, Mr. Stuart tipped his hat to us and started back in the direction of the plantation as casual as you please.

"You can never tell where the next friend might appear," I remarked to Philip.

"I'm always constantly surprised," said Philip with a chuckle. "We better get on to Charles before Captain Clark catches up with us."

With that, we spurred our horses on to the Charles Road and at an easy canter made our way toward Charles.

We arrived at Charles mid-morning as the sun began to warm the March air just a little. The townspeople were all bundled in their winter clothes, yet most went about their business with smiles on their faces, assured by the prospect that spring was just around the corner. As we rode down the main street, gentlemen nodded to us, tipped their hats, the ladies smiled, and some even managed slight waves of the hands. What a friendly town. Unlike Frederick, Charles was more city-like, refined, it had somehow changed for the better.

Our first stop and only stop for that matter was the apothecary. We tied the horses up to the hitching post in front and entered the front door. The bell rang as usual to announce our entrance. Instead of the booming baritone voice of Dr. Wilson, a lady's voice called from the rear, but with the same message.

"Now make sure you close the door behind you. I'll be with you in a moment."

This time I answered, "Yes, ma'am," as Philip pushed the door closed ringing the bell.

A polite "Thank you" resonated from the rear of the apothecary.

Philip and I gazed around the apothecary, looking at all the different jars lined up on the wall behind the counter. Some of the words I recognized, but others were most difficult. Philip was busy reading each label, one at a time. He hardly stumbled on any of the words. I, on the other hand, stood there silently and read along silently, pronouncing the words in unison with Philip if I could. Those I didn't know I repeated silently after he did.

"Well, my goodness, what two fine-looking young lads."

Neither of us had heard the lady enter the room. Her compliment completely startled us.

"My goodness, lads, I didn't mean to startle you. Let me introduce myself. I'm Mrs. Wilson, Dr. Wilson's wife. And you two young lads are not from around here, I take it. Otherwise, you wouldn't have such wind-burned cheeks."

Philip answered first. "No ma'am. We're from Frederick and we came to pick up some medicine for Mrs. Kelley. Her chest is awfully tight and congested."

"And we brought the post, too!" I added.

"Well now, let me see. Two postriders from Frederick? Let me guess who is whom. You must be Philip," she said as she pointed to him.

He nodded.

"So, I guess that makes you Will!" she said with some excitement in her voice. "My goodness, I am so glad I finally got to meet you young lads. The friends speak very highly of you. I had no idea both of you were so young. I guess frontier life means growing up quick."

Without warning, Mrs. Wilson moved over to us and embraced both. With the exception of my mother, I had never been hugged by another woman – well not really. I was surprised by her tight squeeze and the faint scent of lilac in her hair. She smelled so sweet, just like a fresh field of flowers in the spring. All of a sudden, I felt a warm rush.

As she released us, I looked at Philip and noticed he had a grin on his face just as big as mine. The only difference, I don't think he was as red in the face as I felt.

"Now lads, first things first. I need to take care of that windburn on your faces and then we'll talk business. So, follow me back into the office. I have some special cream that's good for cow udders and windburned faces."

Philip and I dutifully followed Mrs. Wilson back to the apothecary office. Over the next half-hour, each taking his turn, we were treated to a wonder application of cow udder salve to our faces. Mrs. Wilson seemed quite content to rub cream onto our faces as she talked about a thousand different happenings in Charles. It did not bother her in the least bit that we didn't carry on our part of the conversation very well. Just as she was finishing my right cheek the door to the apothecary opened and a very baritone voice bellowed a friendly greeting.

"Alicia, it's me, darling. I see we have guests from the country!"

"Back here darling, I'm just about finished taking care of

two very bad cases of windburn," she exclaimed.

The imposing Dr. Wilson entered the office and immediately decreased the usable space by a considerable amount.

"So darling, how do our young post riders from Fredrick look now?" she said proudly displaying her handiwork on our cheeks.

"They look like freshly creamed cow udders!" Dr. Wilson couldn't contain his deep resonating laughter.

"Harry, you ought to be ashamed of yourself," said Mrs. Wilson as she stood up and confronted Dr. Wilson with a handful of udder salve. Reaching on her tiptoes she smeared his cheeks with the same salve. "There, now you look like a freshly creamed cow udder too!"

Dr. Wilson broke out in laughter again. "Just what I needed, my love, a little salve to make the wrinkles go away and make my cheeks as smooth as a baby's rump."

"Now Harry, the boys have some business with you. Would you lads prefer coffee or some nice black tea from India?"

"Coffee, if you please, ma'am," Philip responded.

"That will be fine with me, too," I added.

"Coffee for patriots, darling. Tea is for ladies and Tory dandies," offered Dr. Wilson.

"You men just don't know what you are missing," laughed Mrs. Wilson as she made her way through an adjoining door.

As Mrs. Wilson attended to the coffee, Philip and I related the morning's events to Dr. Wilson. We tried not to embellish, but it was evident that we did. At those points where our embellishment was about to stray beyond belief, Dr. Wilson's rather generous right eyebrow would arch upward. It was our cue to rein in the tales. He didn't interrupt us, but rather sat back in his comfortable chair and smoked his pipe.

"Good report lads," he said as we ended our report. "Now let's get down to the facts so that I can write a report to send to Richmond." Dr. Wilson pulled out a piece of fine bonded paper which looked like it had already been written on. Next, he opened a small concealed compartment in his desk and produced a small blue vial of liquid. He then took a fresh turkey quill from his pen stand and sharpened it to a very fine point.

"Lads watch carefully what I'm doing. You are about to learn the fine art of private correspondence. As you notice I have already written a letter to a friend in Richmond. A seemingly unimportant letter between friends recounting my activities since I last corresponded. Now the artful part. My little blue vial contains a very special ink that is invisible when it is dry. Nothing can bring out the writing except a certain formulated reagent. Neither heat nor light will pick up the hidden writing. Only a very few people know the formula for the ink and it will stay that way. All you have to know is how to use it when the need arises. Notice that I carefully begin writing between the first line and second line of the letter."

We watched as Dr. Wilson began to write the substance of our report on the sheet of paper. Within seconds the ink began to dry and the writing disappeared. It was pure scientific magic. Soon he had completed writing on the lines between and then turned the paper and began to write along the right edge.

"As you see, write between the lines, then continue to the right edge, then to the bottom, and then on to the left edge. Use no more than one letter. You have to make it look real. Too many pages are suspicious. Not only does good bond cost money, but the post fees you lads charge are most prohibitive." Dr. Wilson laughed at his own joke and we joined him. "Remember, never write on the back of the sheet. If the back were to be used and then developed with the reagent, the writing would be virtually impossible to read since the writing would bleed through to the front of the sheet. Another important consideration is to always have a nice roaring fire available just in case an uninvited guest arrives. Spare nothing from the writing kit. Everything goes into the fire. The paper, the ink, and the quill. Security is of the utmost importance. Now we will let this dry thoroughly and enjoy our coffee.

On cue Mrs. Smith pushed through the door with a tray of steeping hot coffee and biscuits saved over from their morning breakfast. It was then my stomach growled loud enough for everyone to hear. Somewhat embarrassed, I apologized. "Sorry, but Philip and I didn't have time to get breakfast this morning,"

"Then I must go and get a bit of sweet Virginia ham to put between those biscuits," said Mrs. Wilson as she quickly returned to the kitchen.

She returned shortly and we all feasted on fresh biscuits and ham, washed down with fine trade coffee.

Our feast ended and Dr. Wilson gave us our instructions. "Philip, take this letter that I'm sealing up to your post contact in Richmond along with the regular post you deliver. Pay no special attention to it. As he goes through it, he will separate the letter to one side. When he finishes, he will thank you for your 'diligence.' That will be your cue that the letter is delivered. If he fails to mention 'diligence', remind him how 'diligent' you were. If that doesn't jog his memory, hit him over the head with a club." We laughed; Dr. Wilson roared.

The laughing subsided, he continued, "Will, take your post to Anderson's Tavern on Duke of Gloucester Street. Give the post either to the tavern keeper, Robert Anderson or one of his barmen. You will be given a bed in a back building for the night. Careful about your association with Captain Clark. While he may be a gentleman of some refinement, he is still British and a potential enemy to our liberty."

The words "a potential enemy to our liberty" rang hard on my ears. Dr. Wilson was right. Captain Clark was refined, but he was a dedicated British officer. I had to be wary.

"I'll be very careful of my contact with him, Dr. Wilson. He did say he would help me see Father," I half-pleaded.

"Yes lad, let him assist you to contact your father, but understand he has ulterior motives. He will expect something in return. If he asks, do not commit to anything, ask for time. Come back here if it is appropriate or seek the advice of Captain Griffin in Frederick. Just be careful, lad. Clark is a very intelligent and resourceful man. He would not hesitate to use you against the cause if he thought it would serve his purposes. Off both of you, be on your way, to your next appointment, whichever. Philip, don't forget to take the medicine for Mrs. Kelley, I have it sitting on the counter for you."

With that adieu, both Philip and I stood up and shook hands with Dr. Wilson. Before we could scoot by, Mrs. Wilson gave each a hug and small peck on the top of our heads.

"Boys, please be careful and ride like the devil is after you!"

Out the door Philip mounted quickly, tipped his hat to me, and trotted off in the direction of Richmond. I grabbed the reins of my horse and walked toward the town square to wait for my luncheon appointment with Captain Clark.

As I leisurely walked the streets of Charles to the town square, my head pounded with the warning that Dr. Wilson had given me about Captain Clark. I tried to put everything into perspective, but it was too difficult. All I knew in my limited world was that my father had befriended a neighbor and because of that he was sitting in prison awaiting trial. Mother, the family, and I had fled to Fredrick with the wounded Farmer Brown and been taken in by the very nice people of the community. That's where things got confused. The people of Fredrick were good people, English by most accounts, who never spoke ill of anyone much less the Crown, yet there was a noticeable undercurrent of hostility when the redcoats had arrived, which for the most part had subsided initially when they intermingled with the townspeople. It erupted again when the redcoats attempted to seize the militia's weapons. Then added to the mixture was Captain Clark, a genteel British officer of some refinement, who seemed to be very understanding and supportive of the basic rights of everyone. I had to steel myself to the fact that he may not be who he appeared to be, but a very capable and resourceful manipulator. And that I, being such a young lad, was the object of his attention.

Rounding the corner of the square I came face-to-face with an old man using a wooden cane, obviously a well-regarded servant or slave of some rich well-to-do family by the way he was dressed.

"Ah, how wonderful! Master Will, I am so glad to run into you this fine morning," he said, greeting me while tipping his hat to me.

"Morning," I replied and in return dutifully tipped my hat to him.

He turned a little and came up to my side. "So, you're meeting that rascal Captain Clark for lunch. Be careful, son, he is a true viper in gentleman's clothing. He'll use you for all you are worth and then cast you out like a worn-out shoe."

"I'm not sure what you are talking about," I pleaded, trying to be as uninformed as possible.

"Master Will, Moses is a very close friend of mine and we are all bound in this struggle for freedom together. It is every patriot's duty to watch out for our young brethren to make sure they are protected. Listen carefully. Captain Clark is a very capable spy in his own right. He is recruiting agents throughout the countryside. Rich or poor, planter, freedman, or slave, he doesn't care. He wants information on the committees and he's willing to do anything to get that information, including using your father as leverage to get you to cooperate. He thinks that since you are a post rider you must be a courier for the Committee and therefore a possibly valuable asset for his ring of informants. We don't have time for you to verify my association with Moses, but you are going to have to trust me. Be cordial with him, treat him no differently than you have before, answer his questions truthfully. Just don't mention anything that deals with the Committee nor who you might think is on the Committee."

"I'm truly sorry to say that this is very interesting, but I have no idea who you are or what you are talking about. I'm the post rider from Fredrick and I deliver letters and other posts on the route from Fredrick through Charles and even on to Williamsburg occasionally. Captain Clark is a friend of mine and he has been very helpful. In fact, he is going to arrange for me to see my father tomorrow if I'm lucky," I said as I put my very best blank expression.

The old black man examined my face carefully. "Master Will, just you mind yourself, be careful." He gave me a wink of the eye and added, "Keep that front up and you will do just fine." He touched my arm lightly and started to hobble off down the street in the opposite direction.

"Wait, I don't even know your name," I said as he left.

He looked over his shoulder, smiled a toothy grin, and replied, "No you don't, now do you?" He turned and continued on his way.

The old man turned down an alley and disappeared from sight.

"Will Jones!" came the shout from behind me.

I turned quickly back to the street ahead of me and saw Captain Clark, dressed in fairly standard riding clothes, waving to me from a storefront not 30 yards up the street. I took a deep breath to regain my strength, smiled, and waved back vigorously. I urged my horse forward and we trotted the remaining distance to the Captain.

"Good morning again, sir. Hope I'm not late," I said, still a little short of breath. "Sir, did you see that old slave I was speaking to? Do you know him? Curious fellow, I believe he is a bit touched in the head. Spoke nonsense. I couldn't make out what he said really." I looked back down the street to the point where the old man had disappeared and maintained a puzzled look on my face to add emphasis to what I said.

"I wouldn't bother myself with the old man. Probably just an old slave past his years and not quite right in the head, if you know what I mean. Come, Will, it's lunch and I am famished. The inn on the corner is rumored to have an excellent venison stew and fresh bread."

I tied up my horse next to the Captain's and jumped up to the broad wooden boardwalk and fell in step with the Captain as we made our way to the end of the street. As we walked, he put his arm around my shoulder in a fatherly manner. It was not an unpleasant gesture and I even managed a smile, but still in the back of my mind, I knew I had to be on guard just in case he proved to be less than what he appeared to be.

The inn, whose name I cannot recall, was located on the northwest corner of the town square. Its southern exposure ensured it had a warm and comfortable atmosphere in winter. The interior was dark wood paneling with numerous rectangular tables spread around the room. Their built-in benches in the wall; spindle armchairs of several different styles provided the remainder of the seating. No tablecloths, nor curtains on the window. Not that I was used to it. Mother had only one tablecloth and used it only on special occasions. I first saw curtains when I arrived in Fredrick, so the inn was both comfortable and charming to me.

"Looks a little sparse on the furnishings," remarked the Captain as he entered behind me.

"Reminds me of home, simple, practical, and comfortable," I retorted.

"I must invite you to England Will and let you see what a real establishment looks like."

Rather than be argumentative I softened my response. "Really, you'd invite me to England to visit? Could we visit Buckingham Palace and maybe see the changing of the Guard? I heard a man in Frederick talk about that and it left me spellbound," I said with enthusiasm.

"Absolutely Will, although I never really thought that would be of much interest to an outdoorsman like yourself. I thought perhaps fox hunting on horseback, or perhaps punting on the Thames."

"Yes, by all means, I guess. But why would people hunt foxes on horses? It's much easier to trap them in a good snare if you know what you are doing. I never heard of punting, although I do know the Thames is a river that runs through London."

Before the Captain could answer, the rather rotund, well-fed proprietress pushed into the room from what I imagined was the kitchen.

"Good morning Gentlemen. If'n you're looking for a hot meal, it will be a little while before the stew is ready. In the meantime, I can serve you some refreshment, a grog of ale for the Master, a nice apple cider for the young Master, and a nice fresh loaf of farmer bread with butter."

"That will be fine," answered the Captain.

The lady waddled off back to the kitchen humming to herself. Obviously, a happy and contented person by most measurements.

The Captain chose a seat in the far corner of the room, away from the kitchen and what I supposed would be away from other patrons who might arrive later. At the time I thought it was nice to have the privacy in a public place, only later in my experiences did I learn it was a necessary precaution for privacy needed for another reason.

The Captain continued and explained to me that punting and fishing on the Thames were his favorite pastimes. To me, fishing as he explained it was perhaps too boring. I preferred using a fish weir like the Cherokee. To me that was much more fun and practical. But I kept my opinion to myself. I was determined to be the perfect lad and keep my comments in a positive light. I was determined to find out what the Captain was up to.

Soon thereafter, our lady returned with a piping hot loaf of bread that smelled heavenly and a tub of creamy butter. Although not famished, since I only recently eaten at the Wilson's, I nevertheless dug into the bread, but only after I remembered something called manners and offered the bread to the Captain first.

A well-mannered man, the Captain accepted the bread and sliced two thick steaming pieces from the loaf, offering me the first, the end-piece as a prize. I gratefully accepted with the customary "Thank you, sir."

As we consumed the bread, the Captain began to relate his childhood to me, I guessed in an endeavor that I would understand him better. He paused and asked about my childhood. Such as it was, since I was only 16, I related some of my most memorable recollections. He was certainly a conversationalist, but I noted a certain preference for things English as opposed to our modest offerings in the colonies.

Later as the venison stew arrived, I felt captivated by his demeanor and personality. He was truly a charming and by all means a captivating gentleman from England. I laughed easily at his jokes, asked the appropriate questions when it was convenient, and acted contrite when he recalled my escapade with the rifles at Fredrick.

Lunch must have lasted a good hour and a half, during which time the tavern started to fill up with local businessmen in search of a grog of midday ale, tradesmen looking for sustenance while away from home, and the occasional gentleman farmer in town to conduct business. The smoke of fine Virginia burley tobacco began to fill the air. All during this time our corner was a private world inhabited only by the Captain and myself. I was his and he used it to his advantage.

"As promised Will, this will be my treat. Now though we must refocus our thoughts and ride on to Williamsburg. I have a few arrangements to make before you can see your father."

I felt a pang of disloyalty, I had completely forgotten about my father's plight and been absorbed in being wooed by Captain Clark. "If I haven't said it recently sir, I do appreciate what you are doing for me. It means everything to me to be able to see my father," I replied and suddenly regretted that I had shown a weakness that the Captain might try to exploit. No doubt I had a worried look on my face.

"Be confident Will. I will personally make sure you see your father."

Now I felt further obligated to him. It was the master at work and I feel like the fly being slowly drawn into the web of deceit.

"Thank you, sir. When we get to Williamsburg, I have to deliver the post to the Anderson Tavern on Duke of Gloucester. I have a small room out back for the evening, but basically I'm free after I deliver the post."

"The Anderson Tavern, previously known as Southall's, is located just across from my favorite place, the Raleigh Tavern. I'll meet you at the Raleigh at six o'clock. I shall have us a table reserved in the Apollo room. I should have more information about your father by then. So young man, off we go to Williamsburg."

Chapter 20

Williamsburg

The ride through the Virginia countryside on the road to Williamsburg that late winter day was refreshing as well as invigorating. For the first hour or so we ambled along at a quick walk letting our stomachs settle from all the food we had consumed. After a short break to answer nature's call, we remounted and galloped on towards Williamsburg. We arrived on the outskirts just as the sun started to set in the West. It had been a pleasant ride devoid of any substantial conversation.

"Will, it's probably about 4:30 now and I have to check in with my unit first. I'll freshen up a bit and meet you at the Raleigh at six o'clock, give or take a few minutes. Do wait for me and don't bolt and run if I'm not there promptly at six."

"I promise I'll wait, sir, at least until they throw me out for loitering," I responded with a grin on my face.

Captain Clark laughed and turned his horse to the British post. I spurred my horse on into Williamsburg proper.

Williamsburg was really a town; houses with picket fences,

multiple streets, some of which were paved with brick, large brick buildings, people everywhere, a church, the assembly hall, a blacksmith, a gunsmith, even a millinery shop. I was overcome with awe. It was not long before I spotted the Anderson and Raleigh taverns.

As I tied my horse to the hitching post in front of the Anderson, I noticed the inn was bustling with clientele even for this early evening hour. I grabbed the post satchel and ran up the four steps to the front door and was reaching for the knob just as two gentlemen chose that time to exit. I literally flew into them causing them to be propelled backward a step or two.

"Sorry sirs. I'm really sorry. I didn't mean to barge through the door, it's just that I didn't see you coming out." I reached down and picked up the taller gentleman's hat and handed it to him.

"That's quite all right young man. We mustn't stand in the way of the post, now should we Thomas," he replied looking at his companion, a somewhat younger man, equally as tall with bright blue eyes.

"Absolutely not, especially if he has a post for me. So young man where are you coming from?"

"I'm just in from Frederick by way of Charles, sir."

"Then you probably won't have anything for me, I was expecting a letter from Richmond today."

"I could check if you like me to, sir? We sometimes pick up mail in Charles that has come from Richmond."

"Why thank you lad, the name is Jefferson; Thomas Jefferson."

"Right away Mr. Jefferson," I said. As I slung the bag over

my shoulder to get a better grip on it so as to look into the pouch, the gentlemen continued their conversation.

"Thomas, I must take my leave. Martha is expecting me back home by midday tomorrow. I have a carriage that will take me to Yorktown this evening, and it's getting late. I'll take a skiff up the Potomac early tomorrow morning. With any luck I should be home by one o'clock, three at the latest."

"George, take care of yourself and have a safe journey. I do hope that you have an escort as far as Yorktown?"

"No need to worry Thomas, I have some very fine friends who have asked to ride along with me."

With that the two gentlemen shook hands and then embraced briefly. It seemed there was true friendship between the older gentleman and the younger one.

"George, I mean be careful. There is no telling who might be out and about this evening."

"Thomas, stop worrying. I'll have the best company on my way to Yorktown."

The older gentleman sprightly descended the steps and jogged toward a waiting covered carriage that had just driven up. Instead of getting into the carriage, the gentleman went to the rear of the carriage and detached the reins of a large bay gelding. The man effortlessly mounted his horse. As he settled himself in the saddle, several other riders came alongside and tipped their hats at the gentleman, who returned their greeting. Without another word the carriage departed with the gentleman and his escort of friends following along behind it. I could not help but notice that as the group rode along Duke of Gloucester Street they were joined by more riders. In all there must have been 10 to 15 riders in the escort party.

As they rode off into the distance and the fading light absorbed them into the darkening background of Williamsburg, I remembered my duty to Mr. Jefferson. "Mr. Jefferson, sir. I'm sorry sir, but there are no letters for you."

"Thank you for looking young man. I'm sorry I delayed you." He prepared to leave the Anderson.

"Sir, not meaning to be too inquisitive, but who was the gentleman that just left."

"A very good friend to both you and me, young man. That was Colonel Washington."

It took me a moment to place the name, but then it struck me like a bolt of lightning. Colonel Washington was one of the most respected men in all of Virginia, a soldier, a planter, and a statesman, and I almost ran over him. And then the second thunderbolt hit, standing before me was Thomas Jefferson, a noted lawyer, writer, and colonial politician. I was dumbstruck.

Mr. Jefferson saw my state of awe. "Young man, is there anything the matter?"

I stuttered momentarily, and then managed a very brief commentary, "I think I must have just met the two most influential men in Virginia and I didn't even know it."

"Why thank you, young man. What a very kind thing to say. Allow me to formally introduce myself, Mr. Thomas Jefferson, at your service." He extended his hand to me.

"I'm very pleased to meet you, Mr. Jefferson. I'm William Jones from … well … I'm from Frederick right now."

"William Jones, you wouldn't by chance be called Will Jones, whose father I regret to say is being held in Williamsburg awaiting trial?"

I cast my eyes down and felt a tear roll down my cheek. I quickly wiped it away and bravely held up my head and answered. "The very same, sir. But my father has a very good attorney, his name is Mr. Henry."

"Not that scoundrel Patrick Henry, I hope?"

"Why yes, sir." I paused. "He's not a good attorney sir? We heard he was the best."

"Will," he used my given name in a very friendly tone, "Patrick is only a scoundrel because he is one of my very best friends and do not worry, he is an excellent barrister. In fact, he is in the Anderson at this moment holding court for some of our more radical friends. Come with me, I'll introduce you."

"A moment sir, if you please. I must drop the mail with Mr. Anderson."

"Of course Will, I almost forgot you are a post rider," smiled Jefferson.

Mr. Anderson was nowhere to be found, but his assistant, a Mr. Rayles, relieved me of my post pouch. Seeing me with Mr. Jefferson, he immediately assumed I was a young lad of stature. I did nothing to dispel his conjecture. I asked after the care of my horse and he readily offered to send for a stable hand. As I was about to rejoin Mr. Jefferson, Mr. Rayles pointed upstairs and told me there was a bed reserved for me this evening. I thanked him as I left.

"Everything is taken care of sir. I'm ready, I guess, to meet Mr. Henry."

Mr. Jefferson smiled, put his arm on my shoulder, and escorted me through the tavern toward the Great Room. Indeed, it was a great room; sufficiently large enough to hold a ball or a banquet of some size. At the moment it was filled with ordinary tavern tables accompanied by substantial dark captain's chairs. The room was comfortably filled with customers in various styles of clothing, a few backwoodsmen, some planters, and then a large contingency of ordinary townsmen. Off to one side there was a large congregation of gentlemen dressed in what I assume was business attire. A few even had on powdered wigs, which in my opinion, made the gentlemen look slightly ridiculous.

In this group was a very demonstrative middle-aged man of about 35, having a receding hairline of neatly combed and tied-back light brown hair, a patrician nose, and a set of glasses perched on his forehead. In all her shyness, my mother would have said he had a rather handsome face in a classical sense, whereas my Father had a handsome face in a more rugged sense. The gentleman, the center of attention, was no doubt a man of distinction. I could feel it even from this distance.

As we approached this very table, the man looked up, and literally shouted to Mr. Jefferson. "Thomas, I thought sure we were rid of you for this evening, but I am sincerely glad that you have returned to join us in our unworthy discussion of the latest British insults to the colonies," the man laughed as did the assembly at the table.

"Actually Patrick, I wish to introduce to you one of your newest clients, Mr. William Jones, son of Jones, who is at the moment incarcerated here in Williamsburg."

The gentleman literally jumped to his feet, came quickly around the table, and extended his hand as he gave a slight bow. "Young Master Jones, Patrick Henry, Esquire, lawyer, barrister, and orator of some renown at your service."

He was definitely theatrical, but I think he was only doing that for the benefit of his audience and not necessarily me. I extended my hand and received a firm and friendly grip.

"Now Patrick, take care of the lad. I've done my duty and now I have other affairs to attend to." Jefferson turned to me and with the wink of the eye, "Will, don't be too spellbound by this rascal, he is more bark than he is bite. Even so, he is a very fine lawyer. If anyone can help you, Mr. Henry can." Mr. Jefferson patted me on the back, tipped his hat to the assembly of men, and left the way we had arrived.

"So gentlemen, allow me to introduce you to a very fine young lad from Frederick, who if rumor serves me correctly is a true patriot at heart. Gentlemen, young Master William Jones."

"Here, here," cheered the assembly in unison, and to a man, each raised his mug to me in my honor.

I must have turned three shades of red in total embarrassment. I had never done anything to deserve such adulation from what I calculated was an august body of prominent men. A simple "Thank You" was all I could manage.

"Modesty, gentlemen is a character flaw that I surely do not exhibit, but I assure you in this case modesty is a mantle this young lad wears like a royal robe. Will, we have heard snippets of your exploits, now you must give us the gospel of what really happened in Frederick when the dragoons came to seize the town's rifles?" Mr.

Henry leaned a little and whispered, "Always embellish the story, if need be, to maintain the interest of your audience."

Mr. Henry asked the gentlemen at the table to clear me a place so that I could be situated practically in the middle. A cold mug of apple cider was produced to wet my whistle.

"All set lad, the floor is yours," said Mr. Henry.

I took a deep breath and remembered the story Philip and I had spun for Captains Hawkins and Clark. Only this time I started at the very beginning. I'm not sure how long I took to relate the events, but by the time I finished there was a fairly large crowd assembled around me, somewhat spellbound by my tale. Pride they say is a sin, but at this moment I did feel a wee pang of pride in telling the tale and felt none the worse for it.

The confrontation with the Sergeant Major drew laudatory remarks, "Good show son," "Should've winged him just for good manners" came another. When I came to the part about the capture by the Cherokees, one man gasped, and said, "Oh no, those poor boys." At this particular point realizing I was talking to a group of town dwellers who could not tell a Cherokee from a Shawnee and perhaps did not understand the complicated relationship between frontiersmen and Indians, I modified the story a bit and painted the Cherokee in the benevolent mood which they really were, contrary to my first impression at the scene. I did, in fact, reveal for the first time the ruse the Cherokee had played on us. The group laughed and cackled. The climax of my tale, I rested on Richard's triumph over the ruffian. That elicited the remark, such as "Great shot, should have taken off the right ear as well." The remark was seconded by a resounding, ``Here, here" from the group.

I quickly concluded my story at our arrival at the Fredrick towne square, not forgetting to mention that a British officer just happened to view our triumphant march into the village.

There was a moment of silence as I concluded. As everyone prepared to clap, a resounding voice from the back of my audience spoke up. "Gentlemen, I assure you that these boys did indeed make a very triumphant return to Frederick. I personally observed it and attest to that fact."

The crowd parted a bit to see who had made the remark. There, framed by townsmen, stood Captain Daniel Clark of his Majesty's dragoons in all his splendor; white cotton gloves, red wool dress uniform, and polished sword by his side. "Please gentlemen, there are so few examples in recent memory of such bravery and élan that have been shown. Even I, who was to some extent tarnished by this incident, applaud it as a fine example of all things good and decent." Captain Clark began to applaud with his gloved hands and was soon joined by the other men.

Needless to say, I was stunned by the appearance of Captain Clark. I did manage to nod in his direction. Immediately after the applause died down the crowd drifted away. That was the cue for me to slip away, but such was not to be my fate. Captain Clark glided through the departing mass of humanity like Moses parting the Red Sea.

"I must say, Will, each time I hear that tale it gets better and better. You do have a knack at storytelling," grinned Captain Clark.

"Well, if it isn't our most distinguished Captain Clark of his Majesty's Royal dragoons," said Mr. Henry in a somewhat unfriendly tone.

"Why Patrick, I thought we were surely on a first-name basis by now. After all, you have managed to extract, what is the count now, 22 miscreants from my clutches?

"I rather think of them as maligned Englishmen who have been afforded the due process of law. And besides, it is 25," smiled Mr. Henry.

"Well, I hope that you will, at least this time, add a worthy Englishman to your list of successes. I understand you represent Mr. William Jones." Without waiting for an answer, he continued. "I was on my way to see if I could find young Will. An opportunity has presented itself and I can take you to see your father immediately. Seems like the Colonel has gone to Savannah for a few weeks, which leaves me in charge of our small detention facility. If we hurry, you can have at least an hour with your father. Will, it is up to you whether or not you wish to extend an invitation to Mr. Henry. Although I did note on the access log, Mr. Henry has visited your father on a very frequent basis."

Mr. Henry turned to me. "Go ahead alone, Will. I try to confer with your father at least three to four times a week. You need time alone. Perhaps later this evening we can talk."

"Why Patrick, Will and I are having supper a little later, we would love for you to join us."

"Thank you for the invitation Daniel. I will regretfully have to decline the offer. But I do need to talk to Will whenever he is free."

"Then tomorrow morning will be good enough. I'll show Will your office and he will be there by eight o'clock," smiled Captain Clark. It did not even occur to him that he might allow me to make my own appointment.

Mr. Henry noticed my perplexed look, winked, and replied, "That is most suitable. Will, I'll see you then. Have a good conversation with your father. And remember he is represented by the best barrister in Virginia."

"I'll attest to that, Will," added Captain Clark with a grin on his face.

"Thank you, Mr. Henry," I said and extended my hand to him. He took it and I added, "I'll see you, bright and early in the morning." I stood up from the chair and accompanied Captain Smith out of the Anderson. I could not help but feel that these two men were in a tempestuous struggle for every soul and who was I to deserve all of this attention?

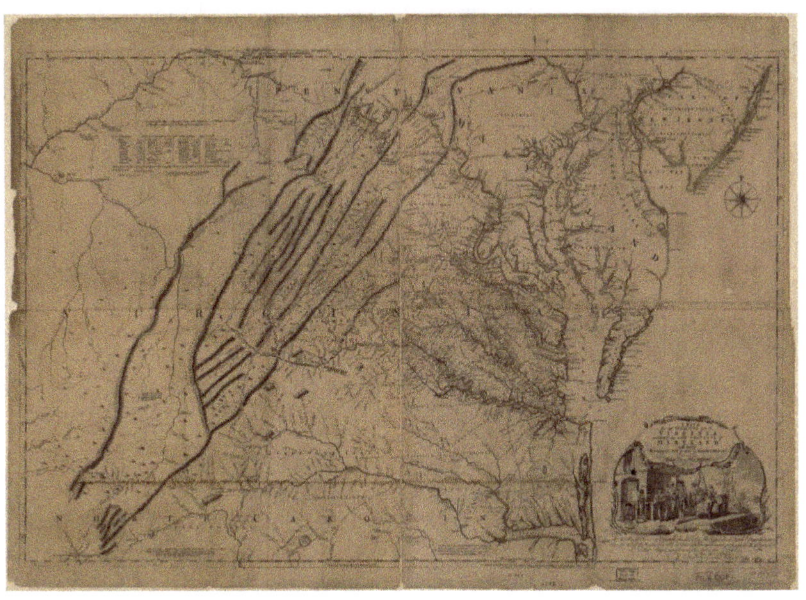

Virgin and Maryland   Credit: Library of Congress, Geography and Map Division

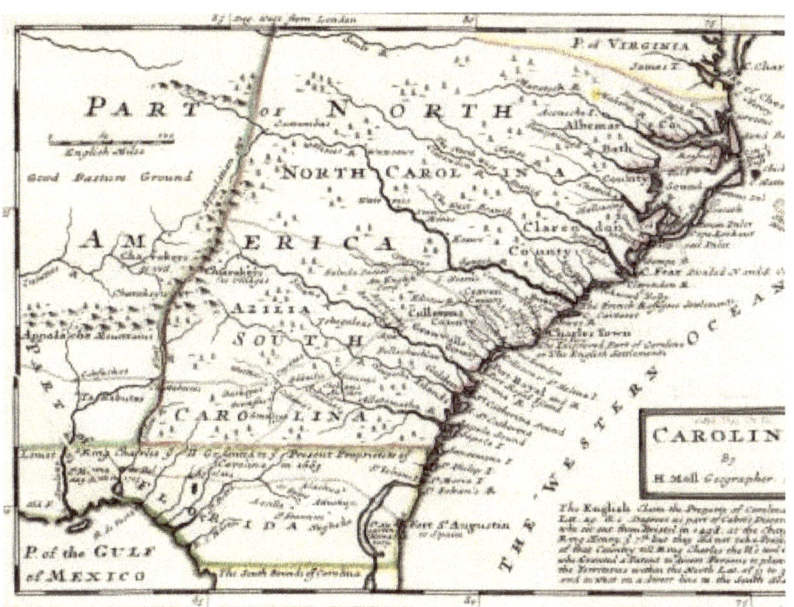

North Carolina   Credit: Library of Congress, Geography and Map Division

Baltick   Credit: Library of Congress, Geography and Map Division

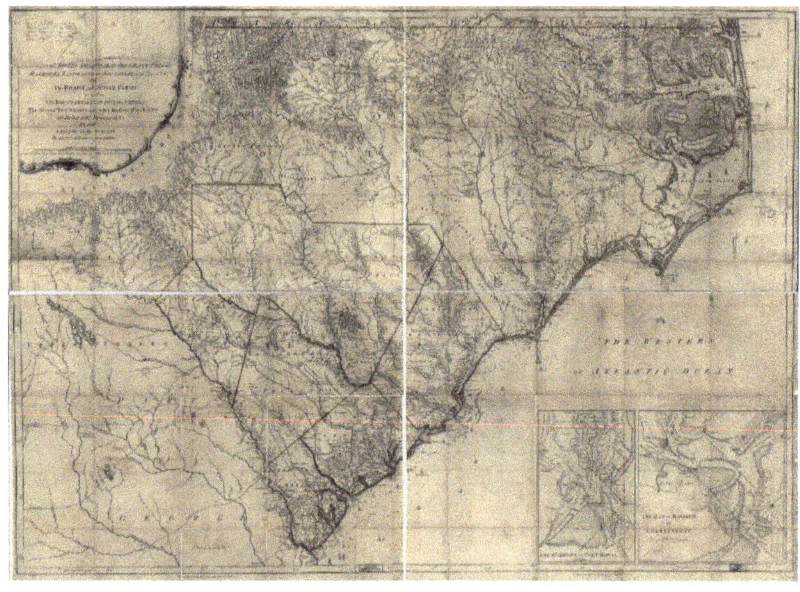

Henry Mouzon - Carolinas 1775
Credit: Library of Congress, Geography and Map Division

Chapter 21

Father

As the Captain and I walked down the dimly lit boardwalk to the British detention facility I had no idea what to say to my father when I saw him. Finally, the Captain broke the ice.

"Will, your father is adjusting well to his situation. He should not be detained too much longer. I frankly cannot see why he was detained in the first place. Your father is a fine, upstanding citizen. It was just the set of circumstances that landed him this mess. It's up to you to show him how strong you have been and how … responsible you have been. I'm not too sure he would approve of your escapade with the rifles, so spare him the story. He needs to know that neither you, your mother, nor your siblings are in any danger. Do you understand Will?" he questioned.

It had never occurred to me that I was in any kind of danger. My adventures were at the most boyish pranks. Not until then had the thought of danger ever occurred to me. "Yes, sir," I replied, knowing that my answer was a little slow in coming.

"Good that you understand Will. Anything you do can have an adverse effect on your father, so practice a little more restraint in the future."

The Captain put his hand on my shoulder and we walked the rest of the way to the detention facility in silence.

The facility came into view in the fading light of early evening. The Captain pointed out Mr. Henry's law office. It was a nicely appointed white cottage at the edge of the street with a business sign announcing to the public that the Law Office of Patrick Henry, Esquire was within. I knew where I would be when the sun rose in the morning.

The facility itself was a nondescript wooden building. It had the character of a tobacco barn, which it may have been in a previous life. As we approached two British redcoat guards snapped to attention. They greeted the Captain in unison, "Good Evening sir" and greeted him with a mandatory arms salute with their Brown Bess muskets.

Neither guard paid attention to me as I entered the jail. The foyer was a large room with three doors, one on each wall. The oil lanterns were already lit. The faint smell of the burning lamps mixed with the now very prevalent smell of drying tobacco. A British non-commissioned officer sat at a small desk to the right-hand side making notations in a ledger book. As the sergeant noticed the Captain, he quickly jumped to attention and saluted.

"Good evening sir. Sorry sir, I didn't hear you come in." The sergeant was still at attention holding his salute.

The Captain threw a short salute at the sergeant. "As you were sergeant. The young lad and I are here to see the prisoner, Mr. William Jones, per my previous arrangements."

"Yes sir. I have it here right in my ledger that you and a

young man will visit the prisoner this evening. The visiting time noted on the ledger is to be one hour." The sergeant still standing, looked down at me, "Wish it could be longer lad, but them's my orders from the Colonel."

"I'm sure the Colonel feels he is being generous, Will. I only regret I could not get you more time." said the Captain.

I tried to be optimistic, but I was disappointed that my time was limited to an hour. I managed to squeak out a "Thank you, sir."

"Now Will, don't be too disheartened, you have a very capable lawyer. And you can count me as your friend."

At that moment I felt entirely alone and incapable of making any difference in my father's life, much less secure his freedom.

"Sergeant, do you have the basket I sent over earlier?

"Right here sir," said the sergeant and he handed the Captain a large wicker basket full of bread and other things to eat and what appeared to be a good size bottle of apple cider.

"Sergeant, you can take us back to the prisoner now. Will, I thought you might like to have supper with your father and I had this basket especially made for you. Enjoy it together. And don't worry, I'll get the Sergeant involved in a card game and make sure you have at least a little more time with your father."

I can't recall whether I thanked the Captain or not. All I can remember after that is a long walk down a dimly lit corridor with hastily constructed wooden cells to either side. Father's cell was on the end, right-hand side. The sergeant inserted a large iron key into the door and opened it. He and the Captain stood aside to let me enter with the large basket in both hands.

There was no light in the cell, only the light from the lantern hanging in the hallway. It was totally dark and I couldn't even see my father. Somewhat apprehensive, I stood at the door to the cell. "Father," I said in a soft yet clear voice, "it's me, Will."

I heard someone shift their body on a rope bed somewhere in the dark enclosure. "Will? Son, is it really you?" said an excited voice.

Almost immediately a match was struck and the interior of the cell flickered to life. As the apparition lit the candle on the low stool next to the wall, my father appeared as an unshaven, shaggy-haired vagabond in filthy clothes. I hardly recognized him, but at that instant, I knew it was him, I threw the basket on the bed and leaped into his arms. Oh, he was so smelly, but to me, it was the sweetest smell I had ever encountered. It was my father. I must have squeezed with all my might because Father made a mock protest.

"Don't squeeze so hard son. Remember I'm an old man." He laughed. "It appears that you have put my absence from the family to good use. You've gained at least a stone it seems."

I tried to answer, but I couldn't. I refused to let go, and then I started to sob like a little child. I don't know what came over me, but I completely broke down. I barely heard the cell door close and the two soldiers walk away.

Father, although he had lost weight during his confinement, held me with all the strength and warmth that I remembered. He never wavered. Finally, I restored some of my self-control, sobbed one big one, and loosened my grip on his neck. I leaned back, still in his grip, and peered at the wooly man who was my father.

"Father, I don't want to be critical, but you do look a fright.

The beard makes you look like one of those trappers from over-the-mountain.

He laughed, which was contagious and I started to laugh too. He embraced me again and this time he gave me a great big bear hug.

"Now Will, I smell some freshly baked bread in that basket. So how did you come about that?"

I released my grip on Father and he let me down. "Father, the British Captain, Captain Clark, gave it to me for us to share for our supper."

"If I hadn't heard about your escapades, I would think you were taking aid and sustenance from the enemy," he said with an arched eyebrow.

"What escapades Father? I've been a very responsible son. I even have a job as a post rider. All the money I earn I give to Mother so she can care for herself and the children," I protested.

Father sat down on the rope bed and motioned to me to sit down opposite him. Without answering my protest, he reached in the basket and pulled out the half loaf of farmer's bread and tore off a large piece for me and an equally large piece for himself. We both started eating the bread, although my eyes were slightly downcast for I had not really told my father the whole truth.

"It was only a small escapade Father," I continued while chewing on my bread.

"What did your mother tell you, 'Never speak with your mouth full,' but she's not here right now, so go ahead and tell me about your little escapade. I want to hear it from the horse's mouth. I've heard mighty wild stories about your escape from Fredrick with an entire arsenal of rifles."

I swallowed quickly, "It wasn't the entire armory; close, but not all of them." Without further hesitation, I launched into the tale, careful this time to stick to the truth, since I was telling my father and he would know when I embellished it.

He let me talk uninterrupted. I talked and he ate. I would pause, take a bite and then continue with my tale, mouthful of food and all. It was a man thing. As I finished, I noticed the smile of approval on Father's face.

"I must say, Will, that was a delightful tale. Based on the other versions I have heard from other reliable sources, I'm quite pleased with your actions." His face turned serious, "Son, I know this has been quite an adventure for you, but you must understand the bigger picture of what is going on. This is not just fun and frolic across the countryside as you play chase, hide and seek with the British dragoons. This is serious business. I realize that you are only 16 years old, but you must grow up quickly if you expect to reach full manhood. It appears the Committee holds you in high regard and you have shown yourself to be resourceful. That's all well and good, but you need to learn as much as you can as fast as you can. Listen and learn from those that can teach you. Absorb all you can. Learn from other people's mistakes so you won't have to learn from your own."

Father's words might have seemed a little too hard for some, but to me, they were words of wisdom that he was imparting to me because he knew harder times were coming. He wanted me to have my eyes wide open and be fully prepared.

"The British officer Captain Clark seems like a decent

enough man, but he is still British to the core. I'm not sure he wouldn't use you if he thought he could disrupt the Committee. Be careful of his motives. There may be a time you have to sever your relationship with him. Do it and get on with it. Don't look back. Although I'm counting on you to be a man, you must still listen to Mother. If she makes a decision contrary to what you want to do, I expect you to be big enough of a man to accept her decision and follow through with it. Will, do you understand?"

"Yes Father, I do understand. I will accept Mother's decisions. I know the family is the most important thing and wouldn't do anything to jeopardize it."

"Good boy, Will. When you get back to Frederick make sure you tell Mother what I have said. Now for yourself, work on your fieldcraft with Philip and the other boys. Make sure they all know the woods and how to fend for themselves. Go up into the mountains and visit with Philip's uncle and learn from the Cherokee. Tell Captain Hawkins it is an order from me. Someone else can fill in for you and Philip for a few weeks or so. Times are going to be tough and you are going to need to be even tougher than you are now."

I felt myself trying to take Father's words to heart and show a tougher exterior. I must have tried to look tougher, but it didn't succeed.

"Will, toughness comes from within. Just because you want to look tough doesn't mean you are tough. You have to work hard and learn fast. Try to understand people's motives, why people act the way they do. Learn who can be trusted, learn who can't. Now let's finish up the rest of this basket before they come back."

Father divided the rest of the treats up; a couple of apples, some biscuits, and even a small portion of venison jerky. The bottle of apple cider we saved until last.

Almost two hours had passed before the Sergeant and the Captain came back to the cell.

"Will," said Captain Clark as the Sergeant opened, "it's time to go."

Father and I stood up together and embraced. As we did Father said in a low voice only I could hear, "Will, no matter what, you and the family must stay safe. Do you understand?"

A little perplexed by what Father said, I nevertheless replied, "Yes sir, I'll make sure we stay safe."

I remembered the cell door closing and the long walk back down the corridor to the foyer. Then the world seemed to sink into a fog as Captain Clark and I walked back to Anderson's tavern. We didn't speak at all along the way. I didn't feel like it and I assume he understood my mood and didn't push the issue. He was good at reading moods, something I needed to learn. It was a lesson Father told me to learn.

Chapter 22

Friends

As we arrived at the tavern, Captain Clark spoke first. "Will, I know what you are feeling like right now." I could feel he was on a path to try and mitigate Father's imprisonment. I listened intently, while outwardly trying to maintain an air of detachment.

"Your Father's predicament is not so bad. I know it is hard to believe that after seeing him, but you have to admit he is in good spirits. He will be released in no time at all."

I was waiting for the kicker, the part where I could help my Father's plight.

"You know you can help him, Will. Think about how you can help him tonight and we'll talk tomorrow morning before you see Mr. Henry. I'll meet you here at the inn at seven o'clock. We can have breakfast and then we can talk some more about your father and your future. I know you are a bit confused right now, but deep down I know you are a loyal subject to the King."

I thought quickly for a truthful phrase to appease the

Captain, "Sir, thank you for your concern and your help. I don't know what I would have done without it. And I do so dearly love England and what it stands for." I extended my hand and firmly shook his hand. Captain Clark seemed to appreciate my gesture.

As we ended our handshake, I backed away from the Captain and looked into his eyes. They were the same steel blue eyes, which showed no emotion. Even the slight smile of concern on his lips could not erase the real lack of compassion in his eyes. He was truly a man who sought to control through subtle manipulation. I was learning, but I feared the risk of losing my sense of compassion.

"In the morning then sir," I said and managed a less than crisp salute.

"Try to sleep tonight Will. But do take time to think about what I said."

I nodded, slipped past him, and walked slowly up the tavern's steps. I didn't look back.

Once inside the tavern and the door closed behind me, I took a deep breath. It was then that the fog lifted a little and I became aware of the din of the tavern. People were laughing, the conversations were loud and demonstrative, and the smoke curled to the ceiling where it hung in a light bluish cloud. There were only men in the tavern except for a couple of serving wenches, which I preferred to call ladies. As I approached the desk inside the foyer, a gentleman looked down at me from an open half-door that appeared to lead to a small office.

"So young master, what can I do for you? Lost your father and been sent to bring him home?" he smiled and laughed at his own joke.

I was curt. "My name is Will Jones. I'm a post rider and Dr. Wilson in Charles said you would have a place for me to spend the night."

He immediately stood erect and changed his expression. "I'm sorry I made such a joke Master Will. It was in poor taste. Please accept my apology." He then leaned through the open door and extended his hand to me, "I'm Anderson, the owner of this fine establishment. Would you like something to eat before I get Elijah to show you to your bed?"

"No thank you sir. I've already eaten. I have to get to bed early, I must leave at first light. Oh, could I have the post satchel for Charles. I'll need to be ready to go in the morning?"

"Sorry Master Will, the post is not quite ready. I'm expecting a couple of more letters this evening, but I will have them ready in a bundle for you to check in the morning. Elijah will make sure you get the proper fee." Without further comment, he pulled a cord behind him. He barely heard the bell somewhere in the inn.

Momentarily, a young black boy appeared out of nowhere.

"Yes, sir, Master Anderson?" he questioned looking at Mr. Anderson.

"Will, this is Elijah, my tavern boy. He takes care of things around here and makes sure everything works properly.

I stuck out my hand, "Pleased to meet you."

"The pleasure is mine, Master Will," he said, executing a very slight bow.

I was uncomfortable with all this "Master this, Master that." All I knew was that in front of me stood a boy perhaps a year or two older than myself, well-groomed and wearing a hand- sewn natural cotton hunter shirt, a pair of dark brown knee breeches, white stockings, and black leather shoes. His skin was the color of coffee and cream and his hair was curly and dark brown, but not black. His eyes were the most striking. They were a piercing, vivid green. Besides, he was squeaky clean! I looked like a hayseed compared to this cosmopolitan lad.

"Come with me please. You will be spending the night with me upstairs in the attic above the kitchen. Do you have a kit with you?"

"A kit?" I asked.

"A bag with extra clothes and such," he replied.

"No. All I got is what I got on."

"Oh," he said, looking a bit perplexed. He turned to Mr. Anderson, "Sir, would it be alright if Master Will availed himself of a bath before retiring?"

I saw Elijah squinch up his nose as if to say I smelled. I took the opportunity to sniff myself. I smelled normal; horse, tobacco, and sweat. Besides, I had had a bath. And then I tried to remember when exactly I had my last bath. It must have been ... Well, I couldn't remember. But I know I had one around Christmas. Heck that was only two months ago.

"Tell Aunt Charlotte to warm some water and give Master Will a bath. That is if he wants one," he said looking at me.

I shrugged my shoulders. "I guess I'm due a bath and it would be nice to see how city folk take one." I felt adventurous.

"Master Will come with me. As a matter of fact, there is warm bath water already drawn in the bathhouse just waiting for you. I'll get Aunt Charlotte to come give you a good scrub."

"I'm sure I can scrub myself." Only my mother had ever scrubbed me and I wasn't too sure about some stranger, especially a woman doing it.

"Oh, you must. Aunt Charlotte gives such a good scrub and besides, it's part of being in the city."

I doubted that Aunt Charlotte's scrubbing was a city thing, but I relented. Elijah showed me out back to the bathhouse, which was actually a small structure almost as large as our log cabin. Inside was a roaring fire and nearby was a large round wooden tub of steaming hot water already for me. I had the feeling this was a pre-arranged ritual; the opportunity to scrub a little bit of wilderness off the country boy on his visit to the city.

"Go ahead and get your clothes off and jump in the tub. I'll get Aunt Charlotte. Let me have your clothes and I'll get them washed too.

"I need my clothes. I don't have no others. Besides, I need them early in the morning. I got to deliver the post to Charles."

"Don't worry, I got an extra set of clothes there, over on the chair. And we'll set the clothes to dry before the fire and they will be ready in the morning."

True enough this was a planned event. There on the chair near the fireplace were a set of clean clothes all neatly folded and just waiting for a newly scrubbed farm boy to put them on.

I disrobed quickly and threw my well-worn clothes to Elijah, who cautiously held them at arm's length. I eased into the hot, steaming tub careful not to damage more delicate parts of my anatomy. As I settled in, the warmth of the water almost overwhelmed me. I could have fallen asleep in an instant, had it not been for the voice that came through the door.

"So young Master Will Jones has come to the city and consented to take a bath."

The voice was angelic with a slight Gaelic touch. I peered over the rim of the tub to see the most beautiful woman I had ever seen before. Her dark red hair was partially stuffed under a white cook's bonnet. Her skin was creamy white and she was absolutely tall. She must have been five feet eight inches or maybe even taller. The only criticism I had about this truly Gaelic beauty was that she was a might thin. She could have used at least a stone or more weight. But I was not complaining. I must have been staring with my mouth open.

"So the cat's got your tongue or is that mouth open to just catch flies?" she joked.

"Sorry," I closed my mouth. "It's just that I wasn't expecting anyone quite so beautiful." I regretted saying it the moment the words slipped from my mouth. If I had not already been red from the hot water I would have turned red from embarrassment.

"Now aren't you the nicest little gentleman to say such flattering things to this old worn-out girl from Ireland. My, if you were just a bit older, I'd run away with you with all your sweet-talking."

I restrained myself because I wanted to invite her to run away, age difference or not!

"I'm sorry ma'am, I didn't mean to be so forward. But it's been always a fault of mine to tell the truth." I couldn't stop myself. My mouth was in full motion and I had no control.

"Oh my, what a charmer and a real frontiersman to boot. I'll certainly have to watch myself." She smiled and let out a chuckle. "Now we have to get down to the real work and try to scrub off some of that accumulated country grime."

Elijah came back into the bathhouse and pulled up a chair just opposite me.

"So Master Will, tell us about the frontier. We want to hear about everything, the Indians, the redcoats, the robbers, the militia, and the bears."

"Uh, wouldn't that be a good tale to tell, while I scrub you down? I'd love to hear it myself," added Aunt Charlotte. She moved a low stool over to the tub and picked up a bar of lye soap and a big scrub brush. It was time for her to go to work.

Now my mother always tried to instill in us that "cleanliness is next to Godliness," but Aunt Charlotte took it a few steps further. I have never before and never since had such a good scrubbing. She must have taken three layers of dirt off me, plus at least two layers of skin, all the while I spun tales of life on the Virginia frontier. Some tales were second- and third-hand, a few were my own personal experiences. She must have scrubbed me for a good half an hour. It was long enough that Elijah put another bucket of hot water in the tub.

I kept my audience of two spellbound with my snippets of frontier life. They laughed and asked questions, accused me of fabricating, all in jest of course. It was a wonderful time. I came to appreciate a bath as a relaxing social thing. Then came time to wash my hair.

My hair, which I had never particularly paid any attention

to, was always pulled back in a ponytail and tied with a piece of rawhide, as was the fashion at that time, although mine was perhaps a bit long since it was down between my shoulder blades. Mother had occasionally trimmed my hair, but only to keep it a modest length. Now it was time to actually get it washed and cut to a more acceptable length. I had even noticed Philip had his cut shorter but never commented. Elijah, due to the curly texture of his hair, wore a very short ponytail that looked like it had been curled with a curling iron. I sort of wished I had hair like Elijah. It was extremely interesting to have curls, I thought.

Aunt Charlotte took some special soap and rubbed it in her hand and then began to rub it into my hair and scalp. The scent of lilac spread throughout the room. The scent, combined with the wondrous feeling of having someone massage my scalp, called for a halt in the storytelling. I asked for a brief pause while I enjoyed the pleasure of this new experience. I felt I had ascended into heaven.

As she continued to wash months of grime and a little bear grease out of my hair, Aunt Charlotte picked up the storytelling and treated Elijah and me to tales of when she was a young girl in Ireland. As a young girl of 10, she had been indentured to an English lord to pay off the debts of her family's small farm. Although her indenture was to last only three years, the lord finagled an extra two years by claiming before the local British magistrate that he had been forced to spend an enormous amount of money on medical expenses when she caught

pneumonia one winter after she was forced to sleep in an unheated room in the lord's manor house. Although her father had protested, she knew that she had no chance. Irish peasants were not afforded fair hearings in the English judicial system when it involved a controversy against an English peer.

She related some of the fun times she had had as a servant, so not all was bad. In fact, she was able to earn a few pennies by taking in sewing for some of the salaried servants. When she reached 15, she had acquired nearly a fortune of five English pounds, unknown to her master or anyone else.

Her escape from that servitude was somewhat anticlimactic, as she explained. As the day of the terminus to her sentence was approaching, the lord was called away to London for a meeting of Parliament. Prior to leaving, he gave the overseer strict orders not to allow Charlotte to leave until he returned. The overseer, being the beneficiary of several exquisitely sewn shirts and a pair of Sunday pants was in no mood to betray the friendship of his best servant girl. On the appointed day, the same magistrate who had indentured her for an extra two years arrived at the manor house early that morning. Called to the kitchen for a hearing on the matter of her indenture, Charlotte could not help but notice how elegant the magistrate looked in the dark linen suit she had sewn for him. The hearing was quick and conclusive; there being no formal request for her further services Charlotte was given 30 minutes to gather her belongings and present herself to the magistrate at his carriage out in front of the manor house.

All of the servants of the manor appeared and wished Charlotte a *bon voyage* as she rode away with the magistrate back to her family's small farm. The lord seems to have lost some of his influence in the community and was never heard from again. Charlotte, then faced with the prospects of a hard and weary life, chose to immigrate to America and find her fortune.

It was at this point Charlotte paused. My hair was deemed clean enough to be rinsed and prepared for a little trim. Now clean from head to toe, I was obliged to remove myself from the tub. Preserving what dignity I had, Aunt Charlotte averted her eyes as she held up a big cotton blanket in which I wrapped myself. She called it a "towel," something city people used to dry themselves with. Whatever it was, the cotton fabric was thick and soft to the touch and it did, in fact, have the effect of drying my skin.

Aunt Charlotte sat me down in front of the fire, still wrapped in the towel thing. She then proceeded to give me a haircut. First, carefully combing my hair straight, getting out all the tangles. Once that was accomplished, she began to snip the ends of my hair. Her story continued.

"Yes, those years at the manor house were hard. I, being the youngest of the servant girls, was given all of the hard duties. Now in the grand scheme of things the duties at the manor house were light work compared to my chores on the farm. I performed my duties, confident that I was working toward a better life. I always kept that in mind. By the time I left, not only was I an excellent seamstress, but I could also read and write."

She combed my hair sideways and clipped a little more.

"Now after I left and went back to the farm, I immediately knew that I had to go to America. Not that I had any idea what I would find, but the lure of this great land was more than I could resist. Like many young girls, I had no future in Ireland and the prospect of finding something in America was all the more reason to come."

She paused for a moment in thought, rubbed her nose with her scissors in hand.

"Now what I'm going to tell you boys does not go beyond this room. And both of you must swear on your dear departed ancestors that you will forever keep your secret. Now do you swear lads?"

Elijah and I looked at each other, overwhelmed by the possibility of a secret we were about to be privileged to. We both answered "Yes" and crossed our hearts to seal the pact.

"Now lads, a little lesson for you; life is not too pretty sometimes. It can be full of traps and snares. I, being a young girl without means or support, had a very difficult decision to make. I had to find some way to get to America. The more I thought and the more I learned it looked as if I was never going to be able to acquire the necessary funds for the trip. At first, I cast aside the idea of indenturing myself to a ship's captain; two terms of indenture had been enough. I decided to go to Dublin to find a solution, I hoped."

She stopped, put down the scissors, and looked at her handiwork.

"Now Will, get dressed and we'll continue the story over a couple of mugs of hot apple cider. Hurry now before you catch a cold."

I jumped up as did Elijah. I threw off the towel thing as Elijah threw me the clean shirt. In succession, he threw me my pants and then stockings. I was dressed in a flash. Elijah and I were a team of sorts. Elijah and I pulled the tub out from in front of the fire and re-laid a fireside rug back in place. He and I settled down on the rug ready for the cider and the continuation of the story. As Aunt Charlotte poured two steaming mugs of apple cider, there was a knock on the door of the bathhouse. Without waiting for an answer, Mr. Anderson poked his head in.

"Just checking on things to make sure everything is fine."

"Mr. Anderson," said Charlotte in a very friendly tone, "things are just fine. The young lads and I are having a bit of hot apple cider and a private conversation. Now if'n you'll close the door we'll continue."

"Tell me again why I put up with your insolence," Mr. Anderson said teasingly.

"Because!" was Aunt Charlotte's response.

Mr. Anderson closed the door and we could hear him depart down the steps.

*****

Aunt Charlotte handed out the hot mugs of apple cider, "Now, where were we?"

"I arrived in Dublin all full of pride and confidence assured that I would be able to find a right decent job in a matter of days. I tried everywhere. I tried every seamstress in Dublin, I think twice. Everywhere was the same. Prospective seamstresses twice as old and three times as good jammed the shops on Monday morning looking for jobs. Why, some girls were working for just room and board; it was bad. My fourth week in Dublin and my money almost gone I happened upon an ad in the window of a millinery shop for a part-time clean-up woman. Desperate that I was, I applied inside hoping that I might have a chance to later move up to being a seamstress.

"There wasn't much of an interview. The shop owner asked me only a few questions, felt my hands and arm muscles, and declared me fit enough. I moved my bags in that afternoon and immediately began to clean not only the shop, but the lady's upstairs apartment as well, all for room and board. My 12-hour days left little time for looking for another job, but I did have Sundays off and I used those days trying to figure out what to do next.

"Now in my youth, I was what you called a pretty good looker," Aunt Charlotte said.

I had to laugh because Aunt Charlotte was perhaps all of 25, perhaps 30, I thought. Her skin was so smooth and milky white, and her hair was thick and shiny Auburn. Maybe she was a tad older, but not much.

"One Sunday, I was strolling in the park when I happened to meet a gentleman of means. He was young English dandy by all appearances, out sizing up the female population. I, being a worldly girl, knew that if I played my cards right, I could perhaps at least have an interesting if not financially lucrative afternoon. Now lads, I do admit I had a bit of larceny in my heart at that time. After all, I had only a few pennies left to my name and this dandy was probably good for at least 10 quid and change."

The story was getting more interesting as Aunt Charlotte opened the door to her secret world.

"Mind, I had never done nothing like this before. I only heard how it was done. I considered myself a rank amateur, but one desperate enough to try anything once. So, I let this dandy chat me up. It wasn't long before he extended me an invitation to afternoon "tea." I knew he was up to no good when he suggested one of the better-known pubs in Dublin. Now ladies never go to the pubs in Dublin, at least real ladies don't go. I inquired if he was from Dublin and of course he said he had only arrived in town the day before. I suggested another pub, more suitable for my purposes, one that had come in stories other ladies had told. He immediately accepted my suggestion of a pub with perhaps a more private setting.

"We arrived at the pub by hired carriage, which he gleefully paid for. This dandy I thought was getting a little too randy too quickly. As we entered, I asked the proprietor for a private booth in the rear. And mentioned Katy O'Connell had recommended his establishment. That was a sort of code word for other working girls to tell the owner that I would need his assistance in handling my escort. He nodded and though having never seen me before placed his right hand on the bar showing all five fingers. Now that meant a 50 percent cut of any money, I was able to separate from my gentleman friend. I was aghast, why that was highway robbery. I gingerly extended three fingers or 30 percent. He smiled and then added another finger to his demand, 60 percent. I agreed to 50 percent. My only hope was this randy Andy from London was loaded with money or my efforts would be for nothing.

"Now the way the scam normally works is that a self-respecting lady allows herself to be approached, suggests a rather private establishment, and then enlists the assistance of ladies of lesser character to assist in the poor fellow's downfall. As luck would have it, I did not have the luxury of any such support. The gentleman in question was all over me, touching me, trying to kiss me. It was awful. The only redeeming thing about the whole experience is that he did smell lovely, I believe it was spring roses. The barkeeper was having a grand old time laughing at my expense. Fortunately, he did keep the drinks coming and after about two hours my young man was just about finished for the evening. I ordered the aperitif, the last drink of the evening. I had things to do and couldn't waste any more time on this rooster. As luck would have it, it took two of 'em to have any effect at all.

"Now, as we were leaving, the bartender wanted his share or rather his take for the evening. My escort, in a stupor now and not in control of any of his faculties, allowed me, without any resistance, to relieve him of his wallet.

"Low and behold there was a good 60 quid in his wallet. The man was proverbially rolling in money. As both the bartender and I looked at our newfound fortune, caution raised its ugly head. The bartender took 25 for the drinks and his share and he cautioned me to take only 20 for myself. He reasoned that a young man flimflammed out of a bit of change was not likely to complain to the constabulary, however out and out theft could cause quite a stir. There was enough left for a carriage to the train station and a long train trip for my young friend."

We must have had shocked expressions on our faces.

"Well, aren't we the ones to judge a poor young working girl, destitute, and literally assaulted by an impetuous English dandy."

We laughed. After all, the English dandy had taken liberties with Aunt Charlotte and probably had assaulted other young girls as well.

"Sorry Aunt Charlotte, it's just that you look so innocent

and ..." I stuttered trying to find the right word.

"Pure!" chimed in Elijah.

"Aye, that I am lads, never again did I play the trollop; the lure maybe, but never the trollop. Oh, it was a profitable year. At first it was only on Sunday afternoons. I would lure a gentleman to an establishment. My associates would descend on him, I being a real lady would feign disgust and leave the poor leech in the clutches of my partners. For not soiling my hands I earned about four quid a guest. Soon I was going one or two nights a week. Then I quit my job as the maid, got my own place, and started doing it nearly every night of the week. In my prime, I could make a good 30 to 40 quid a night for doing nothing but steering unsuspecting gentlemen to some of the seedier establishments in Dublin."

"Aunt Charlotte, didn't you feel bad about luring those men to places when you knew they would be ... ?" I didn't want to make an accusation of wrongdoing.

"Robbed!" added Elijah with a broad grin on his face.

"You're exactly right lads. To begin with it was all fun and games. No one got hurt and a little money was appropriated for the poor working girls of Dublin. As with any enterprise there are those who get greedy or some that run out of luck. In this case it was a lot of both all of a sudden."

The story got even better. Elijah and I looked at each other with glee as we were drawn deeper into the conspiracy.

"Winter was a slow period because it was so damp and dreary not many gentlemen were out and about. I certainly was not going to find steady callers in my line of business. So, I took in a bit of sewing here and there to bid my time until spring. In Ireland, especially Dublin, spring comes first in the heart and only later in April as they say. It must have been late March when we resumed our 'business,' although my partners had worked throughout the year. I was not as driven as they, since I was still young and had a good 10 to 15 years left to my looks. These colleagues were near the end of their looks and had to make money while they could. This put me into a difficult situation as they took more chances that I desired.

"This one particular day, it must have been a Saturday, I was strolling through the park when I was approached by two gentlemen. These two particular older gentlemen were fairly well dressed and were trying to look like gentlemen. However, their manner of speaking, while quite proper for gentlemen, had an edge. I couldn't put my finger on it, but I thought twice about engaging these gentlemen for further activity.

"As I attempted to excuse myself, one of the gentlemen grabbed my arm and literally prevented me from leaving. I was shocked at his behavior. The other gentleman, surprised by his conduct, interceded and came to my rescue. There was a brief argument and the abusive gentleman left. The kindly man apologized profusely and asked if he could show his regrets by taking me to tea. I reluctantly agreed. Since he was a visitor to our fair city, I chose a tea room not too distant from my sponsored tavern. I should have known something was amiss, but now time was running out for this day and I still had not located a mark. This gentleman was going to have to do, or it would have been an unproductive day.

"Over tea, we chatted about a multitude different things. It turned out he was a real charmer and slowly melted my defenses. After tea, he suggested we visit a tavern for something a little substantial and perhaps a glass of wine. I hesitated momentarily and he quickly renewed his invitation saying how nice it was to meet someone so sweet and innocent in the big city.

"Against my better judgment, I relented. As we walked arm and arm to the tavern, I was almost completely absorbed in talking to him and laughing at his funny stories. It was only by chance that I noticed that we were being followed by two other gentlemen, one of whom was the abusive gentleman."

An air of danger now permeated the evening air. Elijah and I had now switched, we lay on our stomachs, head in our hands, as all our attention was focused on Aunt Charlotte.

Aunt Charlotte continued. "Lads, when danger is about, some people claim to have a sixth sense, and can actually feel it. Well, I'm not a gypsy or a psychic and so I claim no special powers, but that evening things were wrong, awfully wrong. As we entered the establishment, I knew I had to warn my colleagues. The tavern keeper was his usual friendly self and greeted us at the door. As he showed us to a private table in the rear of the establishment, I excused myself and inquired of the tavern owner about the location of the ladies' powder room.

"As I left for the back of the establishment, my escort ordered two glasses of the tavern's finest port. The thought of paying that sort of money for a fortified drink grated on my nerves. My mark was showing he was a man of culture and means. Suddenly the mark was becoming the hunter and the establishment was the mark.

"I passed the lady's room and went straight to the parlor where my colleagues were busy preparing for an evening's entertainment. As I burst into the parlor, all conversation stopped. I tried to explain to my associates that I had an extremely bad feeling about my escort and told them we should all leave immediately. Their reaction was not what I expected. Can you believe that they laughed? They laughed so hard; they were literally roaring. The head associate held up her hand and all quieted down.

"'Sarah,' she called me, because I did not give them my real name of course. 'Sarah, just go out there and do your job and we'll take care of the rest.' She then got up and pushed me back into the main room of the tavern. I felt like a trapped rat and didn't know what to do. Reluctantly, I walked back to my escort and sat down. The evening progressed as normal and inside of an hour, my escort was starting to feel his oats.

"The act began and one of my associates asked if she could join us as she sat down next to the gentleman. He immediately switched his attention to my colleague and ordered three drinks. My associate, looking for a quick conclusion to the play, suggested instead aperitifs. I had a sinking feeling. As my eyes wandered about the pub, which had started to fill with normal evening clientele, I noticed the unknown man from the street had taken up a table where he could observe everything that went on. My time to leave.

"Although the play had not gotten to the point where I was to leave in disgust, I decided my participation was at an end. I excused myself to my table companions and left for the lady's room. This time, I didn't stop; I gathered my coat and went right out the back door of the tavern across the rear courtyard, through the adjoining yard to the street beyond. As I reached the street, I took a deep breath and gave a sigh of relief."

Both of us also gave a sigh of relief.

"But it wasn't over yet. I knew I had to depart the area quickly and I was getting my bearings, I glanced to the left. Standing there was a constabulary wagon and at the very least 10 tall lanky gentlemen of the Dublin constabulary in all their finest. My heart skipped a beat. As I started to turn right, I spied the abusive gentleman turn the corner at the other end of the street. I made an instant decision; I turned back to the advance abuser and ran screaming to the constabulary. As I approached, I screamed as loud as I could in my best highbrow accent, 'He's a monster, he's trying to kill me!' looking back over my shoulder and pointing to the abusive gentleman who was now running after me in pursuit. The constabulary reacted instantly and charged toward my erstwhile assailant. In the confusion, I quietly slipped away into the adjacent neighborhoods. It took me the rest of the night to sneak by to my lodgings."

"What a wonderful story, Aunt Charlotte. I can't believe you escaped the constabulary that easy," I remarked.

Elijah nudged me. "She's only taking a dramatic pause. The story continues."

"Thank you, Elijah. Shall I continue?" she asked.

In union, we gleefully answered, "Yes, yes!"

"My days as a lady of leisure were over. I surmised that if the city officials knew of our activities they probably also knew where everyone lived. I had the advantage of not residing in the area of the tavern, so I considered the chances of them finding me at my lodgings to be remote. Nevertheless, erring on the side of caution and good prudence, I decided then and there it was time to immigrate to America. I wasted no time. I packed what essentials I could in two battered linen bags and tied up a bundle to sling over my shoulder. My beautiful dresses I had made in my spare time and my other accumulated possessions I placed in a variety of wooden boxes that I had acquired for eventual passage to America. I set aside a special box as a parting favor. I finished packing in the early morning hours. I then had to make arrangements for my passage to the colonies.

"Over the past year, my involvement with my associates had escalated. I had an inkling that a hasty departure from Dublin might be called for. To that end I had made the acquaintance of a certain shipping clerk at the wharves. His wife had been the recipient of some of my finest work, to which he was forever grateful. Later that morning, humbly attired in a working woman's dowdy clothes, I hired a wagon to take the 'Misses' baggage to the wharf. The wagon delivered me to my friend's firm and unloaded the baggage in the adjacent warehouse where I received a receipt for my boxes I would send for later. I then made my way into the office and quickly caught the eye of my favorite shipping clerk.

"He was somewhat surprised by my most common attire. Immediately he asked if something was the matter. Such a smart lad he was and will forever be a faithful friend. I merely explained that unforeseen circumstances required me to seek passage to the colonies immediately and that I would have to send for my other possessions later. At that point I handed him the small wrapped packet of ladies' items that I thought his wife might enjoy. He was overcome with gratitude. He then said, 'Last night the constabulary raided a bawdy house and arrested a ring of young ladies that had been preying on visiting English gentlemen for the last year. Might you be one of them?' he asked with a gleam in his eye. Unfortunately, my silence did nothing to dispel his conjecture. 'Not to worry,' he said. 'But you have to be careful. They are looking for a very attractive young lady who might be trying to escape Dublin by taking passage to the colonies.' Their description was very accurate with the exception that I was at least 28. I naturally protested the derogatory remark and assured my friend that I was no more than 19 at the time."

Her lighthearted humor, even in the face of adversity, was charming as well as it was a footnote on her determined character. Again, we changed positions, now sitting, but closer to the foot of her chair so that we could absorb all her words.

"In their way of thinking, such a lady of means would pay for her passage. It was therefore announced that the constabulary would be checking all of the passengers departing for the colonies thoroughly. My heart sank momentarily. Then we put our heads together to come up with my escape plan."

Aunt Charlotte leaned over to us, gently pushed our heads together, and touched her forehead to ours, "But now it's time for you lads to get to bed. I'll finish the story as soon as I check on things in the inn."

How we protested, all to no avail. We helped Aunt Charlotte clean up quickly and then scurried back to the tavern. As we ran up the stairs, Elijah waved at Mr. Anderson and quietly yelled over the din of the tavern, "We're going upstairs!"

Mr. Anderson smiled, returned the wave, and just nodded his head. He went back to the very profitable business of attending to his customers.

*****

The "attic" as it was called was the quarters for the tavern owner and his family. It was a spacious arrangement under the roof of the building with a sloped ceiling that must have been at least 16 feet high in the center. Dormer windows peered out both in front and back. The family living area was the first room we entered. I was surprised at the collection of sturdy wood pieces that gave the area the feeling I was in a very private pub. The only thing missing was a fireplace, but in actuality, there was no need for one.

It was nice and warm upstairs; the heat rose from the tavern below, to include the pleasant mixture of burley tobacco and rich country food. Off to either side were bedrooms, one on either side of a narrow hall. Elijah pointed out Mr. Anderson's room, a plain but functional room, then Aunt Charlotte's room, all bright and flowery, with a hand-made feather bed on a huge four-poster bed.

Both rooms were exceptionally large by my standards, nearly half as large as our old homestead. On the other side of the living area were two more rooms similarly situated. Elijah explained one room was for two of the serving ladies and the other one was all his, which he sometimes had to share with special family friends and famous post riders. I laughed at his joke. His room was more like Aunt Charlotte's room in that it was decorated with odds and ends and had a boyish motif about it. There was an old Cherokee arrow on the wall, a very old blunderbuss hanging nearby, and a brass bugle of undetermined origin hanging over the big bed. A big charcoal seascape framed in old barn wood was hanging on the opposite wall. There were even shelves against the opposite wall, which contained a few precious books and a fantastic collection of rocks, shells, arrow heads, a stone hatchet head, a piece of cane, a tied bunch of flax, a tied bunch of dried lilac – obviously Aunt Charlotte's contribution – and an assortment of other odds and ends. I was overcome with curiosity, but didn't ask any of the thousand questions that popped into my mind.

"You'll find a fresh nightshirt on the chair over there. You'll sleep with me in the big bed. Oh, if you have to go during the night, you can use the commode by the window. Aunt Charlotte had a bunch of them made for the tavern. They are the latest in modern conveniences," Elijah said proudly.

The "commode" looked like a large chair to me. I had no idea how one used it. I must have looked confused as I examined it without touching it.

"Watch," said Elijah, as he came over and lifted the seat of the contraption to reveal a hole in the seat with a bucket beneath. It looked like the workings of an outhouse except inside. "Each morning, it's my job to empty all of the buckets in the inn. If we have a full house, it can take most of the morning."

"Isn't that kind of a nasty job?" I asked.

"Naw, you get used to it. Besides, most guests leave a penny for my trouble. Now that is a lot of money."

"Wow," I exclaimed. "That's what I get paid for three letters and I then have to share it with the postmaster. Do you have to share it with anyone?"

"Absolutely not! It's all mine, to do with what I please," said Elijah proudly. He then added, "Normally though, I buy something for Mr. Anderson or Aunt Charlotte, cause they are so good to me."

Elijah closed the seat on the commode and we both grabbed our nightshirts and got ready for bed. After we got ready, Elijah went around his side of the bed and knelt to say his prayers. Now I came from a fairly pious background, but we never prayed before we went to bed. It just something which we didn't do and it was kind of strange to me.

Before he started, he looked at me and asked earnestly, "Don't you say your prayers before you go to sleep?"

"Never did it before. In our family we normally have a short prayer session in the evening where we all hold hands and mother says a little prayer for us all."

"Then I'll do it for both of us," he said, closed his eyes, folded his hands together, and knelt by his bed. "Now I lay me down to sleep. I pray the Lord, my soul, to keep. If I should die before I wake, I pray the Lord my soul to take." Elijah paused and then continued. "Dear Lord, please bless and watch over my friend Will and his family and make sure his father returns home soon. God bless Grandfather and Aunt Charlotte and Miss Caroline and Miss Molly. Amen." Elijah crossed himself as he ended. "There, you and your family are in my prayers," he smiled.

Chapter 23

Elijah's Story

I could not help but wonder who "Grandfather" was, so I asked as we climbed in the bed on opposite sides. "Who is 'Grandfather' that you mentioned in your prayer?"

"It's a family secret of sorts, but you are my friend, aren't you?" he asked earnestly.

Another secret. Williamsburg must have been the repository for all the secrets in the colonies. I thought for a minute, but again my boyish curiosity got the better of me. "Sure, I'm your friend. And I will keep your secret, cross my heart," I answered, crossing my heart with an "X."

Elijah began his story. "This story begins more than 17 years ago because that's how old I am. Mr. Anderson has a son named Robert, who was smart and ambitious. When he was 19 he took a job as a manager of a small sugar plantation in the West Indies. There he ran face-to-face with the cruelty of the slave system that was prevalent on the vast sugar plantations in the West Indies. Although the British attitude toward slavery was changing, it was still a way of life down there.

"Young Master Robert, being a man of destiny and courage, took matters in his own hands and actually made progress in reforming the system on the small plantation he was running. The working conditions of the workers improved and he gained the respect and admiration of the poor slaves and indentured servants who worked for him. The rest of the white community was less accepting of Robert's reforms and sought to have him removed. It proved to be an impossible task and the other owners and managers eventually gave up.

"Now Robert was able to improve the production on his plantation with the help and assistance of his workers. The profits poured in, which enabled him to purchase more land for his employer. After five years of hard work and effort, his employer was the owner of a substantial sugar plantation that covered over 10,000 acres. Robert received his bonuses and had them deposited in a bank in Boston. His dream was to own a plantation not in the West Indies, but in his native Virginia.

"Things were going well until one day, as a single man, he caught the eye of a beautiful, brown-skinned girl working in the sugar mill. Let me explain a little bit about the social structure in the West Indies. In the upper class, you have plantation owners and rich merchants. In the next class, you have plantation managers and small merchants. And in the lower class, you can lump all of the indentured servants and slaves. Now all of the middle class want to get to the upper class. And the upper class wants to keep its status and therefore limits entry. About the only way to go from the middle class to the upper class is to have a daughter marry into it.

Young men, no matter how ambitious or courageous, have little if any chance of marrying into the upper class. It's against the unwritten rules of snobbery.

"Robert had been considered somewhat of an eligible bachelor in the Indies. However, since he was only a manager, all of the available young ladies, who were either owners' daughters or merchants' daughters, were beyond his grasp, not that any of those women were interested in him in the first place. His undisclosed interest gravitated toward the young beauty he had seen in the sugar mill.

"Hesitant to disclose his feeling because of the taboo against whites and workers mixing, Robert shied away from making his interest known – or so he thought. George, the young lady's father, one of Robert's best field managers, soon heard rumors that Master Robert had been seen gazing at his daughter. This was a matter a father had to take into his own hands."

I propped myself on one elbow as Elijah sat cross-legged in the bed, only halfway covered up. He continued.

"It was the end of the harvest festival when all the workers on the plantation would gather and have an afternoon of celebration and festivities. As normal, Robert opened the festival which was held at the mill. After one mug of good rum, as tradition would have it, Robert excused himself and went back to the main house to sit on the veranda and watch the festivities from a distance. It would not do to have the master consorting with the workers. As Robert made his way to the veranda, he poured himself a glass of fine Jamaican rum and carried it to the porch. Once on the veranda, he relaxed into his favorite oversized wicker chair.

"The night air was cool for the tropics and the sea breeze carried the sweet smell of orchids through the air. It must have been several minutes before he noticed the young beautiful girl from the mill sitting on the rail at the end of the veranda. She was dressed in a light, flowery cotton shirt which exposed her round smooth shoulders. Her dark eyes were staring at him and he stared back. Nothing was said for a few moments until she smiled. 'I understand that some have said that you have been watching me from a distance.' She jumped down from her perch on the rail as lightly as a butterfly floating to the ground. Without another word, she glided to Robert in her bare feet. She held out her hand, which he took as he rose from his chair. 'So is the view better up close?' she asked him. 'Much better,' he said as they embraced."

Elijah paused and waited for me to react.

"No, you can't stop now. You have to go on. This is the good part," I protested.

"There are some things that are public and some things that are private," he teased.

"Just tell me what happened," I was on the verge of begging.

"Well, the romantic part was a little later actually. You see this was not a chance encounter between Robert and Helen. Knowing that Robert would eventually find some female diversion sooner or later, George hatched a plan to secure his daughter's future as well as his own. While George was concocting his scheme, he soon learned that Helen, aware of Robert's interest, had been planning a secret chance encounter. They say George, in a mock fit of anger, berated his daughter for her attempted indiscretion. Then as quick as he had angered, he changed his mood and broke into laughter. 'Daughter,' he said, 'you want your young man and you shall have him, but you will do it properly with my blessing. I shall arrange everything.'"

"So, the chance encounter on the veranda was not what it appeared to be?" I asked.

"No, it wasn't," came the voice from the doorway. Aunt Charlotte came the rest of the way into the room. "Now boys, it is getting late and you really need to go to bed. Elijah, you can tell the story some other time when Will comes back with the post."

"Aunt Charlotte," I said in a very serious tone, "I may not be able to come back to Williamsburg for a long time. I have to go up into the Blue Ridge for a while. My father gave me something to do."

"Now what you be doing up in the mountains Will, there all by yourself?" she asked.

"Father senses trouble coming and told me to go to the mountains to learn the ways of the Cherokee and the frontiersmen. He wants me to learn everything I can in order to be able to keep the family safe," I replied, trying to avoid sounding like an alarmist.

"Oh, you dear poor boy," she said as she came around to my side of the bed and hugged me to her bosom. A tear came to her eye and she stared out into the wide beyond. "Well," she said as I came back to reality and released me somewhat, "as Will said, this may be his only opportunity for a while, so Elijah, go ahead and continue with the story. I always like this part anyway. Now Will, come on scoot over a bit and let me bundle in with you."

"So, are we having a story tonight? I wondered where everyone was," said Mr. Anderson as he peered in the door, with his long parson's pipe in his hand.

"Yes sir, I'm telling the story about Robert and Helen and then Charlotte is going to finish her story about coming to the colonies."

"Well, this looks like it could take quite a while. I better pull in my comfortable chair for this one," he said as he walked back into the living area for his favorite chair. "Now," Mr. Anderson said as he relaxed in his chair, "where are we in the story?"

"I was just getting to the point where George was making plans," gleamed Elijah.

Mr. Anderson nodded his head and took a long draw on his pipe.

Elijah resumed the story. "Robert and Helen were embracing on the veranda, watching the celebration, when he noticed a torch parade winding its way up to the main house. Somewhat puzzled, Robert nevertheless remained silent.

"George appeared on the veranda and walked quietly up to the young couple. 'Nice procession, wouldn't you say, Mr. Robert?' said George to the startled young man. 'I … well …' Robert stuttered as he thought of disengaging from Helen, but reconsidered. He regained his composure. 'Yes, it is a nice procession. What's it for George?'

'Oh, it can be anything that you want it to be, a new beginning perhaps, a glad tidings procession, or whatever,' George replied.

'Daughter, what do you think it might be?'

Helen responded in a soft and alluring voice. 'Well father, if I am to be one with my Robert, then I hope it will be my wedding procession.'

"I can imagine Robert's shock at that announcement. Oh, to have been there to see his expression!" chimed in Mr. Anderson with a huge grin on his face.

"Shocked he was!" blurted out Elijah. "Robert was speechless for a full minute before he recovered. Then he became as bold as a young buck should be.

'If I am to have your daughter's hand in marriage then it shall be a proper marriage.'

'So, it shall be my son,' said George as he embraced his new son-in-law-to-be.

"How simply romantic," added Aunt Charlotte as she gave me an excited hug.

"The wedding festivities had been secretly arranged, but all hinged on Robert's acceptance of the arrangements. Once Robert acknowledged his feelings and desires for Helen, the real work began. Helen kissed her fiancé, took a few steps, and flew back into his arms for a more appropriate kiss. Two maids of the house staff appeared and literally tore Helen away to prepare her for the wedding ceremony. The veranda soon filled with Robert's field managers and plantation staff, there to congratulate him on his sudden fall from bachelorhood.

"Soon Robert was led away to make ready for the wedding, as the workers of the plantation bedecked the main house in flowers, ribbons, and finery. Around five o'clock all was prepared and with the arrival of the local minister, it was time. The wedding party now in their best clothes assembled next to a flower-covered trellis erected in the front yard for the occasion. Robert, now dressed in a fine beige linen suit and with a few rums in him, was escorted to the wedding trellis. Robert looked back to the house and waited in anticipation.

"George, father of the bride, also dressed in a beige linen suit, walked through the front door of the house as regally as any king. He paused, surveyed the crowd, raised his hands, and silenced the crowd. 'The Bride,' he announced and took one step to the left side. There, framed by the door of the house, stood the beautiful and alluring Helen in an exquisite white, low-cut linen wedding dress. A ring of colorful flowers encircled her head. Never had Robert seen such a beautiful bride and she was to be his. Helen stepped forward, took her father's arm and walked down the flowing steps to her waiting fiancé.

*****

"The wedding ceremony was short, the celebration was long." Elijah, the storyteller, paused and yawned. He turned to Mr. Anderson and asked, "Grandfather, would you tell the rest of the story?"

"Certainly, Elijah. Come over here and sit by me,"

Elijah climbed out of the bed and crawled up beside his grandfather and leaned on his chair as Mr. Anderson took the opportunity to tussle Elijah's curly hair. Aunt Charlotte hugged me again and kissed me on the top of my head. There was warmth and goodness; things seemed right.

"They say the love that Robert and Helen shared made the flowers bloom brighter, the winds blew gentler, and the sugar cane grew even sweeter. It was a good time on the plantation. Everything seemed to prosper. The profits were huge and the workers for the first time ever shared in the prosperity. With the money they earned, many workers bought small plots of land near the plantation and built neat, white-washed homes that formed a small communal village. A school was built on land donated by the absentee landlord, who also donated the building material for its construction. Things prospered. Maybe it was due to other factors, but everyone on the plantation and for miles around just knew it was because Robert and Helen had gotten married and that the love they shared flowed forth and blessed the community," said Grandfather Anderson with misty eyes.

"Eleven months after their marriage, a baby boy was born and they named him Elijah." Grandfather Anderson took his right hand and tousled Elijah's hair. Elijah laughed. "Now this little cub was the apple of his parent's eyes. Nothing was too good for him and no one could get enough of him. The midwife who delivered him declared him to be the most beautiful baby she had ever seen. Life was wonderful and the community was happier than anyone could remember." Grandfather paused and sadness came over him.

"As with all good things, they come to an end. One day a Spanish fleet appeared off the coast headed toward the port city, 40 miles up the coast. Robert sent two riders to warn the residents of the city. Although the riders made it ahead of the warships, the town could do nothing to prevent the Spanish from landing. The town was utterly destroyed, refugees fled in panic to other parts of the island. A few of the survivors came as far as the plantation, which had been untouched by the attack, or so everyone thought. Two weeks later the pox appeared among the survivors and quickly spread to the rest of the community to include the plantation. Robert did everything he could to protect his family and his workers. Helen and the toddler were sequestered away in the main house and forbidden to leave. Robert, who had suffered cowpox as a child, was immune to the disease, worked endless hours caring for and nursing his workers. He never knew how or why but Helen caught the pox herself and became very ill. Even little Elijah came down with a light case of the disease."

"See these two pox marks on my cheek?" said Elijah as he pointed to them.

"Helen fell victim to the disease as did over 60 percent of the plantation workers and their families. The community outside the plantation fared no better. A large funeral pyre burned for days cremating the remains of the fallen and the bonfires used to burn the contaminated belongings of the sick and dead. A dark pale fell over the plantation. Even in the grief and turmoil of the days following, all remembered the compassion and caring Robert had given to the sick and dying. Everyone shared each other's grief. As the community tried to recover, Grandfather George, himself a victim of the disease, managed to survive, although his wife and other children did not. Now all that was left of the family was Robert, little Elijah, and Grandfather George." Grandfather Anderson paused, took a deep breath, and reflected for a second.

I felt her sadness as her tears poured forth. I even had a few tears of my own.

"There is an old saying that goes, 'When things go wrong, expect them to get worse before they get better.' Having heard of the calamity that struck the island, for the disease did not spare any part of the island, the landlord made a special trip from London to see for himself the death and destruction the pox had reaped. He arrived just as the hurricane season began and was treated to the whimsical weather that was typical of that time of year. He and Robert were confident that they would be able to harvest enough of the crop in order to meet debt on the plantation. The island had even organized a harvesting schedule for each plantation. All calculated if they worked together and pooled the labor resources they could barely scrape by if only a portion of the crop was harvested from each plantation.

"As the harvest began, workers, managers, and owners worked side by side in the fields cutting and processing sugarcane. Well into the harvest, 10 plantations had already been worked through the schedule. Then disaster struck again. A huge, deadly hurricane struck the island. The sugarcane still in the fields was shredded by the forceful winds. The crops not already harvested were completely laid to waste and destroyed. The mill on the plantation was damaged beyond repair. Grandfather George, who had not fully recovered from the pox, suffered a heart attack and died one evening in his sleep.

"The landlord had to face the fact that all was lost. He had nothing left, no money to cover his debts in London, and certainly not any money to continue Robert's employment. Robert waited until the end of hurricane season and caught the first ship back to Virginia. Let me see, that was how many years ago?" questioned Grandfather Anderson.

"I was two years old then and now I'm 17, that makes 15 years ago," chimed in Elijah.

"And such a joyous occasion for me to have Elijah come into my life," said Grandfather Anderson. Then with a somber tone he added, "Will, now you know our family secret. You may not understand everything, but we try not to remind everyone that Elijah is my grandson. Some people around here do not agree that love transcends normal social bounds at times. I didn't at first. In the beginning, it was hard for me to accept Elijah, but then who could not accept such a delightful and lively grandson."

Chapter 24

Charlotte's Story

"And now it is my turn again to finish my story," intoned Aunt Charlotte. She began without waiting for anyone to respond. "Getting on the boat bound for America presented quite a problem. If they were searching all the passengers, I had to figure out a way to get on board unnoticed. My friend and I thought for hours and finally came up with the solution that I would have to go as an indentured servant and change my appearance to match a lower station in life. Remember I had been indentured before and I had sworn to myself that I would never do that again. So, to escape my 'sorrows' I agreed to consider an indenture for a short time. My friend arranged for me to meet the captain of a ship leaving in two days.

"That evening, properly attired in hand-me-down clothes, a fresh haircut which made a mockery of my hair, a couple of blackened teeth, a smudge here and there, and I was ready to go – Well almost. I still smelled too clean to be really a prospect for an indenture. To help a little I got a mackerel fish and rubbed it on my clothes, ate a big onion, and even smeared a little onion juice under my arms. Oh, did I reek like a washerwoman."

The vision of Aunt Charlotte transformed from a country beauty to a virtual beggar propelled me into her story. I could imagine the scene as she painted a vivid picture in my mind.

"The evening fog was beginning to settle in on Dublin as Charlotte and Henry, her shipping clerk friend, descended the slippery cobblestone street toward the wharf district. Lamplighters were busy trying to push back the growing shadows of the coming night. Shops were closing down as merchants prepared to leave the area for their more favorably located homes up and away from the wharf district. A whole different clientele was slowly easing into the district: people looking to take advantage of drunken sailors, pickpockets after an easy take, lonely women in search of an evening's company; not the sort of district a lady would normally find herself in.

"Charlotte clutched Henry as he led the way to the rendezvous with the ship's captain that was known to look the other way when it came to making a little extra money at a poor soul's misfortune. His lair was located on a semi-dark side street one block up from the waterfront. As they approached the pub Charlotte noticed an old pub sign hanging above the entrance that had seen better days. There was no real name on the sign which had obviously changed names dozens of times as evidenced by the names which all faded into one another in the failing light of evening. The only remarkable thing about the sign was the fact that it hung from what resembled a pirate's cutlass, ergo the local name of the pub, "The Cutlass." Not a good sign, Charlotte thought to herself.

"As they entered the pub they were met by a cloud of smoke and the smell of stale ale. The noise was level, just above a low mumble. There was business being conducted and no one wanted their negotiations to be overheard. The captain had situated himself in the far-left corner of the pub at a big table. Two of his more able sailors stood watch. Charlotte and Henry made their way through the crowd. Charlotte elicited only one remark, 'God what a homely wench and she stinks to high heaven. Don't even think a bath would help that one.'

Charlotte was buoyed by that remark and her spirits rose, assured her disguise was solid. As they approached the Captain's table a sailor stepped forward to intercept them.

"State your business," barked the sailor.

"Mr. Tate," said Henry with an air of authority, 'have you forgotten who you are addressing?'

"Sorry sir, I didn't recognize you right away. Who's the poor hag you got with ya?"

"Mr. Tate, if you continue to insult me and my family, I assure the Captain might be able to find more suitable employment for you aboard the ship," replied Henry in a harsher tone.

'My apologies, Mr. Skeahan. I didn't realize she was family. The Captain is waiting for you."

Tate stepped aside, nodded politely to Henry and Charlotte, and let them proceed. As they approached the table, in a show of courtesy reserved for special customers, the Captain's sailors produced two chairs for his guests.

The Captain stood, bowed politely. "Ah, my good friend Henry Skeahan. I hope you had no trouble finding this fine establishment."

Two mugs of ale appeared out of nowhere and were placed in front of Henry and Charlotte.

"So, Captain, I understand that you are sailing to the colonies tomorrow with the evening tide."

"Henry, always the businessman. You must learn to talk to people, be friendly, and ask about the family. A little small talk Henry, before you get down to business."

"I didn't know you had a family Captain," said Henry inquiringly.

"I don't, Henry," replied the Captain as he leaned forward. "But that's not the point my boy. Engage your quarry in conversation. Loosen the tongue a bit and get to know the mark," said the Captain as he turned his attention to Charlotte. A broad grin spread across his face. He spoke directly to Charlotte. "So, you are Henry's what, sister's daughter, distant cousin from Kilkenny, or perhaps the favorite maid of his dear beloved spinster aunt who just died?" The Captain turned to Henry, and smiled. "She'll be safe with me now, Henry. Bring her stuff down to the ship by midday tomorrow. Mr. Tate will relieve her of the baggage, but not too much; we wouldn't want to draw attention to your ward. Now be off with you."

The Captain reached across the table not to shake Henry's hand, but to claim the mug of ale for himself. Henry stood up, looked briefly at Charlotte, and departed without saying anything. Charlotte all of a sudden felt awfully alone.

The Captain took a big swig of ale, wiped his mouth with his sleeve, and put the half-empty mug back on the table with a loud bang. "Lads, make sure the lady and I are not disturbed for the next hour. We have a lot to talk about."

The lads moved from the table and cleared the table directly in front of the Captain of its inhabitants, who only mildly protested the eviction.

"My, but you do look a fright. And you stink to high heaven." The Captain sniffed the air. "Mackerel and let me see …"

"Onions," replied Charlotte with a superior attitude.

"Yes, you're right of course, onions. Horse shit, oh excuse me, horse manure would have been more appropriate."

"Horse shit is acceptable to me, Captain. I'm quite used to such language."

"You know, try that as you may, I can still see the beauty behind that dirt and smut. You might fool the gentry with your disguise, but not the educated eye. The famous Sarah, even if that is your real name, which I doubt. Do you realize they are turning Dublin inside out? Seems like you and your associates aimed a might too high one evening and pinched the pocket of a royal. Caused quite a stir in Whitehall they say. Dublin, a den of thieves and cutthroats, has to be cleaned up, they said. Quite comfortable I am here. Just my town, even though I am English by birth, I'm Irish by choice. Bloody gentry will steal ya blind all in the name of civility. So ya want to travel on my ship to the colonies? As ya know that will cost ya."

"I have no money to make the trip. I was hoping to negotiate a contract for my fare," pleaded Charlotte.

"Just a moment Missy, you and I are cut from the same cloth. We know a mark when we see one. Now tell me, do I look like a gullible man?"

"No," said Charlotte sheepishly.

"Good. Now that we have established that, here is the deal. The reward for you is 20 quid. I require 30 and in order to give you the proper documentation, I'll also take a three-year indenture. I'm taking a big risk."

"Thirty quid," Charlotte exclaimed loudly. "And a three-year indenture, you're a thief and robber!"

The Captain looked horrified and everyone in the pub became quiet and looked in his direction. He held up his hands to Charlotte to tone down her protest. He then assumed a scowl and looked around the room, "What are ya looking at ya sewer rats. Go back to ya own business." He returned his attention to Charlotte. "One more outburst Missy and I'll collect that reward without hesitation. I'll be lucky if someone doesn't sneak out of here and try to turn ya in."

Charlotte readjusted her worn dress and smoothed down her front pleads. "I will not pay you 30 quid. I'll give you 15 quid and a one-year indenture. You can get an easy 50 quid for my contract from a wealthy plantation owner, I'm sure of it," she remarked indignantly.

"Not the way ya look now. I'd be lucky to get a farthing," laughed the Captain.

"I do clean up nicely, with the proper dress. I am quite attractive, if I do say so myself."

"I'll address you as Rachel from now on if that is acceptable to you?" he asked.

"Fine with me," remarked Charlotte, now transformed at

least temporarily to Rachel.

"Rachel, my darling, your beauty is renowned and your charms reputed to be overwhelming, none of which I have seen so far. Convince me and the deal will be 20 quid and a year's contract.

Rachel took a deep breath, smiled coyly, "Can you overlook my appearance and my perfume?"

"It might be hard, but try me," he said.

Charlotte paused and looked around the room. All of us were spellbound by her tale.

"Needless to say, I proved my worth to the Captain and he grudgingly agreed to the 20 quid and a year indenture. I was able to escape Dublin without incident and landed in Yorktown a mere two years ago."

*****

"Now it's my turn again," chimed in Grandfather Anderson. "It must have been early May 1773 when the Georgiana sailed into the Chesapeake and dropped anchor off Yorktown. Word spread that there were some indentures on board and that some of them might do for tavern work. Now the family and I decided to make a day trip and see if we could find a suitable tavern girl to help my Misses in the kitchen with cooking and cleaning. So, all four of us went, there was the Misses, Robert, Elijah, and me."

I could see them traveling from Williamsburg down the 15-mile lane to Yorktown in a wagon going to market so to speak. The oak trees lining the road created a tunnel most of the way. Although I had never been there, people I met here and there said it was a beautiful road that first went to the shore of the Chesapeake and then followed it on over to the tiny port of Yorktown. I settled back again into the story and watched the visions unfold before my eyes.

"The family arrived in Yorktown and made their way down as far as they could and found a spot near the Yorktown Inn to park the wagon. There were plenty of people about. The Georgiana, which lay at anchor not too far offshore, was a medium-sized, three-masted merchant ship. Her markets were the smaller port towns, not reachable by the bigger merchantmen. There the captain of the Georgiana would sell his dry goods to local merchants and sell the indenture contracts for a tidy sum."

Mr. Anderson continued with his story.

"Now everyone stay together," instructed the elder Anderson. "We are here to do a little shopping and see if we can find a decent tavern wench for Mother. Robert, we have no need of fancy new plow blades or farm implements. Remember we run a tavern, not a plantation. And besides, we don't have room in the barn for any more of such stuff."

Robert, who was an experienced young man, took his father's chiding in good humor. "Father, must I remind you that I would already own that plantation, except for someone's bullheadedness," he joked.

"But for me, you would have bought that swampland in Florida. The Spanish would have loved to pick your bones clean the first time you turned your back. Don't forget that beautiful piece of cleared farmland in North Carolina that turned out to be virgin timber," added Anderson.

"Boys," said Mrs. Anderson in a quiet, but resolute tone, "I'll have none of that bickering. When we find the right land, then we will have found it. Until then we will keep looking. In the meantime, I have a tavern to run and I need a good wench to help me. And I will make the choice. I will not waste money on a pretty face that has no idea of what work is all about. Now off with you menfolk. I have to inspect the lot by myself."

"Mother," lamented Robert, "I should help you select the girl. I had a lot of experience in selecting workers for the plantation."

"Thank you, Robert. No!" replied Mrs. Anderson as she slowly walked away from the group of men. Elijah broke away from his father and went running after his grandmother. When he caught up with her, she stopped, took his hand, and continued to the market.

Mr. Anderson and Robert, now alone, decided to do what men always do when they are left to their own devices, they went to grab a pint of ale and look at the horses assembled in the nearby field that were for sale. "A good plow horse is always hard to find" was one of Robert's favorite sayings.

The selection of indentures was rather large on this day. There must have been 30 people willing to sell their souls to the devil on the chance of one day tasting true freedom. There were young Welch coal miner sons, already hardened by years in the mine with their perpetual sooty faces, sturdy Scot highlanders and their long reddish-blond tresses probably on the run from some long-forgotten warrant, a smattering of deceptive looking Irish lads all young ruddy-faced men with long, thinly muscled arms of iron. Yes, there was a good supply of muscle to tame the wilderness beyond the Blue Ridge and these were the lads to do it.

The women were no less impressive; mostly young, sturdy farm girls from the dying tenant farms of Ireland and Scotland. Mrs. Anderson was looking for something different, she was looking for a girl that was quick with her mind, strong of back, and had a no-nonsense disposition. Most of these girls had broken spirits, whose last great hope was to escape servitude in England in exchange for a shorter servitude in the colonies. They were willing to accept almost any treatment in order to survive. To Mrs. Anderson it was such a sad situation. She had taken in several of these girls over the years and provided them a safe haven. It had been mutually beneficial and she had even managed to match these poor unfortunate girls with suitable husbands. Today she wanted something different. She needed to find a girl that could take care of her family when she was gone.

Mrs. Anderson and Elijah took a seat just up from the area where the indentured servants were being displayed. Mrs. Anderson was more interested in watching each woman and her reactions to the potential buyers. Most of the women were shy and reserved; they accepted the touching and the pawing of the prospective male purchasers. Most of the men had brought along their wives and were content to look at the prospects' teeth, feel their hands, test a grip, feel the arm muscles, and even give the prospect a simple math test on a small slate board to see if she could read and cipher. There were a few, who were there to just get a free feel of a woman. This always disturbed Mrs. Anderson; even the auctioneer kept a sharp eye for such molesters. Most of the young women did not fit her bill, they were either too shy, too dimwitted, or just too large. There was one in this group who might do, she thought.

"Eh, get your hands off me you pig," said Charlotte as she twisted the ruffian's hand as he tried to touch her breast. He jerked his hand away and then came at Charlotte with both hands. She managed to intercept the man's hand and as she barely held him at bay, she gave her attacker a swift kick between the legs. The man crumpled to the ground in agony. Charlotte quickly surveyed the area, found a large barrel stave, grabbed it, and started to swing at the man's head just as two merchants lifted her off her feet and prevented the homicide. "Let me down, he deserves to be beaten to a bloody pulp," shouted Charlotte.

The men finally agreed to release Charlotte if she agreed to give up the barrel stave and leave the man in misery. Grudgingly she agreed and they gently released her, making sure they stood between her and her attacker, who was now trying to crawl away unassisted.

Mrs. Anderson approached the young woman, "Hello my dear, allow me to introduce myself. I'm Mrs. Anderson from Williamsburg, my husband and I own a tavern on Duke of Gloucester Street, the main street in Williamsburg."

"How do you do ma'am," said Charlotte as she curtsied a bit. Charlotte saw an opportunity. "I'm Charlotte and I'm from Dublin. I've worked in a manor house for several years as a maid and a cook's assistant and then I've worked as a seamstress for a while. I can read and write and I can cipher with the best of them."

"And it appears you have some experience with men at their worst, too," added Mrs. Anderson.

"Yes, ma'am. It's not easy being a young female alone on the road. I've had my share of unfortunate incidents with drunks and overly aggressive men. I've learned a few things about protecting myself. But normally I'm a very agreeable person and who would serve you well."

"This is Elijah, he's my grandson. The apple of his father and his grandfather's eye. He's a good lad and helps me run the inn."

"I wish I had references, but I don't. The Captain will vouch that I kept his cabin clean and neat on the voyage over. The others will attest that I made a good stew that kept us fit and healthy."

"How long is your indenture young lady?"

"I've never been called a lady before," Charlotte said as she feigned embarrassment. "It's for one year."

"That is an awfully short indenture. Rare is it that I have ever seen an indenture that short. The normal is three years. And an attractive girl like yourself will cost a pretty penny."

Charlotte was in a quandary. The lady that stood before her had a kind and gentle disposition and was the best prospect. There were problems with the other potential buyers, most of whom were rich planters from the surrounding areas. She knew that most of them would have less than honorable intentions and she was not going to be someone's bed servant. She had to think on her feet and plead her case. "Mrs. Anderson, I do realize my indenture is short and there is the possibility that my contract might be expensive, but I would make an excellent servant for you."

"Mrs. Anderson, woman to woman, you have to take pity on me. Should one of those pompous, old fat gentlemen purchase my indenture, as sure as there is a Saint Patrick, I'm going to end up in a horrible situation that I'll not have control over."

Mrs. Anderson smiled at the young lass as she tried to negotiate her own servitude. She was not without sympathy for the young attractive girl. Many like her had been sold into servitude and ended up in deplorable situations and then cast out when they became pregnant. "I know it is such a sad situation. Why just the other day, poor little Annie McGuire was cast off in Williamsburg by her former owner, six months pregnant and nowhere to go. The parson took her in. No doubt she will have a baby which will be adopted out. But what will happen to poor Annie no one knows," said Mrs. Anderson shaking her head.

Charlotte smiled. Mrs. Anderson was negotiating and Charlotte was the one who was going to have to make the first offer. She had to take a chance since time was running out. "Mrs. Anderson, I see that you are a very shrewd woman and know the value of a good servant. We both know that I'll not get pregnant by some fat old farmer. He would certainly have a fatal accident before that happened. Now to save us both pain and the agony of a protracted negotiation, I would entertain an extra year for every 10 pounds over let's say 30 pounds. However, if I serve in your tavern, I get to keep all of my tips, which I can use to reduce my additional contract period by that amount extra you had to pay."

Mrs. Anderson did like this young lady, the red hair, the bright fiery eyes. Yes, she would do just fine. "I'll talk to the Captain and make him a handsome offer of 50 pounds for your contact if you agree to four years."

"I'll give you 10 pounds immediately and agree to no more than three years, same terms as before," countered Charlotte.

"We are going to have such a good relationship, my dear,"

said Mrs. Anderson as she took Charlotte's left arm and escorted her to the Captain, who was sitting at a table not too far away.

"The Captain knows me as Rachel, Mrs. Anderson," whispered Charlotte.

"A woman with a secret; you must tell me sometime, over tea," smiled Mrs. Anderson as she approached the Captain. "Ah, Captain, I'm Mrs. Anderson, from Williamsburg and I was wondering if perhaps I could make an arrangement to purchase Rachel's indenture?"

"I'm sorry madame, the auction will be in another hour. I expect to fetch a pretty penny for this filly, even if she did disable that lout for life. Shows she has spunk and fire. Lots of gentlemen here around appreciate a strong-willed woman, especially one that's a looker."

"Captain, I will offer 30 pounds for the young woman. I think that is a fair offer considering she only has a year indenture," responded Mrs. Anderson without even acknowledging the Captain's opinion. "Oh, by the way, Captain, did you know Rachel has a case of the French Pox?"

"What?" exclaimed the Captain as he jumped up from the table. "You whore!" he yelled at Charlotte and started to reach over and slap her.

Mrs. Anderson stepped in between the Captain and Charlotte. "No need to get violent, Captain. My offer stands. I can use her in the barn and on the farm. That's about all she is good for."

"I have a lot of money invested in her; the passage, her food, the clothes," he lied. Fifty pounds and not a penny less."

"I'm willing to pay 35 pounds."

The Captain glared at Charlotte like he had been betrayed. "Forty-five pounds and she is yours."

"You drive a hard bargain Captain," said Mrs. Anderson as she dug out her little money pouch. "And I'll require the contract and all of her belongings."

The Captain sat down at the table, now only mildly perturbed, and went through the pile of indentures on his table. He found Rachel's contact and quickly signed it over to Mrs. Anderson for the sum of 45 pounds. "Here, take this over to the sailor and he will release her belongings," said the Captain as he handed the indenture to Mrs. Anderson. "And Mrs. Anderson, don't come begging for your money back if she runs on you."

"I'm sure this young woman has no intentions of running any further Captain. Good Day!"

Charlotte, now holding Elijah's hand followed Mrs. Anderson over to where all personal belongings were being held. As instructed, Mrs. Anderson presented the indenture to the sailor, who checked it as if he could read and then asked Charlotte to point out her belongings. Mrs. Anderson signaled a porter standing nearby to pick up the two bags and the trunk and follow them.

"Mrs. Anderson, true to my word, I want to give this to you," said Charlotte as she handed Mrs. Anderson a 10-pound note and a five-pound coin.

"I don't think you will disappoint me, young lady. True to your word, but I must protest the one-year indenture. You must stay longer, I really will need you longer."

"But the indenture is for only a year!" Charlotte mildly

protested.

"Of course darling, it is only a year, but would you please consider staying a little longer. I'll pay you a fair wage. And remember you will still get to keep all your tips."

"I'll have to wait and see how the first year goes before I will commit to any additional time."

"That means that you'll consider it then. That's good enough for now. So, let's take you to your new home, but first, we need to find the menfolk. No need to delay any longer. I have found the treasure I was looking for." That said, Mrs. Anderson reattached herself to Charlotte and led her away to the wagon.

"One thing I failed to mention, Charlotte, my son Robert lost his wife several years ago. I hope you don't feel too presumptuous of me to say that I think you might find him attractive."

"But Mrs. Anderson, I am an indentured servant," Charlotte said. "I wouldn't presume to take an interest in my mistress's son. Heaven forbid!"

"Charlotte, your present situation is only temporary. And besides, you are no longer in Ireland or England. The rules are a little different here. You must understand, I make the rules in this family as far as your situation is concerned. You have my permission to consider my son as a prospective suitor; everything being properly pursued, of course."

Charlotte closed one of her eyes and grinned at Mrs. Anderson, "Now you wouldn't be trying to be a matchmaker, would you ma'am?"

"Absolutely!" replied Mrs. Anderson with a similar smile on

her face. "My son is still in mourning. He can't get on with his future and that young man holding your hand needs a good woman's touch. I've been searching for five long years without success my darling. You may be the answer to my prayers. I only hope you may feel the same way, given the proper time to adjust to your new surroundings."

Charlotte broke the spell by interjecting her comments. "I tell you, Will, I was both shocked at the prospect of being a bought bride and then never more excited at the prospect of a new life with a good family. All of a sudden, I was free of the clouds which hung over me like a menacing thunderstorm. Mrs. Anderson, I knew, was a charming and endearing lady of some stature. Elijah, well what can I say, even then he was an exceptional young man. I wish I could describe the wholeness I felt. As we got to the wagon, I was dumbfounded. There stood two of the most handsome men I had ever seen. Right, fine looking gentlemen they were."

I noticed that Mr. Anderson was blushing as Charlotte kept on talking.

"The distinguished older gentleman I knew right away was Mr. Anderson and I, with all my heart, hoped the younger one was the young Mr. Robert."

Again, I slipped into the story, listened to it unfold, and could vision it in my mind as if I were there.

"Darling," said Mrs. Anderson as she addressed her husband, "I have found a most suitable young woman to help me in the tavern. Her name is Charlotte. She has experience as a servant in a manor house, sews, and claims to make a decent Irish stew."

Mr. Anderson stepped forward, extended his hand.

Charlotte, still holding hands with Elijah curtsied and hesitantly extended her free left hand. Shaking hands with employers was something new to her. These Virginians were truly a different lot.

"Charlotte, it is nice to have you in our household. I'm sure you will find us to be decent, God-fearing people. I hope you are of the same character."

Without thinking Charlotte responded, "Mr. Anderson, I do consider myself to be a decent person, but I have no reason to fear God. I love Him and I do think that He must love me, or he would have never sent me to this wonderful family." She had managed to pull it out with a degree of charm and diplomacy.

Robert could not constrain himself. He began to laugh. "Miss Charlotte, I must warn you that as Protestants we have a rather strict view of our Lord. Only through His strict enforcement of the rules in the Holy Bible are we able to function as his humble servants, but don't let that bother you. As tavern owners, we sometimes are less God-fearing and lean more toward His softer side."

"Will," said Charlotte as she brought me back to reality, "that man was such a charmer all of a sudden. Even his mother was mildly surprised. I can say that I wish Mrs. Anderson had lived a bit longer. Shortly after I started working, she became ill and died of consumption a mere six months after I came to this loving household."

"During those last few months, Charlotte devoted herself to the Misses," added Grandfather Anderson. "Tended to her night and day. Didn't have much time for any of us except Elijah. It was near the end that Mother called Robert in and gave him an order, "Marry this girl, she'll make you a fine wife. But first, you buy that land and build her a proper home. Once you do that then you have my permission to marry.' This was her dying request."

"I've never seen a son so devoted to his mother. Proposed then and there he did, and I accepted with the provisions established by his mother, God Bless her soul. It's been a little over a year since then and Robert bought land out beyond the Blue Ridge near Sycamore Shoals. He writes that the main house will be completed by early April and it is his intention to come back, marry me, and move Elijah and me to the frontier. I'm girlishly giddy about the prospects," said Charlotte excitedly.

"So, Will, there you have it, the Anderson family in a nutshell. Now it's time for you and Elijah to get to bed. You have an early morning. I'll make sure the mail pouch is ready to go as soon as the twilight brightens the morning sky," said Mr. Anderson.

Elijah and I went promptly to bed and were tucked in by Aunt Charlotte. We whispered to each other for another 10 to 15 minutes before we both drifted off to sleep. It was a truly restful sleep. I don't remember having any dreams that night. I remember just having a satisfied feeling, something you only feel when things are right with the world. It was a feeling I would rarely have in the future.

Chapter 25

Escape

The rooster crowed much too soon. The twilight was just beginning to peek over the eastern horizon. I wanted a few more winks, but I knew I had to get up and leave town before the Captain found me again. Slowly I got out of bed, trying not to disturb Elijah. I was unsuccessful.

"Hey, where are you going so early? It's barely light outside," protested Elijah.

"I've got to run by the lawyer's office and try to get out of town before Captain Clark finds me again."

"I'll help you get ready," replied Elijah as he jumped out of bed and got dressed along with me.

Silently we crept down the stairs to the main floor of the tavern. Elijah opened the small office and true to his word Mr. Anderson had left the mail pouch ready to go. I gathered it up and Elijah accompanied me to the stable. We had my horse saddled in no time and I was ready to leave.

"If you make it back this way, remember Aunt Charlotte

and Father are getting married in early May. Try to make it if you can. You take care of yourself." Elijah extended his hand.

I did likewise and gave his hand a good solid shake. "I really enjoyed the hospitality. Please thank your grandfather and Aunt Charlotte for me. And you take care of yourself too."

With that I grabbed the reins of my horse and led him over to a convenient rail to use as a boost up into the saddle. As I rode away from the Anderson Tavern, I waved goodbye to Elijah. I didn't know if I would ever see him again, but I counted him among my best friends. As I quietly rode past the front of the tavern, I caught sight of Aunt Charlotte in an upper window also waving goodbye. I returned her wave and thought of how lucky Elijah was to have her as his future mother.

I trotted easterly down Duke of Gloucester Street toward Mr. Henry's Law Office. To my amazement there was a light glowing from the front window. As I stopped, I jumped down and grabbed the mail pouch. Williamsburg might be a safe town, but it was still my responsibility to guard the mail.

I walked up the steps to the front door and gently knocked on it to see if anyone was about. I heard someone coming.

"Well look who is here so early in the morning. My, what they say about farmers getting up at the crack of dawn must be the truth. Come in Will. I bet you have not had any breakfast," said Mr. Henry.

"No sir," I replied as I entered his front parlor. "I'd hope to get a biscuit or two down the road a piece."

"I have fresh biscuits and even some coffee for you. Sit and we'll talk while you eat."

Mr. Henry was dressed in a long, white night shirt. His head was bare; his nightcap lay on a chair next to the back door of the parlor. He retrieved a silver tray with a basket of biscuits, a small plate of butter and a silver pot of coffee. It was breakfast fit for a post rider that was for sure.

"I can't be staying too long sir. Captain Clark is expecting me to meet him this morning and I have to leave in order to avoid him."

"Is there something I need to know Will?" he asked.

"Perhaps," I replied a little non-committal. I thought for a second and decided to tell Mr. Henry the whole story about meeting Father in the jail and the conversation I had with the Captain afterwards. Mr. Henry listened intently.

"Will it does seem the Captain is up to no good. I expect he will try to use your father's predicament as leverage to get you to talk to him about the goings on between Fredrick and Williamsburg. Good that you are leaving early. I would advise you to stay away from Captain Clark. He might even take more drastic action if he thought it could make you inform your friends and neighbors, but enough said on that issue. I only need to reassure you that I will defend your father to the utmost of my abilities. Now I'm afraid I need to speed you on your way." With that he produced a small cotton bag and stuffed as many biscuits in it as it would hold and handed it to me. "Here, you may need some nourishment on your way back to Fredrick. When you come back from your trek into the Blue Ridge be sure to stop by and see me. I hope to have your father home with you before then."

I grabbed the bag, thanked Mr. Henry, and hurried to my

horse. It took only a second to get the post satchel fixed on my saddle and mount. I waved to Mr. Henry without another word and spurred my horse down the street toward the edge of town.

As luck would have it, I'd gone less than 100 yards when I encountered a British sentry post guarding the entrance to the town. I could not believe my misfortune. I slowed my horse down to a walk as I approached the sentries.

"That's far enough lad. Now what you be out for this early in the morning?," questioned the redcoat sergeant.

"I'm a post rider on my way to Charles with the mail. I need to get an early start so I can be there when shops open," I replied trying to think of a good excuse to be out this early in the morning.

"Right nice excuse lad, but that won't work. No one leaves the town before the Captain inspects the post at seven o'clock. Just git down off your horse and tie'er up. You've a little wait."

"If I must wait, then I'll just go back into town and wait in a more comfortable place."

"Lad, I said hop down off that horse now. You're not going anywhere," bellowed the Sergeant as he readied his rifle to emphasize his order.

I had to think quickly. "Sorry sergeant I didn't mean to disobey you. I wasn't trying to do nothing. Oh, I got some fresh biscuits before I left, would you like some," I asked, grabbing the bag and shoving them toward the Sergeant.

The Sergeant looked suspicious, then grabbed the bag. "Right warm they are lad. So go over and tie your horse up and me and the corporal will gladly let you have a couple of your biscuits."

The Sergeant turned his back and walked over to the

corporal. They greedily opened the bag and started to divide the biscuits between themselves. Their rifles were now leaning against the wall of their little guard shack. I walked my horse to the side of the road just far enough that I was near the end of the barrier they had extended across the road. I continued to walk my horse around the barrier. The soldiers were too interested in their biscuits and didn't pay me any attention.

I was now about 20 feet past the barrier and knew it was time to make a run for it. I spurred my horse and was at a full run in less than 15 feet. Behind me I heard the shouts of the soldiers and they let a stream of profanity. I pulled my horse hard to the left and cleared the picket fence in front of a small cottage just as I heard the muskets fire. Tree branches behind me shattered as the musket balls thankfully missed their mark. Around the side of the house, we went over the back fence through an open field. It took only a few moments and we were on the road to Charles at a dead run.

I counted my blessings a bit too soon. There looming in front of me was a contingent of British dragoons returning from an early patrol. I had no time to react, I plunged my horse head long into the column splitting it in two.

"Sorry gentlemen, I hollered out! In a hurry!" I howled as I created mayhem.

More cursing and shouts, but at least this time there were no shots. The dragoons were too busy trying to regain control of their horses. As I glanced over my shoulder, I saw one green-coated dragoon get tossed in the air by his bucking horse. I only hoped they didn't recognize me.

The Charles town hall clock said it was 7:45 when I arrived in town. I was actually tired and worn out by the ride from Williamsburg. I was ever alert to the possibility that there might be another British patrol or checkpoint along the way. I had ridden my horse hard the whole way and he wasn't going any further. I headed straight to the stable to take care of him, rub him down, and get him some water and a few oats. Another post rider would be able to bring him back to Fredrick on another day.

Normally bickering over a new mount would have taken most of the day, but the Committee had a veritable stable of horses for use by postal riders. There was always one or two available to the rider who had pushed his mount too hard as I had. Once I had arranged for the new mount, a strong-looking brown gelding, I walked the post over to Dr. Smith's Apothecary. By then it was already 8:30.

As I entered the front door the bell announced my arrival. Mrs. Smith called from the back, "Be with you in a moment."

I responded loudly, "It's Will Jones, Mrs. Smith, I have the post."

Instantly she appeared at the doorway with a huge grin on her face. It was truly a warm and generous smile. "Why Will, you're back so soon. I thought you would at least take a couple of days in Williamsburg to visit with your father."

I hung my head a little, "I did get to see him, but things got a little complicated and Mr. Henry, Father's lawyer, thought it best that I leave town. I left early this morning and had to run through a British checkpoint. Luckily, they were poor shots. Then as luck would have it, I literally ran through a dragoon patrol just outside

Williamsburg. This has not been a good morning. Worst of all, in order to divert the guards at that checkpoint, I gave them my fresh biscuits Mr. Henry had made special for me."

"You poor boy," she said, shaking her head and now holding my head in her warm delicate hands. "Well come on back, the Doctor and I are just finishing up breakfast and I think we might have a little left for you."

As we walked back to the kitchen, she insisted on holding me around my shoulders as if I was on my last leg. Her touch was kind and reassuring. I only hoped the Doctor hadn't eaten all the biscuits.

"Will," the Doctor shouted as he rose from the table, a napkin still stuck in his shirt and a jellied biscuit in his left hand. "Sit down son and have some breakfast, you must be starving. What time did you leave Williamsburg this morning?"

Before I could say anything, he literally stuffed the jellied biscuit in my mouth. Unable to talk with half a biscuit stuffed in, I chewed instead of talked.

Unperturbed he continued, "Let me see, if you are here now, knowing that you are a responsible horseman that means you took care of your horse before you came over here, and figuring you rode hard to get here, you must have left Williamsburg right at dawn. What possessed you to leave so early?"

I swallowed and told Dr. and Mrs. Wilson the same story I had related to Mr. Henry only with the addition of running the guard post and riding through the dragoons.

Mrs. Wilson listened intently all the while cutting open biscuits and filling them with jelly and Virginia ham. I had to lick my lips several times as my mouth drooled for another biscuit.

"Interesting story Will. I am disturbed by Captain Clark's actions. I'm afraid we must somehow neutralize his curiosity. We'll just have to keep him too busy with 'friendly' informants. It will also give us an opportunity to see who else he is either interested in or has already coerced. There is no dignity in these British scoundrels. Seems like we are seeing a change in the British attitude toward us. This is the first I've heard of sentries guarding the entrances to Williamsburg at night. Oh, you mentioned you saw green-coated dragoons?"

My mouth was full of biscuits and ham. Ill-mannered or not, I responded. "Yes, sir. There were about four green-coated dragoons wearing black hats with plumes on the left side, riding near the front of the column. One, I think, was an officer who was riding next to the officer of the patrol. The rest were redcoat dragoons." I swallowed and took another bite of biscuit.

"These green-coats are new to the area. We'll have to find out who they are. We'll have to definitely think of a good name for them. Nothing like lobster-backs to irritate our British guests," he said as he laughed out loud.

The questioning died down and the Wilsons allowed me to stuff in as many biscuits as I could eat. After about another 15 minutes I was stuffed. Seeing my satisfaction, Mrs. Wilson quickly put a cup of hot coffee in front of me. The aroma was delightful. I held the cup in both hands up to my nose and let the wonderful smell invade all of my senses. Although still hot, the dark enchanting liquid was at that moment nectar of the gods. Now relaxed, I filled the Wilsons in on my conversation with Father and told them of his directions for me to go over the mountains for several weeks. At first, I thought Dr. Wilson might object.

"Your father has to be a man of great wisdom, Will. As a matter of fact, word has reached us that something is happening in Watauga that might have a bearing on our situation here. We've toyed with the idea of sending someone reliable to investigate, but could not think of anyone who would not raise attention. You and Philip will be our perfect undeclared emissaries. Eat a little more and I will write Captain Hawkins a message endorsing you lads going over the mountain. Just remember to be careful lads."

Dr. Wilson excused himself and went to write a short note to Captain Hawkins. Mrs. Wilson stayed with me while I finished my coffee. We chatted about different things. I even told her a little bit about the Andersons in Williamsburg and how they had befriended me. I was careful not to betray their trust. Shortly, Dr. Wilson returned with the note I was to take to Captain Hawkins.

As Dr. Wilson was giving me my final instructions for my trip the front door opened and a voice called out for Dr. Wilson with some urgency. We quickly went to see what the commotion was about.

"Dr. Wilson, the British are looking for your post rider there," said the farmer as he pointed at me. "Seems like the lad ran a sentry post in Williamsburg, then attacked a British patrol just outside of town and injured several dragoons. They are mad as hornets. The patrol is only a few miles outside of town. They have been stopping at every farm asking questions. They still don't know the boy there is a post rider, but it won't take 'em long before someone talks. Best the boy skedaddle as quickly as he can."

Dr. Wilson turned to me. "Off with you Will, be careful. The post isn't ready; just leave it here. Farley, go with young Will over to the stable, take the horse he rode this morning, and move it to a farm west of town. Will, you take off as fast as you can. Can you get to Fredrick without going over the roads?"

"Yes sir. It's kind of rough going in places, but I know the way," I lied. I had heard of the old Indian trail that went through the fields and woods, but did not know exactly where it began.

"I'll show him the start of the old Indian trail. It's still used by riders wanting to cut a couple of hours off their ride to Fredrick. Will, it's go'in to test your skills as a rider," joked Farley as he clapped me on the back.

I said my goodbyes to the Wilsons and got a big hug and kiss from Mrs. Wilson. It looked as if she had tears in her eyes.

Farley and I raced to the stable. I was surprised he was so quick. As we reached the stable door, we heard the sounds of horses entering the square. A hurried glance over our shoulders confirmed my worst fears. The redcoats had arrived. I knew I was in trouble.

"Will, listen to me carefully. See that street over there?" Farley pointed to a dirt side street catty corner to the stable. "That street runs for about 200 yards and ends at a rail fence. To one side is a gate. You won't have time to use the gate, make your horse jump over the fence. You'll see the path through the field and see it disappear in the scope of woods beyond. Keep on that path through the woods until it comes down to the stream. Go up the stream about 30 yards and you will pick up the path again. If'n you can read trails you'll make it to Fredrick in a little under two hours. Good luck, son. I have to take your old mount out the back.

Unfortunately you are going to draw their attention. Ride close to your saddle and don't give them no shot."

"Thanks Mr. Farley. I appreciate it and I will be part of that saddle."

I pointed out my old mount to Farley and he swung up on the poor tired horse without a saddle and raced out of the back of the barn with nothing more than a halter and lead rope as his bridle. Thankfully my new mount had already been saddled. The groom held him as I jumped on, prepared to burst out of the barn at a full gallop. I only hoped my steed knew how to jump.

"Ready," I exclaimed as I gathered my reins up short and gave the brown a good kick.

"Godspeed!" said the groom as he gave the brown a good slap on the rump for added measure.

The brown leaped forward like a banshee out of hell. We burst through the open barn doors right into a group of three mounted dragoons conducting for me. Brown hit the first horse broadside which caused that horse to fall over on its side and trap it's rider underneath. The rider on the other side fell off his horse, reins still in his grip. The third rider struggled for control of his horse. I pulled the brown hard to the left and managed to turn him in a tight circle. As we came back around, the one dragoon who was still mounted had managed to control his horse now and had drawn his pistol and was pointing it in my general direction. He fired without warning. The shot zoomed past my right ear and impacted on the barn wall.

Things suddenly seemed to be in slow motion. My assailant shoved his spent pistol back in his saddle holster and reached for his sword. Instinctively, I reached for Anne and felt the comfort of her grip in my hand. As I drew her from her holster, I had to control Brown as I attempted to cock the hammer with the reins still in my left hand. This minor correction put me directly in the path of the dragoon as he mounted his charge toward me, saber held high. Brown steady, held his ground as I aimed and fired almost point blank into the charging dragoon. Little Anne exploded with a tremendous boom and a cloud of smoke. The bullet found a mark somewhere on the dragoon. All I saw was the dragoon fall backwards off his horse, saber flying in the air as he lost his grip.

A clamor came from the other end of the street. "Seize him!" I heard. As I looked right, I saw a confusion of dragoons riding pell mell toward me. One dragoon had already drawn his short musket and was attempting to shoot me as he rode. The rider next to him, probably an officer, swung his saber up under the musket and connected with it causing it to fire high over my head. I heard, "Seize him, don't kill him!"

Suddenly, a hand grasped my right leg and another hand tried to reach across and grab the reins. It was a British dragoon, one of those that was still kicking. Where he came from I can't recall. With Anne still in my grip, I swung my right hand as hard as I could. The butt of Anne's grip made a solid connection with the dragoon's face. He released his grip and buckled at his knees, while gripping his now broken nose. It was time for me to make a hasty retreat.

I spurred Brown toward the side street only 50 yards ahead of the lead riders. As I passed onto the street at a full run, I discerned I was being chased by two green-backs and three lobster-backs. The street seemed exceedingly short and Brown and I approached the end of the street and the rail fence in short order. Brown started to slow down, cognizant of the fence ahead. He was obviously used to using the gate. I had no choice but dig deep into his flanks and push him forward. He responded by surging forward.

As we approached the rails, I said a very short prayer of hope. Brown made a minor adjustment to his gate and then sailed over the rail fence in a perfectly executed jump. I, less practiced, held on for dear life. We hit the other side without a loss in stride. We raced over the field and up a small incline toward the scope of woods. I reined in Brown for a second at the top of the hill to check on my pursuers. Somehow the lobster-backs had managed to squeeze the green-backs to the rear. I noticed a lot of unfriendly shoving going on. As they approached the rail fence the green-backs still behind, pulled up. The first steed sailed over the fence; the lobster-back failed to negotiate the landing and ended up in heap to one side. The second horse refused and that rider went sailing over the rail fence. The third horse, having nowhere to go, made a sudden left turn and threw his rider into the gate next to the fence. The two green-coats laughed out loud and shouted something like "louts" to their fallen comrades. Without hesitation, both green-backs spurred their horses and in perfect unison gracefully sailed over the rail fence in extraordinary form.

Oh, they were excellent riders. I was not out of trouble yet. I reined Brown into the woods and soon found myself racing down a narrow tunnel of trees to a stream below. Brown skidded to a stop at the stream and without waiting for my urging leaped into the shallow stream and turned upstream. He knew where he was going.

I felt as if I was only baggage. Not 30 yards later, Brown exited the stream on to another narrow trail. I again restrained him to gauge my pursuit. I heard them in the distance as they entered the woods. They were not letting up, that was for sure.

Brown and I raced through the woods for a good two miles before we came to a large open field that inclined away from us. We didn't let up. The field was larger than it looked, possibly almost three miles in length while the width narrowed to the trail at the end. This time I rode into the shadows of the woods before I halted Brown. I kept the gelding pointing ahead just in case. As I peered over my shoulder I saw the green-backs break out of the woods below, one at a time. They halted just inside the field. One dragoon took out a long cylindrical tube which I suspect was a spyglass, and surveyed the area. They appeared to discuss their dilemma and finally agreed to continue forward, much to my disappointment. We surged forward again. My only hope was that Brown was well rested and their mounts were already tired from the ride to Charles. I didn't try again to check on my pursuers. I had to get to Fredrick and hide.

Chapter 26

The Preparation

The Indian Trail did not lead directly to Fredrick as thought, rather it passed near the town to the east, some two miles away. It was a small path that I had never seen that threw me onto the road to Fredrick. I did notice the trail no wider than a deer trail picked up on the other side of the road and continued to lead west-north-west toward the Blue Ridge, a fact that I tucked into the far reaches of my mind. I tarried for a moment; an indecisive moment. I pondered whether I should take time to cover my tracks, continue on the Indian Trail, and loop back into town, or just put as much distance as possible between myself and my pursuers. I compromised; I reined Brown over to the side of the road. While not firm his tracks would be partially hidden by the tall grass, I hoped. After a hundred yards I turned Brown on to the road and resumed my pace.

As we approached the sentry post to town, I slowed down. I needed to enlist the aid of the sentries if I could.

"Morning, gentlemen!" I yelled out as I approached.

"Morning, Will," came the reply in unison as the two sentries didn't budge from their seats by the fire.

I reined in Brown over to where they were comfortably seated. "Gentlemen, I seem to have picked up two green-coated British dragoons that are on my trail. I would appreciate it if you did not inform them of my passing. It seems they may be determined to apprehend me and take me back to Williamsburg."

The older sentry, who was in his mid-50s at least, looked with a gleam in his eye, "Say, Will, do you have a price on your head yet, or is this just your first offense?"

"Sorry, first offense. Better luck next time."

The younger, who was almost 20 or so, replied with mock disappointment at this, "You know they are just not making criminals as good as they used to."

"Not a problem Will," laughed the older sentry. "You were never here; in fact, I don't even know who you are."

"Who you talking to Uncle Jake? I don't see nobody!" added his younger partner.

"Godspeed son. You did say green-backs. Never seen any of them around here. We'll keep our eyes peeled. About how far behind are they?"

"Probably not more than five miles behind if that much. They're pretty good horsemen for Brits."

"More than likely, they be some of those Tory Loyalists from South Carolina. Can't trust those bastards. Still don't worry, you go on and take off."

I gave a final wave as I left. I looked back and saw the sentries stand up and stretch. At least they would be standing when the green-backs came by. I reached town a little later and made straight for the barn behind Captain Hawkins' store. Brown was hot and sweaty. I couldn't afford to work him down, so I quickly brushed him with hay, covered him with a blanket, and gave him some feed and water. I put him in the darkest part of the barn. I could only hope. I tossed my wet saddle into the grain bin and covered it with a large piece of heavy cloth they called a tarpaulin. I then covered it with grain in an attempt to hide it. I ran to the widow's house, ran inside, and noticed no one was home. I changed clothes quickly, hiding my dirty clothes in a loose wall panel, washed my face, and then sauntered over to the general store to take up my position as the erstwhile store clerk.

As I entered the back door store, I called out for Captain Hawkins.

"Up front here, Will."

I whistled as I walked slowly up to the store area and grabbed a broom on my way, hitting at a speck of dirt here and there. As I came through the door, I continued to whistle and sweep at spots of dirt. The midday light was streaming through the front windows and I really couldn't see who was in the front of the store. I worked my way down the aisle and noted with curiosity that Captain Hawkins was silent. By now my eyes had adjusted and I could now see the front.

There standing next to Captain Hawkins were two green-coated dragoons much worse for the wear, with scowls on their faces. My legs began to shake. I didn't know what to do, run or face the consequences.

Captain Hawkins broke the silence. "Will, come up front

here and re-sweep by the front door. Seems like these gentlemen forgot to knock off their boots before they came in."

"Right away sir. And I'd just gotten through with that not an hour ago, but that's not a problem gentleman, so long as you buy a little something while you're here." I had recovered a little. At least my legs were moving and not shaking as badly.

The taller of the two, who was a giant at six feet, responded in a gruff, no-nonsense tone. "Boy, we're not interested in making any purchases. We are only interested in information. Where have you been all morning?"

"Well, if it is any of your business, which it ain't …"

"Will, mind your manners. These gentlemen are looking for a rider who ran a sentry post in Williamsburg, attacked a dragoon patrol on the outskirts of the town and then in Charles, and shot and seriously wounded a dragoon in a daring escape. These gentlemen followed him here. Have you seen a stranger or anything unusual this morning?"

"No sir," I responded as I tried to shrink in size. "How do you gentlemen know your highwayman came here?"

"It wasn't a highwayman, lad. In fact, it was a young man about five foot eight inches, about 140 pounds, light complexion, brown hair, about 18 to 20 years of age. He's an experienced horseman and may have done some fox hunting in the past." The younger dragoon seemed convinced of his description. Although he was off about 20 pounds and a couple of inches, I did like the part about being an experienced horseman who may have run to the hounds.

"No one hereabouts by that description. No one rides to the

hounds. If that be true, you'd best be looking more around Richmond and further South. We don't hunt foxes from a horse here." The strength was returning to my legs. "Still, you didn't say why you think he came this way." I was pushing my luck.

The big dragoon nodded toward his companion, "Harry here spent a year with the Mohawk upcountry learning the forest arts. He's practically half Mohawk, so good he's good at tracking. Not bad for a young English dandy from London."

The younger dragoon smiled a little. "He came this way alright. If we'd had another 30 minutes, we would have caught him still in the saddle. I lost the track as we got into town and he mixed the tracks with the normal traffic."

I felt a sigh of relief. I was quick to help them with useless information. "Now if he was from hunt country, he'd rode straight through town and out the west end then taken the road that heads southwest toward Richmond. It's a pretty easy road."

I noticed Captain Hawkins wasn't talking. He was letting me do all the talking. He acted unconcerned and was in the process of packing and lighting his pipe.

"No use of wasting any more time here Harry. Let's go. Maybe he did turn back to Richmond. Don't worry gentlemen, we will catch him and when we do, he'll regret he ever crossed our path." The dragoons turned and walked out the door.

I moved to the door and watched them mount their already tired horses. Instead of turning toward Richmond, the dragoons gave up the chase and turned back toward Charles.

As they rode out of view, I turned to face a stern-looking Captain Hawkins smoking his pipe. "I think you better explain why you shot a British dragoon."

I wanted to deny the charge at first but thought better. I merely said, "Yes sir."

I told my story in parts, last part first and then first part last. It took most of an hour to tell the story, with all the interruption of customers coming in and out. Finally, I concluded with Father's direction to go to the mountains and learn the forest arts as that green-back dragoon had obviously done.

"Dr. Wilson thinks your father is correct and I'll have to agree. There seems to be a change in the mood of the British. They seem just a little testy right now. It might be a good idea if a bunch of you lads took a trip to toughen you up and let you see the backcountry. I'll look around and see who can take you lads."

"I thought only Philip and I would go and stay with the Cherokee for a month or so. I didn't figure there'd be a whole troop of us going."

"Will, ever since you boys took off with those rifles and high-tailed into the mountains, I've been thinking whether or not you boys had been properly prepared to go it on your own. Good that you ran into the Cherokee, even though they did give you a fright. It would be good to spend some time with them, at least them that are friendly to us. But you also need to spend some time with the settlers over the mountain and learn their skills too. Tell you what, I'll send you and Philip on a scouting trip when he gets back from his post run. We'll get together and talk about this trip. Anyway, I need a post rider to head to the backcountry and drop off some mail at Sycamore Falls. They've set up a little settlement and they have a mail collection point there. So, take off, spend some time with your mother and siblings. I know how to find you."

"Thank you, sir. Oh, sorry about not being able to stay to pick up the post."

The Captain just laughed as I scooted out the front door of the store in search of my family. I had so much to tell them and then again it wasn't much at all, but at least there was hope. The first place I checked was the Hawkins house to check up on the kids. It seemed like it had been a month since I had seen them last. I was fast becoming the brother that left home at 16 and disappeared.

As I entered the picket fence of the Hawkins house, I heard my mother reciting a math lesson to the kids. A chill went through my body. I always found math an impossible task. Adding and subtracting was fine as long as the numbers weren't too big, but when Mother spoke of multiplying and dividing, my mind fogged over. I mounted the porch and peeked into the window of the house. There she was sitting in front of a parlor full of children from three to 12-years-old. There must have been at least 15 children in the room. She didn't see me, so I went to the other front room and saw Mrs. Hawkins and some of the other town ladies having a quilting bee. Mrs. Hawkins saw me and waved. She put her index finger to her lips to signal me to be quiet. She motioned to me to go around to the back door. I scurried off the front porch and ran around to the back door.

"My, Will Jones, how long have you been gone? A whole two days or is it three? I never know where you are. It seems like it's been ages since I've seen you."

Mrs. Hawkins grabbed me and gave me a big hug. I wasn't too sure about all of this hugging, but over the past week or so, I had been hugged by more different women than I had in my previous existence. The judgment was still to be made whether or not it was an enjoyable experience or not. There were some feelings stirring deep inside that I didn't know nothing about.

"I haven't been gone that long, Mrs. Hawkins. Just a couple of days, but I have been awfully busy being a post rider. Mr. Hawkins gave me some time off since he wants to send Philip and me over the mountains with the post in the next couple of days. So, I came by to see the little ones. But you are right, it seems like ages since I've been back and I got to wrestle with them."

"Well come inside. I got some biscuits left over from breakfast if you're hungry and we'll be having some stew for lunch. We have a whole bunch of people over today. The ladies have the quilting bee going in the front room and your mother has started teaching a few of the kids their ABCs. In fact, she is so good, I'm going to ask to find a permanent place where she can hold school, so all the children in town can go. This idea that everyone is taught at home just won't do. We're fairly modern around here and we need to make a school for our children just like they have in Williamsburg and Richmond. I think your mother would make a grand teacher. What do you think of my idea Will?"

"That sounds great, as long as I don't have to go to school. Mother already taught me everything I need to know and your husband said he would teach everything I need to know about the mercantile business."

"William, I didn't ask for a long dissertation on the quality of your education. I'm sure you are well versed in the ABCs, reading, and writing. I'm talking about the little ones and the other children in the community. Now I expect your full support, young man. Agreed?"

"Yes ma'am. You have my full support. No questions or further commentaries as long as I don't have to go."

"William!" said Mrs. Hawkins sharply. "Your full support! No quibbling."

"Yes ma'am." I limited my answer this time, although I wasn't too sure what quibbling meant.

"Now sit down. We need to think of a good place to use as the school until we can build one."

I knew right away there was only one building in town not currently in use, but I wasn't too sure Captain Hawkins would give up the old armory. Mrs. Hawkins went over every building in town and discarded each as too cold and drafty, not enough room, or unavailable. Finally, she turned to me.

"All right William. You tell me what you think."

"Well Mrs. Hawkins, there is only one building not being used and that is the armory on the square. It needs cleaning up and the fireplace inside needs a little repair, but that's the only place that's available and fairly weatherproof."

"My, Mr. Hawkins will never agree to that. It's his armory, I mean where would he put all the muskets and powder? Oh, I forgot there are no muskets and powder." She brightened up. "What an excellent suggestion Will. Since there are no muskets or powder left," she winked at me, "then the school would be a perfect use for the building. What a great reflection on our community, turning our armory into a school for our children. The British would be absolutely flabbergasted. Now to tell my husband."

Mrs. Hawkins now had a mission. She jumped up from the table, kissed me on the top of my head, grabbed her shawl, excused herself to her quilting bee, and was out the front door in a flash. I felt sorry for Captain Hawkins. He didn't stand a chance. I only hoped that she didn't attach my name to the idea.

Chapter 27

The Plan

The next two days were a blur. I remember playing with the little ones and taking the opportunity to tell Mother about my experiences and Father's orders to me. She was quiet and affirmed her commitment to following Father's wishes, though she did remind me that she still sewed my pants.

Most of what I remember is the cleaning and painting of the armory, which became the new school. Captain Hawkins had resisted the best he could for most of the day but caved in by nightfall. For my part in the conspiracy, I was detailed to help with the renovation of the old structure. I had the unenviable task of re-mortaring the chimney of the fireplace, which meant it had to be cleaned first. I was a black soot cake for most of the time. I vowed never to be a chimney sweep, that was for sure. I had to endure the laughter of the whole town as I walked from the armory to the horse trough at the front of the square. I jumped in clothes and all. I didn't care that it was only 45 degrees. Of course, I then had to clean and drain the trough and refill it with clean water.

Will Jones

After I cleaned the chimney, it was my job to go back up in there and re-mortar the stack. This was of course a thankless job and I spent most of the second afternoon inside the chimney stack painstakingly mortaring between each brick. I finally reached the bottom of the stack just before sundown. I then had to go back up the outside and put a board cap on the chimney to keep the cold air out so the mortar would dry properly without cracking. Someone found an old cast iron stove and temporarily rigged up a flue to the outside to keep the inside of the new schoolhouse warm overnight. I volunteered to stay the night in the schoolhouse to tend to the fire. After all, I had a passel of siblings that were going to be schooled there and Mother was going to be the schoolmarm.

Just as I was settling in for the night the door of the schoolhouse opened and in popped Philip fresh from this post run to Richmond.

"Nice place you got here Will. Just hope we won't be forced to attend. I can't see myself sitting in one room an entire day. I have to be free to roam the store or do chores in the stable."

"My sentiments exactly Philip. I made Mrs. Hawkins a deal and said I would help renovate this place as long as I did not have to attend. I think I have escaped for the time being." We both laughed.

"I heard you ran into trouble on the way back from Williamsburg."

"Who told you that?" I asked.

"Well, first of all, I ran into a bunch of really mad dragoons in Charles. They actually took me into custody and questioned me for about an hour. It wasn't too bad, since I was carrying several letters to the Governor and could prove I had just arrived from Richmond. When they described the rider, even though they were off by a large margin, I knew it had to be you. Of course, I told them right away, 'It has to be that rascal Will Jones from Fredrick.'" Philip laughed at his joke.

"You didn't?" I asked half-seriously.

"You are too easy! Of course, I didn't. I feigned complete ignorance. After a while, they got frustrated and let me go. Oh, the dragoon you shot was not hurt too seriously, but the bullet broke his shoulder. Dr. Wilson removed the ball and patched him up good as new. He'll make a full recovery in about six weeks if he keeps the wound clean and bandaged. Did you really shoot him without provocation?"

"Oh, so now you believe a dragoon? Of course, I didn't. The bastard tried to kill me. If Brown hadn't been dancing around, he would have shot me square through the heart and besides, after missing, he grabbed his saber and came after me. It was self-defense pure and simple. I rest my case."

"In that case, how did you miss? I thought you were a better shot than that."

I jumped up from my sleep sack and tackled Philip as he stood there. I guess we must have wrestled for a good half-hour or more. We did more laughing than wrestling. Finally exhausted, we both gave up.

"To tell the truth Philip, I tried to shoot him in the middle of the chest. I feel lucky that I hit him at all. If I hadn't, he would have sliced me in two. I can safely say that was a harrowing experience."

"Were you scared?

"I must have been. At the encounter in Charles, my heart was racing, I was reacting to things as they happened without thinking and all I knew was that I had to get out of there as quickly as I could. You have to understand the whole morning was more or less a running battle. I just did things on instinct. I really didn't know that I was scared until I got back here and the two green-coats showed up in the store. I almost collapsed then and there; If I hadn't had the broom in my hand I would have. I must have been afraid the whole time and just didn't know it until then."

"The green-coat dragoon officer gave you a left-handed compliment. He called you a seasoned horseman and damn experienced marksman. He had a very high regard for you."

"I wonder what he would have said if he knew I almost crapped in my pants when the bullet whizzed past my ear!"

"How about a stinking, experienced marksman!"

We laughed again until our sides hurt. If we didn't make fun of my narrow escape, I'm afraid I would have been immobilized with fear. The whole day I had driven myself like a man possessed. I tried to keep my mind from wandering back to the previous day's experience. Every time I failed and thought about it, I realized what a close call I had. I had cheated death this time, but I would learn later he would be only a step behind.

"I understand from my little conversation with Captain Griffin that you and I are going to Sycamore Falls as a scouting party for a large contingent later on," said Philip with an inquiring tilt to his voice.

I took a deep breath and gave him the whole story of what

went on in Williamsburg, my meeting with Father, the Captain's unusual interest in me, and my meeting with Mr. Henry. Then he understood at least as much as I did.

"You know Will, this could not come at a better time. I hear something is going on up at Watauga. That's what they call the community up Sycamore Falls. First let me explain what Watauga is. A group of settlers from Virginia and a failed insurrection, by the regulators in North Carolina, a bunch of them also pulled up stakes and went over the mountains. They rented land from the Cherokee and formed a community of sorts in and around Sycamore Falls on the Watauga River. They eventually wrote up a charter for themselves with basic laws and called themselves the Watauga Association. There's a big meeting going on there right now between a land speculator named Henderson and Oconistoto, a Cherokee chief of some stature."

"I thought the British didn't want setters over the mountains?"

"The British have a hard enough time just keeping us under control here, much less trying to prevent settlers going into the wilderness. They have tried to get the Cherokee to help stop the settlers, but most of my people don't see the settlers as a threat, so long as they keep going. Besides, we are learning a lot of good farming skills from these settlers. Right now, there is a pretty good relationship between most of the Cherokee and the settlers, but there is a faction headed by Cui Canacina who opposes the settlers. You may know him as 'Dragging Canoe.'"

"I heard of him. I understand he is a pretty powerful chief and has a large following. Does he really want to evict all of the settlers out of the Blue Ridge?"

"Yeah, he does. If the English keep backing him, I'm afraid there might be trouble. Our tribe is not a single united tribe as some people think. We are sort of like a confederation of Cherokee tribes, each with a chief and council. It is very hard for any one tribe to dominate the others, but in the same sense, it lets tribes act independently of the others regardless of the impact on the whole."

"Sounds a lot like our colonies. Looked at as a whole by England, but in reality, just a bunch of dissimilar regional groups each vying for attention. We better get some sleep. Captain Hawkins wants us to get on our way early in the morning. He's already got our supplies ready and waiting. I was only waiting for you. At least I get out of attending the first day of school, for which I am very grateful," I added.

I helped Philip roll out his bedroll near the old stove and I put in a few more pieces of wood. I guess we talked and laughed for about another hour before I finally drifted off to sleep. It was a restful sleep brought on by all the hard work I had done during the day.

Chapter 28

Ready to Leave

The next morning came a little too early for me. I had tended the fire several times during the night in hopes of keeping the armory warm enough so that some of the heat would keep the new mortar in the chimney from getting too cold. I think that my efforts paid off, for when I woke at sunrise, the room was fairly comfortable; perhaps on the cool side, but good enough for the mortar in the chimney. I put some more kindling in the stove and then went over and shook Philip.

"Let me stay here just a few minutes more. I need my sleep," moaned Philip.

"Come on Philip, we have to get the horses saddled, get a bite of breakfast, and then we are off on our great adventure."

"Mind if I sit this 'dance' out. I'm perfectly happy right where I am."

I gave Philip a swift kick in the butt, not a hard one, but enough of one to tell him it was time.

"Alright, I'll get up," he said grudgingly.

A few minutes later, we had rolled up our sleep sacks, packed our small kit bags, and headed to the barn. Dawn was just breaking as we entered. Captain Hawkins was already there packing one of the two pack horses we would take over the mountain with us.

"Nice to see you boys up so early this morning. I was worried I'd have to come over and wake you."

"I was awake tending the fire and thought we might as well get going," I said.

"Not me, I was sound asleep until this ruffian kicked me in the backside," laughed Philip.

Captain Hawkins laughed along with us. "Let me give you some final instructions. These pack horses have goods for Mr. Benjamin Peters, the sutler in Sycamore Falls. He has already paid for the goods so you don't need to get any money from him. Here is the inventory of the goods, the cost of the goods, and the remaining credit on his account with me. Just tell him before he orders any more goods, he needs to send me some more money. Do not under any circumstances take any money from Mr. Peters to bring back to me. It is his responsibility to send someone he trusts. You boys are capable and I trust you. It's some of the backwoods riff-raff that I don't trust. They would just as soon waylay you as look at you. Philip, you know where Fincastle is, don't you?"

"Yes, sir."

"There's a small general store owned by a friend of mine, James Brown. You'll meet a guide by the name of Lancaster who's there between the fifth and the seventh of each month. He'll guide you the rest of the way to Sycamore Falls. He is there to act as your guide and added protection for the goods. Now there are four trade rifles, shot, and powder for your father, Philip." Captain Hawkins showed us where they were packed.

"The rifles, shot, and powder you can take to your father once you get the other goods to the sutler. If you should run into a Cherokee hunting party, make sure they understand the rifles belong to your father. That should be enough to keep them from bothering you.

Philip spoke up. "What if the hunting party wants to trade with us? What are we supposed to do?"

"Once you hook up with Lancaster, he is responsible for the goods. He'll make the decision. If you run into a hunting party beforehand, try to keep from trading with them. I'll have to trust you boys to do the right thing if you get in a bind. Since you are your father's son, you should have no problems. I've put some coffee and beans in your provisions. If you have to you can use that to placate any disgruntled warriors. Now get your horses saddled and then we eat a good breakfast."

Philip and I saddled our horses in record time. I picked a small but sturdy roan gelding. Philip picked a similar size mare which was a dark brown with a black mane and tail. Horses smaller in stature were better for mountain work.

"One last time boys, these horses are a valuable commodity in the mountains. Each is worth at least 30 pounds apiece. I don't want either one of you to walk out, but if you get a good price for the pack horses you can sell 'em, but not a penny less than 30 pounds apiece."

In unison we said, "Yes, sir." I was a little confused though.

Could we sell the horses or should we sell the horses? Should we sell only the pack horses or should we sell our horses as well if we got a good price? I decided I would let Philip do the bargaining if it came to that, but I was certainly not going to sell my horse, that was for sure – I hoped.

Breakfast was the usual treat as it always was. I got to see the little ones while I was at the Hawkins' and tussled with them a little while. As we finished up breakfast, I slipped away to tell Mother goodbye.

When I arrived at the widow's house all was still quiet. I slipped upstairs and kissed Mother on the cheek. She briefly woke, stroked my cheek, and gave me her instructions. "Stay safe and come home soon." I kissed Mother one more time and slipped back downstairs and ran to the barn.

Captain Hawkins and Philip were making last-minute adjustments to the saddle and pack girts. I quickly inspected my saddle girt, adjusted it a little tighter, and declared myself ready.

"Here boys," said Captain Hawkins, as he threw each of us a piece of tanned leather. "These are finely oiled cows' knees to cover your flints in case of rain. It will keep your powder dry for a while if you're careful and keep your rifle level."

I'm not sure if the tanned leather was made from a cow's knee or not but it certainly had that appearance and looked as if it would snuggly fit over the flint and keep it dry. We tucked the "cow knees" into our kits and mounted. Captain Hawkins handed us each a smooth-bore trade rifle to take with us to hunt and provide us with protection. Philip also carried a saddle pistol and a hunting knife. Likewise, I carried Anne and a hunting knife. We were set to go.

"What you boys do up in the mountains will determine if I'm going to send the rest of the young'uns back with you later in the spring. Look for good places to camp, places to march to, and areas that have game we can use for food. We want to be able to challenge you boys, not march them to death, but on the other hand, we want them to be pushed a little so they will be toughened a bit. Off you go and above all, be careful."

The sun was just peeking over the horizon as we headed east on Charles Road, intent on picking up the Indian Trail to the Shenandoah Valley and Fincastle.

Chapter 29

The Ride

It was over 75 miles to the Shenandoah by way of Swift Run Gap. The first day we made good time and covered 50 miles. It was a fast pace, much too fast for us to sustain the whole way to Fincastle. That evening we made camp late in the day near a stream running out the Blue Ridge which lay just beyond. It was an uneventful evening, except that the night air turned cold and the ground still had not warmed up from the winter. All in all, it was still a restful evening.

The next morning, we got up early, let the horses graze some, and then started out up toward Swift Run Gap. The way up the hills and into the mountains wasn't particularly hard; It was just uphill all the way. By noon we had made only 15 miles, but at least the Gap was nearby. We rested the horses for an hour or so and then started the climb again. We reached the Gap by two o'clock, I think, and pushed on through. The trail was well worn and little trouble for the horses. Two hours later we came out the other side and were presented with a magnificent view of the Shenandoah

Valley and still another set of mountains beyond. We chose to camp near the entrance to the Gap because of the grazing and the available water.

Now into our third day, we set a steady pace westward down the valley floor. Small settlements and farms dotted the valley floor, but it was far from settled. There was still a lot of timbered land just waiting to be cleared. The people were generally friendly and gave us words of encouragement and refreshment when we stopped at a farmhouse or a small tavern. Surprisingly, there were no British soldiers patrolling this area. The settlers in the Shenandoah were on their own and for the most part, did not seem to miss any of the accouterments of our more civilized society back in the lower country.

I guess we did not seem too out of the ordinary to these mountain people. Two young boys out doing man's work seemed the norm around here. There were plenty of boys out and about our age already doing a share of the work on the frontier, but we also saw a lot of families on the move westward. Philip explained that this was the time of the year people moved farther westward in search of their own land. We must have passed 15 wagons on the way to Fincastle. On the evening of the fifth day, we arrived in Fincastle. It was a small community in the valley bearing the same name. Brown's Store was not hard to find. It was the only general store in town.

We tied the horses to the hitching rail in front of the store and went in to inquire about Mr. Lancaster. The shop owner was behind the counter.

"Excuse me, sir, are you Mr. Brown?" I asked.

"Why yes, I am, young man. And who might you boys be?" he asked.

"I'm Will and this here is Philip. We work for Captain Hawkins in Frederick."

"Well, I'll be. You must be the two lads he sent this way to meet up with Lancaster. Sarah," he called to the back, "Hawk's two boys are here on that supply run. Come on out and meet them."

"I'll be right there, James," came the reply.

Mrs. James came out the back with a baby in her arms. He could not have been more than four or five months. At the moment he was attached to his mother's breast and was not going to let go. He was a big strapping baby he was, rosy cheeks and fat legs and arms with blond tufts of hair on his head. He eyed both Philip and me with suspicion and quickly buried his eyes in his mother's chest.

"Good evening ma'am," we said together.

"So you boys are doing business for the old Hawk."

"Yes, ma'am," said Philip. I nodded. We had never heard anyone refer to Captain Hawkins as "Hawk" before and I guess we had a quizzical look on our faces.

"You boys got to be the politest boys I've seen in a long time. I bet you say 'yes, sir' and 'no, sir' out of habit."

"Yes, sir," we replied.

"Now see, Sarah, Thomas is going to learn those same manners. I like that in a young man. You two boys are right fine lads. Tell you what, why don't you take your mounts around back to the barn. I'll go ahead and close down and we can go next door to the tavern, find Lancaster, and have supper. And don't worry about the cost of the food. A little stew won't break us, will it

Sarah?"

"We would be more than honored to have two fine young gentlemen from the low country dine with us tonight. Maybe you can show some of these men around here what manners really are."

We hustled outside, grabbed our mounts, and went around back to the barn. It took us about 30 minutes to rub down the mounts, feed, and water them. After we put our goods away in the storeroom and locked it, we walked back around to the front of the store and on to the tavern next door. As we entered the log structure the room became suddenly quiet. There was a big great room, not well lighted, and it had an open ceiling all the way to the roof. The air was relatively fresh, I guess due to all the air pouring in from the holes in the log chinking.

"Evening," I said in my friendliest voice. "We're looking for Mr. Brown and his wife."

"Those the lowlanders we heard about?" someone in the back of the room asked.

"Must be," someone else said. "Them stories make those boys out to be a tad taller than what they actually are."

"Slim, I'd be careful if I was you. Last man that made fun of a boy from Frederick is missing an ear. And the little 'un there be the one that already kilt himself a redcoat in Charles, mite more than you done so far."

"I didn't kill any redcoat in Charles, I only wounded him," I replied loudly in an angry tone.

"See Slim, I done told you those boys from Frederick are a mite excitable."

The room busted out in laughter.

"Will, Philip, over here!"

I finally saw Mr. and Mrs. Brown sitting in the far corner of the room. With them was another gentleman dressed in dark brown leather buckskins. His black hair was pulled tight back in a ponytail. His craggy face was tanned and smooth shaven. His eyes were the most remarkable, they were solid black and piercing. We made our way back to the tavern table and sat down at the bench across from Mr. and Mrs. Brown.

"Lads this is your contact, Mr. Lancaster from Sycamore Falls over in Watauga. He'll take delivery of the goods tomorrow and you boys can be on your way back to Frederick," said Mr. Brown in an upbeat tone.

Philip spoke up before I had a chance. "Captain Hawkins wants us to scout out the trail to Sycamore Falls." Philip didn't say anything else. There was a pause at the table.

"What fer?" asked Mr. Lancaster in a gruff tone. "You need to know anything; I can tell you all what you need to know. You want to take wagons; they better be two-wheel ox carts. Them four-wheel horse-drawn wagons only good during early winter and late winter when the trail is near frozen or at least dry. Nothing else to know."

"Mr. Lancaster, we've come to look over the area for Captain Hawkins and meet the settlers at Sycamore Falls. The Captain wants to bring a group of other lads up here later in the spring to learn frontier tradecraft," I added.

"Never cottoned to visitors just wanting to look at things. You want'n to bring a bunch of green-ass country boys up here to harden'em up with real work, now that be a different matter.

There's plenty of people around that could use some help getting the fields ready and maybe clearing some land. If'n that be your purpose then maybe I kin help. Ain't going to be no easy walk through the woods. Them boys is going to have to work if'n they want to learn. Sure'nuf plenty of things for'em to learn. Okay, you boys kin come with me in the morning. Them pack horses coming too?"

"Why yes, sir!" replied Philip excitedly.

"I got my own cart here for them goods, but it'll be faster to take the horses. There's a pow-wow going on now at the Falls and I'd like to git back to it. Jim, could you have one of them settlers bring my wagon to the Falls? It'll give 'em a little more room and help me out too."

"Sure, Lancaster. I'll ask around in the morning. I'm sure some family would be interested in at least letting their children ride instead of walking all the way."

"Thank ya, Jim. And boys, you be too damn polite. I guess it ain't bad and all, but don't expect too much politeness in these parts. These be good people, hardworking, but they ain't got much in the way of manners sometimes. That don't mean they ain't nice, just means they don't know no better. Just remember that. I'm hungry. Are we ever going to eat?"

I guess my focus on food and eating stemmed from the fact that at that stage of my life I was a growing boy and was constantly hungry. Later, during the harder times, I was just plain hungry, so I remember the feasts with extra clarity. That evening's meal was a delicious venison stew. Philip and I were given a big wooden bowl full of venison, potatoes, and even a few slices of carrots from last year's crop. It didn't take long before both of us were finished. And I guess we still had the look of still hungry wolf cubs on our faces.

"Boys," said Lancaster, "it would be nice to thank your hosts for the supper, but it's poor mountain manners to ask for more. Vittles around here are expensive so if'n they be free, as they are tonight, you don't be asking for no more."

We nodded our heads and thanked the Browns for the delicious supper.

"Now Lancaster, those are growing young men and they need their nourishment. I think we can spare at least a little more gravy and bread," said Mrs. Brown. She called out to the tavern wench to bring Philip and me a bowl of gravy and some bread to sop it up with.

Little Thomas, who had been asleep, finally woke up from a nap and demanded to be picked up. Mrs. Brown quickly changed the boy's diaper and dropped the soiled diaper to the floor to claim later.

"Here Will, take little Thomas if you will. He'll help you eat your gravy if you don't mind too much," she said as she handed me the little rascal.

Without any hesitation, I reached across the table, gathered him up, and put him securely in the crook of my left arm where he could sit and still see his mother. Thomas was not particularly enamored by me, but after one suck on my bread, he was my eating partner. Thomas in the crook of my left arm and the bowl in front of me, I was set to enjoy my dessert of bread and gravy. Thomas turned out to be a first-class little piglet, never refusing a bite of gravy bread and on occasion reaching out for my right hand in order to guide it to his mouth. He was going to be a big strapping mountain boy. Mrs. Brown seemed to enjoy watching Thomas and me eating gravy and bread. She had a perpetual grin on her face. Thomas and I finally finished our dessert and waited until Philip sopped the last bit of moisture from his bowl.

"Boys, it be time you hit the hay. We got an early morning tomorrow. I want to inventory those goods before we go to bed. Then we kin load quick and be on our way before sunrise. Jim, Sarah, let me go do what I got to do and I'll be back directly and we kin visit a little more." Lancaster got up, I handed Thomas back to his mom, Philip and I thanked the Browns again for their hospitality, and then we followed Lancaster out the door. Little Thomas, now full of gravy and bread, went to sleep in his mother's arms before we even hit the front door.

As we approached the barn Lancaster put his arm out to keep us from going any further. He put his fingers to his lips to make sure we were quiet. Since it was dark, I couldn't see what he was looking at. Lancaster moved his head back and forth and slipped a large knife out of his belt. I saw the gleam just a little in the moonlight. I then heard a faint noise like metal scratching metal and then heard two men whispering.

"Git that damn lock open now. We got to hurry. If'n we git caught we'll be hung 'fore sunrise."

"Hush up. I almost got it."

Lancaster raised his arm with the knife in his hand and at the same time shouted, "Git away from that door, you thieves." Lancaster, in a swift motion, let the blade fly toward the unseen intruders. I heard the knife hit something hard.

"Damn, he done hit me with a knife, Bob. Run for it before the damn fool gits a pitchfork after us."

We heard the racket of the two intruders running through the barn gangway and out the back side into the dark. Neither Philip nor I saw the men.

"Damn Taylor boys, always up to no good. Jim's going to have to lock those boys up for a few days to keep them out everyone's hair while the settlers come through."

"Do you know them, Mr. Lancaster?" I asked.

"Name's only Lancaster, son. And yeah, I do know them worthless scoundrels. Dad's a no-good drunkard up the creek from here. Ain't got no woman in the house to give any sense or purpose, so them boys roam the county hereabouts just gitting into a lot of trouble. Some day they gonna turn up missing and no one is gonna care, lest wise I sure won't. I already had a couple run-ins with 'em."

"Did you stick them with the knife?" asked Philip.

"Naw, that ain't a throwing knife. That's just my big ole bear knife. Probably hit him with the oak handle. More than likely put a big goose egg on his head."

Lancaster walked on into the barn, leaned over, and picked up his bear knife with the big oak handle. As he lit a small lantern in the barn, I noticed the handle on the knife looked like the handle on a good-sized hammer. All in all, it was a rather large homemade knife.

The inventory was a quick affair. What was surprising was that Lancaster, for all his backwoods demeanor, could actually read, write, and cipher.

"All there, boys. What's them trade rifles for?"

"The Captain is sending them to my father."

"Who might your father be, son?"

"My father is Oconistoto."

"Can't be. You Cherokee, boy?"

"Yes, sir"

"Damn sure could'a fooled me. Thought you looked a little dark, but I seen them foreign sailors who looked sorta dark. Would'a never thought you'd be Cherokee. Done right well by yourself son. Your pa will be right proud of ya. Jest make sure them rifles don't fall into the hands of Cui Canacina. That ole boy don't got no love for us that's for sure."

To a certain extent, I was a little perplexed by Lancaster. I thought that when Philip told him he was Cherokee, Lancaster would have shown some objection or mild distaste for my friend, as did some of the low-landers on occasion.

"What you looking at boy?" asked Lancaster looking at me.

"I'm just trying to understand you. You're a curious mix for a settler."

"Ain't really no settler. More mountain man than anything. I mostly hunt and trap. I do have a little farm over in Watauga. Papa moved to these mountains about 30 years ago. He traded a couple of horses for a mixed-breed woman and set about making a family. I got a couple of brothers up the Shenandoah and a sister not too far further up the Finacastle valley. You see son, I'm part Indian myself, just don't know what kind nor what part." Lancaster laughed at his own joke. Philip and I joined in.

Philip and I got our bedrolls and took them to the hayloft above the horses and made our beds. Lancaster re-locked the storage room and walked back to the tavern. There was no danger from the Taylor boys again that night.

Before we went to sleep I had to ask, "Are you really the son of Oconistoto?"

"Yep," was all Philip said.

"That means that you're a Cherokee chief too?"

"Naw, not yet at least. Maybe someday, if I prove myself. But I got three other older brothers who are already warriors. Besides, I kinda like living in town."

We laughed and finally went to sleep.

We heard the barn door swing open again about an hour later. The horses became restless and were moving around in their stalls. Philip and I paid no attention and went back to sleep as the horses settled down a little. Suddenly there was a crash in the barn and all heck broke loose. The horses were kicking their stalls and it sounded like a dog fight was going on just below us. Philip and I scooted over to the opening and peered down into the darkness. We could see two shapes fighting each other, but couldn't make out what they were. About that time, Lancaster opened the barn door with a lantern in his hand. Mr. Brown was standing beside him with a musket.

"Where're you boys?" queried Lancaster.

"We're in the hayloft," I answered loudly as the fight continued below.

"Damn cub bears. Jim, watch out here for the old sow. She could be real close and I don't want her to surprise me. These cubs are yearlings; they just may be out on their own. Looks like they made a pretty mess of your apple barrel. I'll go in and shoo them out if I can. I certainly wouldn't waste a shot on either of these two little cubs; it'd be a waste of good lead. You boys stay up there and out of the way. Philip, slide on around to the side over here and take this lantern and go hang it on that knob by the ladder. I need some light."

Philip scooted around to the side of the hayloft, reached down, and grabbed the light from Lancaster. Philip quickly scooted back to the ladder and hung the lantern from the knob. The light illuminated most of the bottom of the barn. We could now see two good-sized yearlings going at it. They were fighting over the spoils of the apple barrel. The horses, still restless, calmed down a bit but moved nervously in the backs of their stalls.

"Your turn Will. Come over here to the end of the loft, open the hay door, and throw out the pulley rope. I need to come in and chase these little buggers out. They're just a little too big to tussle with."

I did as I was told, threw out the pulley rope through the opened hay door, and tied the line off on a nearby beam. Lancaster was up in a flash.

"Now I need to find me something I can use to prod those little guys out of here."

I grabbed the wooden pitchfork and shoved toward Lancaster, "This any good?"

"That'll do," said Lancaster, who grabbed the pitchfork from me and headed over to a back feed opening in the floor of the loft. That put him way behind the bears, leaving the door open for their escape. Philip and I ran over to the large opening and stuck our heads down to watch the excitement. There is a whole different perspective to watching things happen upside down.

Lancaster prodded the two fighting cubs and successfully got them separated. One cub having had enough, grabbed an apple and made for the front of the barn, brushing past Mr. Brown in the dark, who screamed at the fleeing figure. Now the other cub was a different story. This yearling positioned himself over the apples and growled at Lancaster. He was not going to leave without his treat. Lancaster prodded him again and the cub reared up on his hind legs. The little cub all of a sudden was about five feet tall and all business. He made a couple of tentative steps at Lancaster leaving his apple stash unguarded. Lancaster eased back to give the bear a little more room. A five-foot black bear was a worthy opponent and not to be played with. As Lancaster tried to back up, he tripped and fell backward. Without thinking, Philip and I jumped down to the barn floor. We were not quite sure what we were going to do, but the cub was just about on Lancaster, who was barely holding him off with the pitchfork.

Philip and I grabbed a bunch of apples and started throwing them at the bear. After hitting him a couple of times the bear finally turned around. We grabbed another arm full of apples. I threw another one at him and it bounced off his chest. He went to all fours and gobbled up the apple. Again, he stood and I threw another apple. The scene repeated itself. After doing this about four or five times the cub stayed on his all fours and started walking toward Philip and me.

"Boys, ease on backward out that door. Throw him an apple or two to keep him coming. Don't let him get too close to ya. He's a pretty big yearling and he sure ain't nothing to play with," advised

Lancaster.

We did as Lancaster advised and the yearling came grudgingly with us; slowly, but surely. By the time we got to the door we only had about three apples left.

"Catch up boys," Lancaster said as he started to toss up some more apples from behind the bear.

We finally lured the cub outside and placed a pile of apples just at the edge of the light coming from the barn. The cub slowly worked his way to the apples, laid down, and proceeded to devour the rest of the stash as all four of us watched.

"Jim, you may have a problem with that old boy. He don't seem the least bit bothered by us. If'n I was you I'd pepper his behind with some rock salt. That ought to sting enough to keep him from coming back."

"Yep, you're probably right about that Lancaster. I got jest the gun for that."

Mr. Brown borrowed the key from Lancaster and opened up the storeroom. He came back with a vicious-looking old blunderbuss that must have been 50 years old. He quickly put in a short charge of powder and then rammed in a small handful of rock salt. After he charged the frizzen, he angled around to where he could get a good butt shot. When he was in position, about 20 feet away from the cub, Mr. Brown cocked the blunderbuss.

"This is going to hurt you more than it does me," said Mr. Brown talking to the cub.

The blunderbuss went off with a tremendous boom, smoke curling out and up into the cool evening air. The cub was momentarily stunned and then frantically tried to reach around to his butt, which to him now probably felt like it was on fire. The yearling was bellowing in pain and terror. It must have stung him good because he started dragging himself on his butt trying to put out the sting. Finally, still bellowing in pain, he ran off into the darkness away from the barn and this little part of civilization.

"He won't be back," said Mr. Brown.

"Nope he sure won't," added Lancaster. "Time, we clean up that mess in the barn and get to sleep boys." Lancaster came over by us and grabbed us by our shoulders as he walked us to the barn. "I want to thank ya boys for what ya jest done. That was mighty brave."

We cleaned the barn up the best we could and put the apples back into what was left of the apple barrel. After we finished that. Philip and I scooted back up to the hayloft and Lancaster escorted Mr. Brown to the door of the barn.

"Jim, we'll be leaving just before sunrise. I need to hurry on back to that pow-wow. Thanks for everything and I'll see ya next month."

"Lancaster, take care of yourself and those boys. Got a feeling you and them are pretty well matched for the time being. Bye boys and you take care of Lancaster for me."

"Yes, sir!" we yelled down to him.

Chapter 30

Trouble on the Trail

"Time to wake up boys," said the head as it poked up in the hayloft.

I was groggy and barely knew where I was, much less recognize Lancaster's face.

"What time is it?"

"Time to wake up and git going. We have a hard ride ahead of us. Ya boys hurry up. I ain't yore papa, so I shore ain't goin' to saddle yore horses.

I leaned up on one elbow and reached up and pushed on Philip. It took a couple of shoves before he even responded.

"Bears? There are more bears?"

"No bears. It's time to go. Lancaster said get a move on."

'It's still dark outside. Oh, I don't like this frontier life anymore."

A rooster crowed in the distance. Yes, it was time to get up and get going. We hurried, rolled, and tied our bedding up in tight cylinders. As we scrambled down the ladder to the barn floor, I couldn't help but notice that our horses were saddled for us. Lancaster was a real tough guy.

"Make sure those cinches are tight. I'd hate to lose one of ya to a loose saddle," he laughed.

As we left the barn, Lancaster made sure the door was closed tight, not wanting any more intruders in Mr. Brown's barn, two-legged or four-legged.

The early morning air had a chill to it. It must have been about 40 degrees because I could see my breath. To our left, the morning twilight was just peeking over the horizon. It would be some time before the sun came out. Lancaster took the lead; Philip was next with his packhorse and I came last with my packhorse. Our rifles were draped across our laps, resting on our saddles. Our pace was measured, but at a quick walk, although the horses had to be constantly urged along. I think they must have been sleepy too.

We must have traveled about an hour when Lancaster motioned us up to him.

"Philip, pass some biscuits over to yer buddy. We'll eat as we go. Don't want to waste any time on stopping for unnecessary things."

Philip and I fell back in behind Lancaster. We chose to ride side-by-side now. The road was not more than a wide muddy trail with wagon ruts. Lancaster rode in the center of the road, between the wagon tracks. Philip rode off to the right side of the trail, which allowed me to follow directly behind Lancaster. The biscuits were a little stale, but in the morning chill, they tasted wonderful. Unfortunately, there was no coffee to warm our insides. I ate one biscuit, decided it was enough, and started to tuck the other two biscuits into my coat pocket.

Lancaster, turned around in his saddle, "Will, go ahead and eat up. Ya need some food on yer stomach. Sides that biscuit will warm yer inside later, so go ahead and eat'em all boys. The day mite not warm up much." He turned back forward in his saddle and continued to survey the area ahead as if he was looking for something.

Philip and I continued to eat our semi-hard biscuits and passed a wooden flask of water between us to wash down the rather dry offering.

Another hour and the sun was finally peeking over the horizon, except that there was a mountain or two in between us and the horizon. Nevertheless, the ambient light was getting better and the shadows were vanishing somewhat. Not being an experienced frontier trail rider, I was somewhat concerned by Lancaster always moving his head back and forth as if was looking for something. I shared my concern with Philip.

"Why does Lancaster always look like he's expecting something?"

"That's because you can never tell what you might run into around here. I'm a little concerned myself because I saw fresh foot tracks cross the trail about a mile back down the road. They went up from that creek to the higher ground off to our left. Look like two men in moccasins. Not a hunting party, they're normally about five to six warriors, so I don't think they are Cherokee, unless they are outsiders."

"What do you mean outsiders? You mean Cherokee from a different clan than what's in this area?"

"Naw, just like any community, there are those who just don't fit in. Sometimes they migrate to another clan if they can, other times they just hang outside of the clan and live on the edge of that group. Sometimes these people are banished for good cause, other times they just leave because of some complaint. But anyway, they're outsiders, Cherokee, but not associated with any clan either by cause or choice. They don't normally cause any trouble, but you can never tell. Bad blood is bad blood. So ya just got to be careful.

I continued to watch Lancaster and I found myself mimicking his movements. Before long I noticed Philip had taken a greater interest in surveying the area.

After a while, the trail began to rise slightly. This part of the trail looked like it had either been cut into the hill or had just worn down into it. In either case, walls started to rise on either side of us. The trail itself went up and over a little knoll. As it did it disappeared from view. Lancaster repositioned his rifle. He now had the butt of the rifle on his leg with the barrel pointed straight up in the air. He slowly and quietly cocked his rifle. Philip and I did the same thing. I had an eerie feeling I didn't like.

As we got near the crest of the hill, Lancaster slid off the left side of his horse. He motioned us to keep moving but slow down. Somehow, he found a rabbit trail up the side of the steep embankment and disappeared into the woods above us. His horse continued on without him.

As we came over the rise and could see the trail ahead of us, we noticed a tree had fallen across the road, effectively blocking the trail. A banshee screamed in the woods off to our left. My skin crawled and the hair stood up on the back of my neck. A rifle fired.

A blood-curdling scream pierced the air. Another rifle fired. I could hear someone running through the woods toward the road just in front of us. Suddenly a figure carrying a musket leaped from the embankment on the road, taking a tumble. As he tumbled over the musket, the stock snapped into just behind the flintlock. He leaped to his feet and stared at us not 30 yards away. It was a young man, about 19, in tattered clothing wearing moccasins, a saddle pistol still securely tucked into his pants. Even though his rifle stock was broken he raised the broken musket and fired at us. The shot zinged between Philip and me narrowly missing. Quickly, the boy grabbed the reins to Lancaster's horse and without any effort swung up into the saddle. He wheeled the horse around and came straight at us, pistol in his hand. This was a bad memory happening all over again. Without any prompting Philip and I both lowered our guns into position and fired together. The vagabond was blasted out of the saddle and fell onto the trail with a hard thump. Lancaster's horse ran only as far as our mounts and pulled up.

Everything was strangely quiet for a moment. Then we heard a voice in the woods shout to us.

"You boys alright?" shouted Lancaster.

"Yeah," shouted Philip, "How about you?"

"Jest fine! No worse for the wear. I'm coming out so don't you boys take a pot shot at me."

Lancaster came out about the same place the vagabond had jumped from the embankment, except he took a couple of steps down before he jumped and landed softly, still standing.

"Come on over here boys. We got some work to do."

Philip and I dismounted and walked over to Lancaster. He

was in the process of dragging the body of the dead vagabond off to the side of the road. We tied our horses and his to the fallen tree.

"You boys git that shovel out from under the cover on Will's packhorse and start digging a hole for this poor bastard off to the side of the road down there where it levels out a bit. The soil ought to be soft enough. I'll take care of the other up yonder. By the way, them's the Taylor boys. I think we just ended a lot of misery here 'bout."

I leaned over and picked up the broken musket, which turned out to be a very high-quality Pennsylvania rifle. The stock was broken and it was dirty but other than that it was in decent shape.

"Lancaster, can I keep the broken rifle? I think I can make another stock for it when I get back to Frederick."

"Keep it son if you want it. Sort of like the spoils of war. That is unless the owner happens to be in Sycamore Falls and then I would seriously consider giving it up. Well, if Will keeps the rifle, I reckon as well Philip you get the pistol." Lancaster handed a well-made British saddle pistol over to Philip. "Same goes for you young man. If'n somebody recognizes that pistol just give it up with an explanation of how ya got it. There be four more weapons up there that we can take with us. Those boys were really into good rifles." Lancaster ambled off and deftly climbed the embankment without any effort.

Philip and I found the wooden shovel and went to find a suitable spot to bury the body. It only took a couple of tries before we found a suitable digging spot.

"That's enough boys." Lancaster appeared out of nowhere

and scared us. "Mite be nervous are ya? Well, that's good in these parts. No need to worry about trying to bury this body deep. The critters will more than likely dig'em up in a day or two."

We got out of the way as Lancaster dragged the body of the boy over to our shallow pit. He stopped and started to search the body.

"Well, what do we have here? I'll be tarred and feathered, a booty pouch."

Lancaster opened the pouch and poured out the contents onto a bed of leaves. There were about four pounds in various-sized coins, a pocket watch, a small pipe, some tobacco, a small flint firebox, a piece of rawhide about a yard in length, and a small gold necklace. He then continued his search, but found nothing else of value, except the moccasins the boy was wearing. Lancaster compared them with his feet and declared them too small.

"Go ahead boys, see if'n them moccasins will fit one of ya. No use of leaving them to rot in the ground." Lancaster pulled off the moccasins and threw them to Philip and me. "Now don't be squeamish, he don't need 'em no more and they look almost brand new. Got a lot of good wear left in them."

Philip and I looked at each other. Neither of us really liked the idea of taking the dead boy's shoes, but we didn't want to offend Lancaster either.

I handed them to Philip, "Here you have 'em. They just fit you, I can tell."

"Nice try, friend," as he held the moccasin up to his foot, which I now noticed was rather large. It was obvious that I was now the proud owner of the dead boy's moccasins. I could barely contain myself. I almost threw up then and there.

"Let's keep everything on the up and up. The thief up the hill there also had a booty bag. He had about five pounds and a lot of stuff too. That's nine pounds altogether, so for our troubles, we'll keep two pounds apiece. That'll leave three pounds to leave for someone to claim in Sycamore. The stuff from the bags we'll leave with the money for someone to claim. These boys have been awful busy, but then again, they been at it for about five years. People'll be awful grateful these boys are gone. Don't need to worry 'bout their dad. He's an old drunkard who won't miss'em for a long time."

Lancaster kicked the body unceremoniously into the grave and started to cover him up.

"Aren't we going to say a few words over him? It ain't Christian-like just to shove him in a hole and cover'em up," I protested.

"Not sure these boys ever even saw a preacher. Don't know if'n they were ever baptized. But if'n you want to then go ahead, but hurry it up, we're losing time."

I don't remember what I said, but it was short and ended with "Amen." Lancaster finished filling in the grave. There was no marker, only a couple of stones on top to keep the animals from digging him up.

We walked back to the horses and Lancaster took out his big knife and cut off the upper limbs of the fallen tree so we could get the horses over.

"The settlers kin clean this mess up when they come by. We ain't got time. Let's mount up and git goin."

I noticed that we had acquired two pretty good smooth-bore trade rifles, a fowling piece, and a Brown Bess, as well as a British army musket. If nobody claimed them, Lancaster stood to make a good bit more money. I wondered to myself if he had really told us all that he found. It was something that could wait until later.

The rest of the day was uneventful, but as evening came on the weather started to turn bad. A mist began to fall and Lancaster called our journey to a halt near a rock outcropping.

"Follow me off the track here, there's a good overhang about a mile around this here mountain where we'll be out of the weather. Just hope there ain't a gathering already there."

We smelled the campfires long before we heard the music from the accordion and the general merriment of the overhang campground. As we approached, it was a lot different than what I expected. True, there was a large overhang, but there were also crude but effective brush arbors scattered all over the place, most of which were occupied by either Cherokee or traders. In the middle of all of this was a large area with a big bonfire. Cherokee and traders were sitting around as the liquor flowed and the music played.

Chapter 31

Rest Stop

“Sorry boys, I'd thought everyone would have been at Sycamore Falls by now. Seems like a few latecomers like ourselves are still on the way. “

“Halt,” came the voice from a tree nearby. “Who are ya and what are ya doing here.” An all buckskin-clad figure emerged from beside the tree, just as two similarly clad Cherokee braves emerged from the other direction.

“Damn near scared the bejesus out of me, Karl.”

“Oh, it's you, Lancaster. Sorry. Someone said you'd probably be coming back this way. Didn't hear you'd be bringing company,” he said nodding in our direction.

“Lancaster,” cried a Cherokee on the other side. “Ya bring anything good to eat? I'm tired of dried venison and beans.”

“Sorry Big Bear, all's I got are more beans and a little coffee. If you're interested, I'll make us a pot as soon as we get settled.”

“Hey Big Bear, I thought you were way down in Georgia,” said Philip.

"Philip!" yelled Big Bear. The tall and bulky Cherokee, who was about six feet four inches and weighed a good 17 stones, trotted over to Philip and literally lifted him out of the saddle in one swoop. Philip disappeared into his cousin's arms. There was a lot of backslapping, hugging, and laughter. The other Cherokee brave meandered over to the reunion. He was not much smaller than Big Bear.

"So little cousin, do you remember me?" he asked of Philip.

"Little Bear, is that you? Gosh, you have grown. Two years ago, you were only about five feet six inches." Gee, you must be six feet three inches now."

"Naw, I'm only six feet two inches," near 14 stones. I'd be bigger if'n I didn't hang around with this big oaf all the time. I hardly ever get anything to eat."

Little Bear was smaller to a degree, but he was also a lot trimmer and looked in a lot better shape. The family reunion was heartwarming.

"You know Lancaster?" asked Philip, remembering his manners.

The Bear brothers moved around to shake hands with Lancaster.

"Big Bear, you git any bigger and we're goin to have to rename you Giant Bear."

"Good to see you too, Lancaster. You're still too skinny though. You ought to fatten up a little. Keeps the chill of winter away.

"Philip, I knew both these braves when they were knee-high to a grasshopper. In fact, I am the one who made them their first bow and arrows and taught them how to shoot them.

"Yeah, Philip. And we are so good with them, we have to use a musket instead," laughed Little Bear. "Worst bow and arrow teacher around."

We all laughed.

"But you know, ole Lancaster is a mighty fine marksman though and that he did teach

us real good. Even with an old musket, I can still out-shoot most of those Pennsylvania riflemen."

Lancaster slipped down off his horse and came back to my pack animal. He carefully slid out the best long rifle he had taken off the Taylor boys.

"You know, Big Bear, I am absolutely tired of hearing that you can outshoot most of those Pennsylvania rifles with that old musket of yours. Here, now you can beat anybody regardless." Lancaster handed Big Bear the long rifle.

"Lancaster, I don't know what to say. It's a beautiful rifle. I can't take it, it's much too valuable." Big Bear pawed the rifle feeling every curve of the stock and every edge on the octagon barrel. He put it up to his shoulder and sighted down the barrel. "This is the best rifle I ever had on my shoulder. But Lancaster I really can't take it." Big Bear made a big production of trying to hand it back to Lancaster.

Lancaster held up his hands in refusal. "Don't worry about it. I got that from the Taylor boys. They won't be needing it anymore."

"Oh," said Big Bear as he cradled the rifle in his arm. "I suppose then, they made a terrible mistake."

"You might say that," replied Lancaster. "They tried to ambush us at Robber's Roost. They were a might too casual about their ambush and I caught 'em just finishing up breakfast. They won't be bothering no one no more. Jest to make you feel better, try it out for a couple of days and if you like, I'll take that old musket in trade."

"Now ya make me feel better," replied Big Bear.

Little Bear was standing there all silent and looking a little downtrodden. Lancaster looked at him and smiled.

"So nephew, why the long face? Think yer favorite white uncle would forget about ya?"

Little Bear didn't say anything; he only smiled a big toothy grin.

Lancaster returned from the packhorse with the other long rifle.

"Thank you, Uncle. You have always been too kind to us," said Little Bear and he too stroked his new rifle with love and affection.

"Here Uncle, take my musket now. I know that this rifle will shoot true," said Little Bear as he handed Lancaster his trade musket in exchange.

"Thank you, nephew. I'll make sure it goes to someone that is deserving.

"So, Karl, why the guard post?"

"Well not everyone is excited about the goings-on at the Falls. Seems like some of the clans are opposed and have made threats of disrupting the pow-wow. We thought it might just be better to post a little guard tonight just in case. Lancaster, your nephews will show you where to set up camp. There's a good dry arbor over to the other side. If'n it keeps up, there could be some real rain by morning."

Since we were in the woods at the moment, I had completely forgotten about the mist. The tall pines around us did a good job of providing a little shelter. The Bear brothers led us off to our arbor for the evening. Our brush arbor was a rather large affair; six good-sized pine trees tied together with a series of poles which formed a roof structure over which fresh pine boughs had been tossed. The end for the horses was a small corral made out of pine saplings and the other open end was for us. A fire pit lined with stones had been dug into our dirt floor.

"Thanks, nephews. Before I forget it, let me introduce my other traveling companion. This here's Will. He may be a lowlander, but he's a pretty sure shot when it comes down to it."

Big Bear idled over to me and stuck out his huge callused hand which engulfed my seemingly small hand. "Tell me Will, are you the Will Jones that we been hearing about? Done attacked and defeated a bunch of Cherokee renegades, skunked a British raiding party, and recently single-handedly shot up a patrol of British dragoons?"

"Nope not me, I only shot one Dragoon!"

It was good to hear the belly laughter of everyone. I had never given much thought to my goings-on, but I guess to other people I was the center of a whirlwind.

"Well cousin, you'll have to add that Will ended the terror of those murderous Taylor boys as well," added Philip.

"That I will cousin."

I wanted to go join the merriment around the campfire, but Lancaster had other things in mind. Besides, just as we got our fire started and our supper cooking in the trail pot, the rains began. The merriment at the bonfire quickly subsided as everyone sought shelter under their own arbor, although some of the arbors continued the merry-making until the wee hours of the morning.

Chapter 32

Sycamore Falls

I woke the next morning to the smell of fresh coffee brewing over an open campfire. There was something about the mountain air; it was cool and moist from the rain that was falling, but on the other hand, it was refreshing and invigorating. I felt almost perky and refreshed. The previous day's experience was long gone although not forgotten. I still had trouble reconciling my feelings about shooting the Taylor boy, but then I had shot in self-defense. I just pushed the incident as far back into my subconscious as I could, knowing full well that I would have to deal with it later.

Father had told me about one of his friends that had gone with the militia to the Indian Territory, participated in a massacre of an Indian village, and was never the same afterward. The mental anguish had eaten his soul and left him as a hollow shell of a man incapable of functioning. Father said the man eventually wandered into the forest and was never seen again. I asked about the others that had participated in the massacre and how they were. Father said each man had to deal with his own devil the best he could and had to go on living and caring for the people he loved. He added, there was a lesson to be learned and he said something to the effect of "sewing a bitter seed, one reaps a bitter harvest." That was all he said and I never learned what became of the other men. I could only imagine they burned inside a little each day they lived for the shameless acts they had wrought.

A moment later I was back to my surroundings as the camp came alive. There were mixed emotions as frontiersmen, woodsmen, farmers, and Cherokee alike woke to a new day; some worse for wear, others anxious to get on the road to the Falls. Lancaster was anxious and had the horses already packed, the coffee on the fire, and camp bread already cooking in the pot. Philip and I were a little slower rising. The warmth of the bag was just too comfortable to leave for the fresh air of the mountains.

"You boys ever going to git out of them sacks? Why it's almost sunrise and half the camp done packed up and moved out. You don't hurry up we won't make the Falls before nightfall," laughed Lancaster as he went about lifting the pan bread out of the pot.

The smell of pan bread was overpowering as it steamed on a flat rock next to the dying campfire. Philip and I needed no further encouragement. We quickly rolled out sacks up, pulled on our moccasins, and seated ourselves next to the fire waiting for Lancaster to divvy up our breakfast.

"Well, look'a here. My two wolf pups sitting waiting for breakfast. Does my heart good to see such well-mannered boys. Here ya go," he said as he cut up the bread into three pieces and handed Philip and me our third. "This here is a pot of bacon grease with pieces of chopped bacon thrown in for better flavor. Now don't you boys be eating all my stash. This has to last me a couple of months. This stuff is hard to come by; bacon ain't cheap that's for sure."

Each of us gingerly dipped our fresh bread into the pot, careful not to take too much fat. The taste was entirely new to me and not too bad. Salt had been added for sure and the bits of bacon added texture and substance. I had to be careful not to take too much on my next dip. We finished up quickly as Lancaster poured us each a cup of coffee. He had used only enough of his precious coffee for one cup each. There was hardly any conversation as we finished up the coffee. I had no idea what thrifty meant until I saw Lancaster produce a piece of stained linen and place it over his cup. He proceeded to pour the coffee grounds into the cup and then squeezed the grounds virtually dry. He was rewarded with a rich dark liquid, which he naturally did not offer to share with us.

"These here grounds'll be good for another pot or two if'n I cook 'em long enough. Back home after they be done, I toss into my vegetable garden. They make the soil a little richer and them vegetables a little greener."

Lancaster savored his last swig of coffee. As soon as he drank the last drop from the cup, he collected ours and proceeded to pack up the remaining articles of the camp. We scurried around our camp to clean up in order to make sure we didn't leave anything behind.

"Now boys, see them three sites over there," Lancaster said as he pointed to some now abandoned adjacent campsites. "Them boys left out early this morning. Go have a gander and see if anything was left behind. Never can tell what you might find."

Philip and I took off and began our search. To our amazement, we found a collection of rifle flints in a small leather pouch, a thin-bladed knife about five inches long, several long rawhide laces, a couple of homemade buttons, a farthing, and a half-filled gallon-sized crock of liquor. We quickly scampered back to Lancaster with our treasures.

We proudly showed him our finds. He seemed pleased at our discoveries.

"Boys, let this be a lesson to ya. Every time ya leave a place always clear the area, so ya won't leave nothing behind. Now divide up ya findings. Let me see the farthing." Lancaster took the farthing from my hand and examined it front and back. "This side," he said, pointing to the nearly rubbed-off face of some forgotten English monarch, "will be heads. You call it Will, heads or tails as I flip into the air. Who wins gits to keep it. Only fair thing to do." Lancaster flipped it into the air as I called out "heads." The coin tumbled to the ground, bounced off a small rock, and landed heads down.

"Tails it is!" said Lancaster as he picked up the coin and flipped it to an eagerly waiting Philip. "Next time ya find a farthing, it goes to Will. Anything else, ya'll have to flip for it. Them's the rules. Abide by and live by it." Lancaster meandered over to his horse. "Boys be sure to put on your cow's knees today. It's going to be wet the whole day. Wanta' keep yer powder dry."

Without further encouragement, Philip and I broke out the cow's knees and fashioned them around the flintlocks on our rifles in hopes of keeping the weather out of our locks. We pulled on our thickest coat in hopes that it would provide us some protection from the rain. Lancaster pulled on a thick, tightly woven cotton fabric coat that had a greasy finish to it. It looked more weather resistant than ours, that's for sure.

We rode hard the whole day in intermittent rain and drizzle, stopping only briefly at noon to take a pause and eat a single, now stale biscuit dipped in now-familiar bacon grease, which Lancaster referred to as "pan drip." We joined up with the Watauga River about five miles out from the Falls and followed the river on into the settlement. As far as a mile out we started to run into campsites of setters and frontiersmen who set up their temporary homes. The Cherokees, it seems, prefer the higher elevations to the south of the valley, Lancaster informed us.

The sun broke through the cloudy sky as we were reaching the settlement. It unfortunately was just beginning to touch the trees on the far horizon. The settlement was dominated by a large, well-constructed log fort built not too far from the lower reaches of Sycamore Falls. A short distance from the post was a stretch of open campground with a lot of campsites around it. There were tents, wagons, and hastily made lean-tos. Inside the fort was a collection of settlers intent on making trades with one another, seeking information, and just generally milling around as if they were waiting for something to happen. We rode up to what was the general store, a log building built into one side of the post. As we tied our horses to the hitching post out front, a man, dressed in traditional lowlander attire came out to greet us. I assumed him to be Mr. Peters, the sutler for the post.

"Lancaster, you old rascal, you made it back just in time. That Henderson feller has just about got the Cherokee to agree to cede him the rights to Kentuck. Can't believe it's really coming about. I'm ready to pack and move west with Boone."

"Pete, I'd be a might more careful. Ain't everybody that likes this here treaty talk. The British done told everyone they can't go and no one hereabouts seems to listen. Them redcoats kin make things a might uncomfortable, just like the French did in the 60s. If I were you, I'd be concentrating on making money selling supplies from here, maybe sending someone to Kentuck to open a small trading post. But you know I'm not you, so jest do what you want. Did get those supplies for ya. These two boys here done real good. The big boy is Philip and the other one is Will. Right good shots too. Oh, member them Taylor boys over around Fincastle?

Mr. Peters nodded his head.

"Well, they ain't goin' to bother nobody no more. Me and the boys had a run-in with 'em and the Taylor boys are no longer among us."

Mr. Peters looked concerned. "You don't think their old man is going to come looking for ya, do ya?"

"He'll never know they are missing. Sides only the four of us know and I'd like you to keep it that way. You hear that boys?"

We nodded in agreement, "Yes, sir."

"See, damn polite boys they are, Pete. Now let's get things unloaded."

We hurried and unpacked the horses. I guess it took us no more than half an hour to do the chore. Afterward, Mr. Peters poured Philip and me some apple cider and he and Lancaster tried the strange liquor from our found jug. Obviously, the liquor was a strong homemade liquor. Both Mr. Peters and Lancaster turned red-faced after they took a sip and declared the stuff fit for neither man nor beast, but that didn't stop them from continuing to take a nip from the jug. It was apparent that the two old friends were not going to do much more for the evening. Philip and I asked where the stables were and took care of the horses and locked up Philip's rifles and our saddles. We returned the key to Mr. Peters, who by now was feeling no pain. He did have the where-with-all to put the key back in his pocket. Now it was time for Philip and me to wander through the campsites and see what was really going on.

We wandered far and wide around the area of the fort. There must have been about 100 camps in and around the fort and an equal number or more in the hills because we could see their campfires glowing in the early evening. Things had calmed down, so everyone said, because it was time for supper, which of course reminded us that we had not eaten very much during the day. To our luck, we happened upon a group of Dutch families from Pennsylvania headed south for warmer mountains.

Now I have to explain something here. The Pennsylvania Dutch are not really Dutch, they were German. The name Dutch came from the mispronunciation of the word "Deutsch" which, of course, to any educated person, which excluded me and 90 percent of the colonies, meant German. It was a name that stuck, but didn't matter because these people were some of the friendliest and most outgoing people I had ever encountered. Even their German-accented English was precise as it was correct. And I had never seen such well-mannered children. As sort of lost waifs in the woods, these good people invited us to eat supper with them.

After a bountiful supper, we sat around the fire and listened to the stories of former lives in Germany and the struggle to immigrate to the colonies in hopes of establishing a better life. There were stories of struggle and deprivation, sadness, and tragedy followed by stories of hope, resurrection, hard work, and success. It seems these were small farmers and mill workers who longed for the freedom to succeed by their own work and not see the toils of their labor go into the pockets of some land gentry. These people were headed to a fertile mountain valley deeper in the Blue Ridge. Much to my surprise, these people had no desire to follow Boone or Henderson into Kentuck. They were headed further south to settle land deeper in Cherokee Territory which had been purchased from the Cherokee specifically for these hard-working wanderers.

Among these pioneers were farmers, a couple of smiths, and surprisingly an apprentice gunsmith. Gustav Muller, who was born to German parents in Pennsylvania, was a strapping young man about 18 years old with broad shoulders, iron hands, and absolutely blond hair worn in a long ponytail. He introduced himself to us as "Gus," preferring the more English-sounding nickname. Philip and I ended up spending the evening getting to know Gus and chatting about life in general. Not mentioning where I got my rifle, I told Gus that I had an old Pennsylvania rifle that had a broken stock and wondered if he could look at it to see if it was repairable. Gus agreed to look at it in the morning after breakfast. Not long thereafter Philip and I excused ourselves and wandered back to the fort to find Lancaster and a place to sleep.

Since it must have been later than we thought, the big gates to the fort were closed, so we knocked on a small door on the side. The guard standing watch, or rather sleeping on watch, finally opened the door to ask us who we were and what we wanted. It took a moment to go through all the rigmarole, but we finally convinced him we really were with Lancaster. We checked for our patron at the store, but it was already closed, so we did the only thing we could and that was head to the barn.

The night air was fresh and cool to the point of getting cold. As we entered the barn, we knew we had found Lancaster. The gosh-awful snoring was coming from one of the empty stalls; it was Lancaster, reeking of cheap liquor and dead drunk. Much to our dismay, the storage room was wide open, but on quick inspection by candlelight, we were assured that all our belongings were still there, still a little damp, but there. We grabbed our sleep sacks, secured the door to the storage room, and scooted up the ladder to the hayloft. It took only a few moments before we were fast asleep.

Chapter 33

Life in the Falls

Morning came early as a flock of roosters in the settlement began to herald sunrise. I stirred and then sat up and stretched to get my muscles working. Philip refused to stir and I could still hear Lancaster down in the stall snoring away. I slipped on my moccasins and went to explore the ramparts of the fort.

Just outside the barn was a ladder that gave me access to the ramparts which encircled the inside of the fort. There was a blue haze over the valley. Now I understood why they called the mountains the Blue Ridge. Even the new grass on the valley floor took on a blue tinge in the early morning fog. The air was crisp and clean, if you excluded the numerous campfires just coming to life. I propped myself on the wall of the fort and gazed out over the panorama. There was something relaxing and at the same time fulfilling about this view. It raised a longing in me that I did not understand. Years later and many miles further west, I would still harbor this longing for something I didn't understand.

I heard someone climbing the ladder next to me. Momentarily, the guard I remembered last night poked his head up and climbed up to join me on the parapet.

"Morning," he said as he lit his pipe and stared out over the valley with me. "Kind of peaceful round here this time of day. Can't think of a better place to be, except maybe at my homestead, but duty is duty. Name's John Sevier, I run the militia in these parts. Who might you be?"

"Will Jones, sir. I'm recently from Frederick, here sort of on a scouting trip for Captain Hawkins, who commands our militia in Frederick."

"What is the old rascal thinking about doing, invading us or just looking for a place that's a little more hospitable?" he chuckled.

"He wants to send a bunch of us boys up here to the mountains to get a feel for the frontier and maybe learn some forest skills."

"So, he thinks the war is actually going to come, does he?"

"He didn't say sir, but things are getting a might touchy in and around Virginia."

"Son, we heard you shot about a dozen redcoats down in Charles; that true?"

"Why no, sir it isn't!" I exclaimed using the best English I could muster. "I only winged one, but I did knock him off his horse."

"Thought it might be a bit exaggerated, but sorry to hear them redcoats put you in that situation. Just be careful around here. There be plenty of people around these parts that are still loyal to the King, even though he doesn't want us here. When you get back to Frederick, tell Hawk to send you boys back up in the last part of April or early May. We could use some help on the farms, as well as teach you lowland boys some frontier tradecraft you might find useful in the future. Just come here to the fort and we'll come around for you. Word gets around these here parts pretty fast."

"Thank you, sir. We appreciate your invitation."

He didn't say much more, just nodded and continued to smoke his pipe as he looked over the valley. We must have stood there for 30 minutes or so in silence as we watched the valley come to life.

He finally broke the silence. "Today's going to be a big day of sorts. A lot of trading, talking, and later this evening if things go right a little merry-making. If things go right and the final provisions are worked out, Henderson and the Cherokees may sign a treaty in the morning which opens up lands beyond the Cumberland to settlement. But today will be just a lot of anticipation and not much will get done. You better go see Gus Muller early about fixing that rifle if you want to get it fixed at all, before they move on off down country. Just to let you and Philip know, we hereabouts appreciate what you boys and Lancaster did back at Robber's Roost. Those Taylor boys have been a real thorn in our sides. I hate that they had to be killed. Always thought that if we could have caught them, we could have straightened them out. We must have tried about 10 times to capture those boys, but they were wily. Harder to catch than mountain lions and seemed to be twice as lucky," he said to my amazement. "News, good or bad, travels fast in these parts," he added as he tapped the burnt tobacco out of his pipe. He left without saying another word.

I imagined nothing went on in his company area without him knowing about it almost as it happened.

I stayed on the parapet for another hour or so just watching. It was like looking down on the world from above. I enjoyed being an observer. There was something soothing about watching the valley come to life and not having to participate. Eventually, my solitude was interrupted.

"Hey Will, what you looking at so intently?" asked Philip from the barn hay door not too far away.

"Nothing, just enjoying the view. Did you enjoy sleeping in this morning?"

"Sun's not even up good. I could have slept a couple of hours more. My stomach is still full from last night."

"How's Lancaster doing?"

"He's still snoring. I don't think we'll see him for another couple of hours at best. Bet he and Mr. Peters finished that jug last night."

"I got to go see Gus Muller about the rifle. What are you up to?"

"My father is around here somewhere. I'll have to ask over at the Cherokee camp. Do you know where they are talking about the treaty?"

"Naw, didn't find that out. But looks as though they may have something ready to sign in the morning if all the details are worked out today. It is supposed to be a humdinger of a day today."

"Bet it will be. I'm going to run off and try to find the clan. I catch you back here after lunchtime."

"Taking the rifles with you?"

"Naw, I'm going to leave them here. I'll get a couple of my cousins to come help me once I find out where Father has set up his camp. See you later. Good luck with your rifle.

"Yeah, take care of yourself and I'll see you later." I waved to Philip as he grabbed the rope on the pulley, slid down to the ground, and wandered off out the now open gates of the fort into the settlement and camps beyond.

I continued to watch him as he walked along the trail out of the fort. I even saw him ask a passerby a question which I suppose were directions to the Cherokee camp. The stranger pointed toward the other side of the valley not too far away. Philip thanked him as the stranger tipped his hat and went on his way. I watched Philip as he walked off into the distance and finally lost him as he passed through a series of campsites and outbuildings.

It must have been about seven o'clock when I decided to get moving for the day. I slid down the ladder and meandered back to the barn. Lancaster hadn't budged and he was still snoring. The man was a real snoring machine. I quickly opened the supply room and pulled out my damaged rifle and the broken buttstock. I hoped that Gus would be able to do something with it for me.

I wandered into the German camp just as they were about to eat breakfast. Needless to say, I was invited to partake of their bounty. Breakfast was a solemn affair until everyone was finished. The children were released from the table and proceeded to do their chores around the camp. There was a certain amount of playfulness in doing their chores, but by and large, the chores were taken seriously. The adults, me included, sat at the table and talked about various things. Some of the private conversations were in German, of course, but others were in English for my benefit so that I could join in.

Eventually, the meal was declared over by Mr. Richter, the obvious leader of this small German community and people went about their business. I followed Gus over to his wagon where he wanted to have a closer look at my rifle. His wagon was a lot different from other wagons I had seen before. The back opened into a small workshop that had a thousand different tools all carefully placed in particular slots and drawers. I had never seen something so organized.

"Will, this is a fine example of an old German Jaeger rifle. It is probably a .50 caliber and made for a man that was about six feet tall. I'll have to put another stock on it for you, but I don't think the butt will be as long. How tall is your father," he asked?

"I don't right know, but he is about this much higher than I am," I answered as I held my hand several inches over my head.

"Humph, he's about five feet 10 inches. How old are you?"

"Almost 18," I lied.

Gus laughed. "Well, you're almost five feet nine inches now and look like you could do some more growing. You should end up at least as tall as your father if not a little taller. Come here and let me measure your reach around a rifle." Gus reached into his wagon and pulled out a series of wooden rifle templates in various sizes. He selected one that he thought would fit and gave it to me.

"This is great. It is very comfortable," I said.

"This will fit you now, but it will be way too short for you when you finish growing. Try another one." We went through a whole series of templates until he was satisfied which one, I needed. The one Gus selected was a little larger than what was comfortable, but I could manage it without any problem. "You'll feel like you are reaching a bit, but you should grow into it in a couple of years. Now let's get to work on the stock."

Gus was not one to waste time. He actually pulled out several stock blanks and compared them to the plank pattern. He finally selected a medium-dark elm stock to work for me. The stock itself was about 90 percent done, all he had to do was inlet the barrel and position and attach the flintlock. I was amazed at how quickly and efficiently he worked. I assisted where I could. Within two hours the stock was completely inletted. Gus disassembled the broken rifle and fitted the barrel into the new stock. After a few minor adjustments, the barrel fit perfectly. I tried it for the fit. It was a bit long, but nothing I couldn't manage. Satisfied, Gus went back to work fitting the flintlock to the rifle. I assisted by keeping the rifle steady as he carved out the pattern of the lock and then drilled the holes. In a little under four hours, I had a new stock for my rifle.

"Will, the stock still needs a little more smoothing out to make it perfect, but I'll let you do that. It's something for you to do in your spare time around the fire."

"What do I use?" I asked sheepishly. I had never worked wood before and didn't know how to get wood smooth.

"There are a lot of different tools to use, but for you, the most useful will be the straight edge of a sharp knife and a palm-sized smooth river stone. With these, you should be able to get a pretty smooth finish on your rifle in a matter of months."

Over the next hour, Gus had me practice on a scrap piece of wood. Not that I was able to master the art, but at least I now knew how to draw carefully, draw the knife to me with both hands in a smooth and deliberate action. The results got better each time I tried. Gus next introduced me to the stone.

"Now I use special files from England and Germany which are expensive and not readily available on the frontier. You, my good man, have to find a substitute, which in this case is a smooth river stone. Here look at this one."

Gus handed me what looked to be a palm-sized gray river stone. It was probably granite but I could not be sure. I felt the surface. Although it was smooth, I did feel a slightly grainy texture to the stone. Gus had me rub it across my scrap piece of wood. I was amazed that it actually could smooth the wood. I practiced a while as Gus gave me pointers. Before too long I was delicately smoothing my piece of wood to near perfection, although I knew it was going to take a lot more practice until I tackled my rifle stock. To protect the stock in the meantime Gus gave me a specially treated cloth to rub over the stock to protect it against moisture and of all things boring insects. This made the stock turn a little darker and even brought a slight shine to the otherwise unfinished wood.

Gus and I went to test-fire the weapon to make sure it shot properly. A rifle range had been established nearby the Watauga, where shooters could shoot into the side of the riverbank without having to worry about stray rounds hurting some poor bystander. We made our way down to the bank to the range just as the activity was starting to pick up. There was a good mixture of frontiersmen and Cherokee dressed similarly in buckskin coats and pants, farmers and settlers dressed in linen and cotton homespun, and a local militiaman or two dressed in what passed for a military-style coat of dubious origin. I followed Gus as he pushed his way through the crowd to get to the firing line. No one seemed to mind and all spoke to Gus as if he was a well-known person in the gathering.

"Good morning gentlemen," boomed Gus to the riflemen standing on the line. "This here is Will Jones and I just got through repairing a rifle for him and if you don't mind could we get a spot to see if I need to make any adjustments to his sights.

A tall man stepped back and waved Gus toward a spot on the end.

"How's it going, Gus? See you're doing a lot of business these days. It's always good to have a gunsmith in the community. Still won't consider going with us to Kentuck, will you?

"Sorry Daniel, I'm still headed on down the way a bit with the others. If you ever need me, just ask and somebody will be sure to point the way. Daniel let me introduce you to my latest customer, this here is Will Jones from the low country."

Daniel offered his hand to me and introduced himself. "I'm Daniel Boone, nice to meet you, young man. Heard a little bit about your run-in with the British in Charles. Just you be careful."

I stood in awe. There I was with a real living legend, Daniel Boone, explorer, soldier, and backwoodsman extraordinaire. "Nice to meet you, Mr. Boone." He noticed my awestruck stare.

"Will, I think it's your time to show us just what you can do with a rifle."

The range was for the most part an open line with boards stuck in the ground beyond at about 50 yards. On further back at a tremendous distance was a series of target boards at 100 yards. Up front someone had built a bench and a rifle-holding device so the accuracy of a rifle could be tested while held securely. I quickly loaded my rifle and gave it to Gus who positioned it in the holding vise. I then set down on the bench and adjusted the vise box around until I had a good sight on the big black bull's-eye at 50 yards.

"Listen up," said Boone. "When I tell you, go ahead and fire as you want. This young man will wait till everyone is finished and then fire for his mark. Once he is done the men on the line will go down and check your shots. Everyone understand?"

The men on the firing line nodded in agreement.

"Go ahead and fire as you want," commanded Boone.

The firing line erupted as 10 rifles exploded and sent hot lead downrange. I could hear the lead balls whining through the air. Several later shooters fired and the line was finally cleared. I then adjusted my rifle one more time and fired. The flash and boom echoed along the river bank.

"Move forward," Boone then commanded.

I left my rifle securely in the vise and walked forward to check the hit with Gus. I had aimed directly in the center of the six-inch diameter circle, but I found my ball a good six inches above the outside of the circle, but directly in a vertical line with the center of the target.

"Shoots kinda high," I remarked to Gus.

"No, I don't think so. I just think that the rifle is set for 100 yards. We'll have to see." Gus got out his knife and dug the ball out of the board as did all of the shooters. Lead was too valuable to be discarded. "If your sights are true at a hundred then let's keep them there. Next time try shooting at a point right here on the target." Gus took the point of his knife and pointed to a spot about five inches below the bottom of the bull's-eye. "Try shooting here Will and let's see what happens,"

As we walked back Gus tossed me the misshaped ball and I put it in a side compartment of my pouch for later re-smelting.

"So how did you do young man?" asked Boone.

"Shot a little high. Gus thinks the rifle may be set for 100 yards, so I have to aim a little under, but it does shoot true to the vertical.

"Can't never hurt to be able to touch something at 100 yards. If this falls good, we'll give you another shot at 100 just to make sure."

"Thank you, sir," I said as I went about the process of reloading my rifle and letting Gus replace it in the vise. I sat down again and scooted up to the rifle and sighted it about five inches below the rim, as Gus had instructed me, and then let Gus tie the rifle down. Boone, seeing I was ready, gave the command to fire and the line erupted again. I waited again and then fired last.

On Boone's command, we walked to our targets. Boone walked with us this time to check out my aim.

Before we even got to the target board, I could see my ball resting in the near-dead center of the circle. The vertical alignment was near perfect.

"Well, I'll be. Now that is an extraordinary shot, Will Jones. I am truly impressed with you and Gus. It normally takes a whole day of shooting to get near this good."

"The boy has a fine rifle, Daniel, made by Wolfgang Schutz

in Pennsylvania. Even with the rough handling, this rifle has probably seen, it is still a very fine long-barrel Jaeger rifle."

"I should say so, Gus. Will, you take good care of that rifle and it will take care of you," said Boone.

I had more than a little pride showing at that point. I now only hoped that my rifle was truly set for 100 yards. I certainly didn't want to be off any less on my next shot. The second spent ball joined my other one in the pouch.

When we got back, I reloaded again and positioned the rifle in the vice. Gus made some adjustments and then allowed me to scoot into a good firing position to sight the rifle.

"Will," said Boone, `` the wind has picked up a bit and it is coming at you from your left front. That's going to slow down the ball a bit and push it right. You have to compensate for it. Instead of shooting for dead center, shoot for the upper left corner of the circle about two inches out. That should do you."

Gus nodded in agreement. I moved the vise a little, taking into account the wind and its direction. Gus tied the rifle down. The line fired as before and I fired last. With the line clear, we proceeded downrange. I was unaware, but there was a whole bevy of people walking with us to check on my accuracy.

Shooters at the 50-yard line quickly dug out their spent balls and came with us. Walking those last 50 yards I hoped and prayed that I had at least hit the target. I didn't want to be embarrassed, not in front of all of these experienced shooters.

As we closed in on the target, I searched the whole area outside of the circle for my ball and didn't see it. I was mortified. I had missed the entire target I thought.

"I'll be damned," exclaimed Boone enthusiastically. "Will Jones done put one dead center," announced Boone to the gathering.

I couldn't believe my eyes. It was true. Dead center in the target board was my ball embedded like a crow's eye. I was practically dumbfounded. I had never shot that good before, in fact, I had never shot at that distance before. Men, much better shots than I, started clapping me on the back and congratulating me on my shot. It was minutes before Gus handed me his knife and gave me the privilege of digging out the ball.

I was extremely pleased with my reconditioned Pennsylvania Jaeger rifle. It was truly a work of art. Now if I could only get the stock to match the quality of the rifle itself. That afternoon back at the fort, I spent most of the time working the stock to make it smooth.

Around three o'clock, a local farmer came to the fort and inquired about me. One of the locals who had seen me directed him to the barn.

"Young man, are you Will Jones from Fredrick?" he asked.

The farmer, dressed in comfortable attire, looked the part of a backwoods farmer. Tall, somewhat spindly, rawboned. His face did look familiar. I thought I had seen him before somewhere.

"Yes, sir. I'm Will Jones, may I help you?"

"I be glad to meet you, Will. I'm Robert Anderson Jr. and you may know my family in Williamsburg. I just got a letter this morning from a post rider which said you were headed this way."

"Of course, I know your family. You look just like your father, except younger and not quite as heavy." We both laughed.

Over the next hour, Robert Jr. and I talked about my visit to Williamsburg and I explained how well his family had treated me. I finally asked if he had completed his house.

"Funny you should ask. I'm putting the finishing touches on the house as we speak. I should be through by the first of April. At that time, I'll return to Williamsburg to claim my bride to be and we'll make a life here in the valley. I hope Elijah will come with me, but I'm not too sure. His Grandfather has become mighty attached to him."

"That's definitely correct. I'm not sure what he'll decide to do. I'm sure between you and the family, you'll make the right decision.

About that time, I saw Philip return with a group of three young Cherokee braves.

One of the young braves, John Red Hawk, greeted Mr. Anderson, "Farmer Anderson, we went by your farm this morning and saw you working on the roof. I'm sorry we didn't stop to say hello. We were actually afraid you'd put us to work."

"That's fine John. The mere fact that you and your friends hunt in around the farm and keep the deer and other critters out of my fields is good enough for me. You don't know how much that helps. With the new crop of corn planted, I'll really need you to help control the deer."

"We're glad to help. It's just we're not too keen on carpentry and woodworking. I know my father has asked you to teach us, but we always seem to be too busy."

"Actually, John, I saw your father the other day, and your woodworking schooling will start in May when I get back from

Williamsburg with my new wife. Your cousins are invited to learn also."

As if on cue, the young braves looked anguished. This was not the news they wanted to hear.

"Those carefree days of youth are almost over for us cousins," said John. "Philip we better get back to camp with those trade rifles and enjoy what little free time we have left."

"Mr. Anderson, it was nice to meet you," said Philip. "Excuse us, but I need to get my cousins back to camp. Will, as soon as I get through there, I'll be back here. What time do you want to leave in the morning? asked Philip.

"Sometime around noon will be good," responded Will.

"John," interrupted Mr. Anderson, "please tell Oconistoto I said hi and that I'm looking forward to teaching you carpentry."

John visibly rolled his eyes, "Yes, sir, I'll tell him." He then redirected his attention to Will. "In that case, I'll spend the night with my father and be here by mid-morning."

Philip and his cousins gathered up the trade rifles Lancaster had promised and returned to Father's camp.

Will and Mr. Anderson watched as the group of young Cherokee meandered off in the direction of Oconistoto's camp.

"Those are promising young men. They have actually been most helpful in building my house and establishing my farm. They do it on the sly so as not to be seen cavorting with a settler too much. John has a real knack for agriculture and if he continues will make a fine farmer one day. Will, now it's time for me to leave and get back to my homestead. I hope you'll be able to come to my wedding in Williamsburg or at least the reception here in Sycamore

Falls."

"Mr. Anderson, I'll do my best to be at one or the other or maybe even both."

They shook hands and Anderson went to his horse to make the trip back to his mountain retreat.

Lancaster showed his head outside the stall. "With all that racket, I'm not sure how anyone is supposed to get any rest around here." Without another word, Lancaster turned around and went back into the stall. It was only a moment before Lancaster was snoring again.

Chapter 34

Back to the Lowlands

It was midday when we started out. Fortunately, the sun kept the temperature tolerable throughout the afternoon. We let the horses have their heads and soon they got into an easy rhythm of slow canters and sprightly trots. Every two hours or so we stopped for about half an hour to let the horses rest and take a moment or two to stretch our legs too.

Now nearly 20 miles into the trip and the light fading, we found it necessary to wait until 10 o'clock in the evening for the moon to rise and light the way. A wide notch in the bend of the mountain path provided enough room for us to get off the trail and stay sheltered from the growing cold.

"Philip, you hobble and tie the horses over by the spring and I'll get a fire started so we can heat up some food and stay warm."

"Big Will, the Fire maker! Last time it took you half an hour to get one started. We'll freeze to death by that time. Besides, the horses aren't going anywhere. I'll just tie them up."

"I'm not worried about the horses running off; I'm more worried about someone taking off with them. If you hobble them, then we can rest a little easier. It'll take 'em a good hour to undo one of your knots. And besides, I picked up a frizzen firestarter from the Lieutenant. It's a neat device to quickly start a fire."

"Yeah, if you can afford to waste the gunpowder it takes to use it. I still prefer my flint and that old piece of file I carry in my starter bag. It takes me about a minute to get something started."

"Okay, we'll have a contest. You tie and hobble the horses and I'll gather some dry kindling for the fire. We'll see who is faster."

Philip quickly unsaddled the horses and led them off a short 10 yards to the small spring, hobbled them, and then tied them loosely so they could easily drink. I gathered all of the squaw wood I could find and piled it near the burned-out spot which had been used by some other traveler in the recent past.

"Now the challenge. I'll get my contraption ready and then we can see who is faster."

"No way Will. We start the same way. I put my bag on the ground and you put your frizzen thing next to it, unloaded. This has got to be fair. No head start."

"Should I put a blindfold on just to make it even?"

"Naw, I don't want you to accidentally grab Anne by mistake and shoot me in the butt."

We laughed until our sides hurt. It was getting colder and the fire was becoming a necessity.

"When I say three Philip, we start. First to get a flame in the tender wins."

Philip nodded as he placed his bag on the ground in front of him as I placed the frizzen firelock and powder in front of my spot.

"Three!" shouted Will, as he scrambled to pick up the powder horn and load the frizzen lock.

"Cheater," exclaimed Philip laughing as he made a mad effort to dump the contents of his fire bag on the ground.

Within a second Philip sent a shower of sparks from his flint into his tender ball. I filled the powder bung on the lock, cocked the hammer, and closed the strike plate. Philip's tender was emitting the first faint whips of smoke. I placed my tender around the ignition hole of the frizzen and pulled the trigger. The small but rather loud puff of the frizzen emitted a huge cloud of smoke that engulfed me. Philip, who by this time had put his tender into his hand and was blowing the glowing embers, fell to one side laughing, carefully, of course, not dropping his tender ball. Now black-faced, I tried feverishly to scrape my tender back into a ball. There was no lack of embers, they were everywhere. We both blew with steady, self-determination.

"Got ya!" Philip shouted.

"Aw, beat me by a hair's breadth," as my tender flamed a second behind Philip's.

We put our tender balls on the ground next to each other and started adding small twigs from the squaw woodpile. Soon a nice campfire was glowing warm, chasing the evening chill away and lighting the small campsite as the sun fell behind the mountains to the west.

"We need to eat supper and get going. The moon will be

out until about midnight and we won't be able to travel on this rutted path safely. Let's warm up some of this good Virginia ham and have a hot meal, then we can pack up and move on."

"We might want to save that Virginia ham for later," said the deep, forceful voice from the shadows of the forest.

Startled, we nevertheless dived for our weapons, just a few feet away. Philip rolled over his rife and came up in a sitting position, gun cocked and leveled in the direction of the voice. I was now lying atop my saddle and had both pistols cocked and pointed in the same direction.

"And I thought I had come upon two bear cubs playing in the woods," said the voice, still hidden by the dark shadows. "Instead, I see two young, but obviously able young warriors, who need to be a little more mindful of their surroundings. May I approach your fire? My old bones need warming."

"Come closer so we can see you," ordered Will.

From the shadows emerged, a darkly dressed man of tall stature with a strong build.

"Closer," demanded Philip.

The shadowy figure emerged into the light of the campfire. He was dressed in dark buckskin pants and long buckskin tunic. A gray blanket draped over his head and covered his shoulder. He was about six feet tall and ramrod straight. In one hand was an old trade rifle with a well-oil dark stock, in the other hand was a darkened hickory pole. On the man's belt hung two huge rabbits.

"Who are you?" questioned Will.

"I recognize him, Will, he's from the Nation. They call him Man Who Walks Alone. He's somewhat of a mystic, not a medicine man or a soothsayer, but a man who sometimes looks into men's souls."

"Most whites just call me Billy Two Shoes. You may simply call me Bill. My Cherokee name has little meaning these days. Everywhere I turn, the forests are full of people. It's really hard to walk alone anymore. Now if you like, save your Virginia ham for another day and share with me these fine rabbits I coaxed from hiding."

We shared an evening meal of roasted rabbits and a little bread. It was not much, but enough to satisfy us. Bill was a storyteller without par. Some of his short tales were light and fanciful and a couple were dark and foreboding. Perhaps the strangest thing about our brief time with him was that he didn't ask us any questions. He seemed to already know us.

Now early evening, the first quarter of the moon shone as brightly as it could. We departed Bill's company and returned to our trek down the mountain. We had a limited time to spend on the trail before we were going to be forced to hunker down for the rest of the night.

The cart trail switched back and forth down the mountain, the grade of the sloping path just with-in tolerance to allow oxen carts and lightly loaded horse-drawn wagons to ascend or descend, as the case might be. Every fourth or fifth turn was a pull-off area to allow the carts to pull over and let the animals rest. No doubt, for settlers going up and over the mountain it was an arduous trek. The path for Philip and me was somewhat different.

Intersecting the cart path was a steeper, narrower horse trail, not straight down but much straighter than the path. Since it was night, we had no choice but to take the slower cart path, which bore the ruts of years of use and no repair. The ruts in some places, where the soil was loose and muddy, were nearly a yard deep; dangerous at night for a horseman traveling the path.

The path got so bad we had to dismount and lead the horses through the rutted trail. This slowed us down to a virtual snail's pace. The only saving grace was the cloudless March sky allowing the moon to shine down unabated.

Now about midnight, we caught a whiff of smoke coming from the valley below. Somewhere below them was a campfire, either a hunting party or settlers on their way up the mountain. At any rate, there was a need for caution. No matter whom it was, there would be an armed sentry or two to ward off brigands and renegades.

"Will, I've got my rifle handy, you better grab one of your Dragoon pistols just to be sure. I wouldn't want to slip up on someone accidentally and be fired on without being able to fire back."

"That's just what we need to do. Shoot some poor startled settler, before the Cherokee even get a chance to lift his scalp."

"My Cherokee ancestry doesn't find that humorous."

"With my white schooling and deductive reasoning, I understand the reality of the situation."

"Just remember, Will, it was the white man who started the scalping ritual. Of course, us Indians refined it into an art. And as a matter of fact, I remember meeting an old trapper at a traders fair that had been scalped by the Iroquois during the Indian Wars and survived to talk about it."

"Is that the old man with the nasty scar that he covered up with a coonskin hat?

"Yep, that's the guy. You know I think the scar kind of added some to his swagger. For the price of a glass of whiskey or a pint of ale, he certainly could spin a good tale."

"All right Philip, I've got my pistol ready, let's move on to see what we run into."

We cautiously proceeded down the path, around a switchback and further down the mountain. As we rounded the second switchback we caught a glimpse of a smoldering campfire two turns below them. A light-colored tarp covered a two-ox cart which could be seen in the moonlight. Still a good mile away by road, but only about a quarter of that as the crow flies, the distance was close enough for the animals in the camp below to hear the clops of the horse's hooves as they stepped on the now rocky trail. Almost as soon as the muffled noise echoed in the valley below, two hounds of indeterminate origin began to bay loudly.

So much for walking up to the campsite unannounced. No sooner had the hounds starting baying than all kinds of commotion began to stir in the camp below. Philip and I quickly sought the protection of a big boulder along the path in order to put something between them and the nervous caravan below. Good that we did, for no sooner had we reached the boulder than shots rang out in our general direction. Two, three, four volleys harmlessly flew over our heads and impacted on the side of the mountain far below our position.

"Hurry, reload. There must be a whole war party up there, above us," commanded an authoritative, yet frazzled voice. The voice, although nervous, carried easily to our protected position.

"Wait, hold your fire!" I shouted. "We're just two riders on the way to Richmond and mean you no harm." Even though I was a strapping young man, the youth in my voice came through unabated.

"Boy, who are ya, and what be you doing around here at this time of night?"

I knew from the intonation that these were lowlanders, not too long off the ship. The accents were from the heartland of England, not long removed. That in itself was enough to ask why loyal English citizens, so soon removed from their homeland, would defy the Crown's order against going over the mountains. No doubt, there was a story there for sure.

"Name's Will Jones, and my friend and I are on our way to Richmond."

"Correction my friend, I am not going to Richmond, you are. I'm turning around at the Two Forks tavern and going back to Sycamore Falls," whispered Philip.

"Don't complicate things right now. Those lame brains will probably shoot again just because they can."

"You that post rider they talk about down in Stafford? Famous you are. Your exploits are known far and wide."

I answered the voice from below without responding to Philip. "I'm a post rider on occasion when they need me. But I'm just going to see a sick relative in Richmond."

Philip could not help but continue his quiet banter. "Yeah right, sick relative. You're just the key to rebel patriots in the treasonous conspiracy to dislodge the King from the colonies."

"We are not opposing the King to free ourselves, only to ensure we have the guaranteed rights of all Englishmen."

"Let me see, free ourselves, guarantee our right, free ourselves, guarantee our rights. Sounds pretty much like the same to me," goaded Philip.

"If that be you, then come on down slowly where we can see you."

"We're up above you about two turns. Do you see the large boulder?"

"Great," said Philip exasperated. "Now they know where we are hiding. Why don't we just make a big fire so they can shoot us?"

"Philip, their rifles aren't accurate at that distance."

"And what distance is that?" asked a voice on the same level as the boys about 30 yards distant in the darkness of the cart path.

"Philip, I thought you were watching for someone sneaking up on us."

"Not me, that's for you to do. You're the famous post rider. I'm only a poor orphaned Cherokee boy who lost all of his woodland skills long ago."

"Cherokee!" exclaimed the voice. The distinctive cocking of the hammer resounded in the forest.

"Wait, whoever you are. We're friendly!" exclaimed Will. "I really am Will Jones and this is my friend Philip. He and I have been friends for years. There's no need to make matters worse."

Philip in the meantime had slipped down into a kneeling position, using a smaller boulder as a rest for his rifle and a little extra protection just in case things get testy. His musket pointed straight down the road. Will hugged the boulder a little tighter, even though he was still exposed.

"Edward!" shouted the voice below, "check those boys out, but be careful."

"I'll be careful Capt'n. You can bet on that. Now, boys, we can do this one of two ways. Either you come over to me, or you can die where you stand. Your choice."

"Not very good options, if you don't mind me saying. We could just wait until daylight and then make good."

"Boys, I ain't got time to play no fool's games. Either you start moving, or I start firing."

"Wait. I'll tell you what, I'll come out alone and you can see me unarmed. And then I can call Philip in. How does that sound?"

"What ya got, a rifle or a pistol?"

"I have a pistol," replied Will.

"Here's what you do, empty your pan of all powder, de-cock the pistol, and carry it in your left hand by the muzzle, butt up in the air."

"I will comply with your directions, as long as you at least put your musket on half-cock," replied Will.

"Done. Now start walking this way. And walk on the right side of the path. I want you in between your friend kneeling behind the boulder and me."

"Will, be extremely careful. That man can see in the dark better than I can. I can't even figure out where he is."

"I've heard of people like him. Most say they are part mystic, like our friend Bill, back up the mountain. I'll be careful, but you stay put with the mounts until I give you the all-clear."

"I'll be here covering you."

Will transferred the de-cocked pistol to his left hand, butt up in the air, and advanced slowly down the road on the right-hand side.

He had gone about 20 yards when the voice spoke again.

"Stop!" commanded the voice. "Turn to your left a quarter turn. Take five more steps forward."

Without saying anything, Will complied with the directions.

"You appear to have grown a bit in stature since the last time I saw you," said the voice.

"When was that?" asked Will.

"You raced past me as if the grim reaper was after you. Maybe those redcoats were trying to be the grim reaper, but they obviously never caught you. Not a bad rider for someone of youth."

"Thanks for the compliment. And if they had caught me, I'm sure the grim reaper would have gotten his sixpence, but as luck would have it, I knew the countryside a bit better."

"One last thing. They say you have a girlfriend that is always with you. Tell me what her name is and where is she tonight?"

"Girlfriend, they say? Oh, you must be talking about Anne. Aye, she is with me tonight. Does that bother you?"

"Where is she lad?" the voice said tersely.

"She's tucked in my belt in the small of my back, under my waistcoat."

"Good then leave her there." The voice then appeared like an apparition from behind a tree.

He was tall in stature and completely dark in appearance. There was not one bit of light clothing on his person. Even his face was covered with a dark cloth with holes for eyes. At night he would be completely invisible. I had never seen anything like this before. Not a bit of brass, nor a glint of metal. I shuttered. This was no ordinary lowlander. This was a man of experience and most of it bad, no doubt.

"No doubt, you feel a bit of trepidation at this moment lad. But you have nothing to fear from me. Now bring your friend in and hurry down to the camp."

I called for Philip to join me.

With that, the masked voice yelled to his friend below, "Capt'n there'll be two lads coming down with horses. There are no more."

The voice Edward spoke, "Now go along lads, and be quick. I'll be staying here to make sure there is no more uninvited company." With that, the form slipped back into the woods and in a moment disappeared.

"I don't know about you Will, but the hair is standing up on the back of my neck. That man actually scares me. I've never seen someone who can just disappear into the darkness as quickly."

"I heard my father speak of men with special hunting skills learned from years with the Indians, who could slip through the woods undetected. He really never explained to me how they did, but we may have just crossed paths with one."

"Slipping through the woods silently is one thing, but a disappearing act is something else entirely. Sometimes I wish my brethren had not been so quick to teach our white cousins our woodcraft."

As they finally approached the campsite, the boys could see

a bustle of activity. Men were stoking the three fires and women were stirring pots of liquid and adding what looked like potatoes to the stock. What struck Will and Philip first was the dress of the settlers. All were dressed in dull, earth-colored clothes or so it appeared. The only light fabric around was that of the canvas tarps which covered the oxen carts.

"Welcome to our little camp lads. My people call me Capt'n. We're a close-knit family of pious Anglicans on our way to our new promised land over the mountain. It's a might early for us, but come join us for a bit of stew for a very early breakfast before you go on your way."

Famished, we gladly accepted two wooden bowls filled with a hot steaming stew of potatoes, vegetables, and venison. There was not a better treat for breakfast.

Capt'n, it turned out, was Captain Horace Worthington, formerly of His Majesty's Royal Fusiliers. His flock was the remnants of the men that had served with him in the battles against France on the continent in the early 1760s. Promised land and prosperity from the Crown for their heroic service, the men fell on hard times when those promised rewards evaporated like a drop of water on a hot skillet. Vowing to take care of his "family," Viscount Captain Horace Worthington had sold his lands and title to his brother and struck out to the colonies to find those rewards they were justly due.

"My little family numbers nearly 100. You'll see our little band strung out below us on several of the lay-bys. We probably stretch out for about three to four miles down to the valley." "Sir," asked Will, "aren't you afraid the British cavalry will ride up into your band and attempt to stop you from crossing the mountains?"

"That's not likely to happen, lad. I was in New York last month and informed Governor General Clinton that I thought the ban was ill-conceived and would personally lead my old regiment over the mountains. Now he was slightly peeved at my stance, but he knew of my record and the tenacity of my men. He would not dare to send those pantywaist lads of his against me. It would be a veritable defeat in no uncertain terms. No, the Crown has done my men and their families a grave injustice and we seek only what we were promised and deserve. As soon as we get to Sycamore Falls, we intend to meet with a gentleman there named Daniel Boone and secure from him adequate lands for a settlement on a major river in the area. There we shall live in peace and prosperity. And we have the means to ensure that by force of arms if needed. And as for the chance of British cavalry riding amok into our rear, I have my own troop of experienced fusiliers performing a rear guard. No lad, I have no fear of the British Army at this time."

Chapter 35

Later in Williamsburg

I made my way to Williamsburg, the capital of the Virginia colony, and went directly to see Squire Patrick Henry. Unfortunately, he was not in his office. I then went to see Squire Randolph at Tazewell Hall on South England Street. George, his manservant, greeted me at the door and escorted me to Randolph's well-appointed office on the first room off to the right-hand side to the front door. A few minutes later, Squire Randolph arrived, greeted me warmly, and made me to sit down in a comfortable chair next to his desk.

With little formalities, Randolph immediately launched into the incarceration of my father.

"Will, the main issue is that your father was named as a rebel and significant numbers of his neighbors either stated their opinion as such, or even more damning, remained silent, failing to stand for him at his hearing."

"But Mr. Randolph, as the Crown prosecutor, you know there wasn't a hearing. My mother said there was a mob in front of the Royal Magistrate. My father, in shackles and severely beaten, wasn't even allowed to speak in his defense. The major accuser was Henry Wallace, a notorious brigand and Royalist. His motivation was to make sure the Magistrate labeled Father as a traitor to the Crown so our farm could be seized and sold."

"Will, I do understand what you're saying, but all we have to go on is the rather explicit record of the proceeding"

"There the hearing only lasted five minutes, there was no record. The record in front of you was a fabrication after the fact."

"The record is very explicit, names of witnesses, summary of testimony, findings of fact, the judgment of the Magistrate, and sealed by the Magistrate under his hand. The six-page record speaks for itself and there is nothing we can do to overcome the presumption of a legal proceeding absent an admission by the presiding Magistrate, under seal, that there were substantial errors in the proceedings. Since Magistrate Wickham has fled to England there is nothing we can appeal to the Royal Governor. All Squire Henry can do is petition the Royal Governor Lord Dunmore for your father's release based on his service to the Crown during the Indian Wars and his substantial standing in the Church and the community. We were able to get several letters of support from his former British Commander, the Parson, and several substantial citizens in your community."

"Henry and I presented the petition to the Governor and requested relief, however, the Governor failed to act on the petition. They did inform us that your father was now under the jurisdiction of the British military authority, which meant he had no authority to grant us any relief for your father."

Randolph continued, "Will, the only advice I can give you is to stay above the fray and do not get involved in the current hostilities. I know where your loyalties lay, but do not act on them. In fact, as a bitter pill, you might be able to do more for your father by volunteering for the Royal Home Guard."

I sat there, dumbfounded. How could Randolph even think that joining the Redcoat Loyalists could help my father? I hardened my posture but held my tongue. It suddenly became apparent to me that Randolph was playing both sides, if only to preserve his status as a Virginian and a Royal solicitor. Disdain welled in my emotions, but I had to carefully choose my words.

I questioned, "I don't understand what happened to Father, but to swallow my anger and join the Tories, the very people who put Father in irons and stole our farm, I ask how could I do that?"

"I fully understand your feelings Will, but if you want to help your father, this may be your only option. I can assist you, but only if you can agree to submerge your feelings and take a neutral stance if you can. I will petition for a pass for you to visit your father in Charles Town. Keep in mind there is no guarantee you will see him, but at least there is a chance."

"How will it look when I travel the breadth of Virginia, through the Carolinas on a Royal Pass? I'll be seen as a Tory and Royalist, a traitor in the eyes of the colonial militia."

"With a Royal Pass, you can catch a skiff from Yorktown down to Charles Town. Once you are there, you'll at least be safe within the city. Afterward, you can return to Yorktown, with no one the wiser."

I was caught in a dilemma. I desperately wanted to see

Father, but I fully understood the repercussions of accepting a Royal Pass. I let my emotions override good judgment. Dejectedly I responded.

"Squire Randolph, please assist me in obtaining a Royal Pass. I will abide by whatever terms are required. I have to see my father.

Randolph eased back in his chair and relaxed his manner.

"Will, while I did not personally know your father, members of my family speak very highly of him and his service to the Crown during the Indian Wars. The pass, however, will cost 10 pounds. The fare to Charleston normally costs 15 pounds. Then you will need about 50 pounds to survive in Charleston."

I was devastated. I had no more than 10 pounds on me and no way to earn any more. But then, something clicked in my head. I had recalled seeing a bulletin on the signboard at a tavern in Williamsburg which listed fares to ports along the Coast. I distinctly remembered the fare to Charleston was only three pounds. I quickly realized something was amiss and I should have my wits about me if I was going to unravel the scheme Randolph was presenting me.

Seeing my consternation, Randolph continued without a beat.

"Will, if you are short of funds, I will arrange through friends to make up the shortfall, mindful that you will need to pay back the sum in kind or through a service agreement.

That was the shoe I was waiting for and it fell hard.

"What service agreement?" I asked curiously.

"I meant that for an advance, you agree to perform services for me or friends for a period of time. In your case, I am in need of a trusted courier to take legal papers to the Royal Governor in South Carolina. If you agree, you will carry a sealed package to the Governor as an official courier. Not quite like a Redcoat, but you would be viewed by others as part of the Royal Colonial Administration and as a trusted loyalist. There should be few if any risks whatsoever since you will be traveling from here to Yorktown and then directly to Charles Town. So, the big question is, ``Are you willing to undertake this excursion and see your father?"

I understood what an indentured servant was, for Father had been one as a young man for a period of time. His tales of wonder, woe, mistreatment, and the joy of freedom reverberated in my mind. Through his eyes, I knew what could await me and I took solace in the fact Father had prepared me.

In an agonized manner I responded, "Father is my primary concern. I'll do whatever I have to do to get to him."

"You are a smart lad, Will. A word of caution, I do realize your situation, but you must carry out your duties without fail. The pass will give you some Royal status as a courier, but it is not a complete grant of any type of immunity. That settled, go to the Southall Inn on Duke of Gloucester Street and take bed. Tell Mrs. Dawson you are a runner for my office and need a bed for three nights. I will send a note with you and he will put you up at no cost to you. My office will pay the bill. Be mindful to be thrifty with your meals at the inn."

Squire Randolph took a small piece of notepaper from his desktop secretary and proceeded to write a note to Mrs. Dawson. Finished, he folded the note and sealed it with wax and his stamp, a quite exquisite and distinctive Florentine "R."

As he handed me the note, he remarked, "Do assist Mrs. Dawson at the inn. I do not want you to lay around. You need to work for your keep."

Squire Randolph rose from his chair and extended his hand to me.

As we shook hands he added, "Will, I am sure this is just the beginning of a very worthwhile relationship."

With mild trepidation, I replied, "Thank you, Squire Randolph, I appreciate all that you have done for my family and me and I hope that is truly the beginning of a good relationship."

I quickly departed the Randolph Offices and headed back up England Street. A deal with the Devil. I was acutely aware of my precarious situation. It was an unenviable predicament, but I knew I had only one choice, I needed to see Father. Mild emotional shock began to settle in as I walked aimlessly up toward Duke of Gloucester Street in search of the inn. I passed Francis Street and as I continued to walk, the shock began to wane. It was replaced by a stony resolve to do whatever was necessary to complete the task at hand. Most of all, I realized I had to keep a low profile. Even in Williamsburg loyalties were subject to the ebb and flow of the conflict which was beginning to rage in the Colonies.

*****

The long walk down Duke of Gloucester gave me time to recover from the initial shock. By the time I reached Southall, which had been previously called Wetherburn's Tavern, I was in complete control of my wits and conscious of the hard road that lay ahead of me. As I entered the foyer of the inn, I introduced myself to a rather large stout lady who appeared to be in charge of the establishment

"Excuse me, madame, my name is Will Jones and I was sent here by Squire Randolph. He gave me this note to give to you." I extended the note to her and she took it without saying a word.

She carefully broke the seal, opened the note, and read it with the preciseness of a learned woman. On finishing the note, she gave what I thought was a consenting "Humph!"

Looking up from the note she finally addressed me. "So, you are young Master William Jones, who is, according to this note, to stay with us for the next three nights or more and work for room and board. Squire Randolph will cover any additional costs you incur as long as they are reasonable and required."

Now I was to work for my room and board. There would certainly be no time to lay about and while away the time.

"I'm Mrs. Dawson," she continued, "I expect you to abide by my directions and provide me and my husband with a substantial service for your stay. Is that understood?"

"Yes, ma'am," I responded without a moment's hesitation.

Mrs. Dawson's demeanor was not hostile, but it was far from being friendly.

"Martha!" she yelled.

No sooner had the word left her lips, an equally robust black maid appeared at the doorway of the kitchen.

"Martha, Master Will Jones will be staying with us for several days and he will be under your charge to help you in the kitchen. Make sure he earns his keep. He can chop wood, work the garden, clean vegetables, mop the floors, and do anything else you need him to do."

Mrs. Dawson then looked at me and asked in a very stern voice, "Any objections to taking orders from Martha, Master Will?"

"No ma'am, not whatsoever," although I distinctly understood there was no alternative answer.

Martha chuckled slightly at my response and I realized I must have looked like some backwoods charity case that was just dumped on the Dawsons.

"Now come with me Master Will, I'll show you where you'll sleep. You can drop your pack there and then you can start by filling up the kindling box. Shake a leg, we don't have no time to sit around and jaw."

The days working at the inn dragged into a week and then two weeks. No word from Mr. Randolph on when, or even if, my trip to Charles Town would take place. Squire Henry was noticeably absent from Williamsburg. A routine set in. Rise before dawn, wash up briefly, feed and milk the cows (Bessie and Darling), cut firewood for the cook, gather the eggs from the hen house, help with preparing the breakfast meal, and eat a bite while doing it. After breakfast, go to the various rooms and empty the chamber pots. Just before midday, cut more firewood for the cook, work the garden, help with the midday meal. After the midday meal, the staff was treated to a sit-down meal of the leftovers. Most of the time it was hearty soup, a bit of bread, and a few scraps of meat.

Then it was time to let the meal settle, be it only 30 minutes or so. But I took advantage of the lull in the inn chores to sneak in a nap out in the barn. Back at about two p.m., the routine would mirror the morning to some extent. More firewood to be chopped, feed the cows, muck the pens, and work the garden. At about five p.m. it was time to start the evening meal. One of the little pleasures was the routine of cleaning up for the supper meal. To me this was an unusual ritual, but what Mrs. Dawson had insisted on. Her famous religious quote was "Cleanliness is next to Godliness." So, each evening I fetched a bucket of water and went behind the barn to the wash area and vigorously washed my face and upper body and put on a clean or cleaner shirt than I had on. With the water left in the bucket, I washed out my soiled linen shirt I had worn that day and then hung it out to dry for use the next evening. It was a constant cycle; work, eat, work, eat, work, wash, eat, work, sleep.

In the evening, my work was not done. With a full belly of soup, bread, a little meat, and a small bite of cheese, I went to work in the inn's pub room. My main job was pouring ale, collecting the empty mugs, and washing them for re-use. I had no idea how lively the nights were in Williamsburg. Of course, I had never been in a real drinking establishment, not even the last time I stayed in Williamsburg as a boy. There was little time to worry about a trip to Charles Town.

I had not even had time to go visit Mr. Anderson, Miss Charlotte, and Elijah.

It was one evening close to the end of the second week, which I was faced with a confrontation not of my own doing. A patron, a stranger to the pub, had taken up residence on a corner table, away from the main door, near the hearth with its glowing embers. As I was clearing the mugs from a nearby table, the stranger called to me in a gruff voice, "You lad, go fetch me another pint and be quick about it or I'll box your ears."

Diplomatically as possible, I responded, "Sorry sir, my job is to clean up, not serve customers. Calley, the barmaid, serves the ale."

"You don't understand me, you Tory pup. I want you to bring me my ale and be quick about it."

The hair on my neck stood up at being called a "Tory pup". It was at that moment I realized I must have seemed to be part of the Tory community. Seated in the pub were a smattering of British officers in their redcoat finery, Crown officials in the Virginia colonial government, and notable Tory merchants of the community.

The man, though appeared to be a solidly built backwoodsman, dressed more to suit a frontier tavern than a city dweller. He was gruff and disagreeable.

Against my better judgment, I approached him cautiously. A table of British officers took notice of the situation and had quietly set their mugs down as if preparing to intervene if there was a confrontation.

As I got close, the gruff man grabbed my right arm with a vise-like grip. And he roughly pulled me close.

"Make it look good lad, I need to talk with you briefly outside," he whispered. The man bellowed for all to hear. "You're nothing more than the dirt on the bottom of me shoe." With that, the man threw his remaining ale on me.

In a flash, I reversed the man's grip on his arm and now had twisted it such a way I forced the surly man off his stool and up to the standing position. With his arm now twisted and his wrist severely bent toward his body the man screamed in pain.

"I think sir, it is time for you to leave this establishment!" I shouted.

With a firm grip, I continued to twist the man's arm, pushed him to the front of the inn and out the door.

"Well done lad!" he whispered. I could hear a chorus behind me as I pushed the man outside.

As I grappled the man into the street, I yelled as best I could, "Don't ever come back in this pub again or you'll be the worst for it."

I relaxed my grip but drew the man close.

The man spoke in a whispered tone. "Good for you lad. A bit hard on the arm, but very convincing. Listen carefully. See the smithy at the end of Botetourt Street tomorrow? He has orders for you from the Committee. Will, you'll be working for us too, when you go to Charles Town. Be careful, people will only see you as a Tory. Now be a good lad and give me a good shove to the ground and a few words of encouragement."

Confused, I did as the man instructed. In a violent, convincing movement I shoved the man backward so hard, and with a little acting, he tumbled to the ground with a resounding thud. "Just remember my warning. I won't be so kind next time."

I turned and walked back up the steps to the inn. The excitement over, the small crowd poured back into the pub all fresh and lively from the brief entertainment. A British officer, in the redcoat finery of a British captain of the dragoons, tarried a moment and engaged me as I came onto the porch.

"Ah, Master Will Jones. What a curious turn of events. I thought sure you would clobber him with a mug or two for calling you a Tory pup. Obviously, you have had a change of heart and I hope for the best. Just remember your current situation is less than sealed. We are watching you. Remain loyal to the Crown and increase your chance of seeing your father in Charles Town." The officer turned and walked back into the pub without a further word.

Chapter 36

The Meeting and
New Clothes

"Good morning, Colonel," chirped Captain Harold Bakersfield as he entered the headquarters of the King's First Dragoons stationed in Williamsburg. "I had a most interesting encounter with Will Jones, the young rascal formerly known to have rebel sympathies. He was cleaning tables at the Southall Inn when he was accosted by backwoods trash. He handled himself fairly well and dispatched the ruffian without much ado."

"Remember Captain, you and your dragoons have specific orders to stay away from Jones, and only observe and report. I hope you did not have any interaction with him!"

"No sir, none whatsoever. Only observed and now reporting as ordered."

Less than sure of the substance of his Captain's response, Colonel Highcliff, nonetheless, accepted his statement at face value and then turned to his Sergeant Major. "Make sure to note the

421

incident in his folio." Turning to the Captain, he said, "That will be all. You can return to your men and mount a patrol down to Yorktown this morning and make sure the road is open to all traffic."

"Yes, sir. As you ordered." Captain Bakersfield saluted smartly, turned quickly, and left the headquarters without further delay.

"Sergeant Major, as I recall you had a run-in with young Will Jones some time ago. What do you think? Is he a spy or has he reformed his rebel ways?"

"Sir, if I may speak freely?"

"Of course, Sergeant Major. Speak your mind. More than likely, I will not hold it against you."

Both men chuckled. The Colonel was known far and wide as a man with little tolerance for opposing views.

"Well sir, young Will is in a bit of a predicament. His family has been scattered to winds. The family farm was taken after his father was arrested for an unsolved murder and labeled a rebel sympathizer. He is now on a prison ship in the port of Charles Town. Will's mother, brothers, and sisters are in the mountains somewhere near Cherokee territory. We don't know their exact location. Will himself put down his rifle and wandered into Williamsburg several weeks ago seeking the counsel of the Randolph brothers, solicitors to the Governor and the Crown. His former solicitor Patrick Henry has left for parts unknown. There appears to have been some connection with the senior Jones and one of the elders in the Randolph clan back during the French and Indian War. Something about an unpaid debt, probably a life saved.

That information is murky, but there is a strong sense of obligation by the Randolphs to the Jones clan."

"To what extent does this obligation, as you call it, affect the Crown's connection with the Randolphs?"

"Sir, there is no need to worry about the loyalty of the Randolph solicitors. There are and will remain loyal to the Crown. They would not do anything to jeopardize their status. They would, however, offer as much legal assistance to young Will as is within their capacity as crown attorneys. All legal and above board. The gentlemen would do nothing to adversely affect their contract with the Governor or the Crown."

"What are they doing, legally speaking, to assist Master Jones?"

"From my sources, they have arranged an appointment as a Governor's courier to Charles Town and will give him a letter of introduction to the Garrison Commander there, imploring him to allow Will to see his father. To the Randolphs that would be a debt paid."

"Sergeant Major, I am still not convinced that every soul in these God-forsaken colonies is not a disloyal traitor. Some are adept at playing Crown fools for our enjoyment. As it is, continue to monitor young Will Jones and the other 50 on the watch list. I do not want to be surprised one day to find my headquarters occupied by 'rebel rabble,' and do not comment on my alliteration."

"Sir, I understand completely and would not dare make such an obvious comment."

*****

On the day after my encounter with the backwoodsman, I finished my morning chores early and sought-after Mrs. Dawson. I found her in the detached kitchen cutting vegetables, carrots, potatoes, celery, and such for the daily noontime soup.

"Mrs. Dawson, I need to run down to the smithy and get a retaining nut for the wagon wheel. I noticed that the one on the right side of the wagon is just about stripped of its threads and you need a new one if you are to be safe riding in it. Don't worry about the cost. I can take some of the scrap iron you have laying around and bargain with the smithy for a new one at no expense."

"What a smart lad you are," beamed Mrs. Dawson. "Just make sure you don't take all of my scrap iron. I might need to bargain with the smith later for something else. Now be off with you, but hurry back as quickly as you can. I'm expecting news for you from the Randolphs this morning before noon."

"Yes, ma'am," I replied as I scurried off to pick out a couple of good pieces of scrap to bargain with. Even though the wheel nut was not actually in bad shape, I had to play out the ruse to make the story stick. I grabbed the old nut, which I would trade to the smithy for a newer one. Mrs. Dawson would more than likely take notice of the new one, but not be any further concerned.

With wagon wheel nut in one hand and a few scraps of iron in the other, I started off at a brisk pace to the corner and turned right on Botetourt Street. I was on a mission to find the smithy. Since Williamsburg was not big by Philadelphia standards the business area of the town was compact. I had no problem finding the blacksmith shop. With all the noise of the smithy pounding and shaping hot metal, the location was easy to find.

As I approached, the smith's apprentice shouted something to the smith, who paused his work to look up towards my approach. Not wanting to let the hot metal cool too much, the smith resumed his labor and pounded the metal strap several more times with his 10-pound sledge. The smith then doused the strap into the water to cool it off.

"So, who be you lad? New to these parts, aren't you? We haven't seen you before," inquired the smith.

"I'm Will Jones. I'm working at the Southall Inn temporarily and do various jobs around there. Mrs. Dawson needs a new wheel nut for her wagon. This one is old and the threads are almost stripped." Will held it up for inspection by the smith.

"Sure son, if'ns you say so. How you're going to pay for a new one."

"I brought some good scrap. I thought I'd trade for it."

"I'll take the scrap and the nut. Johnny boy, grab the scrap and put it over in the pile. Master Will, come with me and I'll find you a better wheel nut, but it will be used, not new, if that's alright with you?"

"Yes sir, that will be fine."

"No need to 'sir' me son. I'm not a snot-nose dandy planter in purple pantaloons, I work for a living." The smith laughed at his own joke as he led me into the dark cavern of the smith shop.

Out of the dark, came a familiar gruff, backwoods voice. "See Smithy, I told you he'd be here just after the dragoons left town."

At that moment, I had a sinking feeling in the pit of his stomach. I had not even considered the consequences of my action of going to the blacksmith shop and talking with the backwoodsman, whom I had thrown out of the inn the previous evening.

The man noticed my cold sense of hesitation. "Laddie, your awareness is something you need to get better at. Truth be known, you could be labeled a spy for just coming here today to talk with me. You better start thinking about your actions and the actions of others around you. Here in Williamsburg, you are in the thick of Tory country. Anything you do or say will be noted. Cover your actions with a plausible explanation. Good that you need a wheel nut, but bad that you didn't know about the dragoon patrol. If you want to live, you better start learning."

The man continued and handed me a sealed letter. It looked all official; an expensive envelope, a wax seal of a Crown notary, and precise handwriting noting the intended recipient of the letter. "Will, don't worry about the name on the letter. Take this to the owner of the apothecary on King Street in Charles Town. His name will be easy for you to remember, it's Will Williamson. Sort of coincidental, if I may say so. But be sure it is him. Mr. Williamson is approximately 45 years old, has natural chestnut hair pulled in a fashionable ponytail. He's your height exactly, broad-shouldered, with a Roman nose, and weighs about 12 stones. When he asks what you want, you tell him you need 'bitters' for an achy stomach. Now repeat the directions."

Without hesitating, I described Will Williamson to a tee and then added, "I'll tell him I need 'bitters for an upset stomach.'"

"Wrong," bellowed the gruff man. "You're dead. Period. No going back. The phrase is 'I need bitters for an achy stomach.'"

With that, the man thumped me on the forehead with his index finger. "Think Will, remember what you are supposed to say, without exception. This could mean the difference between your life and an early grave."

"Yes sir," I responded without any additional commentary.

"Now laddie, what's missing from this whole situation? Got a clue for me."

I was frazzled, but thought quickly, "A response as an acceptance."

"Oh, pretty good young man. We call it a response code. His response will be, 'No, but I do have a small bottle of bismuth, which should do the trick.' Remember the whole response, not just part of it. If he answers correctly, hand him the letter, so long as you are alone, otherwise he'll take you in back to retrieve the bismuth. Make sure you give him the letter. Also, make sure you pay for the bismuth. It must look like a real transaction. Any questions?"

"What else does the Committee want me to do?" implored Will cautiously.

"Nothing. Nothing more at all. And be careful, the redcoats are a might tricky. Someone may approach you and tell you they're from the Committee and ask you to do something, say take a package and deliver it, or even take a message and deliver it. It'll be a trap. It's a false friend approach. We've lost several good men to that type of tactic. Just remember, no one will give you another task until you have delivered the letter in Charles Town. If someone is foolish enough to approach you and ask for help, you have two choices; refuse or refuse then report it to the redcoats. Those are your only two choices. If'n it was me, being the old veteran I am,

I'd mosey up to the Redcoat Garrison and ask for money in exchange for information. No harm in making money off a fool's mistake. Don't get me wrong, I wouldn't turn in any patriot if I knew them to be one. A fool that asks a stranger for help is just that, a fool or a spy for redcoats. Don't under any circumstances be dragged into a situation that will compromise your welfare. Oh, and laddie, you, being a good, stout-hearted young buck, should also worry about the proverbial 'damsel in distress'. There is nothing more vulnerable than a young man being pursued by a young and beautiful Redcoat agent. Them's that do get paid five quid for each patriot they uncover, regardless if they be true patriots or not. They prey mostly on the newcomers in town, 'cause the townies know who they are. They be truly 'painted' women. Be careful, you're ripe for the pickins."

"Thanks for the lesson sir. I don't even know your name. What do I call you?"

"'Sir' is good enough. If you don't know my name, then you can't tell someone who I am. It's as simple as that for now."

"Okay, sir, what if there is an emergency and I need to contact someone from the Committee? Do I go back to the apothecary and contact Mr. Williamson?"

"You do that Lad and you'll surely get him and the members of his Committee hanged. Once you deliver the envelope, your work for us is done. It's over for the time being. The only person who will direct you ever again will be me. If'n I get caught or killed, your journey as a secret courier for the Committee is over."

"But how —" I tried to start the sentence, but "Sir" raised his hand to silence me.

"After you finish in Charles Town, take the road west toward the Cumberland Gap. Somewhere along the way, in some inn, pub, or whatever, I will meet you. And if I don't, join up with one of the patriot groups around the Cumberland. That's it, lad. Now be off with you and not another word. Smithy doesn't even know who I am or what I am."

"Sir" turned, walked further into the dark gloom of the smithy's shop, and disappeared. All I heard was the creak of a rear door opening and then a gentle breeze on his face from the wind coming through. The backwoodsman was gone.

I left through the front of the blacksmith shop with my "new" wagon wheel nut clutched in my left hand. The smith and his apprentice were hard at work on a piece of hot iron. The smith used his 10-pound sledge and forced the iron to bend to his will. The two didn't even acknowledge my departure.

I walked briskly back to the inn in a circuitous route. Stopping only once to look into the carpenter's shop at a new inn bench being made.

"Mrs. Dawson, I'm back with the wagon wheel nut," I announced in a confident and somewhat fake gleeful tone.

"Good boy, Will," Mrs. Dawson replied. "Just in time, a package from Squire Randolph just arrived. It's on the bar in the pub."

I hurriedly put down the large nut on the foyer table and made a beeline for the package.

"A package of clothes? Why clothes of all things?" I questioned out loud.

"Will, read the note attached. It'll explain everything.

Impatient youth, too quick to see the writing right in front of him," remarked Mrs. Dawson as she turned and walked back toward the kitchen out back.

The clothes consisted of a forest green military-style waistcoat with six bright, shiny brass buttons. The lapels were wide and made from black velvet-like cloth, actually, much to my liking. The shirt was a normal beige slip-over, with a four-button front instead of the usual lace-up shirts most often found in the backwoods. This was certainly a move-up in fashion. The pants were a different matter altogether. White, below the knee pants with a button on either side to close the pant leg shut. Too much a dandy for my tastes. And then there were the stockings. At least they were forest green to match the coat. Added to the ensemble was a pair of black, low- style utility shoes, the type worn by merchants and tradesmen in town. Not suitable for the road or mountain paths where I wished I was at the moment. Rounding out the ensemble was a new, black felt tri-corner hat. That was the most impressive item in the lot.

After touching each garment and getting a feel for the cloth, felt, and stitching, I had a sense of elation. My trip to Charles Town must still be in the works. Then I noticed for the first time a note from Mr. Randolph in precise cursive handwriting.

"Will, the bundle of clothes is your uniform for your trip to Charles Town. Unfortunately, we could only afford to purchase one full set of clothes. We recommend you save the finery; the pants, coat, stockings, and shoes for Charles Town and your call on the Governor there. If possible, have Mrs. Dawson dye your light brown jacket forest green. There is a small packet of brass buttons for your coat. I'm sure you can sew them on. The buttons function as a sort of identity badge for those who are observant. Whiten out your homespun shirts as much as possible to make the whitest you can. Your tan homespun pants will have to do. Just make sure they are clean and mended. Blacken your boots as much as possible. We can't have you looking like a rag-a-muffin while you are on the Crown's business. Those minor modifications to your daily outfit should suffice for the trip there. But remember when you arrive, change into a proper courier's uniform before you go to the Governor's office. You are due to sail from Yorktown on Thursday next week, seven days from today. You'll have a horse and a rider to escort you to the port. You have to be there the Wednesday evening before since the tide goes out at seven a.m. the next morning. Come by our office next Tuesday for your final instructions. Sincerely, John Randolph, Esq."

I literally jumped for joy and let out a muffled gleeful shout.

"Well Master Will, it seems like you are going to Charles Town," remarked Mrs. Dawson, who was standing behind me.

"Yes, ma'am. I'm too excited to explain. There are some things I need your help on."

"I'm ahead of you on this. Squire Randolph already sent me a note. I have the dark forest green dye ready. We'll use the cauldron out back by the kitchen. First, we boil your 'nasty' coat, get it cleaned and then we dye it. As for shirts, there should be no problem. Over the years I have accumulated a shirt here and there from non-paying customers. I'm sure I have several that may fit you. I hope you have no aversion to frilly cuffs! The best shirts do have a few frills."

"Mrs. Dawson, I am at a loss for words. Your kindness is overwhelming."

"Kindness? I expect you to work extra hard these last few days to earn your keep," she said humorously. "Oh, and there's one other surprise. It seems some thoughtful soul in the garrison here dropped off an excellent pair of riding boots for you. He wouldn't give his name and he was dressed in civilian clothes, but I think I've seen him around in a uniform. I think he may be the Garrison Sergeant Major. Might you know him?"

Stunned, I thought about the only Redcoat Sergeant Major I had ever known. He was the one who tried to intercept the boys and me as we fled to the mountains with the rifles. I actually had stared down my rifle barrel at the Sergeant Major. I remember it was a tense moment, as both the Sergeant Major and I took each other's measure. It was the Sergeant Major who defused the situation and allowed my friends and me to escape into Cherokee territory with the rifles.

"I'm not sure, Mrs. Dawson. I'm sure he will make himself known to me in good time."

"Well, young man, be off with you. No one is going to fill the cauldron and start the fire for you!"

I quickly embraced Mrs. Dawson and gave her a peck on her rosy cheeks, "Thank you for everything,"

"Be off with yourself and get to work before you make me tear up," scolded a red-faced Mrs. Dawson.

I labored hard and fast. I cut the kindling for the fire, moved the cauldron onto several bricks to elevate for a fire underneath, and dug a small trench underneath to add space for the air to circulate.

Then I hauled 30 buckets of water to only half-fill the cauldron. It wasn't until two o'clock that I got the fire going and the pot began to boil. At that point, I threw in my heavy cloth woodsman linen jacket and began to stir the jacket in the water. It only took a couple of minutes for the water to turn mud brown from all the accumulated dirt and previous dye used to darken the jacket.

Mrs. Dawson appeared at the kitchen door. "Will, it's been about 20 minutes, you need to pull the jacket out, wring it out thoroughly, and then refill the cauldron with clean water to rinse it out. Lad, you still have about another three hours of work ahead of you, so get at it." She walked back inside.

"Young Master Will, give me the jacket and I'll wring it out for you. You tend to the cauldron. Just be careful trying to empty it. There is no easy way. You might want to use the bucket and a pair of sturdy gloves. It's going to be hot and messy. And whatever you do, don't make a mud puddle right there. Take the water to the drainage ditch. I don't want to be walking in mud for the next two weeks." Cassey, the part-time barmaid, took the coats on the stirring pole and walked away to the barn to find a place to properly wring out the coat.

Not an easy task, I spent the next hour emptying the cauldron bucket by bucket as the fire slowly burned out. Now down to last water at the very bottom of the cauldron, the bucket no longer was of any use.

"So, lad," commented Mrs. Dawson from the door. "You can now tip it over and let it drain. A little water there won't hurt Cassey. Just be sure to tip in the direction of the ditch so it'll drain downhill that way as much as possible. Then you won't have to contend with a wet fireplace." Without further comment, Mrs. Dawson went back inside.

I looked around, found the best place to tip the cauldron, and began to work it off the bricks.

"Hi Will," came the voice from behind me.

I turned and there was my best friend, Elijah Anderson, smiling from ear to ear.

"What are you doing with that big caldron?" he inquired.

"I'm dying an old coat of mine to look more official. I'm going to Charles Town as a –" I didn't get to finish my sentence. Elijah held up his hand.

"Rumor has it that you accepted a temporary appointment as a Royal courier so you could get the Charles Town to see your dad. This is a very small community and everyone talks to everyone else."

"So much for secrets in Williamsburg," I said.

"So let me help you. We can talk and catch up on things while you dye your coat."

Luckily the cauldron slipped easily off the brick and as if on cue. We tipped it over in the right direction. The remaining water flowed easily toward the ditch, without making a big mess. Empty again, Elijah and I replaced it on the bricks and went through the process of filling it up and restarting the fire.

"Here," said Cassey as she appeared from the barn with a large homemade brush in her hand. "You'll need to scrub the pot out and rinse it with clean water, so you don't dirty your coat again. Oh, you've recruited Elijah to help you."

"Hi Miss Cassey, I thought I'd help Will and catch him up

on the news about Williamsburg."

"Well, I hope you young men work well together. There's no time to spare."

It was not easy work, to say the least. Clean again, Elijah and I replaced it on the bricks and went through the process of filling it up and restarting the fire. It was much easier with two people doing the work.

Cassey returned, took the coat, and went to wring it out again. We emptied and cleaned the cauldron again as we had previously done and returned it to the firepit. With the fire going again and the cauldron filled with water or at least halfway, we waited for the water to get hot.

As we waited, Elijah and I traded news, information, rumors, and gossip. I learned that the redcoats were miffed; they had not caught the escaped rider, but none of the soldiers could accurately describe the "man." None acknowledged it could have been a youth. Most describe the rider as a large burly man with exceptionally dark hair and with a three-day beard. I laughed of course. No one wanted to be bested by a gangly teenager. Elijah said Captain Stewart left Williamsburg several days later, supposedly headed for New York.

I told him about my trip to Sycamore Falls but left out a lot of details. Time was of the essence. I did tell him that I met his father. He was extremely excited when I told him that his father had invited me to the wedding with Miss Charlotte in May in Williamsburg.

"Well, I might as well tell you. Grandfather has found a buyer for the inn. It looks like all of us will be moving to Sycamore

Falls after the wedding. We plan to start a tavern and inn there," explained Elijah.

"They really could use a tavern and inn there. At the moment there is no place to stay except under the stars or in an empty stall in someone's barn." We both laughed.

"I hate to say it, but I've got to run back to our inn. If I don't see you before you leave for Charles Town, stay safe and make sure you come back here for the wedding in May." Elijah waved to me as he scooted out of the yard and headed back to Anderson Inn.

As if on cue, Mrs. Dawson appeared with a large covered light gray ceramic canister.

"I hope you enjoyed your visit with Elijah. We're going to miss the Andersons when they move to Sycamore Falls. Now back to our work. Here is where we see if we can renew the color in your jacket. This is my special dark forest green dye I only use for special things and you be one of them," she laughed. "Let's see, it looks like you have about 20 gallons of water at best and it takes about one spoon per gallon. You get 20 spoons of dye and a couple for good measure. We want it to be extra-dark forest green. And believe me, lad, you will have to do a little extra work for this costly dye," she smiled.

"It will be my pleasure, Mrs. Dawson."

Mrs. Dawson added 20 spoonfuls of dye and a few extra. With a big poplar stick, she quickly and expertly stirred the mixture. After about five minutes she removed the stirrer and carefully eyed the color.

"Perfect, just the right color." The stick had absorbed some of the color on the lower end and was now a deep rich forest green. "Put the jacket in and begin stirring it around. We have to make sure it gets good coverage or else you have a splotchy pattern on your jacket. We don't want to look like a bunch of bushes on the side of the road, now do we?" she cackled.

Now late in the day as the sun was falling, my coat was drying on a line strung between two posts in the inn's kitchen. At least here it might absorb the pleasant smells of the kitchen rather than the odiferous smells of the barn. Even though I was nearly exhausted, I pushed through to help as I could in the kitchen and clean up tables in the inn. About nine o'clock as the crowd was beginning to thin, Squire John Randolph came in and surveyed the area. He spotted me and walked briskly across the room.

"Will, good that I caught you. Just wanted to make sure you come by the office tomorrow. The schedule has been moved up. Be at our offices by eight o'clock in the morning. We'll give you the Governor's packet to take to Charles Town and give you your final instructions. You'll accompany the dragoons to Yorktown on their normal schedule to the port. So, are you all set? Oh, by the way, your attorney sent a brief note to me saying he was sorry he could not see you, he's busy with business in Richmond. Frankly, Will, this was one time I don't think Squire Henry could have been much help. Are there any questions?"

"No sir!" I replied. "I'll be at your office at eight o'clock. Will I need to get a horse and tack for the trip on my own?"

"No, we'll have one of our best horses there, all saddled and ready to go. The dragoons will bring her back when they return to Williamsburg on Wednesday. That settled, get some rest and be at our offices on time tomorrow morning. Bye, Will."

With that, Squire Randolph turned and walked out of the inn. I'm not even sure he heard me say "bye" in return. I was sorely disappointed that my solicitor was unavailable. But I had heard that he was becoming more of a nuisance to the Crown, giving speeches all over Virginia promoting the equal rights of Englishmen for all colonists.

Mrs. Dawson came up behind me and put a hand on my shoulder. "Man of few words," she commented. "Not sure how sociable he is. Anyway, finish cleaning up what dishes you can and then hit the hay. You're going to have a long day tomorrow. And Will, it has been a pleasure having you around here. If'n you decide to settle down, I would gladly take you back here and teach you the tavern trade." She gave me a motherly hug, something I had not felt in a very long time, not since I saw my mother last.

One would think that on the brink of a great adventure with the real possibility that I would be able to see my father, who was rumored to be interned on a prison ship in Charles Town Harbor, I would have been unable to sleep. In actuality, exhausted, I fell asleep almost instantly and stayed that way until "King George" crowed his first call for morning sometime about five a.m. I know I dreamed, but for the life of me, I could not recall any of the wistful moments, only that my dreams must have been peaceful because I felt fully restored and ready for my journey.

By 5:30 I was cleaned and dressed. As I entered the kitchen, Mrs. Dawson and Cassey were hard at work. On the kitchen table in the corner, was a plate of eggs and sausage. I eyed them hungrily.

"Well just don't stand there," laughed Mrs. Dawson. "If'n you don't eat them eggs, I'll have to eat them myself."

Without a word, I eased onto the bench and devoured the eggs and sausage. Cassey brought me a cup of coffee rather than tea. The dark, bitter liquid tasted like nectar from heaven. It almost instantly warmed my body and lifted the remaining sleep fog from my brain.

"Master Will, when you get to Charles Town, if'n you have time, you will be more than welcomed to go visit my cousins, the Charles'," said Cassey. They work for Governor Bull. Just go around back and tell them Cassey sent you. They be good people and if'n you need anything, they will know where you can get it."

"Thank you, Cassey, I will be sure to stop by and give them your greetings and love." My first twang of apprehension, I was surely becoming paranoid and questioned whether Cassey was just being nice or did she have a hidden agenda.

"As a token, would you give my Uncle John this Guinea? This would mean a lot to me and his family."

The gold Guinea shined even in the dim light of the kitchen corner. With trepidation, I took the guinea from Cassey's hand. "I'll guard this with my life and make sure it gets to your uncle in Charles Town without fear." In my gut, I knew I had violated rule number one and would have to be careful that it did not have adverse consequences. I tucked the Guinea into the small hidden pocket on the inside of my vest pocket.

Cassey scurried away with a smile on her face. As if on cue, Mrs. Dawson slid into the bench beside me.

"Will, you be careful on your trip and come back to us if'n you can. We'll miss you. I know Cassey has relatives in Charles Town and she will be thrilled if you stop by to see them. Their situation is not the same as Cassey's situation with me. Her cousins are servants to the Governor, slaves by any other term. I just don't know how they are treated. Use a modicum of caution and don't disturb the apple cart, if'n you know what I means." She paused and then began again, "I too have a relative in Charles Town; my sister, Gayle Stevens, lives there and by happenstance runs a small coffee house down by the battery, naturally it's called Stevens. Not a quality place like mine, but she does let rooms, which are comfortable enough if you come recommended. Here, give her this letter of introduction and she will treat you right." Mrs. Dawson extended a small wax-sealed letter to me with her sister's name, "Mrs. Gayle Stevens" prominently scrolled on the front side of the letter.

Instantly, my stomach churned as I counted mistake number two on what appeared to be a growing list of judgmental errors on my part. As I extended my hand to take possession of the letter, I had no idea what was in the letter or what sort of information it might contain. All I could think about was my neck was feeling the tightness of a noose being slowly wrapped around it.

I smiled and jokingly retorted, "If her hospitality is even half as good as yours Mrs. Dawson, I'm sure my stay in Charles Town will be memorable," as I thought to myself that a hangman's appointment would be perhaps less than memorable.

I tucked the small letter into another pocket of the vest, secure enough to withstand most anything which might occur. Still, a nagging suspicion played on my soul, a suspicion that I was being used by one or both women for nefarious purposes. But then it was custom for trusted travelers to take items like money or letters to distant relatives or acquaintances rather than trust them to the royal post. I tried to soothe my hesitations and prepared to depart the inn in a jovial frame of mind, at least on the surface.

*****

"Well, Mrs. Dawson, I know it is still early, but I need to get my kit together, grab my newly-dyed coat and meander over to Squire Randolph's to get my final instructions." With that, I rose from the bench at the same time as Mrs. Dawson, gave her a hug, and then walked over to Cassey and gave her a parting hug. Neither woman could tell I was concerned about my new "directives" to make separate contacts in Charles Town. Maybe I was paranoid, but I had to be wary.

"Wait Will, Cassey put together a small packet of food for your trip. Better to have your own food, rather than pay a shilling or two for vittles." Mrs. Dawson handed me a sizable packet of wrapped food about the size of a small watermelon. "If'n you are thrifty, this should last you until you reach Charles Town."

By my calculations, I left the inn shortly after 6:30 a.m., with my knapsack on my shoulder and Queen Anne neatly tucked away in an inner vest pocket of my vest. I was not going into the unknown without some protection. Of course, my hunting knife was situated on the left side of my waist belt under my vest with its handle slightly angled to the front for easy access.

The morning chill was noticeable and not unappreciated. Yet, it was the persistent humidity, which made the air heavy and moist. I strolled along the side streets toward Squire Randolph's office. As I came into view of the Governor's Palace, I noticed a troop of dragoons meandering about, some in full regalia, most with open vests and hatless as they tended to their mounts, fixed their tack, and engaged in small talk, oblivious to anything around them. Even from a distance, I recognized Captain Bakersfield. He was talking to another "old friend," the Sergeant Major. It made my skin crawl. I felt one step closer to the hangman's noose. I quietly and unnoticed slipped away to wait for Squire Randolph at his office.

On his office porch, I took a seat on a comfortable bench and waited patiently. As the birds chirped and sang their morning melodies, I watched Williamsburg slowly come to life. Near seven o'clock, I guess, the streets were filling with merchants on their way to their stores and farmers bringing produce and wares for sale.

Mixed in the milieu of the citizenry and barely noticeable was a lone backwoodsman, riding low in his saddle with his rifle slung on the saddle in some sort of scabbard, headed out of Williamsburg, south toward Yorktown. It was remarkable, in that normally, rifles were either carried cross-saddle or hung across the back like the dragoons normally did. The only scabbards I had seen before were pistol scabbards hung on either side of a dragoon saddle. It was intriguing to see a small change in carrying a weapon safely, securely, and apparently comfortably. I did notice the woodsman had a cow's knee securely wrapped around his lock, frizzen, and trigger, which meant he wasn't concerned about any immediate threat because it did take a few seconds to present the rifle, disengage the cow's knee, and ready the rifle to fire. I did take solace knowing full-well that underneath the black sheep's skin covering his saddle there were probably a brace of Pennsylvania flintlocks ready for use. He continued out of sight, seemingly unconcerned about the events beginning to unfold.

"Master Will, so good to see you here so early in the morning. I had hoped you would show up a little early. Captain Bakersfield informed me late last night he wanted to leave for Yorktown by eight o'clock. So come on in and let's get you prepared for your journey. Your horse should be here shortly." Without further ado, Squire Randolph strode into his office without another word. I was unable to even mutter a "Good Morning, sir," before he disappeared into the doorway. I scampered in behind him.

Already seated at his desk, he motioned me into his office and took a seat as he rummaged through papers on his desk. "Just a second. Ah, here it is, your commission as a King's courier, duly stamped and signed by Governor Murray, Lord Dunmore. Now for your packet to take to the Acting Royal Governor, Sir William Bull. Don't concern yourself with the contents, just personal letters to the Governor, official correspondence, and other official matters. Do take care not to lose this packet and make sure you keep it sealed. Is that understood?"

"Yes sir," I quickly and succinctly responded.

"Here is your official pouch, our key to the lock, the packet, and 20 shillings for your expenses. You will make an accounting for all expenditures with Sir William in Charles Town and turn over all unused funds to him. Get a receipt from him. At the conclusion of your duties, you will be paid appropriately. For you personally, here is a letter from our Governor to Sir William instructing him to allow you to see your father if he is present in the environs of Charles Town. This is no guarantee he is there or if Sir William will honor the request. Any questions Will?"

"What shall I do about lodging in Yorktown and passage to Charles Town?"

"Ah, lodging should cost no more than a shilling for a bed at an inn. Your commission will serve as your passage authorization. Anything else?" Without waiting for a response from me, he rose from his desk. "Now let's get down to business. Let's get your horse and introduce you to Captain Bakersfield, your host for the trip to Yorktown." With that, he strode out of his office. I fell in right behind him trying to keep up with his pace.

The horse turned out to be a beautiful roan mare, about 16 hands high with the build of a jumper. The tack and saddle were fairly standard, although the saddle had extra attachment points for tying down bags and such. There was also one pistol scabbard on the right-hand side of the saddle, loaded with a Dragoon pistol. Mr. Randolph noticed my attention and remarked, "The pistol you will keep with you until you get to Charles Town. It is loaded and ready to fire, if necessary. You will turn the pistol over to Sir William upon arrival and delivery of the packet. On your return, you may pick up the pistol and return it to me. Understood?"

I nodded my head, "Yes, sir."

The short walk to the Governor's House was solemn as it was quiet. Just the noises on the street were all I heard. The horse's steel-shoed hooves clopping, the cartwheels churning on the street gravel, our boots keeping a rhythmic pace. As we neared the Governor's House, Squire Randolph decided to give me one more piece of unsolicited advice.

"Will, mind your manners, watch your language, and don't

engage any of the dragoons in any erstwhile political discussions."

Rather than attempt to clarify the instructions, I took the simple way and retorted, "Yes, sir."

As we approached the troop, I could tell all the dragoons were making their final adjustments to their tack. Captain Bakersfield greeted Squire Randolph with a sharp salute and nod of his head.

"Squire Randolph, I see you have our young courier in hand. Most appreciated that you got him here on time. We need to proceed with our patrol to Yorktown immediately." Turning to me, he addressed me rather friendly, "So Master Will Jones, you've become somewhat of an enigma, rascally, rowdy colonial youth, and now if we are to believe a Royal courier on his way to Charles Town. Quite a switch, which I have been assured has been fully vetted and stamped with the Governor's approval." Less friendly, and more sinister, he continued, "Mind your manners and just remember we will keep our eyes on you at all times. Is that understood?"

It seemed at the time that I should have at least shown some backbone, but the admonitions of my backwoods friend suppressed any outspokenness. "Yes sir," I responded feebly.

The Captain turned to my nemesis, the Sergeant Major, now in full redcoat regalia, and commanded, "Sergeant Major prepare the dragoons to mount."

Quickly, without discussion, the Sergeant Major turned to the dragoon who had hastily formed their mounts, and yelled, "Dragoons, prepare to mount."

Captain Bakersfield casually mounted his horse and the dragoons awaited their order. Comfortably seated on his horse, the

Captain nodded to the Sergeant Major, who quickly shouted, "Mount!" In unison, the dragoons mounted in perfect precision. I quickly jumped to the side of my mount and climbed onto my mare. Captain Bakersfield extended his hand to Squire Randolph, said a quick goodbye, and left at a quick trot. The Sergeant Major looked at me, motioned me to join him by his side, and signaled with an upraised hand for the troop to move out. I could not help but be somewhat impressed by the sight. Twenty horses all starting on the right leg as if tied together by some invisible rope.

I quickly pulled alongside the Sergeant Major, nodded to him without a word spoken. We rode silently for several miles on the 15-mile trip to Yorktown and then finally he opened our conversation, "So Will, it has been a while since we last encountered each other. Good to see you have grown a bit and still have your hair on your head. From the stories we have heard, you have had quite a few adventures and even survived a run-in with our Cherokee friends. Now it does seem a bit confusing to see you at my side rather than looking at the business end of your rifle. You do have my permission to speak."

Hesitantly, I began. "If truth be known, Sergeant Major, the rifle wasn't even loaded and it was meant to be no disrespect to you or the Crown. We, the boys and I, saw it as our duty to run away with the rifles in order to make sure the town could still defend itself against marauding Cherokees and Sioux. There were rumors about Indians being restless and using the troubling situation between the Crown and us as an excuse to raid outlying settlements. As far as the other rumors, tales, or adventures, I have no knowledge of any action on my part or of those who may have been with me which would constitute any disloyalty to the Crown. I volunteered to be a Royal Courier in order to curry favor with the Governor, in hopes I could see my father, who is being wrongfully held in custody in Charles Town. I did not have the means or the influence to undertake such a journey without official support or authorization."

"Well said, young Will. It does seem that you and your merry band of juveniles did, in fact, carry out a march from the backwoods and returned to your homes as a fairly organized armed and effective militia."

"That is entirely explainable. As a group, we were lost and without an ability to make a safe return home. By happenstance, we came across a group of settlers headed west, some of whom had previously had military experience. They offered and we accepted their hospitality and accompanied them a few leagues into the wilderness. Along the way, they taught us basic military skills and improved our marksmanship, although they did not have much powder to spare. At least we had some. Anyway, once we reached Gap, we took the trail back southeast in order to return to our homes, then assured we could at least handle ourselves if set upon by war parties or brigands. Surprisingly, we encountered no difficulties on our return, which turned out to be more arduous and tiring than adventurous. Once we reached our homes, we disbanded and returned what rifles we had back to the village militia. That's the end of it."

The Sergeant Major bellowed loudly, "You little rascal, what an understatement of your journey. Reports have you and your band of boys escaping capture by the Indians, dispatching brigands on the way to Sycamore Falls, consorting with Daniel

Boone, shooting up a tavern in the highlands, and then like ghosts on the moors of Scotland, vanishing into the green valleys of Northern Virginia never to be seen again. Obviously, a rumor, but we had reports your little band of brigands numbered close to 200, with three cannons, a troop of 15 cavalries, and a brace of wagons."

"Pure conjecture Sergeant Major. We never numbered more than 15 boys, although we all had rifles and pistols at our disposal. We did acquire a small cart for our bedding but nothing else. Perhaps we did have a few narrow escapes, but nothing historically significant. The tavern incident was merely one well-placed shot from a squirrel rifle that detached the ear of a tavern provocateur. In fact, that was our only shot in anger. It was highly effective, given the fact we formed a skirmish line immediately in front of the tavern and dared any miscreant to engage us. You see, we were defending ourselves. Nothing we did had any hint of aggression against the Crown. We actually looked at our journey as a rite of passage from boys to young men who acquired backwoods skills."

"Well, I'm glad to get your version of the rumors. The fact is, the Crown viewed your adventures as merely troubling and not anything rebellious. Although I do have to admit, the ear your lad detached belonged to the brother of a British Colonel in New York. He was highly motivated to send a troop of his dragoons all the way to the Cumberland to hunt you down. Cooler heads prevailed once the whole truth of the matter was disclosed. Truly, one should not disparage a young sharpshooter in such a menacing encounter. And compliments on your skirmish line. Reports have it that several noteworthy brigands bailed out the back of the tavern, never to be seen in those parts again."

Chapter 37

Yorktown

The remainder of the patrol to Yorktown was uneventful, more or less. Not five miles out from Yorktown, with the smell of the sea on the breeze, we passed the tattered-looking woodsman on the side of the road taking what appeared to be a break. As we passed, he rose and politely nodded to the Captain, who in return tipped his hat to the stranger.

We arrived by the bay road straight onto Water Street. One of the more prosperous ports on the South Chesapeake Bay, Yorktown was active and vibrant. We turned on Ballard Street and made our way to the Customhouse, my drop-off point on this part of my journey.

The Captain dismounted and walked toward me as I dismounted and grabbed my gear. "Young Will, this is where we part ways. Hopefully, we won't meet again. Behind you is the Swan Inn, possible accommodations overnight. To your front left is Smith Street, which should take you to the wharf. There you should be able to find passage to Charles Town on a coastal schooner or another ship. Private Goddard will take your horse and return it to Squire Randolph." Without further conversation, the Captain abruptly did an about-face and marched into the Customhouse. A dragoon, more than likely Private Goddard, took the reins of my horse out of my hand and led the horse away. Nothing was said, no acknowledgment whatsoever. Rudeness seemed to be a trait among the dragoons on this day.

"Well, laddie, looks like you are on your own; not that the dragoons are the most hospitable riding companions, but then again, your saga did not sit well with them," intoned the Sergeant Major.

"No use in trying to set the record straight. It would seem their minds are firmly set in stone," I retorted,

"These are trying times for us British. We don't know which colonist to trust and which to be wary of."

"Sergeant Major, lest you forget, we, the colonists, are British also. The only difference is that we, being residents in the colonies, have no voice in the government back in England. We are, because we reside here, denied the basic rights of representation enjoyed by our cousins in England."

"If Parliament would include representatives from all our colonies, where would that put the good people of Britain in the pool of government? Outnumbered and at the mercy of self-serving colonists from the four corners of the world. A totally unacceptable situation. Could you imagine that colonial representatives, who would dominate Parliament, could force all kinds of measures to their advantage and disenfranchise those who stayed in Britain? Why, the colonists could insist that the capital of the British Empire be moved to say, New York or God forbid, Delhi."

"Obviously, Sergeant Major, your mind is set and no one can persuade you. I appreciate your company on the ride to Yorktown, but I have a lot to do before I board a ship to Charles Town." With little formality, we tipped our hats to each other and I strode back down the street to the Swan Inn. A shilling secured me a bed in the upper floor communal room. That done, I quickly left and wandered down to the wharf to see if I could book passage on the morning tide to Charles Town.

This undertaking proved to be more of a chore than I had anticipated. There were numerous boats at anchor in the bay and a few tied up at the wharf. Two impressive warships, the HMS Augusta and the HMS Essex, both with two decks bearing 64 guns, rode easily on the smooth waters of the lower Chesapeake. Other smaller commercial ships were anchored nearby, mostly two-masted, shallow draft, coastal schooners. At the wharf, I engaged a British customs official and inquired about ships headed to Charles Town.

Much to my disappointment, most vessels currently in port were headed up the Chesapeake to Baltimore or out to sea and then on to New York or Boston. The HMS Essex and Augusta were temporarily "on station" at Yorktown performing harbor duty, which according to the official, meant performing short coastal patrols in and around the mouth of the Chesapeake. Only one small coastal schooner tied up at the end of the wharf offered any hope. As I approached the small two-masted schooner, I noticed the name Baltick carved into a wooden plank on the starboard bow of the ship. I hailed a deckhand on the ship. "Is this ship headed to

Charles Town on the morning tide?" I inquired.

The scruff-looking sailor looked at me, sized me up and down, and merely said, "Wait there." He quickly disappeared below deck.

Shortly, a portly, middle-aged man, wearing a worn, red coat of the British Navy, appeared on deck and addressed me. "So, laddie, ye wish to sail to Charles Town, do ye? Well, Charles Town is the third or fourth stop on our journey back to St. Eustatia. We have a hammock or two free for the right price. There be no room in my humble quarters for even a well-heeled guest, such as yourself."

Naively, I took a chance. "I'm a Royal Courier on my way to Charles Town and in immediate need of assistance to get there as quickly as possible."

The portly man laughed heartily. "Well, don't ye be thinking of pulling that on me young squire. I could give a barnacled bum, who you are or what ye be. If'n you sail with us, ye pay for your keep and ye have watch responsibilities. There are no free rides on the Baltick. The trip will cost you five schillings; with food that'll be seven schillings. The trip, if we are lucky and don't encounter no pirates or customs schooners, should last no more than seven days. I'll not be sailing in the dark and we'll lay anchor at night in the coastal waterways. That's where the watch is most important. It is necessary to ask, can ye and will ye be able to fire a musket? I know some of you young squires have no taste for the flint. Now, who do ye be?"

Now I was faced with a problem. I could not use my status as a courier with the captain of the Baltick and my food rations wouldn't last seven days. "I can pay the five shillings for passage and the two shillings for food, but I'll need a receipt for the cost. The Crown is very strict about what I can spend. As far as a musket, I prefer a Pennsylvania rifle to a Brown Bess."

The portly captain roared with laughter. "Be here in the morning at five o'clock so we can make the morning tide. And I'll take three shillings now to hold a hammock for ye. Just to keep us on a formal footing, ye can address me as Captain Thomas during the voyage.

At that, the scruffy seaman descended the gangplank and put out his hand. Dutifully I placed three shillings in his grubby hand. Then to my surprise, he responded, "Thank you, Squire Will Jones. We hoped you'd be sailing with us." He winked at me and scurried back up the gangplank to hand the shillings to the captain. "In the morning, young squire, and don't be late or we'll sail without ye and I'll damn well keep the three shillings," yelled the portly Captain, who then retreated below deck. The scruffy seaman returned to working on the repair of one of the ship's lines.

I could not help having a sinking feeling in my stomach. It was an eerie sensation and an unanswerable question of how could someone know about me and my trip. My senses were on full alert, paranoia taking the upper hand. I wandered through Yorktown and savored the sights and sounds, mindful to keep an open eye out for any unusual activity. No one paid me any attention. Mindful of my financial status, I soon tired of roaming the town and settled down on a patch of green just off Water Street with a view of the bay.

The wharf was in the distance and I could see the Essex and Augusta riding quietly in the bay. The wharf was filled now with small, shallow-draft coastal schooners, the Baltick riding low in the water on the leeward side. A procession of longboats was scurrying back and forth from ships anchored off the port or to a landing adjacent to the wharf. There, crews of longshoremen were loading barrels and bales of goods onto awaiting freight wagons or unloading freight wagons and loading the longboats. To the naked eye, it seemed to be organized chaos. As each longboat arrived at the wharf, a tall, lean, well-dressed man in a black tri-corner hat holding a writing board in his hand met the boat and scribbled something on his hand-held board and then signaled to one of four longshoremen crews to move forward. Later I would learn he was the stevedore, the sole person responsible for the commerce on the wharf. With precision and full command, the crews followed his directions without question.

Only one other man seemed to have any responsibility in the wharf area. He was thick of stature, at least 15 stone, and with a head full of black shiny hair pulled back in a stylish ponytail wearing a dark blue naval style coat, without rank. It appeared he had an office at the foot of the wharf because he came and went frequently up and down the wharf and in the longboat landing area. I pegged him to be the wharf master. In other ports, he would have been called the harbormaster, but since Yorktown lay at the foot of the Chesapeake Bay and had only a wharf and not a harbor, he was by default the wharf master. His job, it appeared, was to control the ebb and flow of boats, ships, and schooners in the adjacent area. Several longboats landed next to the wharf and British Naval officers climbed the short distance up to the wharf. There they smartly saluted the wharf master who returned their salute.

Greetings were exchanged and the bevy of officers would disappear into the master office.

My observations lasted most of the afternoon and enlightened me on the operations of a small port. More importantly, the afternoon entertainment was free of charge. As the sun began to set, I was joined by a familiar face, my backwoodsman, now clad in more cosmopolitan clothes of a mid-level merchant.

"So, young Will, you've been enjoying the free spectacle of the Port of Yorktown. I'm sure your British pay clerk will appreciate your frugality. Now if someone were to later ask you to sketch a street map of Yorktown, could you do it from memory?"

"Sir, I think without a doubt I could sketch one without much effort. Should I do one now?" I inquired.

"If you value your life, I would refrain. Surely you don't want to be called out as a spy. Only when you are in safe company of the Committee should you undertake such an endeavor. Just remember as much as you can. What do you see as being significant about our host port at the moment?"

I was a little perplexed. I didn't know what my erstwhile mentor wanted me to explain.

"Just give me your impression of the port and its ability to handle commerce in and out of this area."

I started slowly, hoping I was on the right track. "Yorktown is the only major port for the colony of Virginia, which has easy access to the Atlantic via the Chesapeake Bay. Probably small by comparison to other ports such as Boston and New York, it nevertheless is an important access point for British shipping to Virginia and the surrounding countryside. Because of its small size and limited wharf space, commerce in and out of the port is restricted. If more than two or three ocean-going vessels arrive, then the compilation with the flood of coastal schooners and river longboats would cause chaos. From a naval point of view, the port is basically indefensible. There are no defensive works, no cannons, and no fortified positions, much less any type of breastwork. British naval ships arriving in the harbor risk being blockaded by a superior naval force since there is but one way in and one way out. That Yorktown is considered an important British asset on the Chesapeake shows the short-sightedness of the British. A blockade of Yorktown and the Chesapeake from the sea means Baltimore, most of Virginia, and the tidelands are at the mercy of those who are able to maintain the blockade. Yet it would appear the British seem unconcerned about any foreseeable disaster."

"Not too bad, my untrained analyst. Yorktown needs to be and will be considered to be a British redoubt in these troubled times. Even though they don't equate the current situation in the colonies as critical. As long as Yorktown remains open and not pressed by colonial forces, the British will continue to be lulled into a false sense of security, seeing Yorktown and the surrounding area inviolable. And too, it remains open to commerce, which benefits our cause. What better place to land critical supplies and munitions than right under the noses of the British. Patriots of all kinds roaming this area, quietly and unnoticed, bargaining for critical supplies and information. You continue on your journey and leave the future of Yorktown to those of us remaining here. Your report later will confirm our assessment and go a long way toward ensuring this small port will remain vulnerable when the time comes."

The woodsman rose without saying anything else and walked back into the main section of Yorktown. I retreated to the Swan Inn, ordered a pint of ale, and sat in the corner devouring one of the food packets Mrs. Dawson and Cassey had prepared for me. Almost too excited or anxious, whichever it was, I retired early to the sleeping room upstairs and claimed my bed for the night. In the soft glow of the candlelight, I could make out several other travelers preparing for a restless night. Nothing was said, no greetings or salutations. It was as if all wanted to be anonymous and mere shadows in the dim light. One thing I did notice, which caused some mild trepidation, was that each traveler somewhere close by or within easy reach had either a pistol or a knife. I tucked my dragoon under my coat which I used as a pillow and Queen Anne found a comfortable place in my waistband under my untucked shirt.

Chapter 38

The Baltick and Abigail

Shortly after four a.m., a local rooster began his morning serenade. That was my cue to quickly dress, gather my belongings, and head to the port. No one else at the inn, or at least no one I could see, was stirring. Of course, there was a quick stop at the privy.

As I entered Main Street, I would learn later from the ship's captain, I was witnessing the early morning light, or for sailors, it was the beginning of morning nautical twilight (BMNT), just light enough to make out shapes and movement. As I observed, there was a slight movement on the street. Several shapes with bags were proceeding in the same general direction as I was. Further, but in darkness, I could hear the distinct sound of several carts coming into Yorktown. And then there was the chorus of competing roosters announcing the arrival of a new day.

When I arrived at the wharf, the shape of the two-masted Baltick loomed eerily in the morning fog. The portly captain stood at the head of the gangplank and was greeting several passengers boarding the ship. The crewman, who I recognized from the day before, was struggling up the ramp with a load of baggage. I felt somewhat embarrassed that I only had my knapsack and courier bag. I guess I was not much of a seasoned traveler.

"Ah, there you are lad. Glad that you came when you did. Now that we have all on board, we can leave a wee bit early and avoid some of the morning chaos," said the Captain.

"At your service, Captain. If you need my help, I will be glad to assist in any way I can, just as long as you tell me exactly what to do," I replied.

"Well, first of all, come with me below to my luxurious quarters and I will put your belongings under lock and key. Lord help us, if'n any of your things were to come up missing during my watch. I'd not like the Crown poking around my ship if'n your kit comes up missing. Too, you can store your pistol in our weapons chest. And that cute little Queen Anne can go in there, too. You can retrieve them later, once we get under full sail."

"Aye, aye Captain." How he discerned that I was carrying a Queen Anne was a mystery to me. I purposely hid the Anne in my waistcoat, I thought, away from any prying eyes.

As we descended the ladder into the bowels of the ship, small candle lanterns cast a faint light on the interior hold. I could see stacks of cargo lining the walls with small spaces carved out as open quarters for the few passengers traveling southward. These were austere accommodations, just a rung higher than sleeping in a cattle barn. There were no beds as such, only a few hammocks strung between ribs and support beams, and some rather ancient-looking sleeping mats spread out between the bales of cargo.

"Squire," addressing me in a less than respectful tone, the Captain pointed to a hammock adjacent to a door. "Here be your assigned sleeping quarters, I suggest using the hammock, rather than a mat on the deck, less chance of a rat pestering you during your beauty sleep." He unhooked a ring of keys from his belt and opened the squat door, which was not more than four feet in height. "Come inside my quarters, as such. The weapons chest is on the port side. To your left, for flatlanders." The Captain laughed at his own joke.

The room was small by all standards. It was no more than 18 feet wide at its widest point and then narrowed to the canoe stern of the ship, making the length of the room no more than 16 feet in length. On the right side, starboard side I would learn, was a five-foot captain's bed built into the bulkhead of the ship. Besides the weapons chest attached to the port side entrance wall, there was only a small table, which completed the furniture of the captain's cabin. The rest of the space was filled by cargo bales. I quickly placed my dragoon and Queen Anne on the top shelf of the chest. I did notice there were 10 well-maintained muskets in the chest, along with a variety of long knives and several cutlasses. This ship was ready to defend itself from most intruders.

"Not the Captain's quarters of the Exeter, but it is my home on the sea and at sea, I answer to no one but God and myself. So, laddie, let's go topside and get underway. Your only task will be to pull in the lines once we cast off from the wharf. My crew will be in the longboat and will tow us out in the bay until we can catch the outgoing tide and morning wind. Hop to it and earn you keep, young squire."

Without a word, I retreated out of the Captain's cabin and made my way up topside. Along the way, I noticed there were five other passengers, four gentlemen of distinction, and one young lady also well attired. I nodded in their general direction as I climbed the ladder to the deck. The Captain was right behind me. As he made the ladder, he addressed the other passengers.

"We're shoving off. I need all of you to stay out of the way, so stay below until I give the all-clear. Make yourselves comfortable. It will be a while before you're allowed topside."

A young lady's voice spoke up, "What about the young boy, why is he allowed on deck?"

It was obvious, at least to me and I think the Captain too, that this young lady was not used to taking orders from anyone. Spoiled, entitled, and perhaps a bit self-centered, but that was just a quick assessment.

"My dear," the Captain addressed her in his Oxford accent, "the young boy you refer to is actually a seasoned frontiersman, who walked all the way from Sycamore Falls to the far west to Yorktown. He is an experienced young man, not a boy, and by all measures will, by the end of this journey, be a very capable sailor. He above all else knows how to listen and follow orders without question. That is the reason he is topside with my men. If you please, wait until I return for you," gruffly said the Captain.

On deck, the Captain shouted the orders to get underway. Two longshoremen cast off the lines. I proceeded to take the stern line in while a sailor on the bow started to pull in that line. "Circle the lines," commanded the captain.

I had no idea what he meant, but I looked to the sailor on

the bow, and he demonstrated how to make a circle with the line, obviously to keep it secured and out of the way. It took me a moment to get the hang of it, but I succeeded, sort of. The rest of the crew, five men in all, were in the yawl, pulling the Baltick into the bay. It was a slow and laborious task, but the sailors were more than up to the challenge. I moved forward to the bow to watch briefly. In perfect unison, the sailors rowed at a steady pace. Their strong and well-rehearsed rhythm inched the ship away from the wharf and out into the bay.

"Squire, come join me at the helm," roared the Captain happily. I joined him without haste. "Now laddie, you stay with me here while we prepare to set the sails. Not much you can do at this point. As soon as we clear wharf and distance ourselves from the Essex and the Augusta, my lads will scurry back on board, secure the longboat, then set the sails, and we'll be on our way. No use you getting in the way. Just watch and learn. My boys are seasoned sailors and know what to do without much talk from me."

True to his word, as soon as the Baltick had cleared the British warships, the crew scurried back on board. Two of the sailors raised and secured the longboat while the other four crewmen climbed the masts and unfurled the sails. The first to catch the breeze was a small triangle-shaped sail, a jib attached to the top of the first mast, and the foremast out toward the bowsprit. Another sail, also triangular in design, attached to the foremast was the staysail. It too caught the wind and the Baltick picked up speed. The next sail up was a large square mainsail attached also to the foremast. The last sail to go up was a large rectangular sail attached to the rear mast, the mizzenmast. With favorable winds, the Baltick was soon headed to the mouth of Chesapeake Bay.

Once the ship had its full complement of sails set, the Captain sent word below that the passengers could come on deck. Will was soon joined by the other four gentlemen and the young lady. While the gentlemen seemed to be complacent with their status on the ship, the young lady appeared to be irritated. Will avoided her the best he could, but it was not to be.

"So, you're a frontiersman. I thought frontiersmen always dressed in buckskins and carried tomahawks," she said in an aggressive tone.

Will took a deep breath and turned to face her. Awestruck by her close proximity which was well within his personal space, Will noted the young lady was nearly five feet nine inches tall, almost as tall as him, had beautiful blue eyes, dark brown hair peeking out from under her bonnet, and had a summer-tanned face with freckles on her nose. She was no wallflower. She carried herself well and appeared to be a formidable person. Just by her statue, Will quickly calculated she must have weighed between nine and 10 stones. Not heavy, just sturdy.

"Well, do you talk, or are you a deaf-mute?"

"I can speak just fine. And I know my manners apparently better than you. Allow me to introduce myself. William Jones, at your service." Will nodded his head slightly.

"Oh, a proper English frontiersman. Well, in that case, I'm Lady Abigail Farnsworth. My family was originally from Farnworth near Bolton, England. My distant uncle left England and immigrated to Massachusetts and established a textile enterprise there. After my parents died and no one wanted to take me in, at

10 years of age, I was shipped to Boston to live with my uncle. There I enjoyed the distinct pleasure of working 10-hour days, six days a week in one of his textile mills in order to earn my keep. When I turned 15, through the good fortune of a family solicitor in England, an inheritance was sent to me, which freed me from my uncle's servitude. Now I'm on my way to Charles Town to live with other relatives until I determine what I want to do. How is that for a proper introduction Mr. Jones?"

"The title, where did it come from?"

"You do pay attention to details. It came with my inheritance. The title of Lord Farnsworth belonged to my father and his noble status was passed down to me, much to the chagrin of my uncle, who coveted the title. He kept my status secret from me until the papers arrived from England and a solicitor in Boston announced to the Court that I was entitled to be addressed as Lady Abigail and from that point on I was emancipated."

"A court hearing to emancipate you from your wicked uncle? That must have been a spectacle."

Abigail, now relaxing and taking a seat on the forward hatch continued, "Oh, it was quite a show. Unbeknownst to me, my solicitor, who I had never met, had to take my uncle to court, just to force my appearance. In fact, on the day of the hearing, the judge sent a magistrate to the mill where I was working, basically abducted me, and presented me to the judge while I was wearing my tattered and filthy work clothes. I was obviously a sight for the Judge to behold. He immediately ruled my uncle in contempt of court and locked him up. My solicitor was granted my immediate guardianship and instructed to present me to court in proper attire befitting a lady the next day.”

Without taking a breath, she continued and scooted closer to Will, who had taken a seat on the hatch. “It was magical. One moment I was a textile mill scrub and spindle changer, filthy, wearing rags, and bare-footed, and the next moment, I’m being fawned over by a bath lady and doused with perfume. I was a true *Cendrillon*, of sorts. I never really had anything to do with my uncle’s family, so they had no impact on my life and there was no prince in my life, until now.”

Will, all of a sudden, was embarrassed and turned beet red in the face. Abigail laughed out loud.

“Don’t worry, I won’t bite. At the moment, all I need is a friend and since you are traveling alone and the other gentlemen are more concerned with their business ventures in the rice fields of South Carolina, you are elected.”

Will, inexperienced in affairs dealing with women, had never met a woman so bold, forceful, and provocative. On the one hand, he was disconcerted and on the other, he found her exciting.

“Lady Abigail, I will be most honored to be your friend and if you will allow me, I will also escort you to Charles Town.”

“How noble of you William. You may now call me Abigail. You can drop the Lady part. It’s sort of snobbish in these surroundings. What I’m really interested in is learning about the schooner. Do you think the Captain would teach me?”

“I’ll check and ask, but it might be better to dress in something less frilly.”

“Done. I’ll be back in a moment.” Without waiting for an answer, Abigail swung her legs around to the open hatch and jumped down into the hold. It was an athletic move Will had never seen a woman perform.

"Will, where has Lady Farnsworth gone?" asked the Captain as he approached.

"She wants to learn more about the schooner and wants me to ask you to teach her, and I guess about how she sails."

"Hum, an English Lady wants to learn sailing? That's quite the undertaking." surmised the Captain.

"She is not what she appears to be. From the age of 10 until she was emancipated at 15, she was a charwoman in a textile mill outside of Boston. She was held there by her unscrupulous uncle until she was freed by the Court. She is more substantial than she might first appear."

"A good recount of her life, Will. I was aware of some of her background; obviously, a young lassie ready to sow her oats and enjoy her newfound freedom. I would be glad to have the company of ye two to follow me around the ship as long as ye don't get in the way. I might even make you pull a few chores here and there, just to keep both of you in touch with reality."

As if on cue, Abigail appeared in men's brown cord knee-length pants, a tan floppy frontier shirt, dark brown stockings, brown shoes with her long hair braided into a ponytail.

"My, Lady Abigail, if I didn't know it was you, I would say you were fresh from the frontier after clearing your homesite," laughed the Captain.

"Exactly the look I was going for, frontier or the sea. Whatever works. So where do we begin?" gleamed Abigail.

Still awestruck, Will just stood there in amazement and

stared.

"Well, if we can get Master Will's attention, we'll start an orientation of the schooner beginning with the Quarterdeck." The Captain ambled off to the rear of the boat toward the wheel and quarterdeck.

"Come on, Prince Charming, let's get to work or at least on with our orientation. I wonder what he'll have us do to earn our keep? All I can say, it will be a far better experience than working in a textile mill 10 hours a day, six days a week. In fact, anything would be better than that." Abigail headed after the Captain and as she passed Will she gave him a friendly nudge.

The days that followed were a mixture of fun, excitement, and pure drudgery. The Captain pursued his "earn your keep" message. We learned how to swab a deck, secure the lines, climb the rigging, peel potatoes, steer the ship, and how to navigate coastal waters. As toiling as it was at times, it was a rewarding experience. Will, already a stout frontiersman, grew even more rugged. Abigail grew in her knowledge of the world and saw her fitness improve likewise. The two seemed to bond and enjoy each other's company. Although in the back of Will's mind, he still remembered his mission and was not going to let anything interfere with it. He had to find his father.

Chapter 39

Roanoke

The sailing days were just that. The Captain refused to sail at night unless there was a full moon, and on this voyage, there was only the new moon. The waxing crescent had not yet begun and there was always the possibility of pirates lying in wait along the voyage, something the Captain was very concerned about.

At anchorage that first night just inside the Roanoke Inlet, the Captain called the crew, the passengers, and me on deck.

"Tonight, we anchor in this inlet for safety and a little relaxation. We have to be concerned about pirates. Some call themselves privateers, but to me, they are still pirates. The crew and passengers will stand watch during the night. Passengers will stand starboard and port watch for the first watch from 2000 to 2400 hours. Misters Allen, Wentworth, and Jackson will stand from 2000 to 2200. Misters Dreary and Jones will stand watch together from 2200 to 2400. The crew will pick up the watch from midnight until dawn. All on watch will be armed with a cutlass and pistol. I want to emphasize how important this is. We can't afford to be boarded by hostiles in the middle of the night."

"What about me, don't I get to stand watch?" intoned Abigail.

"Lady Abigail," responded the Captain, "I realize you have shown remarkable skill and fortitude in pursuing duties around the ship, but I would not think of putting you in harm's way. I'm not sure you are familiar with the use of a pistol or a cutlass."

"My dear Captain, I assure you that I can use a cutlass just as well as I can handle a scythe and as to using a pistol, I may need a refresher, but as a wee lassie, my father taught me how to load and fire a Queen Anne. So, if you are prepared, I am more than willing to pull my duty on watch."

The crew and passengers joined me in somewhat suppressed laughter at Abigail's commentary. The Captain was not amused.

"Very well, since you and Master Jones have worked well together, he will be responsible for your initial saber training and pistol marksmanship. Master Will, Lady Farnsworth will only get three practice shots. We have to conserve powder and shot."

"Aye, aye Captain, I understand," replied Will.

"Now for a provisioning trip, three of the crew and those who wish may go to the sandbank and go floundering in the early evening. We'll take on fresh flounder to supplement our supplies when and where we can. Now everybody is back to their duties or leisure. Master Will, come with me and I will issue you a pistol, powder, and shot. Don't set up any targets on my railings. Throw a chunk of wood over the port side and use that as your target. I'll not have you shooting up my ship needlessly."

I followed the Captain to his quarters to secure the pistol. Again, in the Captain's quarters, I had a feeling of quiet calm. The Captain quickly opened the weapons cabinet and pulled out a Dragoon pistol, a powder horn, and a handful of shot.

The Captain turned, "Will, take care with that young lady. She may be hardy enough, but she is still a lady in at least her title. Treat her with respect and be aware she may have different goals in mind. Remember you are the King's courier and there is a certain code of conduct to be maintained. I would hate to see you have to stand before a military judge and explain an allegation of reprehensible conduct."

"Aye Captain, I'll continue to maintain a respectful distance from the Lady in accord with my commission as a King's courier."

Back on deck, I secured a scrap of wood to use as a target. "Lady Abigail, if you will, follow me to the port side so we can train you on the loading and firing of a Dragoon pistol."

It only took a short lesson on the loading and firing to get Abigail familiar with the Dragoon. I loaded the pistol first and let Abigail shoot at the scrap wood I had tossed in the water. Her aim was fairly good, but her first shot went over the wood and created a foot-high plume as it hit the water. I corrected her barrel and sight alignment, instructing her to look down the barrel at the end sight and making the sight appear as the top of a circle, no barrel showing. This leveled the gun for an accurate 15-yard shot. Her second shot nicked the wood, her third shot was dead center.

"Well, that was an interesting orientation. I've never seen someone take to shooting a pistol so quickly."

"My father took great pleasure in teaching me to shoot as a

child. If he had lived, I am sure I would have been a very competent hunter. Even as a child he would take me into the field to hunt birds. Those were special moments I still fondly remember. He may have wished for a boy, but I was most glad to accommodate him as a tomboy. Are you going to teach me how to use a cutlass?" asked Abigail.

"We'll have to get the boatswain's mate to instruct us. I'm not good with a long blade. A hunting knife, maybe, but not a cutlass."

I engaged the boatswain's mate, who had served in the Royal Navy to give both Abigail and myself basic moves in cutlass fighting. His instruction drew spectators, not only the other passengers but the crew as well.

"The key to any fight with a cutlass is to keep your blade in front of you to guard and parry and attack. Formally there are seven different moves with a cutlass. You can start by holding an engaging guard. Hold your sword shoulder high with your blade inverted downward. That protects you from a strike. Now if'n your opponent wants to follow the rule of cutlass fighting, you continue to lash at him in somewhat of an X pattern, with an occasional horizontal slash and then an overhand slash to the head. But just remember, while the Royal Navy manual for sword fighting has instructions and examples, there are no rules in a cutlass fight. The more you practice, the better one becomes. You have to be able to slash your enemy as well as defend yourself against his attack. Be careful that your opponent doesn't fight with a cutlass in one hand and a dagger in the other. I myself prefer a large hunting knife as my second weapon. Some prefer even to use their Dragoon as a club instead of a knife. Whatever you do, be aware of who you are fighting and how they are armed. As a mate, don't ever miss the opportunity to help out a fellow shipmate with a slash or two at his opponent. It's a life and death situation with a cutlass. There is only one winner, make sure it is you. Now, those of you who want a little practice, grab a stick and divide up. Pirates on the right, Royal Navy on the left. This will give you an idea of what a melee is like. Easy on the stashes and no poking eyes out. I just want you to get used to fighting in a crowd."

The crew divided up, with passengers alike taking different sides. Abigail, not to be denied, teamed up with Will on the pirate side. At the mark of the boatswain's mate, the melee began. Screams and shouts ensued. Slashes found their marks and bruises were doubled. Soon the whole deck was involved in a practice fight that had even the Captain concerned. As the fight progressed it was apparent that it was getting out of hand and serious injuries were about to be inflicted. The Captain raised his Dragoon and fired.

"Enough!" he shouted. "Belay any further fighting or I'll bring you all up on charges. If'n I didn't know any better, I would have thought there was a real mutiny on hand the way you were wailing away on each other. And you Missy Abigail, intentionally aiming at a man's privates was very uncalled for under the circumstances, although in a real fight I would have commended you for your actions."

The crew and passengers all now sweaty and smelling like wet dogs began to take stock of their injuries. There were plenty of bruises, a few minor cuts in need of stitches, a broken finger, a bashed nose, and a Royal Navy actor with a minor injury to his privates.

Without hesitation, Abigail jumped on top of a closed hold and announced to all, "If any of you need medical attention, I'll be glad to attend to the cuts and bruises. When I worked in the mill, I assisted the practical nurse with injuries to the workers. I was even trained to be a midwife, but I'm sure none of you need that service at the moment. Unfortunately, any injury to men's private parts, well you'll need to see Cookie for assistance. And I do apologize for that injury."

The crew, passengers, and I laughed alike, as those who needed treatment lined up. Cookie produced a box similar to the aid kit which contained medicinal alcohol, needles, thread, and salve to cover wounds. Abigail went about her work, a couple of stitches here, a swab of alcohol there, salve on minor scrapes. She even straightened the broken nose, much to the relief of the injured sailor. All stood in amazement of her skills and banter to go with it.

As the medical treatments were concluding, there came a call from the starboard side. "Ahoy, are things alright on board?"

Off to the starboard side, a yawl was approaching Baltick with seven men on board, six men on the oars, one man on the rudder, all armed with muskets. The Captain quickly gave the order and the boatswain's mate grabbed the keys from the Captain and headed to the gun cabinet below followed by the crew as they prepared for a hostile encounter.

The Captain responded, "Everything is in order on board. What is your purpose?"

The apparent lead in the yawl stood and addressed the Captain, "We spied what we thought was a mutiny on your ship and we came to assist you. Our only intention is to secure your ship from a hostile takeover by your crew."

"We were merely conducting cutlass training for the crew and passengers in case we were to run into pirates in the area. Sorry to have distressed you with our riotous behavior. I assure you all is well on board," answered the Captain.

It was at that moment the crew poured back on deck armed with loaded muskets and cutlasses in their belts. They quickly lined the starboard side and held their muskets high in the ready position, hammers cocked awaiting the Captain's orders. The other passengers and I moved in behind the Captain in a show of support. The display had an unsettling effect on the crew in the yawl. Quickly, the lead in the boat instructed his men to stow their weapons.

In a Cockney accent, the yawl lead yelled, "That's reassuring. We have had some problems in the area in recent months. We weren't sure what was going on. Glad that all is well. In that case, would you accept our invitation to eat with us this early evening onshore? We'd like to hear the latest news from up the coast. We wouldn't detain you long. It's best to set your watch as the sun goes down."

"Aye, invitation accepted. There'll be six of us who'll come to shore. The crew will remain with the ship if that's your wish," bellowed the Captain.

"Come anytime. The sooner the better. We're anxious to hear everything that has gone on." With that, the yawl began to turn back to shore as the six rowers found their rhythm and set a quick pace toward a distant shoreline. The Captain watched the yawl as it left carefully, noting its course and direction.

"Boatswain mate, prepare to launch the yawl. The passengers, you, and I will be going ashore for bit of conversation and a bite to eat. The rest of the crew will tend the boat and set a watch. If anything is amiss, fire the cannon and we'll return quickly."

As the Baltick yawl approached Mill Landing on the southern end of Roanoke Island a small group of people was waiting. When the Captain and our entourage landed, pleasantries were exchanged and we were led to a nearby community building where a fare of fish, shrimp, oysters, and baked potatoes awaited the guests.

Abigail, the four gentlemen, and I were somewhat isolated during the conversation because the islanders were speaking in Cockney, a type of brogue called "hoi toid" which was for the most part unintelligible to us. The Captain and the boatswain mate were having a high time since both adapted to the conversation and engaged the islanders in their peculiar language. I could pick up bits and pieces of the conversation, which mostly dealt with the state of the hostilities between the British colonial government and the rebels. There was an exchange of some seriousness when the word "pirate" was clearly enunciated. The port town of Edenton was mentioned and all the islanders shook their heads in despair. Obviously, the port, a short distance up the inlet was of great concern.

The feast and conversation lasted no more than a full hour before the apparent leader of the islanders stood to conclude it. The group which had escorted us again took the duty to escort us back to the landing and their yawl. The last word from the islanders was "God Speed!"

On the way back to the Baltick the Captain was silent, in a contemplative mood. He was concerned, but kept his thoughts to himself during the row back to the ship. Once on board, the Captain assembled all of us.

"Aye, there is trouble brewing in these parts, especially along the Coastal Tide region. Privateers, which they call themselves, pirates by any other name, are boarding merchant vessels, taking goods, money, jewelry, weapons, and any other valuables all in the name of the fight against the British. One of the key ports for these brigands is Edenton, just at the mouth of the Chowan River from Roanoke. So far, they have left Roanoke alone and have, in fact, enlisted their assistance to give warning of any encroaching British Naval vessels. At the moment, the islanders want to be left out of the fight. They did advise us that we were probably too small to catch the attention of the pirates, but we should steer clear of the Hatteras channel and sail out beyond the shoals, just to be safe. There is little margin for error in the channel at low tide and easy pickings for pirates. We'll be safe here tonight. Their main vessels, the Grand Turk and the Dolphin, left for Hatteras on yesterday's morning tide. Likewise, we'll leave early on the morning tide. Now I suggest we all get as good a night's sleep as you can, but make sure the watch is vigilant." The Captain turned and went below deck to his quarters to chart a course around Cape Hatteras.

"Will," inquired Abigail, "who are those pirates? And what are they doing raiding up and down the Coast?"

"Abi," I chose to shorten her name as a term of friendship,

"if they are privateers as they claim, they have been given authority under some 'Letters of Marque' by a government authority, by the provisional state, or continental government to attack and secure goods, money, and other bounty to be shared between the privateers and the authority. In other words, they are the 'Navy' of the continental government. Disorganized, but authorized to act on their behalf. Perhaps the only difference, and it is a minor one, is that they are not supposed to molest those who surrender, and each vessel captured becomes part of this disorganized navy. Those unfortunate enough to be captured are either carried to the next port or marooned on the outer banks. Sailors who are captured are either recruited to join the privateers or ransomed for their return. British Naval Officers are a prize capture. They are often ransomed for hundreds of pounds."

"The way you explain it, they don't seem too bad and they seem to have a degree of civility," responded Abigail.

"Normally, the capture of a merchant ship is a quick and mostly bloodless event. There are reports of merchant ships who choose to fight, ending up in costly pitched battles with the privateers, costing an untold loss of men, merchandise, and ships. Some have been successful in fending off the pirates, but those who weren't suffered the consequences. Captured crews and passengers were said to have been made to 'walk the plank.' Too bad if they couldn't swim to shore. These are not gentlemen privateers. They can be ruthless and unforgiving pirates reminiscent of the old pirates of the Caribbean, only these pirates are not subject to any law or justice, as long as they share the booty with the continental government."

Chapter 40

Sloop Point

The crew, as well as the passengers, were aroused at the end of the watch by eight bells, which denoted it was four o'clock in civilian time. Cookie quickly began a breakfast broth of fish and grits while the rest of the crew prepared to make way. Breakfast was on the run for the crew as they grabbed a bowl of gruel and chomped down on hard biscuits. We had to wait for our breakfast until Cookie could make a proper breakfast for the Captain and passengers.

By the first bell, the crew was ready to weigh anchor as the ship's yawl was positioned to pull the Baltick out into the channel to catch the outgoing tide.

The Captain gave the order to "weigh anchor," which was repeated by the crew in unison. Four of the crew began the arduous task of raising the anchor using a large wooden windlass pulley. As the ship moved forward propelled by the raising of the anchor and the tow of the yawl, the outgoing tide caught the ship and soon the Baltick was in the channel headed to the Roanoke inlet and the coastal waters. As the yawl quickly returned and was secured, other sailors scrambled to set the sails at the Captain's command. Now under sail, the Baltick began its measured progress through the inlet and into the Atlantic Ocean's coastal waters. As the breeze picked up, the Captain turned south and set more sails. Now on an adjusted course to skirt the Hatteras Channel and sail around the shoals, the Captain turned over the ship to the boatswain mate to continue the journey.

From his position, by the wheel, the Captain announced, "Lady and gentlemen, please join me in my quarters for breakfast. This will be the only formal meal for the day." With that, the Captain descended to his quarters followed by Abigail, the four gentlemen, and myself.

By most standards, and given the unique situation, Cookie had outdone himself. There set in the rather cramped refines of the Captain Cabin was a table for six with china plates, coffee cups, and a full place setting of polished silverware. As all were seated, the young mess steward in a clean white waistcoat, who was no more than 12 or 13 years old, served each guest two fried eggs, two pieces of bacon, and a soft biscuit. Miss Abigail was the recipient of not only two eggs but also three pieces of bacon and two soft biscuits. Her cheeks flushed as everyone chuckled about her bounty. Cookie came next with the pot of coffee which enlisted an explanation from the Captain.

"To all, I apologize that we are serving coffee instead of tea. There seems to be a shortage of tea due to taxes, which are the root of our present hostilities. Coffee is a substitute and, in many ways, symbolizes our desire to plot our own destiny. Those of you who have not drank coffee before, ye might find a spot of milk or sugar to make it more palatable. I myself, prefer the brew straight, so that nothing interferes with the flavor, no matter that it might be bitter. Oh, 'To the King,'" said the Captain as he raised his coffee cup in a toast.

The humor was not lost on the gentlemen or either Abigail or me, although no one commented, cautious not to reveal where one's real opinions lay.

This was a good sailing day. Favorable winds propelled the Baltick down the coastline, around the Hatteras shoals on toward Cape Lookout. Bypassing those shoals, the Baltick took a west-south-west course. The Captain and crew had kept watch all through the voyage, wary of any privateers that might be lurking about. Several times, sails were spotted along the coastline. Close examination confirmed they were small coastal trading schooners and not a threat to the Baltick. Twice the crew spotted sails out in the Atlantic more than 10 leagues away. These appeared to be Royal Navy ships headed north to New York or Boston. They were warships, either in the Dublin class or the Arrogant class carrying 70 or more guns. They were definitely not something coastal privateers would engage.

The Captain gathered the passengers together. "We have made good time and with God's will, we shall make berth at Top Sail Inlet just before nautical sunset. We have a delivery to make at Sloop Point and I need to pick up a couple of barrels of salt. All will stay on board. I have no idea what we will encounter there. It's not a big landing, but it has been known to have hosted pirates in years gone by."

As forecast by the Captain, the Baltick arrived at the Top Sail Inlet just as the sun began to set in the west. Still under sail with a light landward breeze, the ship coasted into Sloop Point. There to the amazement of the crew and passengers alike was a lively coastal port. Dozens of small single-masted sloops lay at anchor, others were even beached on the shoreline with gangplanks connecting them to the beach. Ahead at the two wharves were two large, two-masted brigantines, which appeared to have been modified and carried two swivel cannons each mounted on the deck and visible for all to see.

I was standing next to the Captain as we arrived at Sloop Point. "Will, make sure everyone stays alert. The Dolphin is in port and another brigantine alongside her does not bode well. I'm not sure what flag she flies. Best that we stay as quiet as we can and not draw any attention to ourselves."

The Captain turned next to the boatswain's mate. "Once we dock, have several of the men go below and load all the muskets and pistols. Keep them ready, but out of view. As much as I would like to load our cannon, we'll have to forego that option."

The Baltick slowly coasted into the far wharf, away from the two privateers. As ordered, the crew went about their business in an orderly and circumspect manner. The passengers, as ordered, remained below decks. Only I was allowed topside since I appeared more associated with the crew than did the other passengers.

With the ship securely tied up to the wharf, the crew began to bring large bundles from the hold and put them on deck. In all, there were 10 large canvas bundles about three feet square, weighing approximately seven stones and each numbered with a large black numeral. Soon a small convoy of open wheelbarrows descended on the Baltick to take charge of the cargo. The Captain descended to the wharf with his cargo manifest in hand and talked to the wharf master, who took charge of the offloading of the cargo. A crude tackle and crane were rigged up by the crew and each cargo bundle was transferred from the ship to the waiting wheelbarrows on the wharf. The whole procedure only lasted 45 minutes and was complete by the beginning of the evening nautical twilight (BENT).

Wharf lights were lighted to illuminate the gangway. As soon as the cargo was unloaded, two wheelbarrows returned with caskets of salt. As the Captain and the wharf master shook hands in concluding the transaction, a sailor approached the Captain and delivered a written message. The Captain opened the message and seemed somewhat disturbed. It was obviously not good news.

As the Captain returned to the ship, he had the boatswain mate assemble the crew. "The passengers and I will be going ashore to meet with some merchants about trade prospects in the upcoming months. We should be back by the end of the first watch. All hands will in the meantime stay alert. Remember we are humble colonial seafaring traders. We have no quarrels with any of the belligerents in this area."

"Will, come with me. We need to talk with the others. I'm not comfortable with this invitation. It seems someone knows exactly who is on our ship and our intended destination at least as far as Charles Town."

The Captain and I descended below decks to the waiting passengers. The Captain didn't hesitate in addressing them. "We have a dinner invitation from two respectable merchants in Sloop

Point for all of us, by name. I'm not sure how they know who you are or how they came by that information. All I know is that it is highly unusual for anyone to know who is traveling on my ship, much less extend them an invitation for dinner. Since this is a questionable invitation in a questionable port, we will arm ourselves. I am not comfortable with two privateers docked across from us. The wharf master assured me the port was quiet. Crews from both ships are, for the most part, behaving themselves. We won't take any chances. Each man will carry a pistol and a blade. Miss Abigail, you will carry a purse that will conceal a small Queen Anne inside. You will also, if you please, conceal on your person somewhere discreet a small dirk or folding knife; your choice."

"Captain, if it pleases you, I prefer a small Scottish dirk to a folding knife. If I need it, I don't want to take time to fumble around opening a folding knife. And please rest assured I know how to use a dirk effectively. Boston was at times a very unruly city, especially for women."

Properly attired, the Captain, the other passengers, and I descended the gangplank and proceeded up the wharf to the business of the merchants, Masters Haldron and Palmer. Their office and emporium was a multi-use building. It housed the shipping office, a dry goods store, a warehouse, an open tavern, and off to the side a small but quaint eating establishment. The main entrance was already closed for the evening, so we proceeded to the west side entrance and entered the tavern. Immediately, the rather full tavern became quiet as sailors, fishermen, and local landsmen gawked at the newcomers. The mostly male crowd was especially taken by the appearance of a lady in the group, although not one man commented.

"Captain," bellowed a tall, balding, rotund giant of a man, "so good of you to accept our invitation for dinner. Allow me to introduce myself. I'm Peter Haldron, half owner of this fine establishment and by default the so-called mayor of this community." He held his hand out for the Captain to shake.

As introductions were made, another man appeared by Haldron's side. Tall, thin, and wearing a green waistcoat, he appeared more martial than Haldron. "Allow me to introduce myself since my partner has forgotten his manners," he said with a smile on his face. "I'm George Palmer, the other half of this firm and for all intents and purposes, I also serve as the magistrate, attorney, and counselor for this community. Our other guests are waiting for us in the dining area. If you would please follow my big friend and me to our small gathering."

As we entered the candlelit dining area, several men in naval officer attire stood up. "Allow me to introduce you to our new friends, Captain John Kirkwood of the brigantine 'Jeanie' and his ensign Mr. Sanders, and then Captain Robert Hosea of the brigantine 'The Dolphin' and his ensign Mr. Falsworth. These gentlemen ply the waters from the Chesapeake to the Caribbean and for now at least, under British letters."

The Captain's demeanor immediately changed as he acknowledged each officer and exchanged greetings.

As the evening proceeded over a minor feast of wild turkey, flounder, venison, sweet potatoes, and corn, the group talked about a variety of subjects from the growing conflict, pirates, shipping lanes, current trade trends, and other shipping opportunities. The assembled ships in Sloop Point were due more to safety concerns than trade opportunities. Several privateers had been spotted in the area and many of the trade ships sought the safety of coastal ports in order to "weather" the danger.

Captain Kirkwood spoke with concern. "If I can speak for myself and Captain Hosea, our brigantines are normally fast enough to outrun most privateers. So, as a matter of practice, we sail further out in the Atlantic where we can see approaching ships and take evasive maneuvers when necessary. However, on this voyage, we are both laden with goods bound for different parts of the Caribbean. It was our joint decision to stay closer to the coast until we get past Saint Augustine and then head out to the open seas and more favorable winds."

Captain Thomas, who was now relaxed with several glasses of madeira under his belt, spoke with authority and commitment. "Our load is light and we can sail as fast as any privateer in these waters. If'n they get close at 300 yards of the Baltick, Master Will will make short work of them. He's my insurance, a real frontiersman, and renowned marksman."

Suddenly, Will felt a pang of ambiguity. His whole demeanor had been one of restraint and circumspection. Now the Captain had pushed him to the center stage.

"Tell them, Will, about your exploits on the frontier. No need to be shy in this company," bellowed Peter Haldron.

Will knew he had little chance of escaping without spinning a tale or two, but he had to be selective so as not to betray his true loyalties. Will told the tale about shooting against Daniel Boone in the backcountry, the attack by the two bandits on the mountain trail, and the escape from the Cherokee camp. Will did not mention any of his run-ins with the redcoats. Everyone seemed to be enthralled with the likes of a young man on the frontier, able to take care of himself and survive. Abigail was highly attentive and her attention hung on his every word.

The dinner and conversation ended at 2100 hours, when Mr. Palmer announced the need for the sailors to return to their ships in order to be ready for the morning tide. At the same time, in an unusual move, the tavern began to clear as the visiting Captains gathered their respective crews and headed back to their brigantine. Sailors from the sloops did likewise. The few landsmen quickly finished their ales and departed.

Mr. Palmer commented to Will on his way out, "We close down the public house at 2100 each night in order to preserve the peace and serenity of our little community. Any later than that, the amount of trouble from "demon rum" increases tremendously. Better to have a little restraint than no restraint at all." Palmer left Will's side.

The peaceful stroll back along the wharf was pleasant and enjoyable in and of itself. Abigail and I brought up the rear of our small group. As Abigail took my arm, she merely smiled at me without comment. I felt a sense of warmth and familiarity I had never experienced before. It was both exciting and refreshing, but lingering in the background was my commitment to my mission; find my Father.

Chapter 41

Southport

The Baltick weighed anchor early the next morning just as the morning twilight was shimmering over the outer banks. Other vessels were also slipping their moorings. Soon a procession of sloops, the Baltick, the Dolphin and the Jeanie were making their way to the open sea. The sloops, which had shallow drafts, turned south in the channel between the mainland and the outer banks. While this was a calm and protected lane, it also required expert seamanship and oars on occasion. The open sea was more suited to the larger ships like the Baltick, the Dolphin, and the Jeanie. Once clear of the Top Sail Inlet, all three turned southward. The Dolphin and Jeanie took a south-southeast course toward more of the open sea. The Baltick turned due south to hug the coastline.

As the day progressed the Captain pointed out landmarks to Abigail and me as we passed; Broad Inlet, Shovel Inlet, Cabbage Inlet.

"We'll cut our sailing time short today and pull in at

Southport. We'll need to drop a few more bundles off. This will give you a little extra time to see the port and get used to the surroundings, Lady Farnsworth. As you can tell the climate is much milder here than even Yorktown. The mix of people will no doubt intrigue you. You'll see a mix of red-headed Irishmen, pious Scotsmen, swarthy Spanish sailors, civilized Coastal Indians, bonded slaves, indentured servants, and rich dandy planters. While it is fairly safe during the day, be back aboard before nightfall. As with every port, it's not safe for a lady to be out and about after dark, no matter that she is accompanied by an experienced frontiersman." The Captain chuckled at his own jibe.

The Baltick was able to find a berth at the middle wharf and docked easily. As with Sloop Point, the cargo wheelbarrows quickly showed up, ready to take the cargo to a waiting warehouse. Abigail noted the laborers were a mix of both slave, indentured servants, and freedmen. All were fairly large men, extremely muscled, and glistening from hard-earned sweat. They were all focused on the job at hand and went about their work with purpose and resolve. In a short time, the ship had off-loaded another eight bundles of cargo, which disappeared up the wharf toward the commercial part of the port. The wharf master and the Captain settled the accounts and it was now time for the passengers to roam the port for a couple of hours.

The port itself was about three times the size of Sloop Point and actually had streets and even an avenue built into the port plan. Most of the commercial establishments were centered on sea trade. There was an assortment of ship chandlers, carpenters, ironsmiths, and taverns throughout the four-square blocks of the port. A complete tour of the port only took us less than an hour. With time to spare, we settled on a better-looking establishment on the east side of the commercial district, The Gull's Wing.

As it turned out, the Gull's Wing was also the only tavern that had overnight accommodations and those were attuned to the visiting landed gentry. The building was a two-story affair that took up almost half of the block on the front and extended three-quarters of the way back to the next block. The high-pitched roof of gray slate shingles covered a second-story balcony that wrapped around the building. Painted a traditional gleaming coastal white, the tavern stood out as a very noticeable and substantial structure. Inside in the dark recesses of the tavern, the bar was set off to the left side with a dining area arranged along the right side to take advantage of the breeze offered by the series of double-louvered doors opening onto the covered porch.

Courteous to a fault, the portly, vested tavern host bowed discreetly and showed us to a table near the front corner of the tavern, which had a nice cross breeze. This was a welcome pleasure due to the increasing heat of the day.

Master Allen, who had spoken but a few words during the whole trip, commented on their current situation. "Be thankful our host gave us perhaps the best table in the house. As the day wears on the heat and the humidity will increase almost exponentially."

Mr. Jackson laughed. "For those of us who do not have a Boston education, our good friend is trying to say it will become hot as hell by three o'clock."

"Mr. Jackson, I implore you not to use such language around Lady Farnsworth!" exclaimed Mr. Wentworth.

Abigail raised her ungloved hand politely. "Gentlemen, I am not offended by Mr. Jackson's remark. My time as an indentured servant for my notorious uncle exposed me to much worse banalities of the human experience." As the host delivered tanks of ale to the table, Abigail raised her tankard. "Gentlemen, a toast to our voyage and may it stay as pleasant and uneventful for the remainder."

Over a light afternoon feast of fresh flounder, corn, peas, and cornbread, we continued our conversations about our respective travels, adventures, and plans for the future. I entertained the group with a couple of non-political tales of adventure. Abigail expressed her desire to establish a school for young ladies in Charles Town, while the four gentlemen revealed their plans to purchase land to establish rice and indigo plantations south of Charles Town on Johns Island. I expertly deferred revealing my future plans. Best to keep my mission to myself.

As the meal drew to a conclusion, the Captain strode into the tavern and walked deliberately over to us. "I do hope all of you have enjoyed your brief excursion. I'm afraid it is time to return to the ship. I realize there seems to be more time to spend onshore, but I'll have news to share with you."

The bill was paid and as we left the tavern, each of us paused and thanked our host for his hospitality and remarked on the excellent quality of the fare. The portly host glowed with all the compliments.

Back on board the Baltick, the Captain beckoned us below deck and into his tight quarters. The men stood, as Lady Farnsworth took the chair in front of the Captain's table. "News from up North. We have all heard about Patrick Henry's address to the Virginia Burgess. There is trouble brewing. In '73, there was the so-called Boston Tea Party. In South Carolina Governor Bull, thinking better of the tax, moved all the tax stamps to Fort Johnston for safekeeping. For a while longer, we will still enjoy tax-free tea. However, as a protest, most residents of Charles Town have made the switch to coffee. I'm not sure what we will find when we reach Charles Town. I'd caution each of you to be guarded about your political views."

Chapter 42

Charles Town

Early next morning, the Baltick shoved off from the wharf before any other ships even awoke. Solitary fishermen already on the water gave way to the schooner as she and her cargo made for Charles Town. The cruise was swift and uneventful across Long Bay, past the Pedee and Santee rivers. Again, the Captain pointed out notable landmarks and coastal landings to Will and Abigail. The Captain skirted the Cape Romain Shoals as a small fleet of fisherman busily trolled the shoals for sea bass, speckled trout, and snapper.

Around noon the Baltick entered the North Channel and sailed past Fort Sullivan on the starboard side and then Johnston Fort on the port side. Both forts still boldly flew the Union Jack of the British Empire. The Captain steered the Baltick to Lloyd's Quay, also known as the Lloyd's Bridge, on the eastern side of Charles Town on the Cooper River. Here too the British flag flew unimpeded.

Abigail and I stood together on the small bridge of the

Baltick and watched the crew moor the boat to the wharf. As before, a small company of cargo wheelbarrows descended on the Baltick. Within 30 minutes the Baltick was unloaded.

"Now you two, what do you plan to do in this fine port?" inquired the Captain as he handed me my sealed courier bag. "Will, you'll be looking to turn in that bag down at the Exchange, just down Bay Street, on the second level. The Acting Governor William Bull is presiding at this time. The new governor is due in from England any time, but of course, the establishment has been saying that for the past year." The Captain continued, "Lad you can find a suitable bed over at Mrs. Stevens' place," as he pointed to a three-story brick building off to the right at the end of the pier. This was something I already knew.

"Now Lady Farnsworth, your situation is somewhat different. A lady of your standing, no matter how independent you may be, needs suitable accommodations."

Abigail held up her hands. "Captain, thank you for your concern, but I will be staying with Squire Rutledge and his family on Broad Street. He is a family friend from England. My father befriended him while he was studying law and he became part of my family. When my troubles were resolved, he contacted my lawyer in Boston and offered his assistance in helping me start a new life here in Charles Town. If Master Will is amenable, I will allow him to accompany me to the Rutledge house. Captain, kind sir, if you would, could you arrange to have my baggage delivered there?" With that, Abigail handed the Captain a small coin purse. "I hope it will be enough to cover those expenses?

The Captain quickly looked inside, "A bit, too much, if I

might be so bold."

"No, what is left over, please have a tankard on me."

The Captain left and proceeded down the gangplank to find the wharf master to arrange Abigail's delivery to the Rutledge House.

"Now don't you look all official in your courier uniform," said Abigail. "I didn't suspect you would be a Tory. I thought you would be one of those wild rebels from the mountains. Do you realize you have destroyed my fantasy?"

Will blushed. "My position as a courier is only temporary. I needed this position as a way to get Charles Town in all haste. I have private matters to attend to and being a courier gave me just the opportunity I needed. And I would gladly escort you to the Rutledge House, but first I must find accommodations and then drop off this bag at the Exchange."

"I accept your invitation and will be glad to follow you dutifully around Charles Town as long as I can arrive at the Rutledge's by dinnertime."

As Abigail and I departed the Baltick, goodbyes were said to the crew and the four gentlemen, who were still sorting out their baggage for transportation further up the adjacent Ashley River to their eventual destination.

I intended on a brief stop at Mrs. Stevens's, but it turned out to be a little longer. Unaccustomed to escorting a lady around town, I left Abigail sitting on a wooden bench in front of the shop.

As I entered her coffee house, I inquired about Mrs. Gayle Stevens. From the back of the shop, a stout lady about five feet six inches tall appeared. She was almost the replica of Mrs. Dawson.

"Mrs. Stevens, I'm Will Jones, just arrived from Williamsburg by way of Yorktown. I have a letter from your sister, Mrs. Dawson. Such a wonderful lady."

"Well, I'm not sure either of us are real ladies, but I do appreciate the compliment. Thank you so much for the letter. Do I owe you anything young man?"

"No, nothing at all. Mrs. Dawson was extremely nice to me in Williamsburg and treated me with respect and dignity," I replied smiling.

"Knowing my sister as I do, she probably put you to work in the kitchen and outside as well. Am I not right?" she questioned with a grin on her face.

"My meager efforts in helping around the inn were nothing to compare with the warmth and hospitality I received in return."

"Such a nice young man. Can I do anything for you while you are here in Charles Town?"

"I do need a room for several days, but only if it is at the Crown rate. I'm supposed to be mindful of my expenses."

"I shall have my son Henry select a room upstairs for you."

I was able to meet her son, Henry, the Crown's postal clerk, and get directions to the Exchange.

"Well, that was interesting. I almost left without you. She seems like a very nice inn proprietress," said Abigail. "I guess I should have come in and introduced myself, but that might have been a little too risqué. You know, a young attractive couple coming in for a tryst."

"Abigail, you are so full of yourself and mischievous to boot," I replied.

Twenty minutes later, Abigail and I climbed the stairs to the second floor to the Governor's temporary office. There I announced myself to the secretary in the outer office and requested a moment of the Governor's time. Abigail found a vacant bench and seated herself, prepared to endure the wait. Surprisingly, I was quickly ushered into the Governor's office without delay.

"Well young man, what do you have for me?" asked the portly Governor Bull.

I quickly handed him the sealed dispatch case. The Governor without delay broke the seal, removed the contents, and searched the enclosed sealed envelope for a specific one, personally addressed to him.

"Ah, the very package I've been waiting for." The Governor quickly used his sterling letter opener, sliced it open, and removed to my amazement approximately 1,000 British pounds. "That rascal Lord Dunmore, I never thought he would pay off that bet. It just goes to show you, young man, an honest man always pays off his debts. The rest of this mail you can return to my secretary. I don't have time to go through it. I'm too busy trying to hold this colony together. You wouldn't believe the intrigue I have to put up with each day."

I just stood there waiting for an opportunity to speak.

"Is there something else young man? If not, gather this mail and give it to my secretary." Governor Bull relished the feel of 1000 pounds in his hand.

"Pardon, your Grace, but Lord Dunmore sent you a personal letter on my behalf. It explains that my Father, William Nathaniel Jones, was wrongfully convicted of a crime in Virginia and sent to Charles Town as a rebel for incarceration. I'm here to ask for your assistance to gain his release."

"What a bold adventure young man. And what is your name?"

"William Jones, sir."

"Ah, see we have started off on the right foot. William is a good name, one we share. I can already see that we have something in common. I am not personally aware of the number nor disposition of rebel prisoners sent to Charles Town for incarceration. That is solely in the domain of the acting Garrison Commander, who at this time is Colonel John Stuart. Since you dutifully brought me the rewards of my well-placed bet, I will accommodate you, read the letter from Lord Dunmore, and get back with you within the next day or two." The Governor rifled through the letters from the satchel and found the other private letter from Lord Dunmore. "Yes, here it is. Give me chance to review it and I will send you a note for an appointment. Where are you lodging?"

"I've found lodging at Mrs. Stevens'," replied Will.

"I'll note that. Be sure she gives you the official rate since you are a courier. Now take the rest of these letters to my secretary." The Governor again turned his attention to his ill-gotten gain and chuckled to himself.

I hurriedly collected the letters and departed the office disappointed. As I passed the secretary's desk, I deposited the letter in a large wooden box labeled "new mail."

The secretary looked over his glasses and just shook his head. The box, already full, was now almost overflowing.

"What happened?" inquired Abigail.

"I met the Governor, had a brief private conversation with him, and now I must wait for his reply. It could take several days. Until then I'm at your service." I forced a smile. Behind that smile, my stomach was churning. He had no idea whether my father was dead or alive, or even if he really was in Charles Town. I knew I had to put on a good face for Abigail. She was the only bright spot in my life at the moment.

By all standards, Charles Town had a very English charm about it. The houses were neat, well-appointed, and seemed to exude a sense of wealth. Most were at least three stories with well-maintained yards. Even the Ramadge Tavern on the corner of Broad and Church Street was well maintained and appeared to be a step above the taverns Will was used to back in Williamsburg and especially those in the backcountry.

Now free of my "official" duties, I wandered with Abigail over to King Street to find my appointed apothecary. It wasn't too hard. There were only three on the street and only one advertised Wm. Williamson, proprietor. As I entered the shop, another bell signaled my entry.

"May I help you?" questioned the tall, chestnut-haired man with a Roman nose, who appeared to be about 45 years old, a little over 12 stones, and who was standing behind the counter.

Quickly, Will surveyed the room and discovered to his amazement, he and Abigail were the only customers in the store.

"I'll have a look around while you attend to your business," said Abigail slyly.

As I approached the counter, I repeated my code, "I need

'bitters' for an achy stomach. Do you have any?"

The man smiled, and replied, "No, but I do have a small bottle of bismuth, which should do the trick."

Will reached into his courier vest pocket, pulled out the sealed letter, and handed it to the man.

"Well, forgive me if I'm somewhat surprised that a Royal courier would deliver an important letter from the Committee," said the man quietly. "Just for the sake of a formal introduction, I'm William Williamson, proprietor of this apothecary. And who are you? Wait, I don't need to know. The mere fact that you delivered this letter to me is sufficient enough."

"Thank you, sir. Now if I can have the bismuth, I would be most appreciative."

"Of course, one must follow through," He replied.

Abigail joined him by his side, "Achy stomach? I hope you aren't anxious about meeting my benefactor."

"No, of course not. Just an achy stomach, nothing to be concerned about," I replied.

At that time another customer entered the store.

"So young man, here is your bismuth. That will be a tuppence."

I dug into my coin pocket and produced two pennies and laid them on the counter as William Williamson handed him the small bottle of bismuth.

"I hope your achy stomach settles down young man," he said with a smile on his face.

I picked up the bottle, nodded to the gentlemen, and casually left the store with Abigail on my arm. Outside I broke into a temporary cold sweat. It was an easy mission, yet I could not understand why I had been so nervous. This business was going to be more than what it seemed.

"I must say, that was a bit of intrigue in the ole apothecary," said Abigail. "I like the way you introduced yourself, assured it was the right person, and then handed him the letter. I'm impressed. I just hope I didn't interfere."

"Interfere with what?" I asked.

Abigail squeezed my arm, "Such a complicated young man."

We finally made our way to the Rutledge House up Broad Street. The house was a two-story, red brick house with a pitched slate roof, built over a raised basement with a spiral staircase to the front door. The front porch and second-floor balcony were supported by square wooden columns which gave the house a particular English country flair. Off to the right side was a carriage way to the back of the house. No doubt, there lay the kitchen and carriage house with stables underneath. To me, this was indicative of a well-regarded family and a successful lawyer.

"So glad to see your attorney is a substantial member of the community," I remarked casually.

"Yes, there he is at the top of the ladder. Not to be snobbish, but my father's estate back in England included a main house with 14 bedrooms, a stable for 20 horses, a separate kitchen house, a solarium, and a greenhouse for mother's plants. Of course, I ended up as a factory worker in Boston. From the top to the bottom. Well, okay, not entirely to the bottom. At least I had a job and plenty of friends. We all shared the same attribute; we were poor and helpless."

"Not to be judgmental, but things are different now. You'll be in good hands and if your luck continues you will be the belle of the ball here in Charles Town."

"It will take some getting used to, but I will recover my graces along the way, I hope. My manners may shock my guardian and his family, but I'll have time to remake myself."

"I like you just the way you are. Not many young ladies have experienced your trials and tribulations. For all the rough times, you are definitely a better person for it."

A shout came from the front porch. "Lady Farnsworth, is that you darling?" The sweet dialect of the South carried ever so clear.

There, standing on the front porch, was a tall, raven-haired lady dressed perfectly in her afternoon attire with a fan in her hand.

"My goodness, sugar, you must come inside and meet your new family. And bring that nice young man with you if you like. We are always up for news."

Without hesitation, I touched my hat, "I have to go. I have private things to attend to. It has been a pleasure traveling with you over the past several days. I wish you the best of luck in the future. But I know you'll make your own luck."

"Not so fast Will. You're not going to leave me that easily. I gather you have private matters to attend to, but you will meet me for coffee tomorrow. I'll come down to Mrs. Stevens' at 10 a.m. Now that I have found you, you are not escaping my clutches." Abigail grabbed me by the shoulders and kissed me full square on the lips.

I could feel my face turn beet red. My first kiss, in public of all places, in front of a lawyer's wife.

I heard Mrs. Rutledge exclaim under her breath, "Well I'll be. Isn't that just the sweetest?"

I headed back down Broad Street. My mind was in a whirl. Complications were all I could think about. As I drew up to the Ramadge Tavern, I spotted Captain Thomas in the company of what appeared to be a Royal Navy officer. The other captain was somewhat younger, perhaps 30 to 35, tall at six feet, and maybe 12 stones thin. The cut of his uniform gave him the rank of a captain. His tailored blue frock over a white vest, white shirt, and white silk ascot fit him perfectly. The gold embroidery on his sleeves showed his rank was perhaps a lower grade captain, maybe the captain of an ocean-going schooner or cargo ship.

Captain Thomas spotted me right away, waved a hand to me, and beckoned me to join them. I quickened my pace and was soon in the company of two sea captains.

"Will, allow me to introduce you to Captain William Pond of the Royal Packet ship Le DeSpencer. He just arrived from Falmouth and has all sorts of news for us. I bet if'n I buy him a tankard; we'll get the scuttlebutt from merry ole England and then more."

The relatively young captain extended his hand, "So nice to meet you, Squire Will. I've heard you are a real frontiersman, but the way you are dressed you look more like an up-and-coming young Royal Ensign."

As I shook his hand, I replied, somewhat reserved, "Thank you sir for your compliment, but I'm truly more at home in homespun, moccasins, and roaming the mountains than I am here in this busy port."

Both captains laughed heartily. "Will," replied Captain James, "Charles Town is but a very small example of a port. I'll have to take you to Boston or New York to see a real port. But for our purposes, it is a home away from home. Now enough talk, it's time to have a tankard or two."

As the three of us entered the Ramadge late in the afternoon on April 19, 1775, a small crowd had already gathered. All had heard that the Le DeSpencer had arrived and were anxious to hear the latest news from England.

"Gentlemen, and I use that term loosely," bellowed Captain Thomas, "the good ship Le DeSpencer has just arrived in port. I'll buy the first tankard for Captain Pond, you'll stand in line to buy him the next and the next. With a little persuasion, I'm sure the good Captain will fill our evening with news, stories, rumors, and other delightful entertainment."

The crowd gave a small cheer as tables were rearranged. Near the fireplace, a table of honor was arranged for Captains Pond and Thomas. Will chose to move to the back of the room and observe. The crowd was mixed; merchants, lawyers, and planters all moved to the front as working-class men mulled around the edges of the congregation.

Soon I was joined by a middle-aged man with rolled-up sleeves, wearing a printer's bib over his clothes. I noted his hands were stained and he did, in fact, smell of ink.

"Peter Timothy, printer and owner of the South Carolina Gazette, local politician, and observer. Normally, I'd be upfront with the squires, but today I'm filling in at the press and so I'm not suitably attired. I do have a couple of lads near the front taking in the conversation. So don't worry, I'll have plenty to report in Friday's paper. And who might you be?"

"William Jones, currently on temporary assignment as a Royal Courier from Virginia to Governor Bull," I replied guardedly.

"Are you also known as Will Jones, the young frontiersman?"

"I might have been called that a few times," I answered. The game of cat and mouse was on and I was very uncomfortable.

"Not to worry young man, we all have to live each day as it presents itself. But I'm not sure why such a personality would all of a sudden become a Royal courier, even on a temporary basis. I'm sure there is a story behind all of this charade. In time, I'm sure you'll confide in me, but for now, you need to take note of who is here and their dispositions."

Without further encouragement, Mr. Timothy began to identify each person by name, position, and disposition.

"Up front to left is Squire Edward Rutledge, lawyer and patriot; next to him is Major Peter Boguet, patriot; then Thomas Lynch and Christopher Gadson, patriots; Squire Thomas Heyard; a little apart is Squire Joseph Robinson, loyalist; Thomas Fletchall, loyalist; and Mr. John Mayfield, a visiting loyalist. The room is about equally divided and though it may be strange to you, there are no secrets here. Each knows the persuasion of the other. You might say there is a tense truce at the moment."

At that moment, the door to the tavern was opened and a party of men entered, escorted by two British soldiers. The assembly went quiet.

"Mind your manners lad, the Governor and Colonel Stuart have arrived. Governor Bull is the acting governor and Colonel John Stuart is the acting garrison commander and Crown Representative to the native population. Watch the dynamics as the room adjusts to our new audience."

It was Captain Thomas who spoke first. "Gentlemen, so good of you to come to our little gathering. Come up front. Please make room for the Governor and the Colonel, our most esteemed guests this afternoon."

As if on cue, a small table was placed in front of the two captains, about six feet away. Chairs were produced and two tankards of ale appeared out of nowhere. The crowd moved to the sides to accommodate the two honored guests. Patriots on the left, loyalists on the right. The room seemed evenly divided. This meeting was purely for news and information, not for political discussions.

The two men proceeded to the front and happened to pass by where Mr. Timothy and I were standing. The Governor stopped briefly in front of Mr. Timothy and acknowledged him. "I hope Peter you will accurately report the news from England and not insert any of your seditious leanings."

"I will do my best, Governor. If you like, I would be glad to add any comments you might have," challenged Mr. Timothy.

The Governor averted his eyes and looked straight at me. "Ah, good to see Squire Jones. I sent a note to your lodgings. I've given you an appointment with Colonel Stuart and myself in the morning at my house on Meeting Street at nine o'clock. Please be on time." The Governor did not wait for a response and walked to his place of honor followed by Colonel Stuart.

"A personal friend of the Governor's I see. The plot thickens and I sense there is a story to be told. Would you accept an invitation for a light supper and refreshments over in the other section of the tavern? I'm sure we have a lot to discuss."

Before I could answer, Mr. Wentworth, a passenger from the Baltick, interrupted.

"Will, it's so good to see you. Why it must have been at least three hours since I last saw you? Mr. Timothy, allow me to introduce myself. I'm Robert Wentworth, from Virginia. My friends and I accompanied young Will on the voyage down here and we have been looking for him all afternoon to take him somewhere quiet to have a decent meal. If you will excuse us."

I was thankful for the rescue and didn't hesitate. I quickly accepted Mr. Wentworth's invitation and we left the tavern.

Outside, Wentworth spoke first. "Timothy is a good patriot, but he is a renowned gossip. Anything you would have told him would be all over the port by morning and the rest of the Carolinas by Sunday. I recommend you go back to your lodging and be prompt to your meeting with the Governor in the morning."

"I appreciate your assistance back in the tavern, but why?"

"Will, you ask too many questions. Complete your mission and follow your instructions. Do you understand?"

I was thunderstruck. I suddenly had the realization that I might not be alone in my quest to find my father. It was apparent to me that my mentor was keeping watch over me. I dutifully replied, "Yes, sir."

Wentworth strolled away as I turned toward Bay Street and casually walked towards Mrs. Stevens' coffee house. As I passed the wharves, I noticed several more coastal schooners had been tied up and had been in the process of either unloading cargo or taking on cargo. The port, while small by other standards, was nonetheless extremely busy. I noticed a somewhat large vessel docked near the Baltick. This sailing ship had three masts; two square-rigged with three booms of ascending size near the stern, which carried a spanker furled on a long horizontal boom. It appeared to have three decks. The upper, open deck, a mid-deck, probably for passengers, crew, and the officer quarters, and a lower deck just at the waterline for cargo. Noticeable on the upper deck were six brass Falconets capable of firing a one-pound ball over 4,000 feet. Each was mounted on a wooden carriage with wheels, which added to the mobility of the battery. These small, but effective, cannons were more than capable of keeping pirates at bay. The nameplate on the bow of the ship identified her as the Le DeSpencer, Captain Pond's packet ship.

As I approached the DeSpencer, I noticed Henry Stevens walking down the gangplank with a large satchel. "Mr. Stevens!" I yelled as I approached him, "I see you have secured the mail for the port,"

"Oh, Mr. Jones."

"Please call me Will. No need for formalities in our case."

"Then please call me Henry. Actually, this is the last of four satchels of mail. No doubt it will take me several days to go through each bag and sort out which correspondence goes to which person or office. This particular satchel is for official correspondence. I had to personally pick it up and sign for it. There is always excitement these days to see what new and unusual directives are being placed on us. It's almost as if London completely ignores the fact that we are Englishmen. They treat us more like stepchildren."

"That does seem the case, doesn't it? Mind if I walk with you the rest of the way to the coffee house?" inquired Will.

"Not at all. It's somewhat comforting to have a Royal Courier escort me to the Post Office, even though it is only a dozen or so yards from the wharf. There are enough rumors floating around these days for some to want to have advanced knowledge of the contents of the Governor's mail."

The short walk to the Post Office and Mrs. Stevens' coffee house/hostel was uneventful. I did note, with suspicion, there were several men dressed as workmen hanging about the street near the Post Office with no particular business to attend to. As we entered the building, I noticed the men, almost in unison, departed in the direction of the Exchange, separate, but still at the same pace, not in a hurry, but at a steady, measured pace. Henry proceeded directly to the small corner office which served as the Post Office as I entered the coffee house. As I entered, Mrs. Stevens, with an inquisitive smile on her face, approached me with two notes in her hand.

"My, Master William, you are the most popular young man in Charles Town today. Two notes arrived separately for you. One is from the Governor's office and the other seems to be from a young lady by the perfume smell of it."

Again, I blushed. I made a mental note to myself to learn not to blush at surprises. "Thank you, Mrs. Stevens, I appreciate your attention. Will it be possible to get a light meal later on?"

"We only have a little fish soup left in the pot, but I can also bring out some bread and cheese if you like. I have to serve you now, or you'll have to go somewhere else."

"Now is fine. I will have a bowl of your fish soup and the bit of bread and cheese, if you please."

With a smile on her face, Mrs. Stevens trundled off in the direction of the kitchen. I found a table near the front window for light so I could read the notes. The first note from the Governor was embossed with a seal of sorts. A dead giveaway that it was from the Governor's office. I carefully broke the seal and read the contents. It was, in fact, an invitation, or rather a directive, to be at the Governor's House on tomorrow at 10 o'clock promptly. The short, terse message was signed with the initials WB.

The other note was indeed perfumed with the scent of lilac. It too was sealed with the letter "R," which I assumed stood for Edward Rutledge, at whose home Abigail was currently residing. I carefully opened the note and immediately noticed beautiful and fluid cursive.

Dear William,

I cannot express fully the joy and pleasure I had in having your company on the journey from Yorktown to Charles Town. While not exactly an adventure, it nonetheless was one of my most memorable experiences in my most

recent past. I hope that we can continue our friendship over the coming months and years. I hope you will accept my invitation to come for supper at the Rutledge House on Friday evening the 21st of April in the Year of our Lord 1775. I would like to introduce you to my guardian, benefactor, and his family. You will receive a formal invitation from the Rutledge's on the morrow. With deepest affection,
Abigail

I was a little overwhelmed by the personal nature of the note. Although this was the first note I had ever received from anyone, much less an attractive and alluring female such as Abigail. I was unsure of how to interpret the hidden message in the note, if in fact, there was a hidden message at all.

"Here's your supper for this evening young man," said Mrs. Stevens as she set down a huge bowl of fish soup in front of him and a generous plate of bread and cheese to his right side. "I see you opened the important note first," observed Mrs. Stevens with a chuckle.

"Actually, I opened it second. I saved the best, I think, for last."

"So, there is a question as to the meaning of the message, I take it?" inquired Mrs. Stevens. "Now from a mother's point of view, I'd recommend you talk to your mother for her to read and interpret what the young lady really means. Since your dear mother is not here, I'd be glad to read it and give you, my opinion. I'll be very discreet and keep it in complete confidence." Mrs. Stevens seated herself just to the right of me and politely held out her hand. I hesitated a second and then extended Abigail's note to her.

It took only a moment for Mrs. Stevens to read it. "Not exactly a marriage proposal, but short of that, it is a very interesting note and reveals that the young lady holds you in high regard. She does express herself as being a little forward, but then again, knowing who she is and what she has been through, she is not likely to let polite social graces stand in her way.

"Oh, yes, Master Will, her legend spread like a wildfire as soon as Squire Rutledge announced he was bringing Lady Farnsworth to Charles Town. You wouldn't believe the suitors who have already lined up to meet her and woo her, if I may say so. A young lady, who is by all standards an English aristocrat, regardless of her unfortunate servitude under her uncle, is still extremely attractive. Besides, the size of her inheritance puts her in league with the top 10 percent of the upper crust in all of South Carolina. Squire Rutledge, an exceptionally honest person, will no doubt be a good protector of her wealth.

"There you have it, beauty, a title, and wealth, the very lure for every eligible gentleman bachelor and scoundrel in both of the Carolinas. William Jones, a youthful frontiersman, Royal Courier, and well, that's it, you have her attention. It is my opinion and my opinion only; you could not find a better match in the next hundred years. Play your cards right and you could be happy for the rest of your life. So, if you wish, I will give you a short course starting tomorrow on what you should expect and teach you basic manners and etiquette that will help you survive an evening with the gentry." Without another word, Mrs. Stevens got up from the table, patted me on the shoulder, and went back to the kitchen.

I finished my supper in silence. There was too much going on in my life. Yes, Abigail was exceptional, probably a once-in-a-lifetime encounter, but I struggled. I knew my first mission was to find my father. That was the primary focus. I left the coffee house and went upstairs to my room. The room, not more than both arm's length wide, had a small bed, a writing table with a candle, and a chair. There were a couple of pegs on the wall adjacent to the door where I could hang my clothes. My satchel was neatly placed on the bed. After a brief trip downstairs and out back to the privy, I settled in early for a well-deserved night's sleep.

Unused to the noise of the port, I was constantly awakened by the clanging ship's bells, the horse-drawn carriages traversing the street below, and the noise of drunken sailors returning to their ships. At approximately 10 o'clock, I heard a commotion downstairs in the vicinity of the small post office.

I eased downstairs, dressed only in my nightshirt with Queen Anne in my right hand and a hunting knife in my left. As I approached the landing on the second floor, I heard Henry Stevens arguing with several men. There, standing in the doorway to the Post Office, were three men, casually dressed, but in decent clothing wearing tri-corner hats.

One of the men, the obvious leader of the group, directed his attention at Henry who was deep within the confines of his little office.

"Henry," he said in a commanding, but not threatening tone, "we've come for the Governor's mail from England, which arrived today on the Spencer. We don't mean you any harm, we just need to read his private correspondence. We need to know what the Crown is planning for us here in the colony. Just give us a few minutes to read his mail and we'll be on our way."

"That's against the rules. I can't possibly let you have access to the Governor's private correspondence. If I do, I'll be arrested and thrown in the dungeon in the exchange for treason."

I noticed that all three men had Dragoon pistols in their belts and appeared to be more than capable of using them. The temptation of reading the Governor's mail was enticing.

I spoke up. "Gentlemen, please refrain from moving. I am armed and more than capable of ruining your evening. Poor Henry is correct. If he lets you read the mail and is caught, he suffers. There is another way, which may resolve the situation."

The men cautiously turned toward Will. One spoke. "You be the Royal Courier from Yorktown, why would you help us?"

"It's not to help you, it's to help all of us, Henry included. Are you willing to listen?"

I then quickly explained a plan to secretly open the important sealed letters, allow the men to copy the important information, and then reseal the correspondence. To protect Henry, the men would be allowed to take less important correspondence to make it look like a robbery. The next morning Henry would report the theft by three masked men and present the important correspondence to the Governor explaining to him that he had been overwhelmed, but managed to hide the Governor's mail. The three men and even Henry nodded in agreement. The whole process took more than an hour, but the essential information was gleaned from the private correspondence. The seals were re-attached, unnoticeable that anything was amiss.

The only thing of importance revealed by the whole process was a report of the "Conciliatory Resolution" already reported in the British newspapers, which had been passed by Parliament. According to the letter, the Royal government was willing to offer terms of reconciliation to the colonies so long as they stopped all rebellious activity and accepted Parliament as the sole ruling authority. It encouraged Governor Bull to pursue this avenue and quell any opposition activity.

The men, somewhat disappointed in their find, were nonetheless buoyed by the agreement that Henry would not report the intrusion and "theft" of five pieces of unimportant mail until the morning.

As the men left, Henry turned to me. "I must extend to you my most grateful thanks for interceding. I don't think those gentlemen, who I know to be good, righteous men, would have done me any great harm, but your solution and assistance helped resolve the situation without any real adversity."

"Henry, there are a lot of good men on both sides of the issue. I am glad that I was able to help temper their actions," I said almost apologetically.

As Henry went about re-sorting the mail and cleaning up

from the intrusion, I quietly went back upstairs to my room. Sleep escaped me, but at some point, I was overcome by exhaustion.

515

Chapter 43

Appointment with the Governor and Engagement

At five o'clock, a crowing cock woke me with a start. Disoriented, it took me a few seconds to remember where I was, what happened the previous evening, and to find my bearings. I had plenty of time to prepare for this meeting with the Governor. Not wanting to waste time, I cleaned up, put on my freshest clothes and courier jacket, grabbed a piece of toast, and gave Mrs. Stevens a peck on the cheek on my way out of the house. I spent the morning wandering around the port, learning my way around. Early on I strolled by the Governor's house on Meeting Street, which was obvious due to the two Royal Marines standing guard outside his gate. Feeling a little impetus, I stopped at the guards, introduced myself as a Royal Courier, and announced I had an appointment with the Governor at 10 o'clock.

"Aye lad, we know you be William Jones. Be back here no later than 9:30. The Governor does not like to be kept waiting. 'Tis better you wait than to make him wait. Now be off with you until then and stay out of trouble," commanded the Marine corporal.

I located the State House on the corner of Broad and Queen Street, noting the Church of England was catty-cornered across the street. I proceeded back up Broad Street to find the Rutledge House, which was easy to find. No one was stirring at this early hour, but I did hear activity back in the kitchen. I turned left on Orange Street, passed over a low arch. At the corner of Tradd and Orange, I came upon another guarded house. This one was guarded by two soldiers in their bright red uniforms. Less friendly, they instructed me to "move along." Perhaps this was where Colonel Stuart lived; I would inquire later. As I turned back on Tradd Street in the direction of the port, I looked over my shoulder and noticed someone in a uniform shirt peering out the window at me. Ever polite, I touched my hand to my hat and acknowledged the gentlemen, who in return acknowledged me with a slight nod of the head. The main part of Charles Town was probably no more than six blocks by eight blocks at the most. Of course, there appeared to be other properties further out, but none seemed to be of any significance that I could see.

Precisely at 9:30, a ship in the port rang the time with two bells, a pause, and then a single bell. I walked up to the Royal Marine Guards and presented myself.

"Corporal, William Jones here for an appointment with the Governor at 10 o'clock."

"Aye, that you are. Good manners go a long way laddie. Now, do you have any instruments of destruction on you this morning?"

All of a sudden, I became nervous. Queen Anne was in my pocket and my hunting knife was on my belt. "Corporal, I do have a small pistol in my pocket and my hunting knife is on my belt. Is that a problem?" asked Will.

"Oh, a little pocket pistol and your hunting knife are not exactly going to do much damage. Just remember who you are and where you are. Couriers are allowed to carry their choice of protection. In your case, it's fine. But if you ask me, you be a little under-protected. I myself would carry an additional Dragoon and maybe even billet," the Corporal chuckled at his own humor. "Go around to the Carriage House in back, announce yourself to the downstairs butler, and wait until you are called into the main house. Now be off with you lad and good luck for whatever you are doing."

I followed the directions to a tee. The butler seemed to be expecting me and instructed me to have a seat on the bench in front of the carriage house. Several minutes later, the butler appeared.

"Excuse me, are you Mr. John Charles?" I asked.

"How did you know my name young man?" he asked curiously.

"I met your niece, Cassey in Williamsburg and she asked me to give you this Guinea," I responded as I pulled the gold coin out of my hidden vest pocket.

"Well, I'll be. What a surprise. Why thank you, Squire Jones. It seems we now share some same acquaintances," he said with a twinkle in his eye as he put the coin in his vest pocket.

"Please follow me into the house. Before you go in, please wipe off those shoes or moccasins or whatever they are. We keep a clean house here and we do not allow guests to track dirt into it."

Mr. Charles waited as I grabbed a large brush next to the door, scrubbed my moccasins thoroughly, and then scraped the soles of the mocs over the boot scraper situated off to the side of the back door. "Thank you," he replied as he inspected my handiwork.

The house was finely appointed, as much as I could see. Mr. Charles led me up a back staircase to an office overlooking the carriage house courtyard. He knocked twice on the door, opened it, and announced, "Squire Jones is here, your honor." Under his breath, he said tersely, "Take off your hat!"

The butler stepped aside and I was ushered into the room, hat in my hand. In front of me was the Governor in all his finery standing behind his desk. Off to the right side was Colonel Stuart firmly seated, who looked splendid in this red officer's coat with gold braids on the sleeves, white trousers, and leggings over black polished shoes. The Colonel did not move to stand up.

"William, it's so nice to see you again. Please come, have a seat. I believe you know who Colonel Stuart is. I asked him here as he may have information pertinent to your request." The Governor seated himself as I took a seat in a comfortable chair across the desk from the Governor. The Colonel was eyeing me with distinct suspicion.

"Let's get to the chase, shall we," started the Governor. "I regret to inform you that your father is not in Charles Town. However, Colonel Stuart might be able to add something to that."

Colonel Stuart gave a disdainful glance at the Governor. "William, I met your father briefly during the French and Indian War. I was enamored by his woodcraft and fighting skills. When I learned that he had been arrested and convicted, I was somewhat surprised. I was even more surprised when he was transferred to Charles Town and labeled a rebel sympathizer. The man I knew was a loyal subject of the King and would not have done anything to undermine the rule of law in the colonies. I had friends back in Virginia investigate the circumstances of his alleged activities. I was none too pleased to find that they were all baseless."

"Colonel, my father is innocent of all the charges brought against him. The men who filed the charges against him were part of a plot to steal our farm. He is a loyal subject," I pleaded.

"William, please listen to what I just said. The charges against him were all baseless. However, the witnesses against him have either disappeared or were killed themselves. I convinced the Governor to grant him parole. As a condition of the parole, he will finish out his sentence under the watchful eye of the Crown. I have no doubt he is a loyal subject of the King, but under the circumstances, knowing his military background and his association with now identified radicals, he was shipped to Falmouth, England to serve out his parole. He will remain in England until such time as it is deemed safe for him to return to the colonies. Your father was shipped out on the Swallow on March 13. He should be in England by now. He did leave a message for you with me."

Colonel Stuart handed me the unsealed note. I took the note and read it silently. It was short but insightful.

William, take care of your mother, brothers, and sisters. Be true to your spirit and loyal to the Crown. I will return home as soon as I can. Stay in the upcountry and out of harm's way. Don't do anything that would disgrace the family. You have proven yourself as a young man and stay the course. Give my love to your Mother. Father

The Colonel continued, "As you notice William, that is not your father's handwriting. I had my personal clerk write it for him. At that precise time, your father was nursing a broken right hand and couldn't write. I hope you understand."

"Colonel, I appreciate all you have done for my father and I will be forever indebted to you for his safe journey to England," I said with mock earnestness. One thing Father had always taught me was to be ambidextrous, be able to use my left hand and well as my right hand. Father had entertained the family with his ability to write verses from the Bible with both hands at the same time. I was rightfully suspicious.

The Governor continued, "Now that you know your father is safe, I assume you will be headed back to the upcountry to be with your mother and siblings. Of course, should you decide to remain in Charles Town, I could use a reliable courier to assist my office in distributing official mail to our outlying towns. Let me know within the next couple of days. The Crown will be responsible for your lodging until Monday. That's the least we can do. If you don't have anything further, Colonel Stuart and I need to discuss several issues in private."

I took that as my cue to leave. As I stood, I thanked the Governor and Colonel Stuart. "Gentlemen, thank you for your assistance in helping me resolve the situation with my father. While it is not exactly what I had hoped for, it does give me some peace of mind that he was paroled and sent to England for the duration of these troubles. I know we have distant relatives in England and I'm sure he will get in touch with them. Governor, I will have an answer for you by Monday."

"Good William! Come back to my house a bit earlier, say nine o'clock, with your answer on Monday morning." At that precise moment, Mr. Charles opened the study door and escorted me out of the house, this time through the front door.

As we reached the front door, Mr. Charles slipped me a small sealed note not bigger than the palm of one's hand. "Don't open it here. Wait until you get someplace private away from prying eyes. Your father is a good man. He'll be safe in England. By Christmas, if God is willing, he should be in France by then. We'll not speak again."

The mystery deepened. I had to restrain myself to keep from running back to Mrs. Stevens. As I passed the Marine Guards, the Corporal tried to engage me in a short conversation. "So, Squire William, I hope your meeting with the Governor went well. Shall we be seeing you again?"

"Sorry Corporal, I have to hurry to another meeting down the port. But I will be back on Monday at nine. The Governor offered me a position as his royal courier."

"That's a fine offer for a young lad such as yourself. I'd seriously consider it if I was you. Well, move along. You mustn't interfere with our guard duties."

It took no further encouragement for me to "move along" as the Corporal ordered. I slipped down Meeting House Street until it intersected Tradd Street and then I turned left and headed to the port. As I approached Church Street, someone hailed me.

"Master William Jones?" asked the black-clad messenger.

"Yes, that's me. What can I do for you?" replied Will, a little confused.

"I've been looking around for you all morning. I have an invitation to the Rutledge House for Friday evening. I was told to personally deliver it to you by Lady Farnsworth." The messenger handed him the "R" engraved invitation. "Also please note that the occasion is not formal, but I recommend wearing your Sunday best. And please take a bath and shave. I realize this is none of my business, but the competition is rather stiff. You need to be the best you can be." The messenger tipped his hat, turned around, and headed back up Thadd Street.

To me, it seemed like everyone knew everyone else's business in Charles Town. This was not a town shrouded in secrecy. In fact, it seemed like an open book. Mindful of the note in his pocket, I took a moment to read the invitation.

Greeting and salutations to Mr. William Jones, your presence is requested at the Rutledge House, on Friday, the 21st day of April in the year of our Lord 1775. The Rutledge Family is delighted to present Lady Abigail Farnsworth, recently of Boston, and heiress to the Farnsworth Estate in Lancashire, England. Lady Farnsworth will be receiving guests from 6:30 PM until 7:30 PM followed by dinner

Will Jones

from 7:30 PM until 9:00 PM.

RSVP to the Rutledge House by Wednesday, the 19th day of April in the year of our Lord 1775.

Of course, the invitation was late and the time to accept the invitation was yesterday. I was dismayed until I turned the invitation over to the back. There in perfect cursive was a short-handwritten note.

Will, don't worry about accepting the invitation, I've already accepted it for you. Please come early so we can have time alone.

Affectionately Yours,

Abi

A smile came across my face and again I blushed. There was one thing I could say about Abi and that was that she was persistent, which, under the circumstances, was not a bad thing at all.

When I arrived at Mrs. Stevens', she met me at the front door. "I hope the messenger found you. He was most insistent that he find you immediately."

"Yes indeed, he did find me. And I received the invitation, a day late but according to my friend inside the house, I have a reserved place waiting for me. Please excuse me, I need to run upstairs and take care of a few things."

"Come back down later and we'll start your condensed version of social etiquette school. Don't worry about the finery. I managed to put together some very respectable attire for you. I'm not sure why, but it seems like most of Charles Town is excited and wants you to make a good impression. I received no less than three full sets of clothes and several pairs of shoes to boot."

I excused myself again and raced upstairs. The note from my father was burning a hole in my pocket. Finally, alone, behind a closed door, I pulled out the note and opened it carefully. The paper was frail almost the consistency of onion skin. The note in pencil was hard to read. It had faded over time.

Will, I am fine. Incarceration was bad. Managed to survive. God smiled. Paroled to England for 10 yrs. Soonest to France. Take care of fam. Freedom, we have nothing to lose. F

A new direction, a new mission. I now pondered what my next endeavor should be. One thing was certain, freedom was the cause, and I would do whatever I could to help achieve it. Abigail was a concern. I wasn't sure how I was to approach the situation. She was the one woman in my life that meant anything, besides my mother and sisters. But she had captured my heart. The question was how could I balance the two priorities?

Mrs. Stevens yelled up to him, "Mr. Jones, time for your lessons and I need to do a final fit on your clothes for the dinner."

The two-hour process was a combination of a fitting and an etiquette class. The different place settings were discussed using Mrs. Stevens' set of fine china, which she had secured from privateers years before in exchange for an extended stay in her lodgings. Each piece of the silverware was identified and its use explained. The golden rule was "watch the other guests and follow their lead."

A suit of brown linen was selected from among the donated clothes. The sleeveless waistcoat had 12 finely polished brass buttons along with a gold embroidered band with carefully stitched buttonholes. The brass buttons alone cost at least five pounds. The ruffled white shirt added just the right touch. The dark brown, knee-length breeches made of finely woven linen fit snugly and had a fall-front opening; quite the fashion of the day. A pair of white, thin woolen stockings completed my attire. Mrs. Stevens then produced a pair of lightly worn, black low-heeled shoes to complete my ensemble. The buckles on the shoes were nondescript, more utilitarian than fashionable, but they served their purpose. As a final touch, there was the single-breasted overcoat of light brown wool, again with polished brass, eagle embossed buttons.

"Master Jones, you'll need to wear your own tri-corner. I do recommend you brush it a bit to clean it up. Other than that, you should be dressed very acceptably for the dinner."

"My word," said Henry as he walked in the room, "don't you look the part of a young gentleman. Just mind your p's and q's.

There'll be a lot of observers there just trying to take you down a notch. There'll be stiff competition for Lady Farnsworth's attention." Henry chuckled and left without a further word.

"Thank you, Mrs. Stevens, for your assistance in getting these fine clothes together. I certainly appreciate you and all the others who donated clothes."

"You have at least three more sets of clothes. A pair of used black cavalry riding boots and, of all things, a courier saddle and tack in good condition were just delivered this afternoon with a note." Mrs. Stevens handed him the note. I thanked her and then read the note carefully.

Squire William, we hope you will find this saddle useful in your new undertaking.

Your friends from Virginia

"If you don't mind, I'll just remain here this evening. I have a lot to think about."

"Of course," replied Mrs. Stevens. "I'll bring you out some bread and cheese for your supper.

I took a seat in front of the coffee house by the window and looked out over the port. Fate was not kind to me, I thought. It was sending me in a direction and I had no idea what lay ahead. The note was curious at best. Someone was telling me to take the courier position, but who and why?

Mrs. Stevens brought the bread and cheese together with a hearty beef broth. "Here, you can dip your bread in the broth and enjoy. Just don't do that tomorrow night. Proper manners for that situation." She laughed softly as she walked away.

The answer to my question came quickly. Mr. Wentworth walked into the coffee house and without hesitation took a seat across from me, but positioned himself so he could not be seen from the street.

He addressed Mrs. Stevens, who had started in his direction. "Mrs. Stevens, would you be so kind as to bring me a cup of coffee and a pastry if you have one?"

"It will be my pleasure. Would you like anything in your coffee, sir?"

"No, black coffee is just fine," he answered.

"Will, the big night is coming. You'll have to make some serious decisions in the next couple of days. Of course, your friend in Virginia would be most pleased if you accepted the Governor's offer and became his courier. You've proven your worth to the Governor and he actually thinks you have accepted the story about your father. Let him be none the wiser."

"You know about my father?" inquired Will.

"Only by reports from others. Initially, he was not treated very well. Then Colonel Stuart discovered that he was jailed here and interceded. I will have to give him that credit. Your father was moved to a better cell and given better rations, while the Colonel asked Virginia for clarifications. Your father's cellmates remained jailed in miserable conditions with starvation rations. Patriot groups continue to take food to them, but the Colonel has not seen fit to intervene in their situation."

Continuing, Wentworth went on, "The clarification from Virginia finally arrived and it was decided that your father would be offered parole in England for his assurances that he would not return to the colonies until after these troubles have been settled. The Governor and the Colonel both felt, and still feel, your father would align himself with the patriots. This is a situation the Crown could not afford and yet they could not keep a recognized hero of the French and Indian War in prison on false charges. Mere suspicion at the moment still seems to be insufficient even for the British justice system. That might change, but for the time being, your father is safe in England and if we are lucky, by Christmas he will be smuggled to France and from there back to here. There is a commission waiting for him when he returns."

"As for you Will, there's a decision you are going to have to make. I'm fully aware of your budding relationship with Lady Farnsworth."

"I don't have a relationship with Abi, we are only friends," interjected Will nervously.

"Yes, I know you feel there is a strong friendship growing. Lady Farnsworth has another, more heartfelt opinion. From the Rutledge household staff, of which she has completely enamored, it appears you are the only one on her list of potential fiancés. I know she is only about 16 years old, but she is a strong-minded young lady. I certainly would not want to interfere with your situation. You are in an inevitable position. If you choose to help with our cause, you must postpone any thought of marriage at this time. Will, we need another set of eyes and ears not only here in Charles

Town, but also the Carolinas and the mountains. As a Royal courier, you will have access to important information which could be of great benefit to our effort in obtaining our rights as Englishmen. There will be little time to romance Lady Farnsworth, much less be married to her."

"If I was in a financial situation, I would certainly consider marriage to her, but at the moment my whole wealth is a couple of farthings and a bundle of hand-me-down clothes.

"Yes, yes, we know. Don't forget the saddle and the riding boots. The lady has a sizable estate and should you marry her, it becomes your responsibility to take over the management of that estate. If you can prolong an engagement, then her solicitor will be charged with managing her estates. This keeps you available to help us in a more productive way. Lady Farnsworth and her estate are very important to the cause. Squire Rutledge has invested a sizable sum of her estate in warehousing here in Charles Town and shipbuilding at James Island, Shipyard Creek, and Hobcaw. He has invested heavily with the merchants Thomas Smith Sr. and Benjamin Smith. His friendship with the Scottish shipbuilders William Begbie and Daniel Manson has already seen success with the launching of at least three new coastal schooners. At this moment, Squire Rutledge is fulfilling his duties in an excellent manner. Prolong any engagement until we have reached our goal. Then you can take an apprenticeship under Squire Rutledge and become a respectful gentleman of Charles Town. At the moment we need you to be a soldier."

"My present circumstances are fluid. It would appear I have choices I must make and quickly," I said. "Should I take your advice and Abigail does consent to marry me with a long engagement, what could I tell her about my involvement with the cause?"

"From what little information we have, she seems predisposed to think all Englishmen should share the same rights and privileges. That you would seemingly work as personal courier for the Governor should not be a problem. Should she inquire, you can tell her that this assignment will give you a better chance of seeing the real nature of the struggle and enable both of you to make the right decision, should it ever be required. It will also give you the opportunity to view the landscape for investment opportunities. That should even be a good sell for Squire Rutledge."

Mrs. Stevens brought Mr. Wentworth his coffee and politely excused herself.

"Now Will, there is no need for me to get back with you at this time. I will know your decision if you show up at the Governor's house Monday morning with your saddle in hand. Arrangements for subsequent meetings will be arranged. I've taken a house on the outskirts of town."

Mr. Wentworth quickly drank his coffee, left a farthing, and departed.

I sat there by the window, watching the ebb and flow of traffic in the port, and contemplated my future. An hour passed and I was no further along in making a decision than I had been previously. The coffee house filled with an afternoon crowd and then emptied again as merchants and ship captains went about their business. Unnoticed by all, except for Mrs. Stevens, a young man, or what at first glance appeared to be a young man of some means wearing a dark green overcoat and brown embroidered breeches and riding boots, casually walked in and approached Will, who was still lost in contemplation.

In a deep voice, the "lad" inquired, "Excuse me, sir, do you mind if I sit down with you?"

Shaken from his deep concentration, Will looked up at the lad, took a second glance even closer, and then beamed from ear to ear.

"Why of course young "lad," please have a seat."

"Sorry, for the subterfuge. I was out riding and checking out my investments and literally ran into Mr. Wentworth. I almost knocked him down with my horse. It took a moment for him to recognize me. Fortunately, he told me he had seen you in the coffee house less than an hour ago. I thought it prudent to pay you an unsolicited visit. So, are you going to take the courier job with the Governor?

Abigail didn't mince words and he came directly to the point. "I'm not sure. I've sort of resolved my personal problem."

Abi raised her hand to stop him. "Will, I learned about your father. I am so glad he is safe in England. Just to let you know, I've anonymously donated 50 pounds to help feed the patriots being held in the dungeon at the Exchange. Their situation is abhorrent and it won't change until the British give us our due recognition as Englishmen – or English Women in my case."

I smiled. "You have to understand my dilemma. My father is safe. I.." and I stuttered, "I love you Abigail and don't want anything to come between us." Abi started to speak, but he grabbed her hand, "If I take the job with the Governor, you know what I have to do. I can't stand on the river bank and just watch the water flow by. If I'm caught, I will endure a fate far worse than the men in the dungeon."

"Excuse me, Squire Jones, holding hands with a lad in these parts is not something most people would take kindly to," quietly exclaimed Mrs. Stevens. Turning to Abi, Mrs. Stevens inquired, "Lady Farnsworth, will you take milk and sugar with your tea? It's extremely hard to hide such beauty, but you did fairly well."

"Thank you. I'll take coffee instead with a little milk and half a teaspoon of sugar if you please, replied Abi.

Mrs. Stevens departed the table with a spring in her step.

"So where were we, kind sir?" inquired Abi with a gleam in her eye.

"Do you believe in long engagements? That might give us time to know each other and for me and you also to find our true paths in these troubled times."

"I will not consider any talk of long-term engagements until I get a proposal of marriage," replied Abi with a grin on her face.

"But this is not exactly the surrounding in which I thought I should make such a gesture. I mean, in the middle of a coffee house down by the wharves?"

Mrs. Stevens arrived with the coffee and placed it in front of Abi.

"Mrs. Stevens, what would you think if this kind sir across from me proposed to me in your establishment?"

"Oh, my goodness, I would be so thrilled. Could I tell anyone or should I wait?"

Abi replied, "He hasn't done it yet. But let's see if we can give him some encouragement."

Both women turned their attention to me. I was mildly shocked. Hesitantly I finally spoke, "So be it. Lady Abigail Farnsworth, will you marry me, for richer or poorer, in sickness and in health, in death do us part?"

"That's a might much, Squire Will, but I think she got the message," beamed Mrs. Stevens.

Abi launched herself across the table and kissed me square on the lips and said, "Until death us do part."

The following two hours we celebrated with Mrs. Stevens, who gave us worldly advice about engagements, marriage, family, and life in general.

Later as the initial celebration calmed, Abi turned serious. "Will, I'm only sixteen – well almost – so a long engagement would be most appropriate. This will give us time to get to know each other, you to do the work you need to and for the world around us to become a little more settled. You will need to approach Squire Rutledge and ask for my hand in marriage. I've sort of set you up for that. I've already told him that when the time was right, I was going to marry you. I hope that wasn't too forward of me?" asked Abi.

"I don't think the party tomorrow evening will be the right time. Maybe on Sunday," I said.

"Great, you can attend church with us. I will make sure Squire Rutledge understands I invited you to go with us. Unfortunately, the hour is getting late and I need to return to Rutledge House. I love you, Will." We exchanged a parting kiss.

"I love and adore you, too," I replied as she got up from the table.

The rest of the day I spent in deep contemplation. My world was spinning and I had to untangle it so that I could make sense of it.

I spent a restless night. I remember I dreamed but could not recall any of my dreams except one, the kiss. Was it real or was my imagination playing tricks on me?

Chapter 44

St. James Shipyard

The rooster started crowing at five o'clock as if on cue. After a light breakfast of bread and jam, I found the newly gifted saddle, got directions to the stables preferred by the Governor, and walked there with the saddle across my back.

As I arrived, I noticed a stable boy cleaning up a stall just inside the door.

"I need to see the hostler if he's around," I inquired.

"Mr. Andrews be in the back office. Just so you know, he prefers the English pronunciation. Drop the "h" and just say 'ostler,' if you please," replied the young groom.

"Thank you for the correction and your directions."

"You're more than welcome, Squire Will," said the groom as he continued to muck out the stall.

I thought to myself, does anyone not know who I am? This port has a remarkable gossip tree. I ambled toward the back of the barn where the office was located. Off the left side, I noticed a small sign hanging outside, which merely said "Office."

I knocked on the open door, peered inside, and saw a lanky man sitting at an old roll top desk going over papers. "Are you the ostler, Mr. Andrews?" Will asked timidly.

"Ah, someone who can finally speak at least a little of the King's English. Yes, I'm the ostler. Mr. Andrews is my name. Now, let me see, I'll bet you a farthing that you are William Jones."

Will entered the office and extended his hand to Mr. Andrews. "And you sir, would be a farthing richer."

A firm handshake between us confirmed the introduction.

"I see you are wearing the boots Colonel Stuart sent to you at Mrs. Stevens'. He should have just sent you a note. But no, the Colonel is a man of action, no matter how inappropriate it might be. Now I suppose you will be needing a horse with that saddle. You are going to accept the Governor's offer, aren't you?" asked Mr. Andrews.

"That's my intention. If things go as planned, I will show up at the Governor's house ready to perform my duties. I suppose a horse might be a good addition to the saddle."

Mr. Andrews gave a hearty laugh, "Aye, a lad with a sense of humor. You and I will become good friends no doubt. Now for a horse. A certain young lady, whose name I won't divulge, selected three horses for you to pick from. A good eye for horseflesh she has. Unfortunately, Colonel Stuart narrowed it down to two. You're fortunate he just didn't assign you an old nag, but he was good enough to select two of my better mounts. According to him, you will be required to pay for your own mount. So much for being the personal courier for the Governor. You'd be spending all your pay for a year just to purchase a horse. Fortunately for you, the young lady, through Squire Randolph, has settled on a price for both horses. One for you and one for the young unnamed lady. I must say, she certainly does know how to ride. Not like one of those fancy ladies. She rides just like a true horseman – or woman in her case. Anyway, she prefers the ginger mare; she be a might gentler. The one you might prefer is a light roan gelding. Both are a little over 15 hands high. The roan is a tad faster and is the better jumper. No telling what you might run into in your duties."

Mr. Andrews finally ended his monologue.

"I'm sure the roan gelding would be fine. Could I possibly see him?"

"Of course," laughed Mr. Andrews. "He's in the next barn over. Let's walk over and see if he is ready for a ride."

"I wasn't planning on a ride this morning."

"That's not what I was told," he laughed again.

As they approached the barn, Will noticed two horses being prepared for riding. Abigail was there grooming her ginger mare and a young groom was preparing the roan.

"I thought you might want to go for a ride, get used to your mount, and learn some of the countryside. We could ride to St. James Island and have lunch and look at a couple of shipyards. You know, just have fun."

"That sounds wonderful. Let me saddle up and I'll be ready to go."

Mr. Andrews excused himself as they saddled the horses. He returned quickly with four Dragoon pistols.

"You young people take care. There are two holsters on each saddle. Take these loaded pistols with you. Here is extra shot and powder. I hope you won't need them, but you can never tell. God's speed to you. For your own safety, please return to the stables by dusk."

Abi and I mounted and rode off on St. James just southwest of Charles Town. The trip took only an hour and it was a leisurely, unhurried pace. Along the way, we passed an open marsh, which was showing the first signs of life. As we drew close to Ft. Johnson, we could see two or three small shipyards busy with activity. A community had grown up around the fort and a small tavern was conveniently located on the main road.

We tied the horses up in front of the tavern and went inside. This time Abigail didn't try to hide. Her long hair cascaded over her shoulders and the customers who were all male stared in disbelief. Here was a young girl in breeches and riding boots, casually carrying two Dragoon pistols in her belt. It was a sight to behold. I was no less an object of attention; I too had two Dragoon pistols in my belt.

The barmaid, not at all intimidated, addressed us. "Ah, Lady Farnsworth, we've been expecting you. Mr. Grimes, your ladyship is here."

"Aye, and it's about time," bellowed a husky man rising from a back table. "I must've been waiting a whole five minutes for her ladyship to arrive." He laughed out loud, came forward, bowed slightly, and extended his hand toward Abigail. In accord, Abi extended her hand.

Mr. Grimes bowed again to politely kiss Abi's outstretched hand. "Your ladyship, not often we get the opportunity to meet such a cultured lady in our stretch of the marsh. Please come have a seat with Mr. MacIntosh and myself. We'd like to go over the business at our shipyard with you."

"Mr. Grimes, as you already know, I may have a title, but I'm far from being a cultured lady. My indentured labor in a textile mill taught me the value of good honest labor."

I spoke up. "Mr. Grimes, I'm Will Jones. At the moment my most important job is escort to my lady. I hope that does not interfere with your conversation."

"Quite the opposite, Squire Will. If scuttlebutt be true and most times it has a bit of truth to it, you'll need to be brought into the conversation. Your future position as the Lady's intended is most agreeable."

Over the next hour, Abigail and I went over the books of the Grimes and MacIntosh shipyard. While Grimes took care of the construction of the shipbuilding, MacIntosh, a true Scotsman, kept immaculate books. Everything seemed in order.

Once the review of the books was complete, Mr. MacIntosh spoke up. "Now is the best part. We'd like to show you our shipyard and let you see the three vessels we are working on. Do you have the time today?"

"Only a brief moment," I spoke up. "Lady Farnsworth has to get back to Charles Town for a reception tonight.

"That'll be fine," remarked Grimes. The shipyard is but a five-minute ride from here, just to the port side of the fort."

All of us left the tavern together as the rest of the crowd stared in awe. It was a sight to remember. A real lady in this establishment, looking more like a pirate queen with all the pistols, dressed in breeches and riding boots.

The ride did take only five minutes. As they approached the small shipyard, Abi and I noticed three schooners in various states of construction. In the middle was a nearly completed schooner. To the left, a crew was laying the keel for a new schooner. On the right, the ribs of that schooner were being overlaid with planking. They were almost halfway up the ship's side.

There was no formality in the shipyard. Even though strangers were a rarity, no work stopped and the foul language of the workmen went unabated. The exception was there was no language directed at Lady Farnsworth. A previous directive by Mr. MacIntosh to the crew ensured the lady was treated with respect. After all, her investment in the shipyard was responsible for the new keel being laid.

Mr. Grimes addressed us. "As you'll see off to the left, a new keel is being laid. With permission Your Ladyship, we'd like to call her the "Lady Abigail" after you. It's your investment here that has made her possible. She'll be a fine two-masted coastal schooner when she's completed."

"Mr. Grimes, I would be most honored. I'll return and check on her progress from time to time. If I am fortunate," as she looked at me, "you might consider adding 'Jones' to the name when the time comes."

"Just give the word, and it will be done," replied Grimes with a broad smile on his face.

I spoke up. "I hate to intrude, but I must get Lady Abigail back to Charles Town so she can prepare for the reception."

As we left on horseback, we turned around to see not only Grimes and McIntosh waving goodbye, but most of the workers had stopped momentarily to also wave goodbye. It was obvious that Lady Abigail was a most appreciated benefactor at the shipyard.

Without incident, Abi and I made it back to Charles Town in good time. We rode directly to Rutledge House and exchanged a brief kiss as Abi dismounted. I took their mounts back to the stable and headed to Mrs. Stevens' to "freshen up."

Chapter 45

Abigail's Reception

Much to my surprise, Mrs. Stevens had set up a tub in the back room and had filled it with steaming hot water. A set of clean clothes and shoes awaited him.

"Now Master Will, clean yourself good, no need to smell like a rode horse. There's a bit of lavender water to sprinkle lightly on yourself. It'll make you smell … well … a bit better." Mrs. Stevens laughed as she left me to my bath.

At five o'clock, I started up Broad Street to the Rutledge House, remembering Abi wanted to see me early. Attired as a young gentleman suitor, I drew curious smiles from those I met on the street. As I was passing a millinery shop, an older lady standing at the door directly addressed me.

"My, Master Will Jones, aren't you a sight to behold. Seems like you're missing something important.

"Excuse me?" I questioned.

"Flowers for the lady!" she explained. At that moment, she handed me a large bouquet of fresh snapdragons.

"Why thank you," said Will, a little bewildered. "I guess there are no secrets in Charles Town," I added.

"Not many, young man," the lady replied as she turned back into her shop with a smile on her face.

I arrived shortly at the Rutledge House. There sitting on the front porch was a freshly dressed Abigail in a casual gown of light chintz. The upper square-necked bodice was a blue fabric with printed red roses and three-quarter length sleeves. The ankle-length skirt was a white fabric with large colorful flower bouquets printed on it. She looked beautiful.

Without any hesitation, I made my way up the curved front steps.

"Good afternoon, My Lady. You look beautiful. I guess this is the first time I've seen you in such an attire." Will handed her the bouquet of colorful snapdragons which actually complimented her dress.

"Why kind sir, thank you for your compliment. But if you remember correctly, and obviously you don't, I was wearing such an attire when we first met on the Baltick."

Will smiled, "Was that you? I thought that was a snotty, spoiled girl, who made a scene on the ship."

"Well at least I got your attention," she smiled. "And as for today's dress, it was a battle just to keep from wearing a hoop skirt underneath. I don't care how fashionable they are. They make a woman's hips look huge."

We both laughed. Slowly we moved back down the stairs and around to the courtyard to the side of the house. There we found a bench under a huge live oak tree and sat down together.

I started first. "I hope you understand that I need to take the position as a courier for the Governor. It will be beneficial to us, for me, to become more familiar with the colony and give us the advantage of knowing what is brewing before it happens. Can you wait for me until you are 18?"

"First of all, I do understand the importance of your position. Your absence will give me a chance to apprentice under Squire Randolph and learn about all the investments he has made for me. I'll be able to ensure his bookkeeper keeps proper books. This will also give me time to do some charity work and help the poor prisoners in the dungeon. As to the question, an emphatic 'no.' I'll wait for you until I'm 17 and not a day longer! You know, in South Carolina a girl can get married at 14 with her parents' consent. However, I'll stick with 17. What do you think?"

"That sounds like we have agreed to a long engagement. Just exactly when is your 17th birthday? I guess I should know, but there are so many things we don't know about each other. This long engagement will give us a chance to get to know one another."

"I shall be 17 on the fourth day of July in the year of our Lord in 1776. That will be a fitting day for us to celebrate our wedding. By that time, we shall know everything about each other that matters."

The reception started promptly at 6:30. Guests arrived and passed through an abbreviated reception line as Squire and Mrs. Rutledge had the honor of introducing their new ward, Lady Abigail Farnsworth, to the good people of Charles Town. Notable merchants and their wives came, doctors and their wives, lawyers and their wives, and most of the gentry showed up. Even several of the town's most eligible bachelors showed up, though somewhat dismayed when they spied me standing in the background. The Governor, his wife, and Colonel Stuart and his wife came fashionably late together.

At the appointed dinnertime, those not invited to stay for dinner politely said their goodbyes and left. The remaining guests, with the Governor and Colonel Stuart included, were escorted to the dining room where 22 places had been set. Squire Rutledge was at the head of the table, Lady Abigail was seated to the Squire's right, and Lady Stuart was seated to his left. The remainder of the table was seated man-woman-man and so forth. Will found his seat at the far end of the table just to the right of Mrs. Rutledge.

The meal went well. Mrs. Elizabeth Rutledge was extraordinarily polite to me and made sure I followed her example as the meal progressed. Although uncomfortable, I made the best of the situation and engaged my hostess and the lady next to me in polite conversation.

Near the end of the meal after dessert had been served, Mrs. Rutledge leaned over to me and whispered, "I think long engagements are the best. When Abigail turns 17, we will be pleased to host her wedding at our church and a reception here at Rutledge House. That is, if you are in accord."

Without missing a beat, I responded, "Your kindness is most appreciated, Mrs. Rutledge. Abigail and I would be most honored to have you and your husband stand with us at our wedding when Abi turns 17!"

"Good, I expect you to sit with us in our pew at church on Sunday morning. Services start at nine o'clock followed by a light lunch back here. That will give you and Abi the rest of the afternoon to talk about your engagement and plans for the future with Mr. Rutledge."

Uncharacteristically, after the conclusion of the meal, the guests took their cue and departed without the normal after-dinner drink. The undertones of discord could be felt as those associated with the Governor and the Crown left first. The Carolinians milled around briefly but soon departed. There was no political talk or discussions about the previous day's attempted theft of the Governor's mail. The matter was quietly handled; no one, as yet, had been charged with the attempt.

Abigail and I slipped out the back door of the house. Little was said as we sat under the same live oak tree and held hands. We watched the stars through a canopy of leaves and saw a shooting star.

Finally, Abi spoke up. "Tomorrow is Saturday and I need to go see two other shipyards, one on Shipyard Creek just above town and the other in Hobcaw across the river Charles Town. Would you like to accompany me?"

"Without question," responded Will enthusiastically. "This will give us chance to do something productive and have time alone without prying eyes watching over us. I'll be at the stable at six o'clock and pick up our horses and be back here by 6:30."

"I'm afraid Mr. Rutledge found out about our escapade to St. James. He didn't approve of my attire. Instructions are that I have to act more ladylike, at least for a while. Could you have Mr. Andrews hook up a two-wheel chaise for us? That's more suitable for a skirt."

I laughed. "I hope our adventure did not get you into too much trouble? I'll be sure to show up at 6:30 in a chaise."

"Better make that eight o'clock. No self-respecting lady is seen in public before eight in the morning."

We laughed together. Then as if on cue, Mrs. Rutledge called Abigail back into the house. A brief kiss and Abi left.

As I turned to leave, I literally ran into Squire Rutledge.

"Squire Will, I was wondering if there is anything you would like to talk to me about. It seems you have taken quite an interest in my ward, Lady Farnsworth."

"Sir, I should be most frank with you and not avoid the issue. May I have your permission to marry Lady Abigail when she turns 17?"

"Outstanding young man. A true man of action and conviction. Frankly, I think she made up her mind before you even had a chance. She went on and on about you when she first arrived and without hesitation announced to me privately that she was going to marry you. She actually challenged me to say 'no,' which, of course, I relented."

Mr. Rutledge continued. "After church on Sunday, Lady Abigail, you, and I must have a sit-down in my study. This will allow me to go over her estate and draw up those papers necessary for my continued stewardship of her affairs until you two are married. Once you are married, you will take over the management of her properties and investments. I realize the necessity for you to be the Governor's courier. This benefits both you and our cause. Once your appointment is concluded, I will expect you to complete your education and serve a short apprenticeship with me as a legal clerk, until such time as you feel comfortable to take over those management duties. Tomorrow, I think Lady Abigail has a full day planned for you both. Now off with you, as I understand you have an early day ahead."

Squire Rutledge and I shook hands and I departed.

Chapter 46

Shipyards

The next morning, I rose as soon as the cock crowed. I was finally getting used to city life, sort of. I quickly cleaned up and went into the coffee house for a quick breakfast. Mrs. Stewart was already there, baking something in the five-plate cast-iron stove. The stove was her pride and joy. She had traded a schooner captain a month's lodging for the stove.

As she brought me a breakfast of hot rolls and jam, she casually sat down next to me.

"I understand things went well at the reception last night. My sources say you had a nice conversation with Squire Rutledge afterward. I must say, I admire the way you approached the difficult task of asking for Lady Abigail's hand in marriage."

"Does nothing escape the attention of your sources?" Will inquired.

"Not much," replied Mrs. Stewart with a smile on her face. "I do wish you all the best in the world and hope you and your fiancé have a lively and fruitful life."

As she got up from the table, she leaned over and kissed me on the top of his head, then went about her other business.

At seven o'clock, Will presented himself to Mr. Andrews at the stables.

"Top of the morning to you Squire Will. I understand that you and Lady Abigail will be visiting a few places outside the city this fine day. Too bad that she has to conform to the dress code for young ladies of Charles Town. She seemed much more comfortable in a riding outfit, but I don't make the rules here, I only try to conform to them."

"So do you have a two-wheel chaise that we can use today?" inquired Will.

"Aye that I do. In fact, it's a Boston-style chaise with a movable top if the sun gets too bright. Come along, I'll show you."

Again, we walked to the other barn. There in the middle of the barn gangway was a two-wheel chaise being prepared. A black, well-muscled carriage horse, a little under 14 hands high was being fitted with the harness.

"Daisy is a fine, gentle carriage horse. She's not a jumper as you can see, but she's up to the task at hand. She doesn't spook easily and is responsive to the touch. Have you ever driven a carriage before, Squire Will?"

"I've driven a four-horse team back home in the mountains. They were big German Percherons, and a might too headstrong at times, but they easily pulled a Conestoga wagon. I had to be constantly on my toes just to keep them under control, especially when we got in sight of their home barn. Thank goodness someone had fashioned a long-handled wood break to slow down the wagon."

"This setup is a bit different. You actually get to sit in the chaise alongside your passenger, have a conversation, or whatever, and enjoy the countryside. You might say it's more refined than riding on the back of a big draught horse."

Mr. Andrews continued. "With safety in mind, there are two holsters on either side of the carriage. Two of the Dragoons have been placed there. Come, let me show you something else which is important. Just underneath the seat is a small compartment."

Mr. Andrews released a leather latch to reveal a small double-barreled shotgun.

"Nelly, as I call her, is very dependable at 20 feet. She's freshly loaded and ready to fire. The compartment is weather-tight, so you should have no problems with your powder getting wet. There's also more shot and powder in the compartment. Now be off with you and have a good adventure."

"And… I know, be back before dusk. Thank you, Mr. Andrews. I appreciate your assistance," said Will.

Daisy was anxious to get moving and strained at the harness for the first couple of miles. I took a test run around Charles Town before heading to the Rutledge House to pick up Abigail. I wanted to get used to the chaise and Daisy.

At a little before eight o'clock, I pulled into the courtyard at the Rutledge House. Abigail was sitting on the bench under the live oak tree, dressed in a floral-patterned dress, a bonnet, and wearing, of all things, riding boots under her dress.

"Don't say anything. I know riding boots and a dress look

ridiculous, but we will be traipsing around shipyards today. Shoes would not be appropriate. Besides, I have breeches underneath. Just wait until we get outside Charles Town and I will shed the dress. Don't worry, I have a full set of clothes underneath."

"Actually, I do like the bonnet. It's very cute!"

"Not to worry, I have a tricorn to wear later too! If you are ready Squire Will, would you be so kind as to assist this lady in getting into the chaise?"

It took only a moment for me to jump down from the chaise and then in an exaggerated motion I swung Abigail up into it.

It only took a short while to make it outside Charles Town proper to reach Shipyard Creek. As we arrived at the shipyard, we could see the property was divided into four distinct yards. Abigail directed me to the farthest yard near the end of the harbor. A sign at the entrance announced to all that this was the Charles Schooner Shipyard.

As we drove up to the entrance, a tall lanky gentleman emerged from a small office structure at the entrance. Hatless, he nonetheless bowed to Abigail.

"Lady Farnsworth, what a pleasure to meet you. I'm so glad you had the opportunity to come visit us today. I'm Thaddeus Sherman, chief shipbuilder of this yard. Squire William, you can tie up the chaise over by the water trough. Your horse and carriage will be safe and out of the way.

Mr. Sherman helped Abigail down to the ground. Abi reached back into the carriage and grabbed her tricorn.

"Mr. Sherman, first order of business. I need to change out of this dress into something more suitable for a shipyard tour.

Would you mind if I used the privacy of your office for a quick change of clothes?"

"Be my guest. I'll tell our draftsman to wander off somewhere to give you privacy."

Indeed, Abi was a quick-change artist. It took no more than a couple of minutes for her to transform from a town lady to a rough and tumble lass from the country. I was amazed by the transition.

Mr. Sherman led Abi and me down to the works. There before us were two nearly complete coastal schooners and a much larger ship under construction.

"I'm sure you recognize the two schooners. They'll be for trade up and down the coast and maybe into the Caribbean. The other ship is our first commission for a Royal Frigate. She'll carry 24 guns and have a crew somewhere between 60 to 90 sailors. She'll be a beauty when she's finished. The Governor helped us get the commission and with your timely investment, we were able to purchase all the timber we needed. If things go as planned, I'll be able to turn you a nice profit on your investment."

"I certainly appreciate the attention. Please explain to me the financial requirements for building a ship. I'm not familiar with them," questioned Abigail.

"I'll keep it simple for right now, 'cause I know you and Master Will have to cross the river to the Hobcaw yards. Your boat will be here in about an hour. In the meantime, let me see if I can explain as much as I can. If later you or Master Will have the desire, I can spend as much time as needed to get you familiar with financing a ship."

Will spoke up. "I'd like to learn as much as I can. Between

assignments for the Governor, I'd like to come back and let you teach me."

Abigail smiled. "That would be a great opportunity for both of us to become more schooled in the financial aspects of the business."

Over the next hour in his office, Mr. Sherman went over the various financial arrangements it took to build a ship. The possibilities seemed endless. Some merchants would commission a ship outright and pay sums to the shipyard in installments as the ship reached certain stages of completion. Others would show an interest in the construction of a ship, settle on a set price, and only put a small retainer down, leaving the shipmaster oftentimes the difficult obligation to find funding. Then some shipyards which had enough capital, built ships to sell to the highest bidder. That, Mr. Sherman thought, was risky since sometimes there was a market for a certain type of boat and sometimes not.

Working on a Royal commission was, as Mr. Sherman said, "not a walk in the park." True, a commission came with a sizable down payment and then installments as the work progressed, but there was no room for error and the Royal inspectors were always trying to make changes without authorization. Sometimes it involved protracted negotiations with the use of an attorney to settle the issue. The current commission had the support of the Governor, explained Mr. Sherman, which assisted in keeping the Royal inspectors in check. The current plans for the frigate were a fleet standard used for several years with all previous changes noted ahead of time. So far Mr. Sherman noted the inspectors had only requested minor changes which did not require any substantial refitting.

As the time to leave for the Hobcaw shipyard arrived, Abigail and I thanked Mr. Sherman for this hospitality. The three of us then walked the length of the yard down to the wharf and saw a luger waiting to take us across the river. No sail was set, but there were three sailors at the oars and the helmsman waited on the wharf.

Without further ceremony, Abi and I said goodbye to Mr. Sherman and followed the helmsman to the lugger. The trip across the river was fairly quick. The flow of the river and the outgoing tide helped speed the trip to the Hobcaw Creek shipyard.

*****

There to meet them on the dock of the shipyard were two artisan attired gentlemen.

As Abigail and I ascended the ladder up to the deck of the dock, the men introduced themselves as John Rose and James Stewart, the shipwrights of the Hobcaw Creek shipyard. The men quickly escorted us to the small brick office at the side of the shipyard.

Rose addressed us first. "Here we concentrate on building single-masted coastal sloops and double-masted schooners. This has been our 'bread and butter' over the past several years. Thanks to Lady Farnsworth, we are now seeking a commission to build a frigate for the Royal Navy, in fact using the same plans Mr. Sherman is using to build his frigate. Her funding has allowed us to already purchase the lumber for the keel and mainframe timbers. As Sherman completes phases of his frigate, we'll hire his excess crew to come over and lay our keel. The Governor has assured us the

Royal Navy will give us a commission within the next several months. The dreaded inspectors have already done their preliminary inspection and found us fit to construct a frigate. That a big first step."

The overview of the yard took almost an hour, followed by a walk around to get a better understanding of how a shipyard works. Shipwrights Rose and Stewart seemed a bit more organized than Mr. Sherman. There was a lumberyard attached to the shipyard which contained all the wood they would need to build a number of ships. And as Mr. Rose explained, the lumber was paid for and represented a capital investment for the yard. Buying in bulk, when the lumber prices were low, enabled the shipyard to increase their profits nicely. According to Mr. Stewart, the specialty wood for the keel and frame walls were always hardest to find. That type of lumber was always in short supply. As we went, he explained that Abigail's investment had allowed them to scour the lumber mills from North Carolina down to Georgia to find just the right hardwood. A special site in the yard had already been prepared for laying the keel of the frigate. At the end of the tour, Mr. Rose escorted Abi and me back to the dock to take the luggar back over the river to Sherman's yard.

This time the sail had been set. There were still three sailors and a helmsman, but the trip back was pleasantly powered by the sails. As we landed at Sherman's yard no one was there to meet us, so Abi and I disembarked on our own and walked the short distance to the office. We briefly stuck our heads into the office and said goodbye to Mr. Sherman and his draftsman.

We took a leisurely ride back into town. Along the way,

Abigail slipped into her skirt and blouse so as not to raise the ire of Squire Rutledge. Even in the tight confine of the chaise, Abi displayed remarkable limberness.

As they drew up to the Rutledge House, Abigail replaced the bonnet in mock anger.

"Tomorrow is Sunday and we expect to see you at St. Michael's at nine o'clock. Wear your Sunday best and bring your bible. The Rutledges, I have been told, are extremely religious and read along in the Bible with the minister."

I hesitated. "Abigail, I've never owned a Bible. Our Family Bible is with my mother in the mountains, I hope."

"That's fine. We can share my Bible. My Aunt in Boston gave me my mother's Bible when I left. Someday, I'll have to retrieve my family Bible from my dear uncle."

"One last thing. I need to find a place to stay. The Governor is only paying for my room at Mrs. Stevens' through Monday. I've got a couple of possibilities, but no firm commitments. If you or the Rutledges have any ideas please let me know."

"Silly, don't be shy. There's a spare room over the guest house in the back of the property. I found it while exploring the grounds. It has its own private stairway, so it would be convenient for you to come and go as you please. There is also a spare stall in the carriage house. I'll smooth the way for you. But you'll need to ask the Squire after church in the morning. You know, proper protocol and all that rot." Abi leaned over, kissed me on the cheek and, un-ladylike, nimbly jumped down from the chaise.

We waved to each other as she climbed the back steps to the house and I turned the chaise around and headed to the stables.

From the upstairs windows, Squire Chase and his wife watched the scene in the courtyard.

"You know John, they are so young and carefree. We were once like that. It is so exciting to see them fall in love," remarked Elizabeth Rutledge.

"My dear, we were never young and carefree together. As you remember, I was already a struggling barrister just returned from England and you were an orphan of wealthy parents. Our romance was chaotic and intoxicating."

"Well, I think a two-week romance was sufficient to bind us together forever. Did you have to remind me about the alcohol involved? I still get a headache just thinking about how much wine we consumed during our courtship. It was fun, wasn't it, darling."

"Absolutely, my dear. I'm glad it happened just as it did. For us though, troubled times are ahead. Will is going to be put to the test. In a lot of ways, our success in this colony will depend on his discretion, intelligence, and bravery. We are going to ask a lot of him. I just hope he survives this cruel path on which we are about to send him. We must, as much as we can, protect Abigail from involvement in our calculations."

"Agreed darling. I will keep her as busy as I can with my women's groups and you can keep her busy doing a shadow apprenticeship in your law office."

Elizabeth reached up and gave her husband a peck on his cheek.

Chapter 47

Sunday

Sunday, April 20, 1775, started out much like any other Sunday in my life. The rooster crowed, I got up, and then things went differently. I cleaned up and found a new set of Sunday clothes neatly folded on a chair outside my door. A gift from Mrs. Stevens, no doubt, with a note on top. It read, "Special clothes for a special day. Miss Abigail sends her love, Mrs. S." It was obviously a conspiracy, but it made me smile. My whole life had changed in a matter of days. True, there were things left undone, but my father was relatively safe for the time being and my personal life had surprisingly flourished with my unexpected engagement to Abi. My situation was almost like a dream sequence. I had to pinch himself occasionally to make sure it wasn't all a fantasy.

Downstairs by seven, I was met by a spry Mrs. Stevens, who seemed so happy I thought she had been tipsy.

"If'n, you don't mind, may Henry and I walk with you to church this morning? We attend St. Michaels, too, it being the place where a lot of the notables in town attend," inquired Mrs. Stevens.

"Of course, Mrs. Stevens, I'd be honored to have you and Henry walk with me to church. I do have to be there early so I can meet the Rutledges and Lady Abigail," I added.

"I'll show you the right place to wait. They usually come about 15 minutes before services start. There'll be a lot of greetings exchanged beforehand. Henry and I will slip in and go upstairs to our seats in the balcony. We get a good view from up there."

At the appointed time, the three of us strolled to St. Michaels, which took no more than 15 minutes. As we arrived, I noticed, there were a number of people gathered just outside the main entrance talking in small groups. Some others proceeded directly into the church. Mrs. Stevens pointed to a group of people off to the right, approaching the church. There were the Rutledges coming up to the church. Squire and Mrs. Rutledge lead the way with Abigail, two of the children, John Jr. and Edward, the children's nanny, and an elderly family retainer called Aunt Helen following close behind.

Mrs. Stevens and Henry quickly scooted into the church, headed for the balcony. As I approached the Rutledges and Abigail, Squire Rutledge extended his hand to me in a most friendly gesture.

"Squire William, so good of you to join us this morning. Please join us in our pew. You are most welcome to sit with your betrothed and you may hold her hand during the service. I've instructed Lady Abigail on the conduct of the service and she will keep you informed of what is next during the liturgy."

"Thank you, Squire. I'm afraid my religious education consists of Bible readings at home and a few missionaries who came back to our village every so often. I will follow Lady Abigail's advice."

"That is quite alright. You'll have plenty of time to catch up on your religious education while you are here in Charles Town. We'll make a good Anglican out of you. Have you been baptized?"

"Yes sir. During one of those rare visits by the missionaries, I was baptized. It's recorded in our Family Bible, which my mother has. Does anyone need to see it?"

"No, your word is your bond as far as I'm concerned. Now let's go inside. Our pew is number 43. The family will go in first. You and Lady Abigail will sit next to the aisle."

I had never been in such a magnificent church before. The high ceiling, the stained-glass windows, and the polished wooden pews were a lot to behold. As the family seated themselves, Abigail and I took positions on the aisle. I sat next to the aisle and Abigail sat at my side.

I was able to follow the service through the Book of Common Prayer. The hymns were a different matter. My singing ability was exactly null. Even with the help of Abi, I could only mouth the words. The whole experience was exceptional. The hymns, the reading of the scriptures, and the sermon were all new. The communion was familiar. That's one thing the missionaries had taught our village congregation. When their time came, the parishioners in pew 42 stood up as if on cue and proceeded to join the line for the communion.

Once the communion was over, there was a closing hymn. Abi leaned into me, "There will be a short announcement section. I hope you are not upset, but today the priest will announce our engagement to the church."

"I'm surprised that Squire Rutledge would announce it so quickly."

"Lady Elizabeth was insistent that we do it as soon as possible. She is just as excited as I am. Did I tell you I'm excited?"

"You just did," I smiled. I was also excited, thrilled, and concerned at the same time. I couldn't help but look at the shiny, smiling face next to me and not think about the dark storm clouds forming on the horizon. I only hoped I could protect her from everything.

The Anglican priest came forward to the altar to make a special announcement. He addressed the congregation. "It is a great pleasure to announce the arrival to our congregation Lady Abigail Farnsworth and her fiancé, Squire William Jones. If the couple would please come forward so the congregation can meet you and you can meet the congregation."

My legs all of a sudden felt shaky. Abi firmly gripped my arm as we proceeded up the aisle. There we turned to face a mostly smiling congregation. Although I noted a few previously potential suitors were not smiling.

"May I present to you the couple. Lady Farnsworth, a ward of our esteemed Squire and Mrs. Rutledge, lately from Boston, is fully invested in our community and will assist Mrs. Rutledge with her charitable works in our fine city. Squire Jones, lately of Virginia, will be taking a position with the Governor's staff as a personal assistant. We wish both young people the best in the future. A wedding date has been set for Lady Farnsworth's birthday on July 4, 1776. This will give the couple adequate time to form a union with Christ and our church. For those of you who have time, Squire

Rutledge invites you to come by his house after this service for an opportunity to meet the young couple and enjoy refreshments."

Uncharacteristically, the congregation politely applauded us. I was overcome with emotions and possibly a bit of shock. All I could do was smile pathetically. On the other hand, Abi beamed from ear to ear. This was her coming out into polite society in Charles Town. After years of servitude under her uncle's glare, this was an opportunity to rise to the occasion. Looking at Abi, I felt comfort in her good fortune and mine too!

The remainder of the day was spent meeting the townspeople of Charles Town. Not only did the congregation show up, but other people did as well. The reception turned into a party of sorts as the wine and ale began to flow and the kitchen staff began to put out trays of fresh bread, cheese, and assorted "finger foods." Squire Rutledge and Elizabeth were in rare form. They looked like beaming parents as they held court. Abi and I spent the afternoon wandering through the crowd, meeting new people, seeing recent acquaintances such as Mr. Andrews from the stables, and the shipwrights Stewart and Rose, Mr. Sherman, and Mr. Grimes. The Smith brothers, prominent merchants, dropped by and introduced themselves to us. Of course, Captain Thomas, who was still in port came by with Mrs. Stevens on his arm. Henry trailed a little behind.

As the afternoon wore on, people started to leave and by four o'clock the courtyard was finally empty except for Squire Rutledge and us.

"Sir, I want to thank you again for arranging the reception for Abigail and me. That was very nice of you to do on such short notice."

"You both are very welcome. I take my stewardship very seriously and I want Lady Abigail and yourself to have the best engagement possible. One thing I will adamantly refuse to do is plan the wedding. Mrs. Rutledge will take the lead on that undertaking. And since it is more than 15 months away, more or less, that should be sufficient time to plan a respectable wedding. Lady Abigail, as for your education, you will spend some time with Mrs. Rutledge doing charitable work. Primarily, I want you to work as an assistant in my office three days a week. You need to become familiar with your holdings and the proper way to manage your estate. I am pleased both of you have already visited the three shipyards in which you are invested. That's a good start. Will, as for you, your duties with the Governor may last longer than a year. You will probably not have any days off, so your education in estate management will be delayed until such time as you find yourself free of that entanglement with the Governor. Don't misread me, your work at the Governor's office will benefit us in our cause. I have already spoken to Mr. Wentworth and we are in agreement that you will serve us well, but remember service to our cause has to be in the shadows. Is that understood?"

"Yes sir. I understand exactly what you mean."

"Not to beat around the bush, Abigail has already decided you will stay in the attic apartment of the guest house. You can stable your mount in the spare stall in the carriage house. You two can make the transition now. Please tell Mrs. Stevens I appreciate all that she has done to make things happen. Now both of you go about your business. Wait … one last word of caution … there'll be no late-night visits to the attic, is that understood Lady Abigail?"

Caught before the act. A red-faced Abigail responded with a grin on her face, "I'm sure you must be able to read minds, Squire Rutledge, but given your pronouncement, I will not entice William to break your rule."

"Abi," Squire Rutledge said, getting familiar with her, "it's not Will I'm concerned about breaking the rule. Now be off with you. Will needs to settle in before nightfall. On Sundays, we have a light supper at seven o'clock. Will, since you are now a member of our extended family, when you are in town, you are expected to eat with us."

"Thank you, sir. Abi and I will go fetch my things from Mrs. Stevens."

The move was uneventful. Mrs. Stevens already had my belongings stuffed in my bag. The extra donated clothes were packed in two large cotton bags. It was a tearful goodbye for Mrs. Stevens.

By early sunset, Abi and I had moved my meager belongings into the rather spacious attic apartment. Mindful of the Squire's warning, we didn't tarry too long there together.

As we descended the outside staircase, Abigail wondered aloud. "I wonder if the Squire would consent to us bundling sometime soon. After all, we are engaged."

"I think we might want to wait a few days before we breach that subject," Will replied.

Chapter 48

Monday - The Appointment

Monday morning came unusually early in my mind. The roosters in Charles Town definitely needed to coordinate their morning serenades. I cleaned up, put on a clean set of clothes, dusted off the courier jacket, and headed to the main house. Mrs. Rutledge, already up with her youngest sons William and Charles, met me in the courtyard.

"Good morning, William. The boys wanted to come outside and play on the swing. Such are the duties of a poor, overworked mother. Anyway, breakfast is still a little time off."

"That will be fine. It gives me time to go to the stables and get the Roan ready for today's audition with the Governor."

"Do hurry back. The Squire likes everyone present for breakfast. It's his opportunity to bark out our daily orders to everyone," she laughed.

I returned in 30 minutes on Roan, a name I had given my mount for lack of immediate imagination.

As I entered the dining room, my place next to Abigail was

reserved. Breakfast had already started.

"Good of you to join us, William. It's nice to see someone is up and at it this morning. Oh, by the way, no discussion of bundling at the table. I'll let you know when that discussion will take place and not a minute sooner."

The Rutledge boys at the table stifled their laughter under their breaths. Mrs. Rutledge covered her smile while Abi and I glanced mindlessly at our breakfast plates.

"I mean it," said Squire Rutledge, barely containing his smile.

As breakfast ended, Squire Rutledge pulled me aside. "Today is an important day for all of us, but most important for you. As you get attuned to the tempo of the Governor's business, you'll see where your usefulness lies. Be observant. Ask questions for clarification, not for information. Keep your wits about you."

Without a further word, we shook hands and I rode off to see the Governor about a job.

As I approached the Marine Guards at the Governor's house, both of them came to attention, which was a first experience for me. I reined in Roan and stopped just short of the guard post.

"Corporal, William Jones. I have an appointment with the Governor."

"Aye that you do lad. From now on, you'll have no need to stop for us. You have unrestricted access, so go ahead and start your job."

I nudged Roan into the courtyard and tied him up next to the water trough.

Mr. Charles was waiting for me and without a word

escorted me directly to the Governor's office.

"Ah, there you are, right on time. Sorry, I didn't make the reception at Squire Rutledge's House. I had some important matters to take care of. I'm thrilled you have accepted my offer of a job. Mark my word young man, you and I are going to have a great impact on this colony in the next year."

THE END

About the Author

Cecil Burton "Burt" Jones is a retired US Army Reserve Lieutenant Colonel (LTC), who had a concurrent career as an Army Civilian Counterintelligence (CI) Agent. Recently retired after 32 years as a CI Agent, Mr. Jones saw multiple deployments to the Middle East, tours in Germany and Korea, and numerous inspection/operational trips to Central and South America.

Jones has a Bachelor of Arts in Political Science from Mississippi State University and a Juris Doctor in Law from the University of Mississippi. Upon graduation from law school, he worked as a staff attorney with Legal Services for eight years in Biloxi, Mississippi. While enrolled in the German Language Course at the Defense Language Institute in Monterey, California, Jones, then on active duty, was approached and recruited by Army Intelligence to work as an Army civilian counterintelligence agent. He is not only a German linguist, but also a graduate of the Army General Staff College, the Army Management Staff College, and the Harvard Senior Fellows Executive program.

He retired as a CI Agent in August 2019. Jones ran for Congress in the Texas 23rd Congressional District in 2020 but unfortunately lost in the primary. He has dedicated himself to continued service to the community through his work with the charity Military Families and Survivors First, Inc. and is a part-time political commentator on social media platforms.